Sven Wiederholt

About the Author

ROBERT MAILER ANDERSON was born in San Francisco in 1968, three years before his parents were divorced. He was the fifth generation of his family—a clan comprised largely of railroad workers, San Quentin prison guards, and tamale vendors—to be raised across the Golden Gate Bridge in San Rafael. He spent every other weekend and summers with his father in Mendocino County, reading, playing sports, and accompanying his father to his business, a home for juvenile delinquents, where young Anderson encountered some "hard cases" who were later convicted of, among other crimes, armed robbery, rape, and murder. One former resident, David Mason, was executed by the state. Several others are on death row.

At age fourteen, Anderson moved in with his father "full time" and, due to financial constraints, the group home. He started high school in Ukiah, where he was routinely kicked out of classes. He took a year off from school and played golf. He developed a gambling habit. He began contributing articles to the *Anderson Valley Advertiser,* where his uncle, Bruce Anderson, was editor and publisher. Eventually, he graduated from Anderson Valley High School in Boonville. He played three varsity sports and was MVP of the NCL III in baseball. He was student body president until he was impeached.

Pursuing a career in baseball, Anderson matriculated to the University of Miami, where he did not play. He was then transferred to the College of Marin, where he pitched and played first base for a semester and a half before packing his possessions into the trunk of a "borrowed" Cadillac, cashing his student loan check, and heading to Mexico.

When the money ran out, he moved to New York City, where he had a series of unfulfilling jobs: selling suits, telemarketing, moving furniture, and temping. He did stand-up comedy, once. He played basketball at West Fourth Street. He was accepted into a creative writing tutorial taught by Shelby Hearon at the Ninety-second Street Y.

In 1995, Anderson's short story "36-28-34-7" was published by *Christopher Street*. He began referring to himself as "the heterosexual voice of gay lit."

Anderson lives in San Francisco with his wife and two children, son Dashiell and daughter Lucinda. He is co-owner of Quotidian art gallery and is on the board of the San Francisco Opera Association. *Boonville* is his first novel.

Boonville

Boonville

Robert Mailer Anderson

Perennial
An Imprint of HarperCollins*Publishers*

"I never saw a moor" and *"Surgeons must be careful"* reprinted by permission of the publishers and the Trustees of Amherst College from THE POEMS OF EMILY DICKINSON, Thomas H. Johnson, ed., Cambridge, Mass.: The Belknap Press of Harvard University Press, Copyright © 1951, 1955, 1979 by the President and Fellows of Harvard College.

"Second Fig" by Edna St. Vincent Millay. From *Collected Poems,* HarperCollins. Copyright 1922, 1950 by Edna St. Vincent Millay. Reprinted by permission of Elizabeth Barnett, Literary Executor.

Hardcover publication of this book was made possible by a grant from the Creative Work Fund.

A hardcover edition of this book was published in 2001 by Creative Arts Book Company. It is here reprinted by arrangement with Creative Arts Book Company.

HarperCollins books may be purchased for educational, business, or sales promotional use. For information please write: Special Markets Department, HarperCollins Publishers Inc., 10 East 53rd Street, New York, NY 10022.

First Perennial edition published 2003.

Library of Congress Cataloging-in-Publication Data

Anderson, Robert Mailer.
Boonville / Robert Mailer Anderson.—1st Perennial ed.
p. cm.
ISBN 0-06-051621-6
1. Inheritance and succession—Fiction. 2. California, Northern—Fiction. 3. Young men—Fiction. 4. Hippies—Fiction. I. Title.

PS3601.N546 B6 2002
813'.6—dc21 2002027590

06 07 RRD 10

This is a work of fiction; any character's resemblance to persons living or dead is strictly coincidental. Although the town of Boonville is real and I did live there and graduate from high school and drink beer and play sports and read Dos Passos and write for the local paper there and my first girlfriend (although I never really called her my girlfriend) tried to kill me there by driving into oncoming traffic at the intersection of Highway 128 and Mountain View Road and my heroes have always been cowboys and I do truly love the Anderson Valley, there's no way to accurately portray this place. Nobody would believe the real truth. It's too violent and weird. And this is not some thinly veiled autobiography. I repeat, this is a work of fiction. I tried my best to get at some "higher truth." I think we all know the inherent problems in that undertaking. So, any of the local residents who can read, and do read this novel, and take offense at the descriptions or content, instead of sucker-punching me while I'm in town trying to buy groceries with my wife and son, let me just buy you a drink and we'll call it even. As for the hippies in the county who may be upset at the depiction of hippies, I say, "Tough shit, hippie." Anyone willing to identify themselves as a hippie here in the 21st century has their head up their ass and gets what they deserve.

For
Nicola
and
Dashiell
and
Lucinda
and
the memory of
Joyce Hurley

Acknowledgments

I would like to thank my wife, Nicola, my son, Dashiell, and my daughter, Lucinda, who mean everything to me.

And my friends for their love, strength, inspiration, and support, without which this novel would never have been completed: Mathieu Salgues, Tony Barbieri, Joshua Jennings, Stephen Hulburt, Jason Leggiere, Shawn Phillips, Joe Lucas, Leonardo, Awadagin Pratt, Jonathan Lethem, Klas Eklöf, and Jay Leahy.

And my father and mother for naming me Mailer and getting the ball rolling. My brother and sister, Wayne and Margaret. My Papa. My entire family, especially Bruce, Ling, Zack, Jessica, and Ben. Penny Scanlon, Joy Andrea Larkin, Judy Bernhard, and Byron Spooner. My other sisters, Erin Hurley and Sarah Morrissette. Also, Christina McKay, Bobby Blanchard, Creedence Perkins, and Tom Avvakumovits.

Mary Miner, Luke and Justine, and the memory of Robert Miner.

Laura Jones, for restoring my faith in life.

And the rest of The Tribe, especially Luisa Smith, Tom Stoen, Margaret Hirsh, Timothy "Speed" Levitch, Barry Sherman, Coltrane Gardner, Rod Werner, Jana Giles, Mary Ellen Tseng, Tom Whelan, Jay Berry, Mark Ganter, Sean Foley, Scott and Georgia Thunes, Stacey Hubbard, Geoff Wolf, Darcy West, Dan O'Conner, Walker, Mart Bailey, Andy Shen, Chris Ellinger, Steve Werlin, Mike and Helena Crane, Sunyata Palmer, the

Horowitz family, Donovan Dutro, Paul Ricci, Mark Vronin, and Nick Carr.

The Miami boys, especially Jimmy Glover, Jason Schrift, Brian Wojcik, and Jay Walsh.

Quotidian Gallery, Caffe Valeska, Caffe Trieste, The Columbus Hotel (a.k.a. the Hotel Tevere), Books Revisited, Tosca, the 92nd Street Y, the Presidio YMCA, and the Cypress Quartet.

And Elvis Costello, Tom Waits, Randy Newman, Bruce Springsteen, Coleman Hawkins, Lester Young, Los Lobos, Lucinda Williams, Bob Wills, Cole Porter, John Hiatt, Lyle Lovett, Willie Nelson, Merle Haggard, Waylon Jennings, Janis Joplin, Billie Holiday, the Cowboy Junkies, Beethoven, Bach, Wagner, and the San Francisco Opera for supplying the music.

And to Shelby Hearon, Bill and Em Smith, Norman Mailer, Christina Garcia, Carl Hiaasen, Isabel Allende, Calvin Trillin, Naomi Wolf, Paul Sigenlaub, Jim Stonebreaker, Judith McNally, Alex Peer, Ray Rossen, and Ranney Johnson, whose support and kind words kept me on track when I really needed them.

The *Anderson Valley Advertiser* and *Christopher Street* for publishing my work. And the Northern California Independent Booksellers Association for believing in *Boonville,* and selling it.

My agent, Jack Scovil. Creative Arts Book Company, especially Josh and Emma. HarperCollins, especially Alison Callahan. And Laura Joplin.

And the memory of Michael Arevedo.

And the town of Boonville.

And Panther Pride.

The power of an event can flow from its unresolvable heart, all the cruel and elusive elements that don't add up, and it makes you do odd things, and tell stories to yourself, and build believable worlds.

Don DeLillo, *Underworld*

Which proves again how no man can cause more grief than that one clinging blindly to the vices of his ancestors.

William Faulkner, *Intruder in the Dust*

I

Boonville. John couldn't believe the town was actually named Boonville. It wasn't just an expression, a private joke among his family describing where his whacked-out, alcoholic grandmother had lived and made squirrel sculptures from driftwood. This place existed. He was driving his dead grandmother's '78 Datsun down the main strip, eyes wide with disbelief as the principal attractions shot past: gas station, video store, bar, market, bar, hotel, drive-in, health-food store, open highway. He continued along the two-lane road expecting the rest of the town to appear, more buildings, street signs, traffic, a Burger King for Christ's sake. But there was nothing, a slab of concrete wedged between trees and hills, winding away from what he thought must have been a mirage. Two more miles of pastoral landscape and he flicked on his blinker, signaling for the hell of it, checking his rearview mirror and seeing nobody coming or going in either direction. He steered the car to the skirt of the road, engine coughing and wheezing, dieseling and then farting a cloud of carbon monoxide into the country air. The motor made a mechanical ticking sound. John sat motionless behind the wheel. Tick, tick, tick.

"I'm going to put this as nicely as I can, John," he remembered his girlfriend saying, two weeks before he booked his flight from Miami to San Francisco. "Your grandma was a spent bitch!"

Born a communications major, Christina had a flair for tact. She had recently told John on a crowded bus, within earshot of at least twenty Cubans, she felt like a potato chip dunked into a can of black bean dip.

"Completely fucking gaga," she elaborated. "Growing marijuana at age seventy, shooting a guy in the leg because he had a bad aura. Woodchuck sculptures? Your father said she lived in a shack, and that town Boonville, I read somewhere it's so backward they have their own language."

John had read the same piece on the town's odd lingo, Boontling, which had sprouted around the turn of the century at "hop-pickin' campaigns," a mish-mash of slang that used English as its base. Grandma had said it was as dead as Latin. Only a fistful of locals spoke it, transplants from Arkansas, hard-drinking, tobacco-chewing bullshit artists. In the article there had been a picture of two such men, dirty workshirts, rifles in the gun racks of their pickup trucks, a half-mouth of teeth between them, conversing in front of a restaurant called the Horn of Zeese, which was Boontling for "cup of coffee." Quaint or disturbing, John couldn't decide.

"Christina," he pleaded, unable to recall the last time they had done something spontaneous together, aside from switching long-distance carriers. They never did take those tango classes or learn to salsa. He'd suggest weekend trips without a destination, renting scuba gear, exploring the Everglades. She would agree, and then find an excuse to stay home. Queen of the twenty-four-hour flu. If he argued, she changed the subject to their careers or lack of cash flow.

"Think about it," Christina demanded, with her usual single-mindedness. "Until she died, that woman was living in the sixties. It wasn't even her generation."

Grandma had kept John updated on her protests, weekend attempts to save the spotted owl, the coho salmon, the giant redwoods. The endangered-species cause célèbre. She had been arrested a dozen times in towns he couldn't find on a map, Albion, Covelo, Laytonville, and, of course, Boonville. She had once sent a postcard from the jailhouse of Point Arena that consisted of two Thoreau quotes, "I believe in the forest, and in the meadow, and in the night in which the corn grows." and "What are *you* doing out *there*?" John had found his grandmother's radicalism endearing, transforming her lifelong bitterness into something useful. Christina said, "If she really wanted *change*, she'd pool her resources with other hippies and hire a lobbyist."

Christina had grown more conservative since their college

days at the University of Miami, developing a low tolerance for anything that didn't increase their savings account. It was beginning to dominate the details of their life, the food they ate, the jokes they told, the plays and museum exhibitions they missed. She even dressed differently, skirt suits, hair pulled back and set with a clip. Sensible shoes. Before it was loose T-shirts and loud Bermudas, hair falling unevenly onto her shoulders, eyes that asked, "What next?" She would go braless, sometimes sans panties. "Easy access," she would coo, and they would make love in elevators, parking lots, on the beach. Now it was predictable, clothes, conduct, conversation. And sex only occurred in bed, if they had scheduled a "sex date."

"The sixties are over, the seventies are over, and the eighties are closing fast," Christina told him, demonstrating how history could be disposed of in neat packages. "Your grandma didn't realize that, and now she's dead."

"What does that have to do with anything?" John wanted to know.

He looked around their apartment, pastel furniture and white carpeting. Carefully selected chrome and glass accessories. Television, front and center. A stack of coasters on a coffee table with magazines spread out just so, *Glamour*, *House Beautiful*, *Vanity Fair*. Mood dimmer halogen track lighting, an Italian floor lamp that took six weeks to be delivered, all ordered from one of Christina's catalogs. Over the sofa, a framed Ansel Adams print of a forest of white-trunked trees.

What compromise had led to that purchase? John wondered. It must have been the day he wanted to buy the Diane Arbus photograph of the retarded girl touching her toes.

"Muerto!" Christina spit, and even in another language her point was still unclear. "Her whole way of thinking is done."

Outside the apartment, Florida air hung as hot and tight as a sunbather's butt thong. Through the window, John watched palm trees droop with the weight of the afternoon, Coppertone bodies flashing Rolexes, boutiques and half-empty high-rises. Miami, city of greed and vanity, cocaine and implants, varicose veins and mambo. He had grown up, gone to college, spent twenty-seven years in the Sunshine State trying to believe fun was a large body of water and a pink drink. Whenever you built a city in a place without seasons, he observed, people got strange. At least as a child he was able to walk the beaches barefoot. Now you couldn't take a step without cutting yourself on a broken bottle or syringe. Miami had become an hourglass. Time run out.

"What about rednecks?" Christina asked. "Have you given a thought about rednecks?"

Christina was on a roll that a fancy dinner and a pitcher of piña coladas couldn't stop. Forget trying to make it up to her with flowers, he wouldn't hear the end of this one for weeks. It was as if he had suggested they move straight to hell.

"Remember, I lived in Tallahassee for five years," she reminded John. "Rednecks might be worse than hippies."

Of course he had thought about rednecks, recalling the saying in Miami, "The farther north you go, the farther south you get." But the question on the floor was, "What about west?" California was supposed to be the final frontier for personal expression, especially the San Francisco Bay Area, an enclave of born dissidents. By Grandma's account, Boonville was only a hundred miles north of the Golden Gate Bridge, in Mendocino County, a region known for its stunning coastline and wine grapes. There were rivers and forests, a fertile valley with acres of scrub oaks and apple orchards. Everybody knew everybody by their first name. They still rode horses and raised livestock. People didn't lock their doors at night.

But you never knew what was fact or fiction until you experienced it for yourself. Grandma had also warned, "If you travel fifty miles outside any city in America, it's Faulkner country."

"I need to move," John told Christina.

"Selfish," Christina chided. "Mr. Selfish."

"I can't live here anymore," he tried to explain. "I don't want to start a family in Florida. They'll grow up to be surfers, realtors, lawyers, or worse. There's nothing else here."

"We're here," Christina said.

"That's right," John said, conceding the obvious, but not knowing exactly what to make of it. "And I don't want my kids getting skin cancer or believing life imitates L.A."

"What's wrong with L.A.?" she said.

Christina compulsively reached for one of the bottles of sunscreen left around the apartment, squirting a dollop in her palm and rubbing it onto her arms as if the lotion offered a layer of protection not only from the UV rays, but from her life.

"It could be great," John said, ignoring her question because answering it would begin another conversation about the same thing, and he was trying to build momentum. "We could take the forty grand she left me and fix her cabin. You could work in a gallery. I could take a break from marketing. You said yourself I need a career change. It would be an adventure."

"How about doing the same thing here," Christina suggested. "Use the money for a down payment on a place in Coral Gables?"

"I'm sick of living this close to my parents," John said, thinking, if she didn't understand that, who had he been sleeping with all these years? "I'm starting to wonder how much influence I have over my own life."

"I'm starting to wonder how much you want to be involved in mine." Christina replied, sealing the lid back on the bottle. "You go to Bumfuck, John, you're leaving your job, your family, your friends. And me."

Not quite believing it, John looked at Christina and saw seven years of devotion culminating in a decision that took all of two seconds. Then he told himself a joke that he had always found more frightening than funny, one passed around ceremoniously by his buddies after breakups with wives and girlfriends, inserting their former partner's name for the punch line:

Knock, knock.

"Who's there?"

Not Christina anymore.

The dying California sunlight shredded trees, spreading Fritz Lang shadows across John's face and the Datsun. With each gust of wind, leaves and brittle sticks departed the main to the mulching roadside. Moss covered branches, mistletoe clung in clumps to inner limbs. There were no mangroves or sand. No coconuts or dates hanging oblong and edible, ripe for the picking. No Key Biscayne shimmering through the windshield. This wasn't a Sunday drive to contemplate sailboats and pink flamingos, a down and back to Sloppy Joe's to sit on Hemingway's stool and sip Cuba Libres. John smelled rotting apples, sweat, motor oil. He felt his universe imploding, boundaries pulled in and tucked around his neck like a plastic bag. California didn't feel laid back.

Something compelled him to look out the passenger's window to the drainage ditch running the length of the highway where he spotted the carcass of a decomposing animal. Deer, goat, dog? There was a trail in the dirt leading to where it had collapsed, probably with the hopes of somehow escaping. Every animal believes in immortality, John thought, if only in the moment before they die. He wondered if the thing knew where it was when it took its last breath. Euphoric adrenaline shock of a child falling off a bicycle. Did the rest of the pack so much as pause? He had heard that when dogs had litters in the country, their owners put the puppies in a sack and threw them in a river to drown.

Looking at the dead animal, John thought, What have I done?

"Don't do it," his father had warned, standing in the center of the living room where John had spent countless hours hunkered down on the rug doing his homework and listening to his parents fight.

The Gibson house was a steel-shuttered bungalow in the center of a middle-class block. Hurricane-proof, inside and out. The furniture consisted of cheap antiques and worthless heirlooms. It seemed that in decorating their home, John's parents had pledged to make the same mistakes as their parents, not just with the furnishings but across the board—fear-infused alcoholism with a Republican chaser. Grandma was the exception, departing from the fold. But they refused to acknowledge her second life as a senior citizen and sculptor because it didn't fit into their perspective of appropriate behavior. She was a skeleton in the closet, dead and bone-rattling.

"The devil you know is better than the devil you don't," his father continued. "They got cults out there, Moonies, Bhagwans, Manson, Jim Jones, feminists. Weird alliances."

John hadn't told his father that his bags were already packed. He had splurged on a one-way ticket in business class, paying last-minute prices for a hot towel and a shot of Courvoisier. Christina wasn't coming. Tomorrow he would be on the West Coast alone, manifesting his destiny.

He had just gone through the motions of saying goodbye to his mother. No tears there. She was sherry-glazed and doing the laundry.

"Take care and write," she said, the same farewell speech she had given John when he had moved fifteen minutes away to Coral Gables for college.

His father was more verbose. John was almost enjoying the

alarmist concern. It was a perverse power, knowing that whatever his father said, he could no longer stop him.

"You make a decision like this," his father said, trying to relate to him the dire consequences of embracing the unknown, "and you have to live with it, forever."

John knew his father had once dreamed of his only child becoming an investment banker instead of a manager in the marketing department of a public relations firm. He envisioned his son tearing entire economies a new asshole, not fucking around with pamphlets. John was supposed to own an apartment in Manhattan by now, a house in the Hamptons, a condo in Boca Raton. There were supposed to be brief visits and expensive dinners, beautiful women on his arm, so his father could have something worth looking at across the table from him. How would John get laid without money? Christina was fine, but his father was convinced she was going to leave him if John didn't claw his way into a higher tax bracket. His relationship with Christina had always been a mystery to his father, a wrinkle on a clean pressed shirt.

So, in preparation for his son's future, his father had made John play a game of "fantasy stocks." Choosing shares with a pretend bank account, he taught him how to pick "winners." IRAs, money-markets, futures, junk bonds. There were quizzes and transaction fees. Daily calls. Then he could read the sports page if he liked, unless he would rather make his father happy and scour the rest of the *Herald* for trends. But instead of the business section, John developed an obsession with the obituaries, people's lives laid out in a paragraph. Eventually his mother discovered his notebooks filled with imaginary obits for his family and friends, the neighbors and the postman. John's father concluded that his son was a failure, and it became clear to John that any success he might experience would be looked upon with disappointment by the man who had leaked life inside his mother while simultaneously sucking it out. But his father's real obituary was forthcoming. Men like him didn't see sixty too often. They died of strokes and colon cancer, overdosing on red meat and Black Label. John looked forward to writing his father's obituary. It wouldn't take long or be much of a headline, possibly only the words Also Dead Today. Or a small listing: Survived by. His own name beneath his mother's.

He felt a tinge of guilt as he watched his father's hand shake with a tremor of Parkinson's, a dark prayer answered. His father tried to steady the wave but the quake rolled down his arm, shoulder trembling, face twisting with the sting of palsy.

"You never listen to me anyway," his father said.

John wanted to disagree, tell his father he had heard everything, but it seemed cruel to attack a man whose own body had turned against him. His father backed away, ambling to a rhythm that only the marrow of his bones could understand, and went over to the liquor cabinet to pour himself a drink. Half the booze made it into the glass, the rest ran down his wrist onto the floor. A puddle formed at his feet. His father swallowed the contents of the tumbler, grimacing at his choice of medicine.

John heard his mother in the kitchen, banging pots and pans. Well-done meat, limp vegetables, plenty of potatoes. The menu never changed. John didn't miss eating at the family table, his mother serving the meal, then doing her crossword so she didn't have to watch her husband stabbing the meat with his knife and fork, challenging the food until he defeated every last bite. Gibsons were fast eaters, food defined by texture not taste. His father sat down in his chair waiting for the routine to begin, looking away from his only heir. John turned to leave. No tears all the way around.

So now here he was staring past the dashboard of the Datsun at the swaying trees, their branches swinging with suffusive intent, each limb fighting for space amidst the others. Leaves failing to cover the conflict. The largest of the trees let out a high-pitched creak from somewhere within its bark. That one should be cut down, John thought. What had his father whispered passing the casket at Grandma's funeral? "Damage control."

John recalled the relief in his father's eyes after throwing the first shovelful of dirt at Grandma's grave site. Later, while eating ice cream off a paper plate, he had heard the phrase "self-quarantine," uncertain whether someone was referring to Grandma packing up and moving to California or how his father had decided to stay put in Florida. John still couldn't believe she was dead. He remembered their last conversation, three days before her death.

Holding the telephone receiver in his office at Leggiere and Philips, John didn't hear the condemned roller coaster he had come to know as Grandma's voice, starting low and rising decibel by decibel, lurching upward with regrets and misgivings until it shrieked on its tracks, dropping into drunken grumbling. She had found a pace for her thoughts that carried with it the unsettling notes of finality. Instead of singing like a carnival ride, she seemed to hum an aria of sadness. It caught him off guard, not because she had called him at work—Grandma rarely telephoned him at home for fear of reaching "The Ivory Girl," as she had dubbed Christina—it was her tone that was unnerving. The calm urgency of someone who had prepared for catastrophe all their lives and had finally spotted locusts on the horizon.

John was eating a Cuban sandwich. He tried to do something else when he talked to Grandma, an excuse not to listen closely. If he did, he found himself hearing a kind of truth nobody else spoke, recruiting him into a conspiracy against himself. If any of his colleagues caught him in his cubicle on one of these calls, they teased him. He had told them stories about Grandma and they thought it was hilarious the way he could hardly tolerate a five-minute conversation with the woman. They made sinister Nosferatu gestures with their fingers and drinking motions with imaginary bottles in their hands. They knew it was Grandma because John's expression grew serious like he was contemplating the laws of physics instead of trying to create a mailer. The office secretary thought his discomfort was cute, everybody loving a crazy relative as long as they weren't related. Normally, John welcomed the distractions, but on this day he found their banter caustic and accusing.

Bean Bean, his friend and co-worker, whose real name was Benito Beñes, a Cuban whose parents had fled Fidel in the sixties by floating to America on a makeshift raft of inner tubes stripped from their Chrysler Imperial, called John's name out in the voice John used to mimic his grandmother. John scowled. Bean Bean's hands were full of fliers in three different fonts. Another arbitrary aesthetic decision. He smiled at John and his "abuela loca." When John pressed the receiver to Bean Bean's ear so he could hear the source, it ceased being funny.

"What's that noise?" Grandma wanted to know. "Feeding time at the zoo?"

"Sorry, Grandma," he said, swallowing a lump of sandwich and waving away Bean Bean.

"If you were sorry, you'd visit," she replied, telling him that he sounded older than he ought to be, adding, "It's amazing how people change if they're capable of it. Human beings have a huge capacity to better themselves, although they rarely ever do. But their opportunities never cease."

John glanced at the other Leggiere and Philips employees bustling about with tired eyes. The fluorescent lighting sucked color from everyone's skin, even the sunworshippers who spent their weekends darkening their tropical tans—the Long Island refugees and Jewish girls who now looked Jamaican. He knew half the office was involved in some deadline with an unhappy client. The other half was updating their resumes. Typical Thursday. The custodian changed the lining on the wastepaper baskets. Bean Bean had moved to the water cooler where he tried to avoid eye contact with their boss and a secretary he had slept with on a rum drunk. Everyone wanted to hit the beach or go home. They were pushing sand against the tide. That was one of Grandma's favorite expressions. She used it to describe the first sixty-five years of her life.

"There's so much bullshit to sort through before you get to yourself," she had told John. "I wish I could have started earlier. My race is about run. But you could take advantage of this. And as you go on, I go on. I'm in your blood, probably more so than your father. Sometimes it skips a generation, the desire to be alive."

John turned the key and stepped on the accelerator. The Datsun swung around in a semicircle off the shoulder of the road and back onto the highway. A rear door opened, threatening to spill his suitcase and the cardboard boxes full of everything he had flown out with him from Miami, but the door hit its hinge, springing back before anything was lost. He barely noticed, foot flush with floorboard, eyes fixed ahead. He saw a field of sheep grazing among archaic farm equipment, parted out and left to rust, tillers and thrashers, diggers and planters. Machinery of a bygone era. There was a pile of tractor tires, a stack of industrial pipe, broken cinder blocks. Smoke from a burn barrel gathered in a billow above the remnants of a feed barn. Metal stakes of a new vineyard flickered the reflections of anticipated growth in the periphery of his vision. He didn't bother to check his rearview mirror or feel sympathy for his compatriot left back in the ditch. He concentrated on the road stretching out before him.

And there it was again, the town where Grandma had spent the last twelve years of her life. The town where she had willed him his future. A green sign riddled with bullet holes and dents pounded by beer bottles flung from speeding trucks, said, "Boonville, pop 715." He blinked. Boonville, pop 715.

2

"I'm a feminist, but I can still have fun!" a woman's voice boomed from the dining room of the Boonville Hotel.

John was sitting at the bar. He threw back a shot of whiskey and took a swig of his beer chaser. After revisiting the mile-long strip of Highway 128 that was Boonville, he had decided he needed a drink. Maybe two drinks, stiff ones. Possibly three. Then I can assess the situation objectively, he convinced himself, and call Grandma's friend to get the keys to her cabin or make a run for the airport while my bags are still packed.

"That's the problem with the Movement," stated the voice from the dining room. "I can't be a part of it if I want to get laid."

The bartender shook his head. He had gentle blue eyes and stiff whiskers, his silver hair cut into a style that may have been fashionable some Sunday-go-to-meeting fifty years ago. He wore a wine-stained apron and a denim shirt with embroidery above each pocket depicting two blossoming roses. John didn't know if the shirt was a uniform or something the old man would wear anyway, not every day, but to get gussied up. He reminded John of the wagon-train cook in an old Western, the one the bad guys shot to let you know they were bad.

The bartender checked the room to see if he could be overheard, then fixed an elbow on the bar in front of John.

"Before this was the Boonville Hotel, it was the New Boonville Hotel," he said, voice gravelly, furthering the John Ford effect. "Hands down, it had the ugliest sign of any restaurant in Northern California."

John tried to imagine the sort of monstrosity an entrepreneur in this area might hang to attract passing motorists, thinking about the signs that cluttered Highway 1 in Florida, transforming what used to be a scenic view into a gaudy sales pitch.

"This building dates back to before I was born, which is saying something for anything standin' in these parts," the bartender elaborated. "But that sign was plastic and neon tacked on like an outhouse at the Taj Mahal."

John nodded, pushing his shot glass forward, indicating he didn't need another, although he wanted one. The bartender dispensed of the empty into a three-tubbed sink filled with soapy, clear, and blue-dyed water. He ran the dirty glass through the three pools and set it in a drying rack.

"But now that it's gone, we got her," he gestured back toward the woman's voice, a trail of water following his hand. "Not an even exchange."

John's head began to transmit a serene static. Hard alcohol hit him right away. Maybe he didn't want another. He took a drink of his Boont Amber to keep it rolling, a beer he learned from the menu was brewed across the street at the Buckhorn Saloon, which operated a "micro-brewery" in its basement. By the taste of it, that sounded about right.

He had spotted the Buckhorn on his drive into town, a redwood structure that resembled a hunting lodge, the sort of place where several televisions would be showing marginal sporting events, steeplechasing, kick-boxing, Australian-rules football. They had the same kind of bars in Miami with tropical motifs: "Tommy's Tuna Hut," "Jim's Trophy Room," "Danny's Dolphin Lounge." But the Buckhorn appeared to be a new business; nothing about it sagged like the rest of the town.

John had chosen to patronize the Boonville Hotel because of the fancier cars in the parking lot. He wanted to see the best Boonville had to offer and also check for a vacancy in case Grandma's cabin was unlivable. It was the only hotel he had seen since Cloverdale, another wide spot in the road thirty miles back toward San Francisco. Unfortunately, the hostess of the Boonville Hotel informed him that it wasn't a working hotel anymore, "just a restaurant and bar." John didn't press for details. He'd settle for a drink. But apparently the bartender had taken it upon himself to fill him in on the history.

"The owners of this place were a couple from Frisk," he told

John. "They were the ones responsible for the sign and puttin' art on the walls, fancy wine, espresso, ten bucks a salad: piece of lettuce, rabbit's shit worth of goat cheese. California Nouvelle Cuisine. Told the food critics they grew everything in the garden, organic. Yuppies and hippies love their organics. They came out of the woodwork to eat at the New Boonville Hotel. Then all hell broke loose."

People didn't often share information with John, who had overheard his friends describe him as "fiercely loyal" and "the last to know," the latter attribute lending itself to the first. He had the instincts of a mutt: feed me, pet me, fetch. What facts he had discovered, he had sought out to routine disappointment. The truth hurt. Still, he didn't want to be left out. He waited for the bartender's bone toss, feigning the composure of someone who could keep a secret. The bartender leaned in further, obviously having taken the job for the social aspects, not the paycheck.

He told John the former owners were bad businesspeople, running up debts and burning bridges. The wait-staff began demanding payment for their shifts in advance. A cook once quit three times in the same week, walking out during the dinner rush. They had to bribe him back with a case of wine. One night, tired of the battle, the couple "Z'ed" the register and skipped town without paying anyone. Two weeks later, they hired someone to rob the restaurant, then claimed theft and collected insurance money from a post office box in Mendocino.

"Big goddamned stink," the bartender said. "Locals started lootin' the place. See, your average logger or Mexican couldn't afford to eat here, still can't. They wouldn't let 'em hang out in the bar either. Yuppies in six-hundred-dollar suits don't want to look at rednecks in twenty-dollar jeans. Most folks just took what they thought was owed. I sent my grandkid into the wine cellar, but the half-wit came back with six bottles of grenadine. Been drinkin' Shirley Temples to make my toes curl. But now that couple runs a restaurant up in Seattle or Paris or somewhere. Rich people can get away with murder."

"Didn't the local authorities do anything?" John said, rinsing his throat with the rest of his beer.

"Local authorities?" the bartender laughed. "All we got is Cal, the resident deputy. Other than him, there's no law. He's got better things to do than guard this place. There's a fight pretty near every week at the Lodge, folks drivin' around higher 'n a billy, four-wheelin', shootin' guns. Besides, his response time ain't what I call inspirin'. By the time he gets his slow butt out of bed, crime's been done. Hold up a minute."

The bartender tramped three paces to take a couple's order, waiting patiently while a bald man in a sports jacket asked about the "nose" and "acidity" of various wines on the wine list. After a litany of questions concerning "harvests," "fermentation," and "barrel selection," he inquired about the house red, asking if it was "full-bodied." The bartender answered, "Like Liz Taylor on a chocolate binge." Uncorking a bottle labeled Edmeades, he poured two glasses with the nonchalance of someone who had spent more than their share of time behind a slab of mahogany. The bald man shoved his face into the glass, held it up to the light, swirled it, and then took a sip.

"Jammy," he said, as if he had stomped the grapes himself.

His companion sampled hers, seemingly satisfied. The bartender returned the bottle to its shelf, marked a check with a pencil and set the bill in front of them in a brandy snifter. The two kissed as if the bartender's tip was to witness their affection. He swabbed a wet spot to their right with a towel, wiped his hands on his apron, and slid back to John.

"I should have left them the bottle," he whispered. "And bet they couldn't make it back to the bright lights inside an hour. Highpockety prack."

John wasn't familiar with the expression, wondering if it was a bit of the local language, but as a native Floridian used to tourists making the rounds in Mickey Mouse ears, he felt he got the gist of it.

"Where you from?" the bartender asked, peeking at the couple like he had served them hemlock and was waiting for it to kick in. "You look like you got more sense than to be from around here."

"Miami," John answered.

"Should have known by the tan," the bartender said. "Almost mistook you for a workin' man."

"I work," John replied, not wanting to talk shop about the job he had quit. "But my grandmother died recently, so I'm moving out here into her place."

"Sorry to hear that," the bartender said.

"That I'm moving to Boonville or that my grandmother died?" John asked.

"Both," the bartender told him. "This town is hard on the young and it's never easy losin' family. Plus, bad luck runs in threes. You got somethin' else waitin' on you."

"I'm not superstitious," John said, although he was the kind of person who hedged his bets, throwing salt, knocking wood, avoiding the underneath of ladders. He wouldn't stoop for a penny on the ground unless it was faced heads up. Out loud, he claimed superstitions were for idiots. In private, he read his horoscope and cringed at unfortuitous fortune cookies. Christina once rearranged their furniture for good feng shui, demanding he buy a mirror for the entryway of the apartment to access their "career center." Why pull on trouble's braid? He did as he was told. He didn't solicit occult information, but always felt better if someone was predicting happiness instead of doom.

"Grandma and I weren't close," he told the bartender, trying to distance himself from a woman whose whole life seemed snakebit.

Edna Woodhull Nesbitt had been born in the wrong place at the wrong time, not that there would have been a right place or right time. If you had asked her, she would have told you the world was rigged against all women. But being born eccentric in Arizona in 1915 without a father did her no favors. On her seventh birthday, her schoolmarm widow of a mother gave her a copy of *The Works of Emily Dickinson,* relaying emphatically, "This is our legacy. Stay away from those Brontë sisters." Edna carried it with her wherever she went, sitting for hours in the Tucson sun, reading over and over, "I never saw a moor, I never saw the sea; Yet know I how the heather looks, And what a wave must be." She took long walks and had conversations with dead writers. She was at the top of her class at school, but indifferent to classmates. "Why doesn't she come play?" the other girls would ask. Edna thought the answer was obvious.

When her figure took shape at sixteen, it isolated her even further. Occasionally, a teen smelling of pomade and puberty would cross the cafeteria, eyes of the school upon him, and ask her to a movie. "Are you kidding?" she would say, unsure if the boy was being sincere, thinking to herself, "Wasn't he making fun of my breasts in gym class?" Her confusion sounded like a refusal and the boy would slink back to his lunchtable pals, cursing,

"Stuck-up bitch!" High school ended. She didn't go to prom. She didn't care. She got to go to college, the other girls didn't.

She matriculated at Arizona State to study teaching like her mother. The girls in her dormitory compared her looks to Myrna Loy's and were shocked that she had never dated. Edna was astounded that they had no intention of pursuing a career outside of being a rich man's wife. They called her "the last suffragette." "We already have the vote," they'd say. "What else do you want?" Edna didn't know, something. But to appease them, she dated Wayne Gibson, a business major from Honolulu who kept his tan year-round as captain of the A.S.U. golf team. She went along with the relationship like a guest served burnt food, forcing a look of satisfaction, never asking for seconds. They graduated, Edna with honors, Wayne a scratch golfer. They married and moved to Hawaii where Wayne was handed the family fortune, which he dropped in a series of bad investments. After selling their beach-front property, stating, "Nobody's going to want to vacation here anymore, not after Pearl Harbor," he invested in a chain of miniature-golf-course-Laundromats. They moved to Florida. Babies came, one after the other; Wayne named them, Edna raised them. They bought twin beds. Too late.

"None of it was my idea," Grandma revealed to John after his grandfather had died. "I never wanted to teach, I never wanted children," she paused, taking a pop from her glass of gin. "And I never wanted your grandfather. The only thing he knew how to do was play golf and lose money. I used to sit in our house and pray to God he'd die of heatstroke on the tee of the eighteenth hole. I'd take over the finances, and he wouldn't get to finish his round."

"Imagine," she continued, John transfixed, "We had once owned acres of Waikiki Beach and then there we were in the concrete squalor of South Florida sitting behind that 'Putt and Dry' with only a pocket full of quarters. And once we had children, your grandfather disappeared. I'll tell you, his absence became the only thing he had to offer me. This is a man's world. They don't even let women think about the possibilities. Now that he's really gone, I'm doing as I please!"

She took their bank book and her dog-eared copy of Emily Dickinson and flew to the self-actualizing confines of the Left Coast. The answer was obvious.

For the bartender's benefit, John briefly explained how Grandma had moved from Florida when he was fourteen, communicating through letters and telephone calls. She sent books for his birthday: Grace Paley, Edith Wharton, Dawn Powell. It was part of a deal that hinged on the understanding that he would never visit and she would never return. In fact, he still had to get the keys to her cabin from a friend of hers named Pensive Prairie Sunset.

"Aw shit!" the bartender let loose. "Is your grandmother's place up on Manchester Road?"

"I think so," John answered, reaching into his pocket for a slip of paper ripped from a pad of Leggiere and Philips stationery, the scrawl close to illegible, as if he had hoped to get lost from his own directions.

"I'll be a sonofabitch," the bartender said, when John confirmed the address as either 312 or 317 Manchester Road, unable to decipher the last digit. "Your grandma's the Squirrel Lady!"

"She's just Grandma to me," John replied, but could see the bartender recognized something in his features.

"I know folks come here to get weird, but the Squirrel Lady must have started way before she hit Boont," the bartender insisted. "I never had no problems with her, except winnin' one of her squirrels in a raffle. Pissy lookin' thing, eight-feet tall, still settin' in my backyard, not worth a shit. But that's my luck, same old six-then-seven."

"So you knew her?" John said, wondering if her reputation was going to prevent him from being anything more than Edna Gibson's grandson.

"Everybody knew her," the bartender told him. "But I don't talk about nobody's family to their face. Folks are more sensitive than they care to admit, and quicker with their fists than you'd care to imagine."

"What about Pensive Prairie Sunset?" John asked.

"See for yourself," the bartender said. "But I'm guessin' she's number three in your cycle of bad luck."

John tried to imagine his luck deteriorating more than it already had, clicking along like the insides of Grandma's pocket watch, running neither fast nor slow but at its own unpredictable pace. As a child, he had opened the gold timepiece because he had wanted to survey the works, gears gleaming, gunmetal efficient. He replaced the back and it never kept time again. Sometimes, tapping the crystal, it gave a few irregular seconds. False hopes. Nothing to be counted on. After Grandma pronounced it worthless, she gave it to him as a gift. Later in life, John carried it as a charm to the dog track. Jai alai matches. If I can get it to work, he'd say, shaking it roughly, I'll win. More superstition. There was only one cycle of luck, he had decided. And it was all bad.

"Here's one on the house," the bartender said, setting a fresh beer in front of John. "Welcome to the valley, Squirrel Boy. Bahl hornin'. Drink up though, this place is shut at 9:30 and I'm home with the wife yellin' at me by 9:35."

"How come you close so early?" John asked.

"In case you haven't noticed," the bartender replied, "this is a small town."

John thanked him, but as he drank, his fears reasserted themselves. Everything was becoming treacherous; the bar, the patrons, his buzz. He worried that Grandma had been more than a crazy alcoholic. Even the bartender could tell something else was wrong with her, anyone with common sense, a semi-normal nervous system, could see that. John's father had said Edna Gibson was mean enough to fake Alzheimer's. "Are you sure I have a son who is alive?" Grandma would ask if John mentioned his father, "Well, tell him I said, 'Hello,' and that I'm dying." She had been kind to John, but now he wondered if Grandma didn't resent him too, plotting to destroy her grandson because she could reach him in a way she couldn't her own son. Boonville could be a trap. Her love the bait.

John stared at the bubbles in his beer. He tried to remember the last time he had had a drink without waiting for Christina or a friend to join him. He didn't like to drink alone. But it was on occasions that he did the unexpected that he felt the most alive. Time seemed to stop; hours slowed to minutes, separated into seconds, halted into pictures. Still-life image of emotion. Perfectly framed as any flicker of *Citizen Kane,* only not running reel to reel. It was a slide show his mind flashed to make sense of the shifting world. And in these gluts, John felt he revealed himself, every beer bottle and doubt, cobwebbed corner and regret, shadow and memory in deep focus. This was who he was. This was life.

Everything else was in-between.

John held tight to the vision of himself in the Boonville Hotel, a stranger in a strange land. The modern-day frontiersman. Compared to his parents or Christina or the paper-shufflers back at Leggiere and Philips, he was Daniel Boone. Grandma had said Boonville had been named after Daniel Boone's cousin, so it was appropriate. He'd find a coonskin hat to fill out the role. Grandma was on the right track. He knew what he had to do. In a few minutes, he'd call her friend to get the keys and directions to the cabin, and then get a good night's sleep.

Resolved, he glanced around the bar at the art on the walls, a series of watercolors of dilapidated barns. Unobtrusive as shopping music. He smiled at the red-winers giddy with their outing, happy at how friendly people could be when you spent money. They raised their glasses in his direction and the bald man said, "Cheers." John could tell they thought they made friends wherever they went, the kind of people who used name tags to create one-way intimacies with waiters, bellhops, gas station attendants, ice cream scoopers, whoever had the misfortune of working for minimum wage and with the public.

Pricks, John thought, wishing the couple would gather their coats and drive off to whatever bright corner of California they had come from.

Then he saw her.

She was waiting by the exit, shouting something about how homosexuals were going to be "the negroes of the nineties," AIDS awareness replacing the Civil Rights Movement as a political focus for liberals. She wore a man's dress shirt, showcasing her femininity within a shroud of the masculine. John flashed on Christina, undeniably beautiful, but always searching for center stage. This woman the spotlight followed like a celebrity in rehab. She tossed back ringlets of brown hair with fingers that belonged on the hands of a cellist, then returned to the dining room, possibly having forgotten something. But before she was gone, John caught a glimpse of her eyes. Blue. Sea without wave, sky without cloud.

"Squirrel Boy," the bartender said, "Put your tongue back in your mouth and piss on a fire hydrant outside. Don't fool with her. She was the one doin' that squawkin'. Not to mention, her ex is crayzeek. Make your Grandma seem stone sane. Been six years, and if it weren't for lack of pussy, he wouldn't know they was ever divorced."

The bartender told John how the woman's ex-husband had recently made a visit to her intentional community, drunk and demanding entry into her cabin. She said, "Fuck off!" He produced a chain saw, yelling, "Nobody locks me out of my house!" Then tried to cut a new door in a side wall, forgetting she was the sole resident on the commune with electricity. He hit a power line. Deputy Cal found him unconscious fifty feet away, still holding the Stihl, hands burnt to the color of forgotten toast. She had a restraining order, but nobody had the death wish to enforce it.

"Mr. Cooper the English schoolch took her here for gorms once," the bartender said. "I'm settin' up horns when I hear this racket and go to the window to see what I can see. There's her ex, takin' swings at Cooper's car with an ax. Loggers got a thing for their equipment. Then he punched in the windows, bare-fisted. He said he'd kill Cooper if he saw them together again. Nobody doubted him. He may be jimheady, but he's also a man of his word."

"Why did she marry him?" John asked.

"Why does anybody get married?" the bartender replied. "He's good lookin', makes a decent wage. Around here even the hippies marry young."

"What's her name?" John said.

"Sarah McKay," the bartender told him. "She's prettier than the gene pool of Anderson Valley, but I'm tellin' you stay clear 'less you want to go the way of your grandma."

That said, the bartender began to collect coasters, wash glasses, and busy himself with the procedures of closing time. Fair warning.

"Ever seen a redneck in the city?" a voice asked.

In the reflection of the bar mirror, John spotted a man standing behind him wearing black and smiling like he might leap on him with his teeth. He was of average height but pumping-iron stocky. He had a big nose and his hair was slicked back with gel. There was a scar running across his left cheek. John could tell he wasn't from Boonville.

"They look scared," the man hissed.

John turned his shoulders to face the man, noticing at once the earring in his lobe previously obscured by the angle of the reflection—a silver hoop engraved with skulls, much larger than the diamond studs John's friends had started sporting, and obviously having more to do with piracy than fashion.

"Can they stop a bullet?" the man asked, opening his leather jacket and revealing a gun tucked into his belt. "I came to help these hayseeds harvest early, if you know what I mean. I checked it out, hippies and rubes, that's all that's here. Too stupid to have money, not tough enough to keep it if they did. Don't sweat these hillbillies, they'd last two minutes on concrete. It's a whole different ball game."

Startled by the gun but having enough street smarts from watching reruns of "Baretta," John tried to stay calm and agree with whatever the man said. Despite the firearm, the man seemed friendly; the gun flash wasn't so much a threat, but a confidence.

"The name's Balostrasi," the man said. "See you around."

"Take care," John offered, wondering if anyone else had seen the gun and just how long it would take Deputy Cal to answer a distress call.

"I will," Balostrasi promised, swaggering his way to the exit, earring swinging like a canaryless perch. "Go Hurricanes!"

"Go Canes!" John responded out of habit, realizing Balostrasi must have heard him tell the bartender he was from Miami.

And Sarah McKay appeared again, reclaiming her space with a rail thin woman in blue jeans and cowboy boots. They were both laughing. Sarah stuffed a wad of money into her pocket. The rail said, "Thanks again." Sarah answered, "No problem. I'll be flush in another month when the season's over." The rail responded, "Sorry I can't help." Sarah said, "No worries." Balostrasi held the door open for them, but instead of leaving, the two women filled stools next to John. Balostrasi smiled, giving John the thumbs up sign. Then he was gone.

John believed in the "no blood, no foul" rule of inappropriate behavior. If someone crossed the line of social etiquette, then walked out of your life to wreak havoc somewhere else, it wasn't your problem. Especially when Sarah McKay was gesturing at your beer, and asking, "Doesn't Boont Amber make you feel like you have to shit?"

John stared through the question and into her eyes. Balostrasi, concealed weapons, and idle threats were quickly forgotten. Sarah was even more beautiful up close. She had a distinctive 1940s quality to her, as if she were stopping off on her way home from the munitions factory, or if she held her hands behind her head, posing for a painting to be imprinted on the side of a bomber. She was why men fought wars. Her skin was creamy white, smelling of pine trees, and doobage?

"I guess by your expression it does," she said.

"No," John answered, more flustered by her voice than Balostrasi's gun. "I always look this way when I drink."

"Then I'd hate to watch you shit," she replied, turning to her friend and the bartender, who was explaining that the bar was closed.

John regarded the back of her head, only Beer Nuts and ashtrays between them. He thought about the bartender's warning and his own limited knowledge of logging tools. Even stacking blocks as a child, he never built a structure that didn't topple. That seemed to be the point, the elastic moment before collapse and watching the pile crumble. But he was beginning to feel good, real good, and perhaps subconsciously infected by Balostrasi's confidence, he decided conversation couldn't hurt anyone.

Sarah was talking to her friend about herbal medicine, running her hand through her hair again.

"I can't do that with my hair," the bald wine connoisseur commented.

"You can't do it with mine either," she replied.

The bald man laughed and his partner wrapped her arm through his, trying to regain his attention. She gave Sarah a nasty look.

"What do you suggest?" John asked, realizing his timing was awkward, on the heels of the bald man's remark.

Sarah swiveled toward him, sizing him up, making sure she had previously pegged him correctly. The rail peered past her, intrigued. Attractive women made John nervous. Their beauty seemed to give them standing to pass judgment on his manhood. Not that he thought of himself as inadequate, but there was always the chance of changing his mind.

"Since this bar is closed," she said, more for the bartender's benefit, "I'd change venue. Maybe the Buckhorn, except that's where the closet pervs congregate. If you do go there, remember the faces. Their regulars hot-tubbed with Leonard Lake and Charles Ng, waiters from Philo who hacked up bodies and buried them beneath their house, proving again that closet pervs are the worst, especially if they have video equipment. Guaranteed, somebody eating pretzels over at the Buckhorn will be the next Kenneth Parnell or Treefrog Johnson, digging pleasure pits in their basements with passages of the Bible plastered to the walls. It's true what they say about born-agains, they're even more fucked up the second time around."

"Huh," was all John could muster.

"Huh," Sarah mocked him. "It probably wouldn't be your scene."

None of this was his scene.

"Why do you go?" John asked, trying to regain his balance.

"I take a risk once in a while," Sarah answered.

I bet you do, he thought, the smooth bend of Sarah's neck reminding him of the C plus he received in art history. Postmodern abstract? Preindustrial deconstructionalist? Flemish realism? It definitely reminded him of something chiseled from marble and then rubbed to an erotic luster. *Le Baiser*? To this day, he didn't understand texture, tactility, works of art that you could touch.

"Thanks," he said.

"I wasn't through," she said. "What are you, some sort of a tourist?"

"No," John said, trying not to appear to her like one of the red-winers or as out of place as Balostrasi. "I'm a local."

"Sorry, but I know everybody in this town," Sarah said, holding back her laughter. "Besides, just a tip, around here locals don't wear Dockers."

The rail giggled.

"I'm trying," John said, pretending his feelings were hurt. "I just moved here."

"Whereabouts?" Sarah inquired.

"Manchester Road," John said.

"The Squirrel Lady's place?" the rail asked.

"That's right," John answered. "I'm her grandson, the Squirrel Boy."

"Are you a rodent sculptor too?" Sarah asked.

"No," John said, half-wishing he was because he could see that it might score points, and anything was more interesting than marketing.

But he told the women the truth, apologizing for his former vocation. He said he didn't know what he was going to do now.

That's when Sarah's tone changed from someone giving a grocery clerk a hard time to someone speaking to a lifelong friend.

"I was going to suggest a 'horn of skee,' as they say in these parts, down at the Lodge," Sarah said. "Then me and my friend got a baggie of something that will make you feel real local. You smoke?"

John knew he smelled doobage.

"I stick to the family drug," he saluted with his glass.

"Every drug is my family's drug," Sarah replied.

"Sorry to hear that," John said.

"You know," she looked solemnly at John, reaching for his beer and taking a sip, a foam mustache appearing above her lips. "You can't pick your relatives."

John was struck with the uneasy feeling that Sarah had been to his house, played in his yard, experienced his family's tension first-hand. It sent him spinning to another time and place. He was seven years old again, standing in the living room of his parents' home, his father reading the paper, scotch and soda, his mother fixing dinner, white wine, entering from the kitchen.

Mother: "Does your friend want to stay for dinner, John?"

Father: "We can't be feeding the whole damn neighborhood. We don't send him to anybody's house at dinnertime."

Mother scowls. John feels the weight of her anger.

Father: "What the hell are you looking at? Are you making dinner? Make it. Let me read about the nigger riot in Overtown. Unless you want to invite them too?"

Mother: "I don't know why you talk to me that way."

John, head pounding, tries to leave the room with his friend.

Mother: "Did I say you could go?"

John, no response, returns.

Mother: "You can just stand there. Next time you'll ask to be excused. And what's the matter with you, Sourpuss? Did your mother call? The new office manager giving you a hard time? I told you ten years ago that company would get you nowhere."

Father: "I'm nowhere? Then where are you? You taking us somewhere? You going to watch soap operas and cooking shows to get us somewhere? Sitting on your fat ass, on the couch I bought, watching the television I bought, in the house I bought, here in the middle of nowhere? I worked for all of this, paid for it with my check. Your name's not on anything. Remember that!"

Mother: "You want to take credit for the twin beds too, Mr. Provider? What else? The refrigerator that can't keep anything cold? The promotion to senior vice-nobody you've never gotten? While we're on the subject, how about the reservations at the Travelodge under the name of Johnson? Didn't think I knew? Next time push the twins together, I'll leave for three minutes, and we can spend the money we save, excuse me, you save, to fix the refrigerator."

Friend: "John, I gotta go."

Father: "Tell her she can stay, John, as long as you don't marry her."

John, no response, wishing it all away.

"That certainly is true," he said to Sarah. "You can't pick your relatives."

"Or your relatives' noses," the rail added.

John snapped back to the conversation. He was having difficulty concentrating on more than one thing at a time. He blamed it on circumstance.

"I'm sorry," he said, trying to conceal his somberness. "I was somewhere else."

"Really?" Sarah asked. "Where?"

"No place you'd want to spend much time," John replied.

"Sounds like Boonville," Sarah said.

"I wouldn't know," John said, wondering if she had been raised here.

"You will soon enough," the rail assured him.

John wasn't sure he wanted to, knowing there were experiences in which people consumed too much information all at once, leaving them bloated and immobile, chewing on the indigestible facts for the rest of their lives. A last supper of knowledge. He didn't want this move to overwhelm him.

"I don't think I introduced myself," John said, trying to change the subject. "My name is John Gibson."

He shook Sarah's hand. She watched him, one eyebrow lifting into a lock of auburn hair. The top three buttons of her shirt were unbuttoned and John could see the curve of her breasts. He had to tell himself to look away.

"I'm Sarah," she said. "This is my friend, Lisa."

"I'd shake your hand too, Lisa," John told her. "But I'm afraid I'd fall on my face if I tried to reach that far. I'd like to avoid a scene on my first night in town."

"Then you can't come with us," Lisa answered. "I'm searching for that warm sunken feeling and might need a scene to get there. It's been a long week."

"It's only Tuesday," John said, taking the bait.

"I told you it was dragging," Lisa said, reeling him in.

"Drink up, cowboy," Sarah laughed. "If you want to play the home version of 'Wild Kingdom'."

"You two ready?" he asked, rising unsteadily.

"Is anybody ever really ready for anything they do?" Sarah replied.

John tried to remember when he had been ready for something he had done. In every instance, there seemed to have been a curve catching him off guard, school, puberty, work, sex, reading *The Brothers Karamazov*, leaving home. Never really ready. Even the easy stuff, geography tests, ordering in a restaurant, smiling for the camera. None of it.

He held open the door for his two companions, both jacketless and shivering from the cold air outside. Sarah led the way down the hotel's steps and across the street to the Lodge, Lisa grabbing her arm after a few chilly steps. John brought up the rear.

"I hope we don't run into Daryl," Lisa said.

"Yeah?" Sarah snarled. "Fuck him."

The Lodge was a squat brick building attached to a defunct restaurant and a convenience store called "Pic 'N Pay." There were closed blinds covering the bar's one window, which was lit by a beer sign. Inside was a dark room filled by a pool table and a crowd of drinkers. It took John a moment to adjust to the lack of light, and when he did, he saw nobody was smiling. Cowboy hats and giant belt buckles. The men wore wool shirts and muddy work boots. The women, tight jeans. Cigarettes burned between fingers, in ashtrays or left dead on the edge of the bar. Lower lips bulged from chewing tobacco. Bottles of spit rested near open cans of beer. Dead animal heads hung as decorations while country music played on the jukebox. There were two tables in the back near the bathroom, shimmed with matchbooks.

Sarah made a beeline for the bar and John followed. Lisa stopped to say hello to a few people. Eyes squinted in John's direction. He could tell they were interested to find out who he was and what he was doing in here; a distant relative, a tourist, a dead man walking? When she rejoined them, John could see that Lisa was in her element, more so than at the Boonville Hotel. The Lodge's patrons seemed wary of Sarah. They were outright leering with malevolence at John.

"Don't worry, Squirrel Boy. I talked to Larry and Danny," Lisa said, claiming a stool. "I don't think anybody's going to kick your ass."

John bought the first round of beer and whiskey, thinking it would end right there, "Goodnight, nice meeting you. Maybe we could do this again sometime?" He'd once followed a Cuban cutie into a similar situation in Little Havana. One mohito and he left without asking her name. But his companions immediately ordered and paid for another setup. And another. Then it was his turn again. He didn't want to be a wuss. Nobody had harassed him so far. He was starting not to care as much either. He'd been in fights before. Blood dried. A couple of women from the sticks weren't going to drink a Miami Hurricane under the table. He ordered another round, fumbling with the bills in his wallet, urging himself on with the U of M cheer, "We've got some 'canes over here! Whoosh, whoosh!"

Their conversation started out light, 70s television, favorite foods, mutual appreciation for the film *Badlands*. Lisa didn't say much once the libations had been served, content to drink and listen. But as the alcohol took effect, Sarah switched into a confessional mode, offering unsolicited information about her divorce, dropping out of college, an unhappy childhood, a self-centered mother, an absent father, and living on a commune called "The Waterfall." She had been born in San Francisco and uprooted to Mendocino County by her mother when she was eleven. That's when she had met Lisa. They toasted their friendship. Sarah had moved away from the area several times, for a year, six months, to pursue art, men, a career. She said she hated the hypocrisy of the hippies she lived with and everyone "knowing your shit in this redneck town." But, for some reason, she had always returned.

"Everyone here is a failure, it's just a matter of degree," Sarah said, looking away from John and into the menagerie of bottles behind the bar, as if the truth were something that couldn't be met straight on. "Success is simple, leave and don't come back."

John could tell Sarah was trying to swim free of something

tangled in her mind, past the waves of melancholy that rolled over your finer senses when you drank. They were pounding drinks fast. He had been caught in the undertow of alcohol many times and understood that to escape its influence you had to float in the seam of the pull, ignoring the weight of yourself, until it let go of you.

"Step one is not being pregnant for prom," Sarah explained.

"Numero uno," Lisa agreed.

"Number two, never fall in love with a local," Sarah said.

"Dos!" Lisa chirped.

"And three," Sarah turned back to John, "No matter who you are, wherever you've come from, get the fuck out!"

"Tres flores por los muertos!" Lisa slurred. "Y tres cervezas mas. Melonie, otra vez, por favor!"

"Your head has to be on straight if you're sneaking away from the inevitable," Sarah said, taking a drink of her beer. "But if you stay, you've got to understand *our* kind of insanity. Guys like Jim Jones had to fly to Guyana to get it done. The Kool-Aid group slaughter thing doesn't cut it here. We go for the slow burn: wife beating, child abuse, molestation. Take people down, but do it slowly. Make them wish they *were* dead."

Sarah leaned toward him, her breath on his face: beer, bourbon, the faint scent of peppermint. He watched the space between her lips forming each word. He wanted to kiss her, to tell her he understood, to reduce their confusion to some kind of identifiable conflict. Nature vs. nurture. Inserting tab A into slot B. Then he could fly back to Miami and beg for Christina's forgiveness.

"My advice, Squirrel Boy," she said. "Eat as many meals at the hotel as you can, listen to country music, drink heavily, and drive home fast and fucked-up out of your mind. Boonville is for losers. And we hate outsiders because they have an option we don't, the chance to leave."

She finished her beer and searched down the bar for the next round. John noticed she was blushing. He wanted to believe it was from the embarrassment of revealing intimacies, but it was more likely the rouge of whisky. The result was the same, the color of her cheeks accenting her milky skin and the red hidden in the curl of her hair. Somewhere in her lineage, not too far back, John thought, were a crew of hard-drinking Irishmen who sang loudly and died young.

"It's best not to get too involved with anybody," she added, facing the dull light of an Olympia sign. "Just be nuts and blend."

"I resemble that remark," a voice announced.

John peered over his shoulder into a face that could have been featured in a book on the Stone Age, the words "hunter" and "gatherer" written throughout the margin. It was a face familiar to Boonville, John had already seen four or five, one had spilled a drink on him and bumped him with a pool stick, not apologizing for either transgression. But for that matter, it was a face recognizable in any small town. He thought if you could shake out the bars in deep east Texas, the paper-mill towns of Georgia, the swamps of Louisiana, the hog farms of Arkansas, or the coal mining camps of West Virginia, you could produce a thousand men able to pass for this man's brother or identical twin. And accounting for promiscuity in the jerkwater, they quite possibly were.

"Billy Chuck," Sarah said, glass and spirit replenished, "This is John 'The Squirrel Boy' Gibson, the Squirrel Lady's grandson."

"No shit?" Billy Chuck whistled.

He stuck out his hand for John to shake, the malice in his grip covered by a thin veneer of friendship. Dirt magnified the wrinkles of his palm. Blistered fingers, calluses, cut knuckles. John knew he was shaking the hand of a man who made his living outdoors.

"Don't let these hippies sour you on our town," Billy Chuck advised. "Lesbians are always bustin' balls cause they ain't got any."

"Prince, you are so charming," Lisa said.

Billy Chuck grinned, exposing his teeth, yellowed bits of calcium that had played out their usefulness. He licked his tongue around his extended gum line, seemingly proud that he had any teeth at all. Under her breath, John heard Lisa called him a "crank junkie."

"John does marketing," Sarah said. "I'd tell him what you do, Billy Chuck, but jerking off is more of a hobby than an occupation, isn't it?"

"When in doubt, whip it out," Billy Chuck answered. "You ought to know, Sarah. Must be lonely at the commune without Daryl, havin' a boat on and no oar to paddle."

"You're such a child," Sarah said. "I can't believe we're the same age."

John couldn't believe it either. Bad teeth aside, Billy Chuck was aging like picked fruit. John had gauged him to be at least twenty years older than Sarah, one of her friends' fathers. His hairline was receding, temples gray. Maybe he had that accelerated-growth disease that turned children into old men. John tried to catch a glimpse of the younger man trapped inside Billy Chuck's skin, but didn't want to be caught staring.

"We went to school together," Sarah told John. "Junior high and high school, not to mention the quality time spent drinking at the gravel pits, the Indian caves, and right here. If I didn't know you so well, Billy Chuck, I'd have to kill you."

"I can't believe he was my prom date," Lisa offered.

"Hard to believe I would have asked a dagger," Billy Chuck admitted. "But you were pretty, Lisa. And it's hard to spot a lesbian when they're young."

"It's easy to spot an asshole," Sarah replied.

She told John that when they had attended Anderson Valley High School, the student body was ninety. Forty boys, ten in special ed. Certifiably retarded. That didn't include the shop crowd, which straddled the line between retarded and dull-normal. Girls went to dances with their cousins and brothers. In her English class, combining all the juniors and seniors who had the scholastic aptitude to maybe take an aerobics class at the junior college someday, there was only one boy. And she married him.

"I was against Lisa going to prom with you, Billy Chuck," Sarah recalled. "I fixed her up with a Mendo boy, but he canceled. What was his name, Lisa?"

"Todd Chambers," Billy Chuck said, surprising both women. "Mendocino's the next real town north, Squirrel Boy, and everyone there's named Todd or Morning Starr. Spelled with two D's and two R's. Buncha fuckin' yup hippies. Never did an honest day's work in their lives, growin' dope, sellin' seaweed, spendin' their money fuckin' up the valley. Goddamned tourists. And their kids are second-generation tourists."

Billy Chuck told John that Mendocino used to be good country when his father was young, but tourists had brought in their tourist shit, wine and cheese, art and whale T-shirts, retreats and inns, and now they were overrun by Todds and Morning Starrs who thought they were better than the people who built the county, who did the living and dying before any of them had ever heard of the Redwood Highway. His eyes rested on John, who was tempted to point out that he spelled his name with one N.

"I knocked his dick in the dirt," Billy Chuck said, spitting tobacco onto the floor, smearing a string of saliva across his stubbled chin. "Whenever we played football against Mendo, we picked out who we were gonna hit on the kickoff. Didn't matter if they ran the ball back all the way for a touchdown, the point was to stick somebody. Hopefully someone would choose the ball carrier. I picked Todd, number 82. Hit him so hard his whole family said, 'Ouch!'"

At this point, Billy Chuck reached for a cocktail napkin to make a diagram of "The Play." John knew every man had their own version of "The Play," a last-second shot, called third strike, diving catch, where in their minds they became the testosterone-dripping center of the universe. "The Play" after which lightning flashed, women fainted, headlines were printed, and children were named on your behalf. John's "play" had come prematurely on a game-winning, check-swing single in Little League, leaving him quiet during conversations about sporting glories.

"See, I was over here," Billy Chuck drew an X on the napkin. "That yup was way on other side of the field." He drew an O. "I ran straight at him." He drew a line connecting the two. "I was low like you're supposed to be. Neck up, arms in close. I put my shoulder so far into that pretty boy, I thought they were gonna have to surgically remove him from me." He scribbled over the O, tearing a hole in the napkin. "He flew about six feet. I told him, 'Stay there son, I'll be right back!'"

Billy Chuck chortled. John laughed too, not at the joke so much as Billy Chuck in general, at being drunk in the Lodge in Boonville. John could tell Sarah and Lisa thought Billy Chuck was pathetic and if it weren't for the size of the town and their shared experience, they wouldn't piss on him if he were on fire.

"When I heard Lisa was goin' to prom with Todd, I reminded him how bad it would hurt to get hit again, this time without pads," Billy Chuck said. "'Take a Morning Starr or Sequoia Cooze to your own yup-fest,' I told him."

He wiped his mouth with his shirt sleeve, getting the spit this time.

"I was all-league honorable mention that year," he said, taking a long pull from his can of Coors Light.

"That's sweet in a Neanderthal kind of way," Lisa declared. "How come you never told me?"

"Strong silent type," Billy Chuck answered, ordering more drinks for all of them.

The bartender, Melonie, set another round of beer and whisky in front of them. She was pregnant; tired eyes, sand-bagged posture, inflated body encased in jaundiced skin. Her hair seemed to have been carefully styled and then slept on. She wore a T-shirt with an arrow pointing to her stomach that read: "This one better make money." Her mouth moved wordlessly as she took care of the orders, whispering advice to her unborn in the language of reluctant mothers. The men in the Lodge avoided her eyes.

"Sides," Billy Chuck said, "It don't look good with you turnin' out to be a dyke."

"Will you stop with your homophobia?" Sarah pleaded. "Just because we don't date anybody from Boonville doesn't mean we're lesbians. It means we have standards."

"Guess I hit a nerve," Billy Chuck said. "You better bring that up at one of your clit-chats, if you get past exchangin' dildos."

"Fuck you," Sarah said. "I haven't seen a woman near you since that prom. If anyone's gay, it's probably you. Why don't you take it to the other end of the bar, Big Man?"

John looked to where Sarah was referring, an empty stool near a television tuned to an endless chase scene, no outlaws or cops, just cars following each other across terrain that resembled a Hollywood back lot. A man wearing a Confederate flag bandanna stood at the bar by the open seat, fingering a bundle of butcher paper with one less finger on his hand than the national average. Blood seeped from the package, forming a puddle on the bar. He was delivering a soliloquy on the merits of his smoker, stating he could make jerky out of anything: deer, bobcat, raccoon. A woman was sleeping with her head resting next to the mess. Two men holding beers racked their memories and math skills to figure out which of them had "got" and "kicked" more ass. They debated whether a piece of ass should be counted twice if it had been both "got" and "kicked," or if that constituted a separate category. Meanwhile, a woman in pink overalls climbed onto her barstool to dance to her "all-time favorite song." No expert, John guessed it was Dolly, Tammy, or Reba. Something aside from bleeding meat smelled pungent.

"Just joking." Billy Chuck backed off.

There would be plenty of nights to drink alone, John could see him thinking. This didn't have to be one of them.

"You used to be able to take it," Billy Chuck said, still pushing.

"I can take it," Sarah replied. "I've been hearing that shit since before I had any idea what sex was. Assholes coming on to me and crying lesbian because I said, 'No.' I've had enough of insecure men and their tiny dicks."

"I know you're not talkin' about me 'cause I measured myself this morning," Billy Chuck said, "That must be the way it is at the Waterfall, Aslan with his Ecstasy and eight-year-olds. 'Father of the New Children.' Talk about a 'new age,' happy birthday, there's a six-foot-ten hippie corkscrewin' your ass."

"Fuck you, Howdy," Sarah cursed. "You've never been to the Waterfall. You don't know what goes on there. I meant Boonville, you and these rednecks."

Sarah swung her arm to include the whole bar. John's head rolled dizzily trying to follow her gesture. He tried to control the visual insubordination by focusing on the pool table, but too much motion surrounded it, lights and laughter, players and pool cues. Uh-oh, he thought. Head spins. His stomach churned with the recollections of vomiting in half-forgotten bathrooms, tile and porcelain, splattering alleys with his insides; car bumpers, bushes, dress shoes. Unsettling short orders wavered somewhere between his pancreas and the back of his throat, minestrone and milk, egg yolks and escargot, okra and octopus. It was familiar territory, as common as sticking his finger down his throat to get it all out. John was a puker. He tried to think of cold water and light breezes. But the odor of rancid meat wormed its way from the Siberian end of the bar, snowballing its fragrance with everything else sour and unwashed in the Lodge. John looked to his new friends for support, but they were deep into their discussion, justifying their animosity for each other. He shut his eyes, fighting his reflex to gag.

Why didn't I stop at three? he asked himself.

"Don't wag your finger at me, bitch," Billy Chuck said, oblivious to John's plight. "You don't know Boont from bullshit. Lisa's grandpa and mine drank in this bar when it was called the

Bucket of Blood, logged these forests with plain old axes and saws. When the tourists have gone off to ruin someplace else, me and Lisa will be here doin' what our families have always done here: try to get to the next day. Where you gonna be? Smokin' dope in some other town? Talkin' shit in some other therapy group? You came with the Volvos and you'll leave with them."

"Don't worry, Billy Chuck," Sarah promised. "I'll be here."

They stared at each other, beauty and the beast bickering with no fairy tale ending in sight. A trucker sucked in his gut, strolled over to the pool table and placed a stack of quarters beneath the far rail. One of the cars on the television crashed and caught fire. Someone burped for a solid five seconds. A couple opened a bag of pork rinds and began munching. The man with the missing finger was showing Melonie a bloody hoof. The song on the jukebox wound to a conclusion and Pink Overalls climbed off her stool.

"I'll be here too," John said.

They were the first words John had spoken in some time and nobody seemed certain they had come from his mouth. Billy Chuck was the first to laugh. Sarah and Lisa joined in with a few others who had been eavesdropping. Someone bought him a drink. John again became more concerned with the state of his stomach and the ricocheting of the pool balls. But despite nausea and the unpleasantness of the conversation, something had told him that this was in line with a larger picture; Grandma had led him here for a reason. There was nothing for him back in Miami but the man he had left behind. Boonville was something he had to endure. He had the feeling he was going to be here for a while, a good long while, and eventually he would belong as much as anybody else. Then he could decide to leave.

"I'll be here too," he repeated, emptying a shot glass.

"Damn straight! It takes more than bulls to have a rodeo," Billy Chuck whooped, thumping John between the shoulder blades, almost causing him to expound further and less articulately. "A toast! To the new age of new locals, anyone after us is a tourist. No hard feelings."

"Call me a bitch again," Sarah said, "my knee's in your crotch."

"Don't call me an asshole," Billy Chuck replied. "In this age of equality, I ain't afraid to punch no woman."

"Yeah?" Sarah said, her sternness giving way, clinking Billy

Chuck's beer can with her own. "Sounds like all we can ask for."

She chugged the rest of her beer. Billy Chuck followed suit. Lisa ordered another round so they could all drink to the truce. "Tequiler to seal her," she said, licking the fold of John's thumb and dosing him with salt. After swallowing the firewater, Sarah popped a lime in his mouth. John bit hard, then spit out the peel. He heard everyone claim "no hard feelings." His eyes were heavy. He drooped low in his stool, beer held well below his knees, legs akimbo, room rotating to the baseline of the Wurlitzer. He snatched at a lyric, what sounded like: "If I get stoned and drink all night long, it's a family tradition."

"Bahl hornin'!" Billy Chuck whooped.

Then somebody said something and there was a cheer and the bar was all motion like a fire drill or a hurricane warning and he was being pulled outside. He didn't think he could stand alone. But he had a new family and Billy Chuck was promising that nothing would happen to him as long as there was air in his lungs; Daryl could go fuck himself. John wasn't so sure about the air in his own lungs or Billy Chuck's sudden fraternity or who this Daryl was again and what was everybody hollering about. With each step less steady than the last, but all bringing him closer to the pulsating mob, he crossed the length of the Lodge's parking lot, wiggly beneath the night's sky. The fresh air was helping his stomach, but more than anything, right now, he wanted Christina. Not the woman who cared about what make of car they drove, but the carefree Christina who had made him feel safe and loved. He couldn't believe she wouldn't be in his bed tonight, giving purpose to his life. No more worrying about what's for breakfast, comments about his marketing strategies, arguing over who was hogging the covers. No snuggle-bunny.

Billy Chuck slapped his face and pointed to a figure across the street by the post office making a stamping motion with his leg, bellowing a chorus of moos. John was about to search for change and a telephone to call Christina, when he noticed the guy next to him breathing heavily and doing the same thing as the man across the street, pantomiming a farm animal. "One day, them Kurts brothers are going to kill themselves doing this," a voice prophesied. And the two men ran toward one another, eating up the eighty yards of asphalt between them, throating low-pitched cowcalls and gaining speed, until in the center of the road, on one of the hyphens of yellow that John could see would soon to be covered with blood, they collided with a butt of heads. There was a resounding pop. The brothers staggered, paindrunk. And collapsed.

The crowd applauded. Men exchanged money. They weighed comparisons of past exhibitions. A group bowled cans of beer at the Kurtses from a cooler in the back of a pickup. Others threw open bottles that smashed in the street and covered the two men with foam and fragments of glass. Some couples kissed as if the New Year had arrived. Then, as rapidly as it had assembled, the horde reconvened inside the Lodge, leaving the Kurtses unconscious in the middle of the road with the noise of the crickets.

"What was that?" John asked whoever was keeping him from falling down.

"Oh," a female voice replied, "That's something the Kurts do."

"No it ain't," a voice disagreed. "They're tryin' to stop the tourists from comin'."

"We should help," John mumbled.

"Damn straight!" the second voice confirmed.

And the last thing John remembered was lying down next to the Kurtses in the center of Highway 128 and the coolness of concrete against his face and pebbles digging into his rubbery cheek and holding somebody's hand and an ache in his knee and the smell of beer and the warmth of bodies and wondering what Christina was doing at this exact moment and if Grandma was rolling over in her grave for being buried in Miami instead of Arizona or right here in Boonville and wanting to cry and a soft kiss on his lips and being amazed at the darkness of the night and the brightness of the stars and somebody saying, "I hope that's not a fuckin' car."

3

John's grandma had always smelled of gin and vaginal infection. He remembered crawling onto her lap as a child, careful not to spill her drink, getting a big whiff and then gagging like he'd swallowed a mouthful of vinegar. The scent of heredity. As quickly as he could, he scrambled away from her to hide. From the closet in his bedroom, he could hear her calling to him, "What's the matter, John? Come back to Grandma, my love."

As John awoke, that same smell bit at him, producing memories of holiday dinners, family squabbles, and the first time he had oral sex. Noon sun slashed at his eyes. He realized he was outside on what must be the porch of Grandma's shack, crumpled into a wicker love seat. He shoved his fists into his eyes and rubbed them as two 20-foot squirrels flanking his position came into focus, wearing the same carved expression he had modeled on Grandma's lap. His stomach surged.

After going for the Big Spit, John felt ready to face the squirrels. He imagined how pitiful he must appear to them, red-eyed, unshaven, encrusted in what he hoped was his own vomit. The squirrels were definitely frowning. But aside from their totemic silence, there wasn't much else in the front yard of his new domicile. Grandma's cabin was situated in the middle of a hill, trees rising left and right, madrone, redwood, fir, pine, land sloping ahead of him toward a wire fence covered with brambles of blackberry bushes, then dropping drastically to give him a view of the valley; across to the east were hills of scrub oak; a receding fog bank covered the north; to the south his sight line was obstructed by forest. Down in the flat, he saw an airstrip, a field of horses, a school, a cluster of houses, and part of a small town. Boonville.

His head was pounding. But all things considered, he thought, it wasn't such a bad thing to wallow in your excrement—a certain womblike quality—the way he had felt as a boy discovering he had wet his bed, warm and safe, as long as the morning air didn't get between him and the pee-soaked sheets. But then he moved.

Lifting from the love seat, pain shot through his body, tearing at joints and nerve endings, screaming for him to sit back down. Even his hair hurt. He limped to the shack's front door, which he found to be locked. Fuckup number one, he had failed to get the keys from Grandma's friend Pensive Prairie Sunset. He tried a Bruce Lee entrance, a flurry of kicks and karate chops to the midsection of the door, yelling, "Why, why, why!" But his kung fu was no good here. The outburst made him feel nauseated. He tried another approach, through cracked lips pleading, "Open sesame." Both strategies failing, he sent Plan C into action, the standard "find an open window."

Circling the cabin, John saw Grandma's shack had five windows, one each in the bedroom and kitchen, two curtained picture windows in the living room, and one small screen window partially open in the bathroom that he could squeeze through if he could find something to stand on. He also discovered Grandma's Datsun was parked behind the cabin, smashed and missing parts; gone were the headlights, hub caps, hood, bumper, grille. To compensate for their loss, a mountain of steel had been stacked on the roof. Coming closer, he realized the sheets of metal were road signs, some still attached to their posts.

"Hmm," he said, calmed by the alcohol still flooding his bloodstream. "This, I don't remember."

He tried to open the Datsun's door, but it was locked. All doors were locked, including the trunk, while his possessions remained where he had put them in the backseat. He spied the keys dangling from the ignition and an empty whiskey bottle in the passenger's seat.

Dilemm-o-rama, John thought, staggering off in the direction of a rock planted at the base of a shrub. He dug the stone from the dirt with his fingers. Unearthed and in his hands, it felt as heavy as a mountain. Wasn't there a parable about burden, involving a boulder, a saint, and a bottomless chalice? Or was that the beginning of a dirty joke? Unable to distinguish Bible stories from borscht-belt humor, John carried the stone to the Datsun and hurled it through the driver's side window.

The car started on the first try. He steered it to the cabin's bathroom wall, set the brake, then climbed on top of the car roof and road signs, reading the warning beneath his splattered shoes, "Deaf Child Near," and tore away the window screen. He slid open the window and hopped into the opening. There was a moment of precarious equilibrium in which John was balanced half in and half out of the bathroom before he tipped the scale with a wriggle, dropping to the floor on his head.

He was tempted to lie there on the linoleum, let the day go by, but a miniature squirrel sculpture he had knocked off the window sill glowered at him. He got to his feet and flicked on the light switch. They were everywhere, bathtub, toilet tank, medicine chest, hallway, kitchen, living room, coffee table, bookshelves, bureau, nightstand, various widths and heights, well over a thousand, all with a look of sour disapproval. Squirrels, squirrels, squirrels. John suppressed a scream, hurrying to open the rest of the cabin windows, hoping fresh air might change the squirrels' expression, or more accurately, his own.

Then he piled his belongings from the Datsun into the center of the living room, sweating 120 proof and flaking hardened gastric juices. He didn't feel all there. Or maybe he was "all there," but with more of himself on the outside than he was used to. He looked through his luggage for a towel to take a shower, deciding that the best thing about being hung over was the totality of effort it took to conquer simple tasks. Moving at half-speed, there wasn't enough energy to expand your focus beyond survival, causing you to disregard those obstacles that persuaded you to get swacked in the first place. It was the after-effects of alcohol that helped more than intoxication; John had wanted to get back to basics, to separate the neurotic from the necessary, and now he could accomplish that goal, wash, unpack, try not to vomit, and feel like he had put in a full day.

In the bathroom, the water trickling from the shower head was brown and smelled of sulfur. Enamel had been eaten away in spots from the tub's bottom. Rust stains circled the drain. The sliver of soap in the soap dish was an unnatural color. It took a while for the water to get hot. When John finally entered the spray, it had the effect of smelling salts. Nose espresso, he thought, trying to convince himself that tourists paid top dollar for this kind of free-flowing mud bath.

Toweling off, he negotiated all odors with a splash of cologne Christina had given him. John didn't like cologne, believing natural scents were sexier. He thought he had left it behind, taking only his toothbrush, travel toothpaste, razor, shaving cream, comb, and a few hotel freebies of shampoo and conditioner from their bathroom. Somehow the cologne had made the trip. Today, it was a welcomed accessory. He wished he had snared some of Christina's other products accidentally-on-purpose, a moisturizer, an exfolient, shaving rasage. He wouldn't know where to buy some of that stuff. You might have to speak French to get it. They weren't going to stock it in Boonville.

John dressed, and after bagging his former clothes to be washed or thrown out later, he felt ready to settle into his new home. Someone, presumably Pensive Prairie Sunset, had already swept and vacuumed, mopped and dusted. There were no major cobwebs or ghost turds. The coffee table glistened with a wet sheen. The trash can beneath the sink had been lined with a new bag. The refrigerator was clean. John checked the cupboards, satisfied with Grandma's supply of pots, pans, glassware, plates, and utensils. The telephone was dead. He would have to get it connected. In the bedroom, he stuffed his socks, underwear, T-shirts, and sweats into the chest of drawers, hanging his good pants, ties, and dress shirts in the closet. He made a pile of Grandma's clothes for the Goodwill. When he realized there was no cable, he stuck the TV in the closet as well, finding a shotgun and three boxes of shells sitting in the corner. He remembered the rumor that Grandma had shot someone. He left the gun and ammunition alone, wondering what the real story was and why Grandma felt she had needed a gun.

Feeling motivated, he decided to make a general upgrade of aesthetics. With a whisk of his arm, he cleared a chessboard's worth of squirrel sculptures from the coffee table in the living room. Mud-glazed ceramic forms joined the squirrels in empty fruit crates for storage. There were too many cushions on the couch. He cut the number in half. He took decorative baskets, flowers, and feathers off the walls. He let hang a Georgia O'Keeffe print of an aroused lily and a photograph of Grandma as a girl, staring into the camera like a gunfighter. A painting of a seascape done on cardboard with glue and sand crumbled in his hands when he tried to center it. There was a rusted wheelbarrow full of broken glass standing near the front door as if someone had intended to dump the shards onto the living room floor as a prank. John decided it was sculpture. Instead of rolling it outside, he moved it closer to the front window so it could catch the light. Lastly, he placed a picture of Christina on the nightstand near his bed.

Just a bit of torture, he told himself. Just a bit of home.

That done, John shut the windows and looked for a newspaper to start a fire in the woodburning stove that stood on bricks in the corner of the living room. It had never been cold enough in Miami to start an actual fire. People didn't have central heating there, let alone fireplaces. Children didn't go through a pyro stage in Florida because it was so hot. There was only air conditioning. John's nose twitched.

Not finding any newspaper, he turned to the bookshelves. Except for Grandma's copy of Emily Dickinson's poetry, most of it looked like metaphysics, stuff he could torch without much moral conflict. He selected a book by John White Eagle Free Soul, a discourse on inner peace through intuitive strength. Where did they get their names? What was Free Soul supposed to be? Irish? And White Eagle? He must have picked that up in the seventies when everybody was claiming to be half Cherokee or part Seminole. If they were going to change their names, those authors should be forced to name themselves Horseshit or Asshole, he thought, and then number themselves off like Muslims: Horseshit no. 1, Asshole no. 56.

Another book of poetry caught John's eye, *Puppies Make a Porch More Cute* by Margaret Washington. He knew she lived in the area and Grandma had belonged to her Radical Petunia Arts Community. He also knew the film based on her book *Cecilia* was touted as an important feminist statement. After seeing it, John had wanted his money back and two hours of his life returned. Christina had cried. The theater was thick with Kleenex. Leaving the cineplex, John saw a line of moviegoers wrapping around the block, waiting for their turn to weep. He didn't want to ruin Christina's experience, so he said nothing on the ride home. But his silence revealed to her that he had not been moved. She accused him of insensitivity. He was going to tell her that he cried every time he saw *Dumbo*, but she switched on the radio and turned away from him. They didn't have sex for a month.

John opened *Puppies Make a Porch More Cute* to see it had been inscribed: "Ruth, Remember in order to give birth you have to experience labor pains, Peace and love, Margaret Washington."

Flipping pages, John read a poem entitled "All White Men Are Evil Rapists."

> Our foremothers cooked and cleaned and smiled
> as they stirred the pots that fed us all,
> sweat slipping down beautiful black skin
> while being repeatedly abused,
> though always standing strong.
> But if the world were perfect,
> we would sit in a green field holding hands;
> a calm constructive conversation,
> even the cows would join in.
> But no white men,
> because all white men are evil rapists.

John tore that page out first, feeling it crumple in his hand before he tossed it into the stove. Without reading another sentence, the rest of the book followed. He threw on a dozen squirrel sculptures for kindling, a large one for a log. He lit the fire with a foot-long match, feeling the heat on his face. Lying down on the carpet, he tried not to think about Grandma or Margaret Washington, instead concentrating on the silence that surrounded the crackling flames.

He had only experienced quiet like this on mornings when Christina jogged. Not knowing what to do, he usually fell back to sleep, reawakening to the sound of her shower, a Billy Joel cassette, the steaming gurgle of the coffeemaker. He had been reared on stimulus and distraction; introspection had not been encouraged as a pastime. Silence was as forbidden as masturbation. As a boy, John watched children's shows where men in animal costumes introduced cartoons, lusted after Girl Scouts, and ran around, yelling, "Hold that bus!" In high school, he studied while Meatloaf screamed and Frampton came alive at 200 watts per channel. College was the drone of the campus radio station and students singing the theme to "The Love Boat" outside his door. Even in bed with Christina, Johnny or Dave delivered their late night monologues with the sound of the city as background, boom boxes, screeching tires, stray gunfire. Never silence.

John resisted the urge to sleep, pondering instead the unfinished business he had to complete before he would feel established in his new residence. First, he had to call Christina and let his friends and parents know he had arrived. He still needed to get the keys from Pensive Prairie Sunset so he could lock the cabin. He had to buy groceries, do laundry, get rid of those road signs. Wine tasting was out of the question for a few days, but he could go to the coast, explore the area, write postcards, read that biography on Jim Jones. He also wanted to talk to that blue-eyed Sarah.

Enough quiet time.

Outside, he shoved the signs off the roof of the Datsun. Taking the helm of the battered vehicle, he wound down the hill toward town, his stomach protesting at each turn. He reached for the whiskey bottle in the passenger seat, running it along the edges of the broken driver's side window, eliminating the remaining glass fragments. Unsullied air blew against his face. The drive straightened. To his right, he saw a red house on a knoll and the field of horses he had spotted from Grandma's cabin. The tiny airstrip and the Anderson Valley Junior/Senior High School were on his left, then basketball courts, a pair of strange geodesic domes, a "Home of the Panthers" sign, a creek bridge, a stop sign, and Highway 128. The crossroads.

John looked both ways, letting his sight settle for a moment on the asphalt where he had blacked out. A truck trailing a load of grapes roared past followed by a camper, a logging truck, and a group of teenagers in a green AMC Hornet. Someone behind him honked. He clicked his turn signal and drove, wincing at the sight of the brick building next to the Pic 'N Pay. The Lodge's beer sign winked its neon eye. He steered into the parking lot of the Boonville Hotel.

No alcohol this time, he told himself. Caffeine.

"If it ain't the Squirrel Boy," the bartender greeted him. "Rumor had it, you died."

"The way I feel," John said, the bartender's voice booming between his ears, "maybe I did."

"You don't waste no time takin' over where your grandma left off," the bartender observed. "What can I get for you? Hair of one of the dogs that bit you?"

"You got cappuccino?" John asked, thinking how Christina

would take care of him if he were home: coffee, grapefruit juice, ice pack, kisses.

"Guess you're on the dissie stool," the bartender grinned. "Cuppa cappa comin' up."

John didn't know if he was on the dissie stool or not; his seat looked like all the other empty ones in the bar. He figured the phrase meant something like "on the wagon." He didn't bother asking the bartender to clarify the term. The energy he had generated at the cabin had disappeared.

When his coffee came, he held his face above the cup, letting the steam play against his skin. Cooling slightly, he bottomed it in two gulps. The milk had been scalded and the espresso was bitter. He asked for a refill of regular coffee, which he loaded with sugar. His insides began to warm. On this trip into town, he had noticed the Horn of Zeese, the truckstop from the news article he had read about Boontling. It was across from the hotel and not too far down the road. He thought about braving it for some eggs, but his stomach didn't feel ready.

"You got a pay phone?" John asked the bartender.

"Cross the street at the market, ours is out of order," the bartender said. "But if you're callin' your hornin' buddies, none of 'em got phones. Billy Chuck don't pay the bills, Sarah's too far outta town, and the Kurts ain't good with numbers."

"I take it word travels fast anyway," John said.

"What else do we got to do in this town?" the bartender replied. "Sounds like you had a night. You remember any of it?"

"Up to a point," John answered.

"Which one?" the bartender asked

"How many were there?" John replied.

"I heard you were higher 'n Dwight's flagpole," the bartender said. "Laid out in the road with the Kurts and Billy Chuck, sniffin' after that hippie girl's yeast-powder biscuit when I told you she was trouble."

"Can I ask you a question?" John said, uncertain if he wanted to know the answer or if he would be able to translate the bartender's reply into Basic English. "How did my car get wrecked? And how did I get home?"

"That's two questions," the bartender told him, then inquired if John's car had collected any road signs.

Not wanting to admit guilt, John took a sip of his coffee.

Smiling, the bartender informed him that he was now an eco-terrorist, a soldier in Judy Bari's army. John had never heard of Judy Bari and was even less enthusiastic about being linked to the word "eco-terrorist," thinking it sounded worse than "dissie stool."

"Those hippie girls are environmentalists," the bartender explained. "For kicks they hunt road signs. They think they're ugly and bring the wrong kind of business to the valley. But that ain't all they do. You weren't at any lumber sites or LP land, were you?"

"I don't think so," John answered, rummaging through his short-term memory.

"Good, 'cause they're also monkeywrenchers," the bartender said.

"Do monkeywrenchers and eco-terrorists sniff yeast-powder biscuits?" John asked, letting the bartender know he wasn't following him.

"Ain't you heard of Earth First!?" the bartender said, surprised. "Protesters spikin' redwoods and sabotagin' lumber equipment, savin' old growth and the spotted owl? Ain't you never read *The Lorax*? Don't you watch 'Sixty Minutes'?"

John had read *The Lorax*, but he didn't know how the children's story applied to the topic at hand. But he didn't watch "Sixty Minutes" anymore; Andy Rooney annoyed him and Diane Sawyer was at the top of his list, with new-entry Margaret Washington, as one of the top ten women he would hate to be stuck in an elevator with. All that smug nodding, the person interviewed forced to respond to questions whose answers were later edited into whatever slant the network thought would earn better ratings. John used to fill his quota of Orwellian hate for the week by tuning in, but he saw a segment they did on the poultry industry and to this day couldn't eat chicken. He figured if he watched long enough, he would develop the same reaction to all his favorite foods.

"I try to miss it," John admitted.

"Earth First! is big up here," the bartender explained. "I'm for the trees, but I sympathize with the loggers; like the steel workers, they're losin' their industry to bigger profits made elsewhere, mostly Mexico and Japan. But in a few years there ain't gonna be any trees or jobs left. Everybody loses. I ain't gonna climb up on a soapbox though."

"I appreciate that," John said, then added. "Do you know

how I got home?"

"Eee tah, Squirrel Boy, invite me out with you next time, then maybe I'll know." The bartender extended his hand across the bar. "Folks call me Hap."

"What's your real name?" John inquired, shaking his hand.

"Hap," the bartender said. "That's why folks call me Hap."

"Nice to meet you, Hap," John said, unsure whether he was being made a fool of. "You have a strange way of talking. Is that the local language I heard about?"

"I'm a kimmie can harp Boont," Hap said, proudly. "But lemme tell you one thing before you go. If I heard you was with that Sarah, you can bet her ex did too. Keep your eyes peeled. Leek bee'n. Get me?"

"Leek bee'n," John said, understanding Hap was telling him to watch his ass.

He paid for the coffee and thanked Hap again. In the parking lot, two kids with skateboards were evaluating the damage to the Datsun, one saying to the other, "Dude, he's totally foiled." The other, seeing John approach, observed, "He's the poster child for hating it." John looked at his car, the loser in a demolition derby. With a wave of his hand, the first kid said, "Adios, Mr. Morose," then both teens scooted off down the center of the highway, doing a few tricks as they rolled away.

John drove to the pay phone at the Anderson Valley Market. The telephone booth had a sign above it, "Bucky Walter." John wondered if the booth had been memorialized for some local motor mouth or if it was independently owed. Maybe it was more Boontling. He'd ask Hap about it sometime he didn't want a straight answer.

John searched his pockets for change. Depositing a quarter in the telephone, he remembered when the cost was a dime.

"Hello," he said, into the receiver.

"Peace and love," a voice answered.

"Could I speak to Pensive Prairie Sunset?" John said.

"I am she and she is me," the voice replied.

"This is John Gibson," he identified himself against his better judgment, thinking he shouldn't get involved with anyone named Pensive Prairie Sunset who spoke in Beatles lyrics. "You left my grandmother's car for me at the San Francisco airport."

"How are you?" Pensive cut in. "Did you have a safe trip? I

hope you ordered a vegetarian or low sodium meal for the flight. You can suffer severe autointoxication from just one in-flight meal, especially when you combine it with that terrible recycled airplane air. Last time I flew, I had to fast for a week after I ate the apple pancakes on a red-eye to Cleveland."

"I'm in Boonville," John said.

"Fantastic," Pensive replied, no pauses or pitch change in her voice, coming at you like the flat groan of a Ray Manzarek keyboard solo. "We must be doing O.K. then."

"I don't know," he admitted. "I called to get the keys to my grandma's cabin."

"Where are you calling from?" Pensive asked.

"A pay phone that says 'Bucky Walter' outside the Anderson Valley Market," John said.

"That means telephone," the woman informed him. "I'll be there in twenty minutes."

Click. Dial tone.

Some unwanted force was now bearing down on John like in a 1970s disaster film: *Airport, Earthquake, Towering Inferno, Billy Jack*. There was nothing he could do. He dialed zero, trying to place a collect call to Christina, but the line was busy. 911 seemed extreme.

Stepping from the pay phone, he peered into the Anderson Valley Market past a stand of magazines and romance novels. John's eye caught the headline of the local paper: "Congressman Calls Coasters 'Hippie Potheads.'" The cashier was counting out change for a man with a nylon Bush Hog hat. A woman dragged a little girl whose face was smeared with chocolate from the store, screaming and kicking. Dogs barked from the back of a truck. The woman stopped to swat the girl, but the girl broke loose from her grip and darted toward the truck with the dogs. "I want fudge!" the girl howled. The woman looked on the verge of violence. Nearby, a group of Mexicans in cowboy hats conversed in Spanish, their accents sounding different to John than the Cubans in Miami. They weren't wearing guayberas either or playing dominoes. Peterbilts loaded with logs whizzed past, diesels roaring, chrome nude girl silhouette mud flaps. The man with the Bush Hog hat walked past the Mexicans and joined the woman and girl at the truck with the dogs. With a voice offering no room for argument, he told them both to get into the truck, the girl wasn't getting any more fudge until after lunch.

"When's lunch?" the girl asked, swiftly obedient.

"When your mama makes it," the man said, petting the dogs and looking without affection at his wife. "Sometime before dinner."

"We'll eat when we get home," the woman said. "Fish sticks and chili."

For the sake of his stomach, John tried to put the woman's lunch menu out of his mind. But what time was it? He checked his watch, black and silver, with flecks of green fluorescence. Waterproof up to two hundred feet. "In case you take it snorkeling," he remembered Christina had said, before he could see what it was he had unwrapped. He kissed her, setting the watch aside, and they rolled into wrapping paper. Tinsel reflected bulbs of red and green. Pine needles fell into her hair. She kissed his hairless chest. His hands pushed at soft cotton and lacy underthings. Tiny lights pulsed. He felt the curve of her thighs, her firm buttocks, and the full of her weight came down to swallow him. His body stilled in paralytic ecstasy. She pressed wet lips to his, and whispered, "Merry Christmas."

1:12 p.m.

He had been gone less than two days and he couldn't quite remember why he had left. The air-conditioned nightmare. His eyes blurred the parking lot of cars and high-riding trucks parked parallel to the store, three rows wide. Some were penned in and couldn't leave until other drivers came out of the store and moved their vehicles first. The Datsun was one of the trapped cars.

"Kinda makes you wonder," a voice said. "Maybe aliens really did kill Kennedy."

John turned to see a man sitting on a picnic table in front of the market. His face was serious, almost grim, like he had lost something important but couldn't remember what it was. The man spit a glob of tobacco.

"I'm sorry," John apologized. "Did you say aliens assassinated Kennedy? John F. Kennedy?"

"Haven't you seen the videotape?" the man asked.

John shook his head, half because he hadn't seen the tape, half because he couldn't believe he was entering this conversation.

"Where have you been?" the man said. "I saw that video six months ago. It wasn't really the aliens, it was the show-fer. They slowed that Zapruder film down and you seen the driver plug the president like a fish in a barrel. Blowed his head clean off. That's why Jackie O was crawlin' out the back. She seen it was the driver. The same people coverin' up the UFOs. They had the real E.T. and nobody knew it, except government agents, and when he died they destroyed the body. They got more, but their fingers don't light up. It's complicated and linked to drugs and patterns in cornfields and LBJ not runnin' for a second term. And Incas. But it's really this secret government run with aliens. That's why I wonder if it wasn't aliens killed Kennedy. It would explain the 'magic bullet.' You know aliens got ammunition like that."

John tried to grasp the concept of a secret government of drug-selling aliens assassinating President Kennedy and denying President Johnson a second term in office.

"Kennedy sure is dead," he offered.

"Yep," the man said, spitting. "There's a lot we don't know about. Like Einstein said, 'Anything's possible.'"

"Was that Einstein?" John asked.

"I watch out for 'em," the man answered. "Like you say, Kennedy sure is dead."

"No doubt about that," John replied, entering the market and leaving the man outside to worry about conspiracy-oriented extraterrestrials.

Scanning the shelves of the Anderson Valley Market, John noticed that whoever did the purchasing had gone heavy on beverages and sugar-coated cereals. A shopper told him if he wanted to buy more than Budweiser and Frosted Flakes, he should drive over the hill to Ukiah where they had several supermarkets, including an Albertson's. John saw that the rear section, some one-third of the store, was dedicated to wine. He guided his cart back toward the front, searching hard for merchandise, having logged too much media time not to buy something. He could always be persuaded by packaging, cookies with a midget or an elf on the wrapper, a thirst quencher, a quick-and-easy, light-and-tasty, new-and-improved, thirty-percent-more, half-the-calories, cholesterol-free taste treat. John dutifully filled his cart.

At the checkout there was a wrinkled woman in a green smock manipulating an ancient cash register. Her hair had the pink glow of a home-brewed dye job. Her eyes peered through bifocals at John's pile of groceries.

"Having a party?" she asked.

"No," John answered, riding the consumer high. "It's all for me."

"Lotta food there," the woman observed, bagging the supplies.

"I get hungry," John replied. "Three times a day, at least."

"You ain't the Squirrel Lady's grandson, are ya?" the woman squinted over the top of her glasses.

"Yes, I am," John admitted.

"Ain't that somethin'?" the woman said, like someone had told her that with a good pot of beans, you never added bacon. "Even the devil's got relatives, I suppose."

"That's right," John said, trying to be agreeable, but wondering what the people here had expected. He was Edna Gibson's grandson, not Josef Mengele's clone.

Before he could give the matter more thought, he was outside stuffing his groceries into the Datsun. He heard a car horn and an orange Pacer approached the market looking like something conceived by minds in Michigan overwhelmed by Japanese efficiency. In an effort to cover up their mistake, bumper stickers had been plastered on bumper stickers; "One nuclear bomb could ruin your whole day," "Greenpeace," "Skateboarding is not a crime," "Mondale/Ferraro 84," "Carter 76," "Have a nice day," "Honk if you're Jesus!" The car gave the impression that if someone were to scrape off the bumper stickers, there would be nothing left but a giant fishbowl. It rolled to a stop in front of John. He heard a grunt of physical effort. The driver's side door opened and the car's frame lifted another foot from the ground. Out stepped Pensive Prairie Sunset.

John had seen fatter women before, lying on hotel beaches, cellulite craters digesting sand, naked or with a bathing suit in there somewhere. But they all seemed to have been old. Pensive Prairie Sunset was young. He guessed late thirties as she waddled from the car, flesh rolling against flesh, breasts hanging to her beltline, calves like loaves of head cheese. Her dress defied any specific pattern or culture. It was a freak-show tent, catastrophic paisleys and mongoloid camels drowning in a purple ocean. Was it Indian? Hawaiian? French? He stopped counting chins when he ran out of fingers. She held out her arms for a hug.

John felt his cappuccino rising.

"I'm Pensive Prairie Sunset," she said, as if it were a

reasonable enough excuse to embrace a stranger.

"I'm John Gibson," he said, taking a step back.

"I figured," she said, understanding, not forcing the hug. "Your energy resembles Edna's, but not as released. You also have the same nose. You must be an Aries."

"I guess it runs in the family," John said, unsure which statement he was commenting on.

"Not always," she said. "Spirits circulate, kundalini rises and flows depending on your ability to breathe."

Kundalini? John thought. Kumbaya.

"Edna and I spent six years together at the Radical Petunia Arts Community," Pensive continued. "You've heard of Margaret Washington, haven't you? They made a fabulous movie of her book *Cecilia*. The Radical Petunia Arts Community is an extension of her creativity and her understanding of women's needs."

"That sounds great," John lied. "I'd like to go to a meeting some time."

"You can't attend seminars, they're for women only," Pensive said, adding, "I do abstract pottery."

"I'm sorry," John said, wondering if the ceramics he had trashed had been her work. "I had a long flight and I didn't sleep too well. I don't want to be rude, but could you please give me the keys to my grandmother's cabin?"

"Hey, I hear you," Pensive said. "I know where you're coming from. You don't have to bombard me with half-truths. Be honest, it sets a good vibe. I know you were out last night and that's O.K., men are like that. But could you get past your needs for a moment? I have an inflamed sixth disc and I have to get some bulgur and mung beans down at the Boontberry, and I did come here with Edna's keys, so it would be nice if you could help me carry my groceries."

John's head was throbbing, his car was blocked, the caffeine was gone, and the appropriate response of "fuck you" hadn't come fast enough. He found himself walking at Pensive's side, passing the Lodge with his head down.

Luckily, the Boontberry Health Food Store wasn't far. With the ringing of bells strapped to the door by strips of leather, they entered a shed loaded with wicker baskets containing a strange assortment of kiwis and gooseberries, string beans and red bananas, avocados and cucumbers. There was another room connected to the main store, housing an old-fashioned glass-doored refrigerator, which held cheese, yogurt, tofu, brown eggs, and other perishables. A few hippies milled about barefoot. Pensive filled her hands with an array of edibles and ordered a burrito from the deli. The purchasing counter overflowed as she added to her booty, a mountain of health, on top of which she threw a loaf of Oat Bran Bruce Bread.

Stepping from the front door to the counter in two strides was a giant standing almost seven feet tall. He had a beard clumped into tufts by rubber bands and bushy eyebrows connected at an Arab's nose. His eyes were as dark and watchful as a raven's. John saw his hair had been braided into a ponytail that reached his butt, whose half-smile could be seen grinning from beneath the tie-dyed sarong slung over his shoulder. Holding a key tied to a plunger, he confronted an effeminate man who was minding the store.

"Here's the key to the bathroom, Garrett," the giant said, with a trace of an Eastern European accent. "Tell your gerbil-jamming friends the gel works for extraction and with each dozen, I'll throw in a Grand Inquisitor."

"Let's talk about that later," Garrett said, eyes darting to see who was listening.

"I've got nothing to hide," the giant replied. "This is business. I'd throw God off the Bay Bridge if he fucked with me on this one."

"Let's just talk later," Garrett urged.

"Remember how good that crystal meth was?" the giant demanded. "This is better. This is flesh and blood, something that can sink its teeth into you."

"I'll come up and take a look," Garrett promised, giving John an uncomfortable smile. "Now I have to help the customers."

"I'm helping customers help themselves!" the giant yelled. "My system's so clean if you rubbed watermelon on my head, I could taste it."

John was afraid the giant might try to prove it. He looked to Pensive who was holding a family pack of whole wheat fig bars. She didn't seem alarmed. The other hippies in the store didn't seem worried about the behemoth either, continuing to finger jicama roots and carob clusters. John pretended to be interested in the wheat germ bin, casually moving to the other side of Pensive.

"I'm like this," the giant said, jumping back from the counter, jerking his neck and writhing his body like a break-dancer. "I've been anointed as a seer. And you, Gay-rat, have a front row seat to the end of the world!"

The giant plunged his hand into Pensive's loaf of Bruce Bread, popping the plastic bag and squeezing the ten grain into a ball of dough. He held it above his head, almost touching the ceiling. Crumbs cascaded to the floor. Garrett flinched, ready to be assaulted. But the giant dropped the bread harmlessly. He looked at it on the ground for a moment as if he were reading tea leaves, then leaped a step and a half across the store, out the door. A bleary-eyed hippie poked his head from the dairy room, but seeing nothing, continued to shop. The others noticed nothing.

"How are we today, Pensive?" Garrett said, stepping around the counter, picking up the mess and selecting another loaf of bread for Pensive's pile.

"I'm fine," she replied, John staying behind her, one eye on the door. "But it looks like Aslan's self-medicating again. I hope it's not a solstice-long experiment."

"I try not to be judgmental," Garrett said, returning to the register. He tabulated her foodstuffs, then asked, "Will that be all?"

Pensive said it was, producing a blank check from a pocket of her dress or maybe it came from a wrinkle in her flesh. John wasn't sure which.

"That will be $64.58, Pensive," Garrett said.

But there was nowhere for her to fill out the check. The counter was covered by her bags. Without hesitating, Pensive took a pen from a plastic cup near the register, leaned back like she was looking into a telescope set up too close to her face, and wrote out the check using her right breast as a desk. She handed the check to Garrett who was as unimpressed with her ingenuity as he had been with the giant's outburst. Pensive scooped up the smallest sack, commanded John to take the others, and they were outside tramping back toward the Pacer. Not a giant in sight.

All right, John told himself, enough is enough. It's time to go home and stay there for a while, regroup, detox, sleep. I'll call Christina and make contact with Sarah sometime when I'm more myself.

But with a burst of doors, two men stumbled from the Lodge, one pursuing the other. At first, John thought one was the giant, but he could see they were regular-sized men, although one was much huskier than the other.

"Shit, I was just jokin'," the smaller man said.

"Shut up!" the other told him.

"Sarah ain't even your wife no more," the smaller man argued.

Wham! Crack of knuckles, spray of blood.

"You broke my nose!" the smaller man cried. "My fuckin' nose is broken!"

Wham! Head snapped back, animal grunt.

"My eye! Damn, Daryl, I can't see out of my eye!"

"Get the hell outta here before there ain't nothin' left of you to see," Daryl warned.

The smaller man ran to his truck. Pensive kept walking, uninterested. John had stopped in his tracks. Daryl looked around the parking lot, mad-dog crazy. His eyes met John's.

"What are you lookin' at, yuppie?"

John was unable to move or look away. A grocery bag fell from his hands, a container of hummus rolling to Daryl's feet.

"Wait a minute!" Daryl's voice slammed John's head like a hand against a cigarette machine. "Don't move!"

John was stiff from fright.

"I know who you are!"

Please God, John thought, let it be quick.

"You're the Squirrel Boy!"

4

"Busted flat in Baton Rouge . . ." Music radiated from the main house of the Waterfall commune, bending sound waves, shaking tree branches, scaring animals, sparking acid flashbacks, stirring bad blood, and waking Sarah, who was sleeping in her cabin on the other side of the woods, a quarter of a mile away.

Sarah pulled a pillow over her head, temples drumming beneath the grog and stink of dope and Jack Daniels. She knew Mom was blaring this shit. Nobody else at the commune was into Janis Joplin, not anymore. Too negative. Without a telephone this was Mom's way of reaching out and touching her, person-to-person.

No way, Sarah told herself, feeling half-alive and fully irritable, I'm not trudging up to the main house to listen to Mom in one of her dead feminist moods.

She flipped the pillow over, tugging it tightly to her ears and creating an air vent in the linen so she didn't smother. It occurred to her that mother was smother minus the *s*.

"I swear to God," she grumbled, as the music continued, "if I have to get up, everybody in the main house is going to die."

The main house was the karmic center of the Waterfall commune, where residents connected with their comrades or just vegged out and shuffled the tarot. It was where the community stored its harvested dope and the Bang and Olufsen, a stereo so sound-sensitive and powerful that you could rock out to "Woodstock" and, adjusting treble and bass, isolate the voice of the one guy who booed Hendrix. The other houses, hoagies, lean-tos, yurts, and teepees on the commune weren't wired for sound and didn't have trash bags of Mendo Mellow in their closets, ready to shake and bake. Consequently, they were regarded as places of personal space. The main house was a place to "be." Over the years, Sarah had observed that her comrades chose to "be" self-absorbed assholes. And Mom was obviously up there right now among the brethren, letting it all hang out.

Sarah had gone through enough of these scenarios to know the score. Mom was coming down from a binge of booze and pills, spiraling toward bottom, and she wanted Sarah to commiserate, reassure her that being a horrible mother and completely egocentric was O.K.; choosing this alternative lifestyle and including Sarah in it was the best reality any daughter could hope for. After all, life was unduly harsh and everybody knew Mom was trying her best. There was no reason to feel bad about anything. Sarah loved her, the past was the past, and tomorrow would work itself out. Every day was a rebirth. Mom needed validation. But there was certain music Sarah couldn't listen to anymore, not without reliving the memories, reopening sores linked to a time she still didn't understand. It was the music Mom always played too, Janis screaming, "Down on meeeeeee!"

Janis was a familiar reveille since before Sarah and her mother had moved to the Waterfall. Before they stopped believing in running water, flush toilets, voting, eating meat, table grapes, cooked food, and still went to church on Christmas Eve and Easter Sunday. Back when they were mainstream, living in a Victorian in San Francisco, and Sarah wore a plaid skirt to school each day. The last time she had felt like everybody else. Back when their karma was bad and she couldn't have told you what EST stood for. Before Mom became liberated. Before Dad split.

Sarah was born before the first ripple of the "no-fault divorce" wave that swelled in California and rolled into every state but Utah, spraying alimony settlements and a mist of visitation rights, leaving behind a foam of single-parent homes and cesspools of Saturday mornings waiting for Dad. And when he didn't come, Mom called that "irresponsible bastard" and told him, "Stop fucking that teenager and pick up your daughter!" Sarah was born June 11, 1964, the day Liz Taylor divorced Eddie Fisher and then ten days later married Richard Burton. For the first time.

Slamming the phone into its cradle after one of her verbal assaults on Dad, Mom would go for the records. No explanation, only records turned up two decibels past the point of distortion on the lo-fi; Janis Joplin, Carole King, Carly Simon, Aretha Franklin, Pheobe Snow, Maria Muldaur, Rita Coolidge, Joan Baez. "The pseudo-feminists," Dad called them. But at least the "pseudo-feminists" gave Sarah an idea how Mom was feeling, and, more importantly, how she was expected to react. "You've Got a Friend" meant give Mom a hug; "Think," do a soul dance; "Mockingbird," be funny, cheer Mom up; "Poetry Man," be quiet, Mom was lamenting; "Midnight at the Oasis," cry with her, Mom needed company. And "Down on Me" meant anything was possible, murder, suicide, spontaneous combustion. Sarah hated those "Down on Me Days," feeling like she had to hold her breath and keep perfectly still or else the world was going to explode.

"Down on Me Days" could sneak up on you. They started normal enough, a bowl of granola, English muffins with organic peanut butter, a couple of well-stashed Pop-Tarts, and then into the living room to watch cartoons. On her way to the tube, Sarah would stop at the thermostat and fire it way up, ninety degrees, so she could sit on the air vent and get hothouse warm while her nightgown ballooned around her with each dusty blast of the furnace. Central heating. It was almost as good as one of Mom's hugs, except it turned the ferns brown in their macramé holders and really brought out that dirty shag carpeting smell. In between breakfast, cartoons, and the air vent, there was a jigsaw puzzle: 2,000 interlocking pieces of boats in Venice. She liked the boats, but hated doing the sky. Around 8:30, the narcotic glow of TV and search for edge would be interrupted. Whoever it was that had spent the night with Mom would be sneaking out, zipping up his pants. Sarah thought they all looked like John Davidson. Whenever they saw her, they felt obligated to take a seat on the sofa and watch about five minutes of "Banana Splits."

"When I was your age, we didn't have all these cartoons and health foods," they would say, inevitably. "I used to watch Howdy Doody and eat Cream of Wheat."

"What's your point?" Sarah would ask, looking for an elusive piece of the docks.

"Nothing major," they responded. "Things have changed since I was a kid."

"Not men," Sarah would say, finding the piece. "Not their attitude toward women. Not their macho bullshit."

"Easy does it, huh?" J.D. would say. "How old are you anyway?"

"Old enough to know you're a butthole," Sarah would reply. "And fucking my mother."

That would end the whole getting-to-know-Greta's-kid thing. Even if this week's John Davidson could have rattled off a few advancements in man's recent evolution, they never did. Sarah thought they were too afraid she might cite them and their relationship with Mom as example number one in a lecture on "How Men Are Still Pricks." There would be silence those next minutes, except for Hanna-Barbera's sound effects, which seemed appropriate for both the cartoons and the punch she had landed to John Davidson's pride.

During an advertisement for the Baby Thataway doll Sarah had wanted last year for her birthday, but never got, John Boy would rise from the sofa, saying, "Take care of your mama for me, until I get back."

"Why don't you just not leave?" she would ask.

That stopped them in their Dingos.

For a moment, she almost expected an answer. Maybe they did too. At least a poster catchphrase, "Hang in there, baby," or "Life's a bummer!" But then the door hinge squeaked, the screen door rattled, and John Davidson climbed into a sports car that never started on the first try.

"Butthole," Sarah would say, not watching them leave.

She didn't need anyone telling her to take care of her mother. She knew she would have to do it, maybe for the rest of her life. But she got a break every other weekend, which included this one, because those were Dad's days. Sarah would be gathered up by her father, and for two days Dad became her responsibility. Which was fine, except it was a common catalyst for a "Down on Me Day."

Dad liked to come at nine because he knew Mom would be asleep. Anything after ten was pushing it. Nine was best. That way they could avoid a scene until Dad dropped her off on Sunday, but a scene on Sunday was inevitable. Mom and her friends would be waiting, drinking carafes of Chablis, listening to Janis Joplin, and working themselves into a frenzy like high school boys in a Friday night parking lot.

"If they're so liberated," Dad would mumble, pulling into the driveway, "why do they travel in packs?"

The weekends with Dad should have been great, Slurpees and museums. If Sarah could have vanished and materialized, used the transport system they had on "Star Trek," said, "Beam me home, Dad," then everything would have been all right. Of course, she knew life didn't work that way. As a result, her stress level was high in the a.m. hours of the weekend, the pre-stereophonic prelude to a "Down on Me Day." More often than not, Dad was late, oversleeping with girlfriends, picking up dry-cleaning, forgetting it was his weekend. Lame excuses. The exchange was rarely made without unpleasantries, crying jags, or tossed knickknacks. And Dad would ruin Sunday by doing a play-by-play of his inevitable fight with Mom. Like Sarah needed to go through the whole thing twice.

"You crazy bitch!" Dad would scream.

"You selfish bastard!" Mom would yell.

The argument wouldn't go anywhere. How could it? They were debating two separate points. It was becoming clear to Sarah that both of them were right too, Mom was a "crazy bitch" and Dad was a "selfish bastard." But it didn't make the weekends any easier. The worst part of the fiasco was that it revolved around her. Sunday night at the fights began when Sarah tried to answer the unanswerable question Mom asked when Dad dropped her off. It was the bell that sounded the start of the main event: Pops the Punisher vs. the Maternal Masher. Fifteen rounds, no holds barred.

"Sarah, did you have a good time with your father?"

Ding ding.

If Sarah said yes, Mom freaked out. In her eyes, Sarah had sided with Dad. After everything Mom had sacrificed for her, Sarah had sold out. It was more important to have fun with her father than to remain vigilantly depressed on Mom's behalf. Right in front of her friends too.

"Why don't you go live with the son of a bitch then? I'll sweep in every blue moon to have fun. That's easy, anybody can do that. It's the rest of the job that's hard!"

And if Sarah said no, Mom would throw a shit fit. You had sided with *her*, giving her a license to lay into Dad on your behalf.

"I know you're a bastard, but I can't believe you can't show your own daughter a good time twice a month. All I've been hearing is 'Dad and me are gonna do this. Dad and me are gonna do that.' I didn't have the heart to tell her everything you've ever said was a lie. I kept it inside. I've been hurting inside. But I'm not letting you hurt my baby, you bastard! Not anymore! Not my baby!"

"We're behind you, Greta," one of Mom's friends would say. "You're beautiful, woman. Let that silver-tongued devil know!"

Now Mom would let Dad have it for Sarah and herself, for her friends and all divorcees. For all women. And for the Movement.

That scene would happen soon enough, Sarah could wait. There would be another one occurring in a few minutes if Dad didn't arrive soon. She could hear Mom's waterbed sloshing. The clock shaped like a half-eaten cheeseburger sitting on the television said 11:15. Defcon four. Sarah could smell the melt-down, the husky-musky scent of Charlie and Tab cola. Mom appeared in the living room wearing only an Angela Davis–inspired Afro matted down on one side and puffed out on the other. Vagina proud. She held a pink can of soda in her hand with a cigarette between her fingers. The sight of Mom's breasts made Sarah uncomfortable. Before the liberation, she always wore a robe.

"So, that sonofabitch hasn't got around to picking you up yet?" Mom would ask.

The answer seemed obvious; Sarah was still there watching cartoons. If Dad had collected her, they would be at the Zoo eating pink popcorn or looking at the buffalo in Golden Gate Park. Sarah didn't say anything. She didn't think Mom wanted an answer. Lately, Mom asked a lot of questions she wasn't expected to answer.

"You gonna wait all day for that irresponsible bastard?" Mom said.

There was another one.

"Hon, let me tell you something," she'd say, after taking a drag of her cigarette and depositing the butt in her Tab can. "Your father's never been there for you and he never will be. Let's face it, he divorced both of us. Look around, do you see him?"

That made three.

"He thinks he can send us a shitty check once a month and that's enough? Who buys your clothes? Who takes you to the emergency room when your ankle is broken? Who pays the bills? Cooks dinner? Cleans? Sweats blood and shows up to your school's open house when she's having a monster period and could have gone to the premiere of *Claudine* with a personal friend of Billy Graham's? Who? Huh?"

They were coming pretty fast.

"Not that good-for-nothing, womanizing, shit-fuck, lousy-lay of a man. Did I ever tell you I went two years without oral sex because I had a recurring yeast infection and he refused to go down on me. Like it was my fault! That bastard!"

On cue, Dad. His presence preceded him. Sarah didn't need to look through the window, hearing the sound of his car, motor purring like a cat stalking a bird and then fluttering as if that same bird were flying away. Sarah knew instinctively, working a strong sixth sense. But Mom did too.

"Here comes that rat-fuck now," Mom would say, like that was the answer that filled in the blanks to all her previous questions.

Sarah had never thought of her father as a "rat-fuck," although everything from shrink bills to broken refrigerator doors were routinely blamed on him and his absence. Dad was more a compilation of smells, Old Spice, the San Francisco Bay, sweaty jogging shoes. Charisma. The fast food they ate together not because they liked it, but because it wasn't allowed with Mom.

When Dad rang the doorbell, Mom fired the first blast. Sarah could hear Dad curse on the other side of the door before being drowned out by the voice of the liberated American woman, the one who overdosed, choked to death on her own bile.

"Down on meeeeeee!"

Sarah didn't get it. Something was missing. What had gone wrong between Mom and Dad? How did the recognition of familiar suffering bring happiness? Where was the power in identifying yourself with being left behind, screwed again. What was so great about the B-side of "Pearl"? Someday she would understand, Mom promised. But Sarah hoped it was far into the future before she could sing "I'd trade all my tomorrows for one single yesterday" and mean it.

Janis was playing the day they headed north to Mendoland, Mom gunning her convertible Karmann Ghia up 101, a silver streak against sunburned hills. The divorce was final, alimony and child support checks in her pocketbook. According to Mom, they were escaping from the lost souls living the lies of capitalism at the mercy of men.

"The Movement died," she said. "There's no use sticking around for the funeral."

The torn convertible top flapped in the wind. Sarah imagined

Dad behind the car on a stallion, getting ready to leap into the Ghia, take the wheel and steal her back. But he didn't jump because his good pair of bell-bottoms were caught in the stirrups and he didn't want to risk ripping them. Meanwhile, Janis sang "Bye Bye Baby" on the eight-track, the system Sarah had received a week ago from Mom as a birthday present.

"Hon, lookit, now you can listen to music when we're on the road," Mom had said.

It was her eleventh birthday. The party was the pits.

"You're not still upset about the party, are you?" Mom asked. "I told you my friends were there because we don't have a traditional sexist mother/daughter relationship. My friends are your friends. Besides, I went through with the pregnancy. Don't I deserve something for that? And you got more presents. I didn't get any presents."

To mark the day, Mom's friends had given Sarah a string of love beads, a bottle of root beer lip gloss, two eight-tracks of Carole King's "Tapestry" album, a subscription to *Ms.*, a copy of *I'm O.K., You're O.K.*, and a diaphragm. All of which Mom had borrowed the following week. Dad was a no-show, contracting business in Tahoe. "Contracting herpes, I hope," Mom said. He sent a dress from Macy's, which was Sarah's only decent gift, aside from the eight track, which she did enjoy, when she was in the car.

"You're not on a bummer because we're moving to this commune with Marty, are you?" Mom said, like Sarah had objected to cashing in a winning lottery ticket. "We're finally getting out from underneath your father. We're going back to the earth. I just wish I could have you all over again so you could start off pure, without all this imperialistic male materialism polluting you. We're going to become spiritually aware, hon. We don't know ourselves anymore. We've drifted from our centers. We've forgotten how to love."

Sarah wasn't listening, learning to tune Mom out. She wished life could be as easy as singing backup for Janis, being a member of Big Brother and the Holding Company, coming in with a few "take its" and "break its." But Sarah was certain her life would be more complicated than a four-bar blues. Judge Steinberg's idea of a nurturing environment wasn't going to be realized, "equity of responsibility" was just a phrase written on a court document.

Sarah had custody of herself.

"Besides, it's time for me to do something for myself for a change," Mom said. "And it's nice for your mother to have someone who's there for her. And, hon, Marty's not like your father, he's there for me."

"I'm there for you too," Sarah felt compelled to say.

"I know, hon, and that's beautiful," Mom said. "I got you Babe. It's special. But sometimes Mommy needs someone who is there for her with a penis."

Mom began to steer the car with her knees, reaching into her Guatemalan satchel with both hands, searching for something without regard for the road. Sarah became aware of how fast they were traveling. If the Ghia crashed, tossing them from the car, they would be hurtling at that same rate of speed, 70, 80, 90 mph. She saw herself falling out of this already half-open car and imagined the impact, road removing her skin as she rolled to a halt. She replayed the vision until it seemed inevitable, then braced herself in her seat for that future. Mom produced a joint and a lighter from her bag while her hair danced in the wind, a thousand crazed ballerinas.

"C'mon, hon," she said, taking a toke of the joint. "You looked so stressed. I hate to see you this way. Let's mellow."

Sarah pictured the smoke swirling in Mom's lungs like in the film on cancer she had seen at school. Mom put her knees to the wheel again, snuffed out the joint, reached back into her purse and took out two tiny tears of psychedelic orange paper.

"Better yet," she said, handing one of the tabs to Sarah, spires of smoke floating from her mouth as she spoke. "Let's trip."

Yeah, waking up to Janis was a harsh call.

I don't need this shit, Sarah told herself, removing the pillow from her head. If Mom wants to drudge up bad memories and bad vibes, she can do it quietly and without involving me.

Stepping out of bed, Sarah grabbed her crumpled Levi's, pulling them over her hips. She felt bloated and sick. She wondered whether it was the alcohol or if she was getting her period. Morning air goose-bumped her arms.

God, it's cold, she thought, snagging a sweatshirt and jacket. I better check my patch after I deal with Mom. Maybe with this weather and everyone getting CAMP'ed, I ought to harvest early. The government's Campaign Against Marijuana Planting seizing her crop would be even more depressing than an early frost.

She stepped into half-laced mountain boots, then, sniffing the air, put a cupped hand to her mouth. Is there something dead in here? Or is that my breath? In the bathroom, she swirled mouthwash, swearing off Jack Daniel's for the rest of her life. From the main house she heard Janis howling "Cry Baby." She spit into the sink. "Fuck you, Mom."

Sarah scooped up her Walkman from a pile of laundry. She had a habit of throwing things down when she came into the cabin, sunglasses, coats, keys, aiming for something soft with the delicate stuff, trying to avoid her art projects and board games. Which reminded her, the NEA application was coming due, Parker Brothers had expressed interest in "Hidden Agenda: The Passive-Aggressive Game," and the Trojan company liked her idea of barbecue-flavored ribbed condoms. She had to write letters, highlighting the specifics of each project.

But later for that.

Her cassette player was cued to her favorite bootleg Cowboy Junkies song about a woman finding the strength to carry on after a breakup. In the song the woman spent the day lamenting her loss but invigorated by the power of her new independence, being able to make decisions based solely on her own needs. In the last verse she put it all together, conceding, "Sure I admit there are times when I miss you, especially like now when I could use someone to hold me. But there are some things that can never be forgiven. And I just have to tell you, I kind of like these extra few feet in my bed."

That was the real freedom, Sarah had decided, being strong enough to sleep alone.

She put the speakers over her ears and let Margot Timmons drown out Janis Joplin as she made her way toward the main house. Seeing a splash of vomit on her boot, she thought of the previous night and wondered how the Squirrel Boy was doing. Mr. Local with his Dockers and Miami smile. He would be lucky if he got anywhere close to vertical today. She hoped he made it home and his car didn't get too fucked up. He had been a sweetheart, oddly sincere, cute in his awkwardness, not nearly as uptight as he looked, really seeming to listen when she talked. He deserved better than to be left with the Kurtses and Billy Chuck, but he had wanted to keep going and Sarah had grown tired.

I shouldn't worry, she decided, knowing she would track Squirrel Boy down later. He's probably doing better than I am.

5

John felt the tip of a steel-toed boot. It rolled him onto his back in the middle of the Lodge's parking lot. Concrete cut at his elbows. He tried to cover up, curling himself into a ball, arms over face, unable to fight back. Crash position. He squeezed his eyes shut, waiting for impact. He wasn't even angry, didn't really know what was happening. One minute he had been walking with Pensive back to their cars, the next he was taking a backwater biology exam. Kidneys? Right there, punch! Cerebral cortex? Back here, whap! Groin? Somewhere down there, smack!

"Enough!" Pensive shrieked, like she actually expected this maniac to stop beating him.

Daryl took a two-step running start and kicked him again. Out of reflex, John wrapped himself around the leathered foot.

"Fuck you, fat bitch!" Daryl snarled, trying to shake John loose.

"Fuck me?" Pensive said, obviously having heard that sentiment one too many times. "No, fuck you!"

John heard the release of an aerosol can and felt his throat close. His eyes seared shut. Daryl screamed, falling onto him like a soldier on a live grenade.

"Fat bitch?" Pensive said, losing her usual California-Quaalude-speak. "Don't you ever judge my body."

She began punctuating her syllables with her own kicks, despite the fact that she was wearing sandals. John coiled up tighter. Daryl flailed at his side, trying to climb over him.

"Don't judge my person, my being, my spirit, based on my body," Pensive said. "You have no right to do that to me or any woman."

Daryl continued to curse, but John didn't hear the word

"fat" amidst the litany of insults. Bitch, stanky, hippie, whore, yes. Fat, no.

"I am a radiant being filled with light and love!" Pensive proclaimed, Daryl tasting the back of her Birkenstocks. "I am an open channel of creative energy! My life is blossoming into total perfection! I accept both the size and shape of my breasts!"

After a dozen more affirmations, John heard the spray of the aerosol can again, followed by a blood-curdling yelp from Daryl.

"That's enough physical release for one day," Pensive said, yanking John from beneath Daryl.

John's eyes were burning, blood trickling from his head and arms. He was barely able to breathe let alone stand. Pensive was huffing too. Disoriented, he leaned into her, sinking into the gelatinous expanse of her breasts.

"C'mon," Pensive commanded. "We need to get you some water."

Water? John thought. Ambulance.

"Have you ever done any creative visualization?" Pensive asked, carrying him. "It helps actualize a more progressive situation."

"I have no vision at all," John whined.

"Good time to start," she said. "Beethoven created his greatest symphonies completely deaf. Repeat after me, higher-self surround me in a wall of mirrored light."

John was frightened of this new age voodoo, afraid Pensive was attempting some sort of karmic mouth-to-mouth. He was also concerned that somehow during the melee he had swallowed a mouthful of napalm. His face was on fire, body throbbing with the heat of a hundred bruises. He couldn't stop shaking or dry heaving.

Pensive chanted for guidance as she dragged him off the street, up a flight of stairs and inside a building. John was placed in a chair. Pensive asked someone for water and a wet towel. When the most minimal of medicinals arrived, she forced John to drink from a glass while dabbing at his eyes with a cloth.

"Didn't anybody teach you how to duck?" she asked, wiping a compress against a gash near his temple.

"I only got one chance," John blenched, wiseass mode clicking to automatic pilot. "Lately, my reactions have been a little slow."

"I don't believe in violence," Pensive said, hitting John with another pat of the washcloth.

John winced, seeing static. Molecular activity. Pensive's snowy electric outline disappeared. His brain fired random synapses, signal flares for self-preservation. He saw Grandma. She was administering care to him while giving a lecture on nonviolence.

"Civil disobedience can be effective," Grandma explained. "But so can a left hook. Getting beaten for the cameras is one thing, fighting back is another. Malcolm X said, 'I am not against violence in self-defense. I don't even call it violence when it's self-defense. I call it intelligence.' So, if someone hurts you, John, and you've tried nonviolent tactics and they're ineffectual, kick your enemy square in the nuts. Just don't throw the first punch, unless they leave themselves wide open."

Grandma touched his face, fingers tracing wounds he didn't remember receiving. Birthmarks. She rubbed her thumb against the side of his nose, then across his swelling cheek. She wiped a tangle of hair from his forehead. Taking his hand in her own, she kissed his fingertips and pressed them to his bruise.

"'Surgeons must be very careful/When they take the knife,'" Grandma quoted. "'Underneath their fine incisions/stirs the culprit, life.'"

The lines swam in John's head, somewhere between a lesson and a lullaby. They were words spoken in alphabet soup letters on Fats Waller Sundays. Grandma's dusty anthology of Emily Dickinson and a bottle of Gilbey's gin. Soup and sermon. He never wanted to visit her, and once in Grandma's house, never wanted to leave.

He began to rock on his haunches to the rhythm of his own affirmations: "I am in charge of my own destiny. I will outlast this affliction." The static cleared. He saw Pensive staring at him as if something even more than the obvious was wrong. He stopped rocking.

"John?" Pensive asked. "Are you all right?"

"Yes," John replied, not believing it for a second.

"You've given me quite a scare," she said. "And I'm out of Mace."

"Mace?" John's voice was a panic, worried chemicals would cause him permanent brain damage, more flashbacks. Grandma would stroll into his head whenever she wanted to recite poetry and dime-store philosophy. He would be like David Carradine in *Kung Fu,* convinced Squirrel Boy was a name given to him in a martial arts monastery, every bar he entered, someone yelling, "Hey, Chinaman!"

"The stuff flies," Pensive told him. "In my rage, I shot the whole can."

John felt a rash rising on his face. His heart was beating double-time. The rest of him was numb with shock and adrenaline. But nothing felt broken. On the other hand, nothing felt. He was one dull ache, trying to put an arm back into a shredded shirt sleeve. He tried to move his leg to balance himself in the chair, but he couldn't bend his knee. Shifting his weight, he tried to find a position he could live with.

It might be easier to just stop breathing, he thought.

"You should be thanking me," Pensive said. "Of course, your ego's bruised. Men are so ashamed when they can't defend themselves. But when you pay for the groceries you dropped, I'll call it even."

John held his tongue. He dabbed at his eyes with the washcloth he had been handed. The first couple shots Daryl had landed were to his face, adding to the general swelling. He blinked, trying to clear his vision, but found himself looking through fly eyes, a kaleidoscope of confusion multiplied by a thousand.

"Every time I deek on you, you're lookin' a mite worse," said a voice John recognized as Hap. "Next time I'll be tossin' orchids at you in the Boont Dusties."

"He'll be fine," Pensive promised. "Would you take care of him for a minute while I see if I can save my acidophilus?"

"Should I call Cal?" Hap asked.

"I think he's outside," Pensive said, John able to consolidate his sight into a single smear to follow her figure to the door. "I'll tell him John's here."

Wiping his nose, John smelled food, pizza, lamb, wine. Blood pudding. He realized he was back in the Boonville Hotel and wondered if customers were gawking at him. He could have used some backup from the man he had met at the bar here last night, the one with the earring and gun, Balostrasi. He had said the locals in these parts weren't tough, a bunch of hippies and rubes. He didn't mention giants and psychopaths. Would Daryl have backed down from Balostrasi's gun?

"Gettin' to meet the whole town, Squirrel Boy," Hap said, interrupting John's thoughts. "This here's Deputy Cal."

"So, you're Edna's grandkid," Deputy Cal said. "My heartfelt condolences."

Deputy Cal was as tall as he was wide, and as wide as he was deep, dressed in shorts and a brown shirt from which stretched impressive arms and an imposing beer gut. He wore a mustache beneath a pug nose and reflective sunglasses. Out of uniform, he could have been mistaken for a PE teacher or marine gone to seed. In John's condition, he could have also been mistaken for Imelda Marcos or Sonny Bono.

"It's unfortunate Edna ain't here to show you the ropes," Cal said. "Boonville can be chaotic at times, but out of chaos comes a kind of freedom."

Deputy Cal was the first law enforcement officer John had met to openly promote anarchy. But John came from Florida, the only state in the union where chain gangs were legal and there was a movement to bring back the guillotine. Cops in Miami collected hollow points like bottle caps. Every week an officer of the law was shot, usually walking the thin blue line to serve a simple citation; a Dade County citizen sitting on a million-two worth of AK-47s in the trunk of a stolen Buick Skylark, a Ziploc of coke in the glove box, couldn't stand the suspense, facing twenty years hard time because he didn't know enough names to get into the Federal Witness Protection Program.

"We got a different way of livin'," Deputy Cal explained. "We don't like folks meddlin' in our business, public or private. This town literally has its own language."

"I think I heard Daryl grunting it," John said, beginning to regulate his heartbeat.

"No," the deputy corrected him, "it's called Boontling and it was developed by locals suspicious of outside influences. Hap here can speak it."

"I know," John said. "Leek bee'n."

Hap grinned. Deputy Cal was unimpressed.

"Point is, we do things our own way," Deputy Cal said. "We don't appreciate people pokin' their noses where they don't belong."

"So, because I talked to this guy's ex-wife," John said, looking at the bloodstains on his compress, "I deserved to get my ass kicked?"

"I'm sorry it happened," Deputy Cal said. "Tell you the truth, Whitward looks worse. I think Prairie Mama broke a couple of his ribs. The damage has been done."

"But what?" John asked, trying to see himself from Cal's

point of view, a city boy ground into country sausage. He had got what he deserved. His grandma was a nut, John couldn't have fallen too far from the tree. He should get out of town while he could and save everybody a lot of trouble.

Balostrasi was wrong, John thought. These people were tough.

"If you don't press charges, there's a lot less paperwork," Deputy Cal told him, smiling as only certain rural cops could. "I'm certain Prairie Mama ain't got a license for that mace. You could save folks a lot of hassle. But do as you please. Remember though, everybody who has lived in this town, includin' your grandma, has taken a few punches. But they've also thrown some."

John watched his knees bleed. He hadn't skinned them since he was a child, sliding on asphalt in a game of kickball. His parents had yelled at him, Father complaining about ruined clothes as he spanked John's butt. His mother warned about overcompetitiveness while she soaked him in Bactine. John was sent to his room to "think about what he had done." Lying on his bed, he stared at the picture of Pete Rose his father had tacked to his wall. With two outs in the bottom of the ninth, what were you supposed to do?

"The other thing," Deputy Cal said, "Daryl says he won't start nothing again if . . ."

"If what?" John asked, but knew what the deputy was going to say.

"If you stay away from Sarah," Deputy Cal finished.

No wonder he isn't wearing a uniform, John thought, anybody relaying threats of violence from a sociopath shouldn't be on the force. Maybe I should ask to see his badge?

Fuck it, John told himself. Fuck it all. Fuck being hung over and getting beat up. Fuck Daryl and Pensive Prairie Sunset, this idiot deputy and pressing charges. Fuck Sarah with her blue eyes and fuck Grandma with her faulty DNA. Most of all, fuck Boonville.

"I won't press charges," John said. "I don't plan to be here that long. But tell Daryl if he comes near me again, I have my grandma's shotgun and I'm not afraid to use it. So if you'll excuse me, gentlemen, I'm going to sleep for about a week, and when I wake up, I'm calling my girlfriend and getting out of this shit hole."

John stood to make a grand exit, but his legs forgot the basic one foot in front of the other. They buckled, veering him toward a wall that he mistook for a door, and after reaching for a nonexistent knob, he hit it squarely with his face. John found himself looking up from the floor.

"Maybe you should have another glass of water," Hap said.

"God damn!" Billy Chuck said, entering the hotel, looking exactly as he did the night before, no better, no worse. Not a hair in or out of place.

His children will be born with scales, John thought.

Deputy Cal and Hap seemed to expect John to reseat himself and order a beer now that his drinking buddy had arrived.

"This one's a draw," Billy Chuck announced. "I 'bout fell over Whitward at the Pic 'N Pay. I needed aspirin, but these boys need body bags. We should count to ten and whoever can stand, we'll call winner."

"Squirrel Boy was standin' a second ago," Hap informed him.

"There we go," Billy Chuck laughed. "Now I can collect on my bets. I got five-to-one from Kurts on a buck and ten-to-one from Melonie on a beer. I knew you could do it, Squirrel Boy, you ain't no tourist."

They were betting on me, John realized. But there came a point when things were at their fullest and could hold no more. He was beyond that now, the number that followed infinity. Everything rolled off, part of the same extreme.

"Hold your horses, Meyers," Hap told Billy Chuck. "Our boy had help from Prairie Mama. Doubt your bet was on a tag team match."

"My bet was Daryl wouldn't put his head on a stick by noon today," Billy Chuck said. "Did Prairie Mama put all that hurt on Daryl?"

"She's one mean hippie," Deputy Cal admitted. "Off-duty, I wouldn't mess with no feminist weighin' three-fifty."

"It's the organics make 'em jimheady," Hap offered.

"And the world that makes them mean," Pensive said, returning to the bar.

"No offense, Pensive," Hap excused himself.

"None taken," Pensive said. "By living life as a holistic experience, you find untapped strength in yourself and the world around you. By not indulging in the artificial, you remain pure, spiritually and physically."

She paused.

"What's John doing on the floor?" she asked.

"Taking in the seminar," John answered, pain too intense to bother with. "When are we going to hold hands and burn incense?"

"We don't go for that shit in town," Billy Chuck told him. "That's what the hills are for, personal expression."

John tried to get to his feet again, latching on to Pensive, who was the only one in the group extending a hand. He stood for a moment, and then decided the floor was a better idea.

"Boy's jake-legged," Hap said.

"Anybody got any painkillers?" Billy Chuck asked. "This dog can't hunt."

"Horn of skee?" Hap offered.

John felt ready to faint. On top of everything else, he was dehydrated. He took a sip of the water that Pensive had gotten for him.

"Hell," Billy Chuck said, "I got a .22 in my truck."

"It might come to that," Hap admitted.

Pensive offered to mix a batch of linseed oil and herbs at her house, adding that she had some mushrooms she used as a relaxant.

Suspicions confirmed, John thought. But I don't need any Pensive Prairie Peyote. This is the last place I want to start hallucinating. Isn't there a doctor or hospital? We are in America, aren't we? This is the twentieth century?

"We could take him to Doc Testicles," Deputy Cal suggested, reading John's expression. "But when Big Jack cut off his thumb, Doc just gave him a lozenge. One of those cough drops for sore throats. Said, 'Suck on this, maybe it'll take your mind off the pain.' Big Jack stuck it in his mouth and put his thumb in his shirt pocket. I drove him over the hill to Ukiah General."

"You boys call him Doc Testicles 'cause he holds on too long durin' physicals," Hap asked, "or 'cause he wears those fruity jogging shorts without underwear and you can see all the way to Boulder?"

"Don't talk that way about Dr. Goldberg," Pensive told Hap. "He's a fine doctor and a natural man."

"'Au natural,'" Deputy Cal said, and Hap and Billy Chuck sniggered.

I'm at death's door and they're making puns, John thought. This is funny to them. Something to tell the boys at the Lodge, the one about the tourist who was killed his second day in town. Knock, knock. Who's there? My cowboy-boot up your ass.

"I could take him to Ukiah General." Deputy Cal said. "Personally, I'd rather die in a ditch than check into one of those rooms. I visited Cloris there when she rolled her Bronco. I asked a nurse for her room number and the Grim Reaper himself pointed me down the hall. Makes the morgue look like a dance hall. But we could take John there."

Put me out near the road so a tourist can find me, John wanted to say, his pain receding along with his consciousness. Hee and haw all you want, but get me to the curb. I need my bed. Get me to Christina. She'll make everything all right. I don't even hurt anymore. I just want to leave this town.

"What about Blindman?" Hap asked.

"He has good Valium," Pensive said.

More suspicions confirmed.

"But I heard Blindman beats his wife," Pensive said, reconsidering. "I don't have the kind of forgiveness in me to do business with a wife beater. It would be giving approval to his actions, saying commerce is more important than conduct."

"We organizin' a boycott or tryin' to help Squirrel Boy?" Billy Chuck said. "Get a petition going on your own time. I don't pity any woman dumb enough to let a blind guy hit her. She should be quiet and stand still. He'd never find her."

"The visually impaired often heighten their other senses," Pensive countered. "Didn't you ever see *Wait Until Dark*?"

"No," Billy Chuck confessed. "But I played football against the School for the Deaf. They used to bang a drum on the sidelines to know when to hike the ball. Got every decent deaf player in the state and some fakes that just said, 'Huh?' a lot. Kicked the shit out of us. But you could curse their mothers and all you'd get was a smile."

"Bottom line," Deputy Cal stated, somewhat professionally, "aside from a wife beater, Blindman's a drug dealer, shoplifter, ex-Moonie, ex-Joneser, a contributor to the delinquency of minors, and after that bridge incident, a murder suspect. You can do what you want for John's sake, but as an officer of the law, I ain't consorting with a piece of shit the likes of him."

"What do you want to do, Squirrel Boy?" Hap had the courtesy to ask.

"Snuggle-bunny," John replied, fuzzily. "I need to leave this place. I thought it would be all right, but it's not. I scraped my knees sliding. I should go to my room."

"Let's get him to his grandma's," Deputy Cal said. "Put him to bed. He'll be fine. He needs sleep is all."

"I'll check in on him," Pensive promised. "Billy Chuck, follow me in your truck, I'll drive him in Edna's car."

"Edna's car?" Billy Chuck asked.

"The Squirrel Lady," Pensive clarified.

Deputy Cal lifted John's arm around his neck and Pensive positioned herself beneath the other, John hanging limp between them. They left for the parking lot, passing alarmed tourists. Billy Chuck readied himself to assist in negotiating the steps. Hap held open the door. A wind blustered, carrying the scent of pumpkins, apples, and cut wood.

Grandma, John said to himself, we're not in Miami anymore.

They had to wait as logging trucks barreled past. John's steps were heavy and uncertain. They crossed the highway. Billy Chuck and Hap followed, helping to lean John into the passenger seat of the broken Datsun.

"Too bad his mind's fixed on leavin'," John heard Hap say, as Pensive fished the keys from John's pocket and Cal shut the door behind him. "I think he fits right in."

6

John wondered if waking up in Boonville was the worst thing the world had to offer. Worse than Turkish prisons, worse than being buried alive, worse than reruns of "Three's Company," fruitcakes, heavy metal, herpes, Lee Iacocca, being trapped in an elevator with Barbra Streisand, Liza Minnelli, and Whitney Houston, who all want to sing rounds of show tunes until you're rescued. But you're never saved. And they find you magnetically attractive. Liza thrusts her tongue down your throat, pancake makeup smearing against your cheek, blinded by eyeliner and false eyelashes, as one of Barbra's nostrils swallows your penis, blowing you with her nose, while Whitney becomes so excited she strokes herself into a lather, climactically crying out in Muzak ecstasy, "I believe children are our future!"

"Hey, Squirrel Boy, you wanna buy some codeine? I got codeine, hash, health crystals! Wake up!"

John felt a lump the size of a tangerine beneath his left eye, uncertain whether his vision had been permanently impaired or if it was dark outside. Somebody was banging on the door. He was too exhausted to answer. It was a tough call, one he didn't make immediately because his sleep hadn't been restful. Anytime Liza, Barbra, or Whitney worked cameos into your dreams, your subconscious was doing you wrong. John was sure in his closet of nightmares, probably with their hands on the knob. Glenn Close, Nancy Reagan, and Connie Chung were getting ready to put in disturbing appearances, along with Margaret Thatcher, Jane Fonda, and Lady Macbeth.

Why were his worst dreams filled with women? They couldn't represent the ones in his waking life, he thought. How could his mind, even asleep, confuse Glenn Close with Christina? Margaret Thatcher with Grandma? Baabaa with Mama? He hated his father more than anyone, his subconscious knew that. Why didn't he dream of Richard Nixon, Donald Trump, or Andy Rooney? Running post patterns for Dan Marino in US 1. Fishing trips with Sylvester Stallone, William F. Buckley, and Benny Hill. Sandwiched in a sleeping bag between the Shah of Iran and John Denver, who were rubbed down in marshmallow cream. That seemed more relevant a neurosis than anything the women stirred. Except for John's recurring "subverted flower" dream.

The "subverted flower" dream started with John jogging on the beach, pants chafing his legs, shirt untucked, feet sinking into loose sand. Why am I running? Sand fleas feasting. He knew there was a reason because he wasn't dressed for exercise. Seagull shit baking. He was tired, having run all the way from the far end of the beach. Lubed cocoa butter. Away from something. Squealing rectal wetness. Something he had done, but felt no remorse. Saliva slicked cock. Something that undeniably felt good. Bikini torn Gottex. Purging him momentarily. Fisted scream release. But had followed him. Cunt fuck. And was ready to devour him whole.

John couldn't run any faster. He felt sick and wanted to stop. Then the beach tilted and he fell. Fall, falling, fallen. Forward onto fours, running like a dog. The one in Frost's poem, changing from man to beast because of what he had done to the girl in the field, the subverted flower. A hand hung like a paw, his arm worked like a saw. Women watched, knowing. John wanted to prove them wrong, run on two legs or stop running altogether, but the slant of the beach made it impossible. He fell with infinite dream-like fluidity, again and again and again, pulling at his pants as if his trousers were what tangled his stride. But everybody seemed to understand it was natural for him to run palm to toe, obeying bestial laws. Finally, he gave in, skirting down the beach as much on his hands as on his feet. Panting, John looked and saw the worst.

"Rise and shine, Squirrel Boy! I got coke so pure it'll make you homesick! I'll get the wifeback to cook some arroz con pollo and we'll fiesta! Mexicans are practically Cuban!"

John didn't want to guess who it was on the other side of his door. His worst nightmares, even the "subverted flower" dream, fell short of the terror of dealing with Boonville. He pulled the blankets over his head, closing his eyes.

"Don't, John. Stop."

"What?"

"I'm not in the mood."

"Not in the mood?"

"I'm not in the mood, and I don't want to be forced into having sex."

"We've been sleeping together for seven years and all of a sudden I'm forcing you into having sex? What are you talking about? When do I force you to have sex?"

"Right now, for one."

"Right now? When else?"

"All the time."

"All the time?"

"I'm saying, I'm tired and I don't want to have sex. Do I have to feel bad about it? If we're going to start making it, I've got to get more sleep."

"What's that supposed to mean?"

"It means you're content with your career in marketing, so it's up to me to make changes so we can get somewhere."

"Get somewhere? Where do you want to go? Somewhere we never have sex?"

"Fine. Go ahead, fuck me."

"Christina, why are you being this way? I love you."

"If you loved me you'd get a job with a future. There would be a ring on my finger. We would have children. There would be a spark when we made love. It's time to quit fooling ourselves, we're getting what we settle for."

Blam! Blam! Blam!

"I'm not getting any younger, Squirrel Boy! I know you're in there, open up!"

Instead of waking, John continued his somnolent drift. He heard his father's voice, saw his face, the chiseled rock resting below a Florida Gators hat, flushed cheeks, eyes squinting from the white noise in his head. Most people's First impression of John's father was that he was the kind of guy who had earned the right to drink beer and watch the ball game after a routinely bad day of working outdoors. Despite his resemblance to a member of the road crew, John's father sold insurance from an office in downtown Miami where he had air-conditioning, a swivel chair, a water cooler, and a view of the site where the last "Putt and Dry" had stood before being sold by John's grandfather to overseas investors who built a high-rise, which became the corporate headquarters to the largest advertising firm south of Saatchi & Saatchi. That was reality, savage and mundane. John's father started every day at the office drawing the curtains, standing in the shadow of success, taking a nip of Old Grand-Dad, and flipping off the skyscraper. But the rugged workman image was what he liked to project.

"He'll learn the hard way!" his father yelled.

"Put that belt away!" his mother cried, equally hysterical.

"No Communists are going to live under my roof!"

"He's twelve, Jim. It was a report, a class assignment. Everybody did Cuba."

"He's reading the wrong books. There will be no pro-Castro garbage in my house while I'm paying the bills. I'll show him red!"

"You've scared him enough. Let him be!"

"He's got to learn!"

"Stop! He's afraid!"

"He better be, those cigar-breathed bastards are ninety miles away. I suppose he'll really be scared when they come to rape his mother. You want to watch the Commies rape your mother, John?"

Whap! Whap! Whap!

The way John saw it, he could either relive the day his father beat him with a belt or open his eyes and see which of Boonville's residents was continuing that fine tradition. There was no third choice. This, combined with his recent experiences, seemed like a valid argument for handguns.

"Wake up, Squirrel Boy!"

Green glow of alarm clock: 4:12.

Late or early? John wondered. And on the subject of time, what day was it?

He saw a mysterious figure standing over him, illuminated by the moonlight, swinging a cane whose handle had been carved to resemble the head of a frowning squirrel. The specter wore wraparound sunglasses and had a bald head, pasty skin, white shirt, and white pants. John thought he was either still dreaming or being visited by the ghost of Boonville Past.

"Wake up, Squirrel Boy. I'm Blindman!"

"You hit me with that cane again," John rasped, a strange bitter taste climbing from the back of his throat, "you're gonna be a dead man."

"Tough talk, coming from someone that can't hold their liquor and just got his butt kicked," Blindman said, addressing a spot three feet to the left of John's eyes. "But your grandma was good to me, so I'll cut you slack. Pick your poison, Squirrel Boy."

Blindman tossed a paper bag to that same spot three feet to John's left. The bag crashed onto the nightstand, knocking over John's alarm clock and picture of Christina. The lamp wobbled ovals, found the edge of the nightstand, and fell from sight. There was a disheartening crunch.

"Pick that up, will you?" Blindman said.

Without thinking, John reached for the bag. It was a familiar movement, one he performed almost daily in Miami to retrieve his alarm clock. Maybe that's why he responded with obedience; in his lassitude he thought he was in bed with Christina beginning a day like any other. He never could get a handle on things in the morning, not without three or four snooze bars, half a pot of coffee, and Christina telling him he was going to be late for the fifth time. John wasn't a morning person. Every day he slid from beneath his covers grudgingly. For the illusion of extra sleep, he set his clock twenty minutes fast. It didn't occur to him that he was waking himself up that much earlier. The fact that he didn't use the correct time annoyed Christina. She hated waking up before she had to.

"What time is it, really?" Christina would ask, letting John know this was one of his habits that would never become endearing.

Half-asleep, John would knock over the alarm clock, along with his keys, a pile of change, a glass of water, Christina's diaphragm, and one of the books Grandma had given him, a symbolic collage he didn't have the presence of mind to ponder. Fumbling to turn off the buzzing, he would inadvertently switch the clock's alarm setting from "ringer" to "radio" and they would be blasted by "classic rock radio," most likely the instrumental solo of "Magic Carpet Ride." But during the instrumental solo of "Magic Carpet Ride," you never know it's the instrumental solo of "Magic Carpet Ride." Until the chorus kicks in, you think you're listening to a recording made to communicate with dolphins. In the morning, it's even more confusing. On occasion the alarm lasted to the next tune, usually Neil Young's "Ohio." John was convinced the DJs of "classic rock radio" only played ten different songs, a stack of 45s with grooves deeper than radial tires. "Tin soldiers and Nixon's coming . . ." Any record from the loop was enough to keep John awake and on edge. He would pound the clock with his fist.

"Squirrel Boy," Blindman said. "You there?"

"Yes," John replied. "It's hard to believe, but I am here."

"Between you and me, you're not retarded, are you?" Blindman asked. "I don't sell to retards. I let Bobby Dee buy, everybody knows that. He's got Down's syndrome, but he's not too far down, not after all the speed I pass his way."

"No," John said, noticing he had slept in his clothes for the second straight night. "I don't think I'm retarded."

"Thing is with retards," Blindman explained, "Half of them don't know they're retarded. The quiet ones take me a while to catch on to. They're sneaky handicapped. You pity them like Krishnas or Reagan because they seem harmless, but next thing you know they own every copy shop in California or get themselves elected president of the United States."

John resumed his stretch for Blindman's bag. The movement reminded him of his beating; his stomach felt ulcerated and his body abscessed. He got snared in the tatters of his bloodstained oxford. There was a ripping sound, a loosening, a slight breeze beneath his armpit. Grabbing the sack, he felt relieved his intruder was sightless.

Meanwhile, Blindman was telling him a story about Tim Stoen, the lawyer for the People's Temple, who let his wife and kids go to Guyana flying coach. According to Blindman, Stoen picked out the flavor of Kool-Aid they served at "the last picnic" and had somebody buy generic cyanide so he could put another nickel into his bank account. Stoen got out of the cult the day before the slaughter. Blindman had been deprogrammed a year earlier, confessing to John that he had gone from drugs to the Moonies' chinchilla ranch, to Jones, and then back to drugs.

"Go with what got you here, that's my motto," Blindman said. "My mother was a junkie and that's why I'm blind. Fuck it, two tears in a bucket. But tell me how a sleaze like Stoen can run for Congress and get twelve thousand votes? Don't people remember?"

John asked himself, do I look like a priest? The *Miami Herald*?

Why are people telling me these things? But his concern shifted from Boonville's need of an audience to Blindman's bag, which he discovered was full of drugs.

"Guy like that," Blindman said, "they ought to string up by the balls, cut off his dick, and stick an apple in his mouth."

"Blindman," John interrupted, not asking about the apple-in-the-mouth part of the punishment, although it intrigued him, "this bag is full of drugs."

"There's more where that came from," Blindman assured him. "Mexicans aren't the only ones that can deal in this town. I can't be expected to survive on my state check without a supplement."

"I sympathize," John said, trying to be diplomatic. "But I'm not into drugs."

He tried to return the sack, but Blindman refused to take it. John pressed the portable pharmacy to Blindman's chest. Blindman looked left, then right, tapped at the sack with his cane, but wouldn't take hold of it.

"Blindman," John said, "you can't come barging into my home, hitting me with your cane and expecting me to buy drugs? I don't even know you. The last thing I need is some pixilated pariah giving me a cult update while it's still dark outside."

"What do I care if it's dark outside?" Blindman said. "Night, day, inside, outside, it's all the same to me. Colorless, shapeless, without reason. Pixilated pariah? Fuck you and your *Reader's Digest* enriched word power."

There was something in Blindman's hostility that triggered a vague memory of somebody saying he had once killed a man. Killed as in dead. Not living, not breathing, not just down at the Lodge tipping a few beers back with the Kurtses. Another thought entered John's mind, what if this nut is flying on something from his goody bag? God only knows what he's taking, he can't even read the labels. John began to find that early morning clock radio alertness, ready to break on through to the other side.

"Don't talk to me about dark outside," Blindman said. "I was ready to believe anything to see light, sold flowers, shaved my head, raised chinchillas, gave my money away, special diets, special chants. Nothing. I'm blind. That's the way I like it, because light is an exploded star, something that's already been decided. You see nothing but reflections of particles that don't exist except in a dead moment passing toward absolute darkness. Give me sound. One big explosion! The truth!"

John thought about bolting for the door, but it seemed silly to run from a blind man in your own home. Where do you go at four in the morning when you live in the middle of nowhere? Who was going to help? And how were they going to try to help you? Maybe a preemptive strike was the answer. Violence seemed Boonville logical. Deputy Cal would understand a plea of self-defense and they could bury Blindman out back with the road signs. It went without saying, Blindman wouldn't see it coming.

"Goddamn," Blindman said, calming himself. "I need some more No-Contact."

"No-Contact?" John asked, temporarily holding off his ambush.

"I only do over-the-counter drugs," Blindman informed John, who didn't believe this kind of craziness could come in the form of a capsule. "There's a Raley's in Ukiah open twenty-four hours, and if I'm broke, I can steal what I need. The clerks there would never arrest a blind person for shoplifting cold medicine."

"It's good to know you wouldn't take advantage of the kindness of strangers," John said, reclining to a less aggressive but still siege-friendly stance.

Blindman was still gazing three feet to John's left. It was strange to talk to someone who could only look you in the eye by accident.

"The tough part of No-Contact," Blindman explained, "I need the wifeback to open the Contac* capsules and separate the red balls from the blues and whites. Only the reds mix well with No-Doz. Luckily, she's used to piece labor. I can melt everything myself. Stuff is twice as good as cocaine, a hundred times cheaper, legal, and instead of destroying your nasal passages, it cleans your sinuses. I haven't sneezed in five years."

"You ought to be in line for the Nobel Prize," John assured him. "You could be the first antihistamine junkie to win the award."

"We all got our vices," Blindman said. "You're probably addicted to pain and don't even know it. The noble sufferer. Blame everybody but yourself. Edna told me about you and your family."

John couldn't imagine Grandma having a conversation with Blindman, so it was preposterous that she could have told him anything personal about his family. And, it wasn't true, he wasn't addicted to pain. He just had a high threshold, that's all. Why else would he be tolerating Blindman? He couldn't speak for his parents, it might be true about them. At this point in his life, John didn't care.

"You don't know me, Blindman," John said.

"But I knew your grandma," Blindman told him. "In the biblical sense."

"What are you trying to say?" John asked.

"I'm not trying to say anything," Blindman said. "I'm telling you, I porked your grandma, lunged her doughnut. How clear do you need it?"

In order to have been born, John knew his grandparents had to have had sex, but he didn't want to reflect on any specific grope. Maybe he could handle thinking about it in terms of old photographs, a black-and-white snapshot couple walking hand in hand, spreading a blanket, laying down and coming together to produce his father in a moment of shared passion. But not Grandma without Grandpa. And not Grandma as an old woman. And not Grandma as an old woman taking in the appendage of a blind, petty-thief, junkie, cultist drug-dealer. Not Grandma and Blindman. John didn't need it that clear.

"I don't want to hear this," John said, wishing his telephone worked so he could call Deputy Cal. "I'm sure my grandma would have nothing to do with you."

"Which shows you what you can be sure of," Blindman said. "It only happened once. Edna had read somewhere cum was made up of the same substance as the fluid that protects your brain. She wanted to save it, for health reasons. She believed you could fuck your brains out. The way we went at it, she made a believer of me. She was a strange woman, but she grew the best Mendo Mellow in the county. I was hoping you came here to do the same. That's why I stopped by. The bag was because Prairie Mama told me you could use some help."

John wished Grandma had told him she had slept with Blindman. Not that he had told her about his one-night stands, all three of them, each an awkward entering occurring before he had met Christina. In every case, John had felt like he had done his best, until in post-orgasm depression the women shook his confidence by saying something like, "It's O.K., we can try again later." Christina had been the one that taught him how to "make love," fulfilling his desires and satisfying him with the notion that she would be the only woman he would sleep with for the rest of his life.

John was a sexual throwback, having completely missed the sixties free-love influence. He didn't even get the seventies until the eighties were fully under way. In Miami, a "Look, don't touch!" voyeurism was dominant. Floridians were on the cutting edge of strip shows, phone sex, Bain de Soleil ads, and cheek-to-cheekless dances. His parents, being McCarthy-era, Legion of Decency inspired, believing in one mate, one ejaculation for one child, of which there was only one, were no help either. His father screwed around, but nobody was supposed to know. His mother was an inebriated June Cleaver, the perfect apron-wearing housewife until the sneak-drinks of sherry kicked in and she stalked around the house making lewd comments about Tom Jones's bulge and rubbing against the ironing board to the rhythm of fiercely creased pants and a Vegas version of "I Want to Kiss You All Over." Apparently, Grandma had her kinks too.

John formed the disgusted expression cut into a thousand scraps of wood at the thought of Blindman's seed spilling into Grandma's shriveled sanctum. He hoped they at least had the decency to put a layer of latex between them. Grandma wasn't even supposed to like people, why this man? How many others were there? Didn't you need a special lubricant to have sex with a woman over the age of seventy? Who bought it? What else didn't he know? John was willing to accept there had been hints about Grandma growing dope, her place being a shack, Boonville being rural, all about as revealing as Noah saying, "It looks like rain," but clues nonetheless. He knew Grandma was eccentric, but having sex with this scumbag was something else. What was he to think? What was he to say?

"Do you have proof?" John asked.

"What?" Blindman said.

"Do you have proof?" John repeated. "That you slept with my grandma?"

John wanted Blindman to say something he could refute, that Grandma had a flat stomach and minty breath, or that in the throes of passion she had called out Grandpa's name. John wanted to believe Grandma's dark side wasn't fused with human need. He wanted limits to the dementia of his heredity. He wanted to be told a crude lie.

"Edna wasn't the kind of woman to wear garters," Blindman offered. "I could get specific, but I doubt you felt her up the way I did."

"When did it happen?" John said, skin crawling.

"It wasn't D-Day, it was a roll in the hay," Blindman told him. "The days that matter to me are today and the day I die. You're talking to a man that has never seen a watch. I ask somebody what time it is, I have to take their word for it. When I used to go to the Blind Center it was like going to prison. Sometimes I'd sit in the library reading braille and think to myself this stuff ticking away could be minutes, seconds, or years. When you're in darkness and there's silence, time could be anything. You realize it's in your head. This could be an afternoon in the year 2000, what difference would it make?"

"There would have been a better chance of you catching me awake," John said.

"Be glad you are awake," Blindman cautioned. "I had a friend who used to worry over little disturbances. The night I was with Edna, he walked off the side of a bridge."

"He killed himself?" John said.

"I didn't have anything to do with it," Blindman answered, as if he had been accused before. "We were hunting. We were drunk. It was an accident."

Hunting drunk didn't sound like an accident to John. It sounded like the next closest thing to suicide.

"We were in a car, roadkilling," Blindman explained. "I couldn't get any high school kids to take us out because Cal told them they'd lose their licenses if he caught them driving me anymore. The Mexicans will still do it for twenty bucks and a case of Tecate. Mexicans will do anything for twenty bucks and a case of Tecate, anything but learn the language or drive an economy car."

John wanted to know how this related to him. People told stories in this town, no point, no moral, no reason. He was tired and in pain. The room was dimming. The moon had fallen to the other side of the cabin. Curtains of geometric shapes filled the room from floor to ceiling, stitching corners, embroidering dust. Blindman appeared in the center, a vanishing point.

"My friend Josh had never hunted," Blindman said. "The blind have to look out for each other, otherwise our only excitement is listening to baseball on the radio. I don't let people dilute my life with their conventions and limitations. 'Visually challenged,' I'd never let someone hang that on me. Rock climbing is a challenge, arm wrestling, river rafting. Someone saying they can drink you under the table, that's a challenge. Being blind is fucked. End of challenge. But that doesn't mean I can't get drunk or get laid or go hunting. I'm entitled too, maybe even more so. Why should I conform to a way of life that doesn't accept me? It's my duty as an outcast, as a blind man, to form another order. And Josh, that straight-living dead sonofabitch, him too."

"Was he in the People's Temple?" John asked, yawning, figuring if he was going to get the story, he might as well get the whole story.

"Straight people don't go for cults," Blindman told him. "It's the crooked ones that need order and direction so they can get through the day-to-day. They're the ones that join cults. Josh wouldn't kiss a girl on a first date, so there was no way he'd marry a strange Korean. It was hard enough to get him drunk."

John was having trouble concentrating. This was about the fifth wall he'd hit in the last two days. He turned to Blindman's bag, wanting dreamless, uninterrupted sleep, not worrying that it was self-prescribed. He sifted through the sack of multicolored pills, tablets, capsules, powders, herbs, vials, baggies, rolling papers, pipes, syringes, spoons, lighters, screens, matches, model glue, a piece of quartz, a half-eaten Snickers, a can of butane, a nine-volt battery, baby laxative, and finally, a bottle labeled 'Codeine.' With difficulty, John sprang the 'child-proof' cap and shook two into his palm. Working up a spit, he popped them into his mouth when Blindman's monologue seemed at a temporary pause.

"Go on," John said, preparing for sleep, grabbing the piece of quartz before setting the bag aside, willing to try anything.

"We had a bottle of bourbon and a case of Bud," Blindman said. "God only knows if we killed anything because the Mexies didn't speak English. It was 'gato' this, 'perro' that, while we clicked off rounds out the car windows. Once in a while Paco or Rabanne would yell, 'Bambi!' and we'd blast away hoping for some antlers. Basically it's the thrill of the sound, taking a chunk out of the world. I was happy because I knew Josh had never done anything like this, shooting that gun, making that sound. It's the closest thing we got to color."

"Where did you say my grandma was?" John interrupted.

"Waiting for us to try her new crop," Blindman said, "We were on our way to Edna's when I told The Beaner Twins to pull over so I could pee. But they didn't know the rules of the road, so they stopped in the middle of Millwood Bridge, about a hundred feet long and two hundred feet down without any railing because it's for logging trucks. I got out my side, and you can read the police report if you don't believe me, I pissed and got back in the car. I didn't hear anything but my stream and the stream down below. I thought Josh was passed out. Next thing I knew, the Mexies were pushing me out of the car at Edna's. I must have blacked out. No big deal, black is black. For me, it's like putting in ear plugs. So I get to the porch here, and then I think to myself, 'Where's Josh?' Answer, the Boont Dusties. He walked off that bridge, with his zipper down."

"And in your grief," John said. "You screwed my grandma."

"Edna drove me back to the bridge and, sure enough, Josh was at the bottom of it," Blindman said. "When you're blind you don't have to shut your eyes, but I got a vision of my friend down there, and I looked away."

John watched Blindman replay his only image of the visual world, a friend dead in a half-dried riverbed. He felt something like sympathy for the drug dealer, even if he had slept with his grandmother. It was no wonder he didn't believe in light, the only thing it had revealed to him was death.

"He looked surprised," Blindman said. "Like his sight had been returned to him when he hit the ground, a second or two before he died. He didn't know this was where he had been living, among rocks and shadows. I knew I couldn't help him, never could. I had to go to the car. Edna pulled him out of the river, called Cal, went to the questioning with me, and let me stay the night with her. She was a strong woman."

John thought it would be ridiculous for him to try to console Blindman. He felt sorry for him, but wanted him gone so he could go to sleep and forget the image of this man merging with his grandmother. The codeine was making him woozy. He couldn't blink away the drowsiness. He pictured Grandma in his mind, the way her smile slid into a sneer. He knew she exercised the kind of influence over him that could only take place across a great distance, the space between youth and old age. There was something in her worthy of respect and emulation, but this was where it had got her, Boonville. This was what she had become, a freak on a hill whittling squirrel sculptures, drunk, reading metaphysics, hanging out with Margaret Washington and Pensive Prairie Sunset, fucking Blindman, calling out to her grandson to follow in her footsteps.

"Sorry if you don't like hearing this," Blindman said, and John heard him tapping across the planked floor. "But I wasn't put on this earth for you to like. Neither was your grandma."

John's head sank into the pillow, a quilt of darkness spreading over him with the promise of sleep. The haunting was over. Everything was quiet except for the wind outside the cabin. Grandma's spirit trying to touch him, he thought, in the throes of the codeine. A breeze slipped through a crack to kiss him goodnight. He felt relieved, at ease with himself for the first time since he had left Florida.

Then Roseanne Barr walked into the bedroom wearing a Yankees uniform, a batting helmet and spikes, and holding a Louisville Slugger smeared in Vaseline.

"I'm ready, John," she whispered. "Let's play hardball."

7

". . . Honey, when everybody in the world wants the same damn thing. When everybody in the world needs the same lonely thing. When I want to work for your love, Daddy. When I want to try for your love, Daddy. I don't understand, how come you're gone, man? I don't understand why half the world is still crying, man, when the other half of the world is still crying too, man. And I can't get it together. I mean, if you got a cat for one day, man, I don't mean if you, say, say maybe you want a cat for 365 days, right? You ain't got him for 365 days, you got him for one day, man. Well, I'll tell you that one day, man, better be your life, man. Because you know, you can say, 'Aw man,' you can cry about the other 364, man, but you're gonna lose that one day, man, and that's all you got. You gotta call that love, man. That's what it is, man. If you need it today, you don't want it tomorrow, man, 'cause you don't need it. 'Cause as a matter of fact, as we discover on the terrain, tomorrow never happens, man. It's all the same fucking day . . ."

Sarah stepped onto the deck of the main house and into the full deafening craziness of Janis Joplin's rant. As a child, she had heard Mom sing this song so many times that the two women's voices had become indistinguishable in her mind. It was Mom howling, Mom babbling, Mom on speed and whiskey. Mom close to death. Mom played Janis whenever she came home from dates alone. She would pour herself a drink, kick off her cork-heeled Cherokees, toss the cat onto the beanbag chair, park herself on the couch, and at the top of her lungs, rave after Janis, "It's all the same fucking day!" Sarah would listen from her bedroom, certain Mom would o.d. like Janis. And everyone would blame her for not being a good enough daughter. That was Sarah's ball and chain.

Reaching the main house, Sarah expected to find Mom bumming, the way she had seen her a zillion times, drunk or stoned, waiting for Sarah to arrive to heave a rap into her lap like a lump of shit. Not even, Sarah thought, hot potato that one back to you. Unless Mom copped a whole new attitude, it was going to be a short conversation. Mom would have to join a peyote circle or find a self-help book she hadn't read for solace. But instead of finding her mother, Sarah encountered three Future Primitives crawling around the red leather Roche-Bobois, churning groin butter.

Of course they were naked, of course they were dirty, of course they were grunting; Future Primitives didn't believe in clothes, language, or standing erect. It was their way of getting back to the Earth, fulfilling their "true animal selves," and creating a need for the main house to be flea-bombed. Filthy and foul, howling and humping, they were beyond gross; one had bitten a resident in the leg, drawing blood, and Sarah was certain they were responsible for the epidemic of lice. Not only was their society a farce, but they were a health hazard. She wished the residents of the Waterfall would give them their walking papers, literally. But it wasn't going to happen; people living in glass yurts don't throw stones. Everybody at the Waterfall was into something bizarre. And for a brief period, most of them had "gone primitive."

The Future Primitives had come into existence when Mom's ex-squeeze Marty, now Aslan, Father of the New Children, wanted to screw a sixteen-year-old retro-hippie from Vacaville named Resa who wouldn't be seduced until the Poobah, as Sarah called Marty, created the concept of the Future Primitives. Then ninety percent of the Waterfall went primitive, following the Poobah's "DarJungian Philosophy" encouraging them to "renounce language, revert to all fours, and respond to your sexual instincts." During this epoch, Sarah's sexual instincts told her to carry a marlin bat she had bought as a souvenir in Hawaii, letting everyone know she would use it if anyone so much as growled at her wrong. The men snorted an understanding, then orgied down, Resa and Poobah merging. Most of the residents abandoned the faith after their knees got sore, certain women refused to be mounted, and their children weren't testing well in their English classes. Five members remained, including these three defiling the Roche-Bobois, sniffing and licking each other's butts.

"Hey!" Sarah yelled, shedding her Walkman because her music had been drowned out by Janis's wailing. "Get off the couch!"

But the music in the main house was too loud. The Future Primitives didn't hear her and continued their whiffing. Sarah stalked to the stereo and ripped Janis from the turntable. Startled, the Future Primitives looked up from their hind-nuzzling like a new breed of groundhog.

"Where were you raised?" Sarah asked. "In a dome?"

The Future Primitives piled off the couch, hairy, pale and unhealthy, the three cult stooges. In an act of uncivil disobedience, one of the males, Mancub, showed Sarah his privates. The other male, Jeremy Roth, too busy for anything that political, grappled and shrieked in a mock mating ritual with the female, Saffron. Sarah was set to get a bucket of cold water to separate them, but Saffron regarded her with such a savage smirk of superiority that Sarah had to take a step back.

These weren't dogs, Sarah reminded herself. Dogs smelled better.

The Future Primitives brought to Sarah's mind her favorite Saturday morning kids' show "Land of the Lost" gone porno; Marshall, Will, and the missing link Choco, getting it on in a prehistoric ménage à trois. The Future Primitives were the worst kind of experimental hippies, scraggly, sexual, and in-your-face.

Sarah had decided long ago that hippies could be filed into four basic categories: experimental, retro, bush, and associative. Experimental hippies were marked by their extremist lifestyles. They believed if you were going to do something crazy, it was best to do it in numbers. For example, the land adjacent to the northwest of the Waterfall was occupied by a cult of experimental hippies called the Spinners who believed God spoke to them through Jerry Garcia's guitar. To hear the holy word clearly, they took Ecstasy and spun in circles with their arms outstretched until they spewed. What experimental hippies lacked in common sense, they made up for in intensity. They were the most fanatical type of hippie, prone to jail, premature burn-out, and group suicide. They supported themselves through collective business ventures ranging from T-bill accounts to mass begging. The Spinners sold the standard wannabe paraphernalia, marijuana, bootleg Dead cassettes, tie-dyed clothing, to retro-hippies who, in Sarah's book, were tourists of time.

Retro-hippies, young, white, and predominantly middle-class, saw the surface of the decade they were visiting and shopped accordingly. They littered the sidewalks of Haight Street in San Francisco and Telegraph Avenue in Berkeley, bumming quarters for acid and pizza, acting as if they were homeless instead of bored, and packed the second-hand stores, paying top dollar for paisley vests and torn bell-bottoms, fringed leather jackets that were ugly and didn't fit. They showed up for demonstrations, trying to out-hip each other with their political erectness and stylishly unstylish garb. Their idea of a political statement was to hold hands, form a circle, and sing "Give Peace a Chance." Sarah felt it was what happened when history was taught by MTV.

But maybe that was all that was left of the legacy, Sarah thought, all that had filtered through the ad execs who wrote the final fiction.

Either way, it was embarrassing to see people her own age that clueless; retros didn't know the difference between Che Guevara and Chez Panisse. People had died in the sixties, were beaten and imprisoned, movers and shakers were moved out and shook down. Sarah had seen the scars, dealt with the aftermath. Retros didn't have any idea what it meant to live in a revolutionary environment. Raised in the wreckage, Sarah considered herself a by-product of those times as opposed to waste matter. She had heard the bush-hippies babble, reaching for roaches, pipes, pills, bongs, a copy of *Soul on Ice*, anything that might ease the memory of their failed attempt to change the world. She had listened to them exhale the oral history of how close they had come to a bright new tomorrow, seen the vision of the better times that preceded the fall burned into their bloodshot eyes.

"You should have been there." Unsteady hands struck matches for an encore. "It was cosmic." The Band has played its last waltz, packed up and disappeared into the tranquility of a closing night. "It was like, wow!" Stragglers splayed on the dance floor with cigarette butts and crumpled cups, among dried sweat and lost earrings. "The music, the sex, the love, everybody knew we were winning." A bulb has burned out in the marquee. "If I could do it all over." The W does not flash. "You should have been there." The smell of smoked dope and dissipated dreams. "We were that close." The anonymous odor of a dispersing crowd. "Everything almost changed." A door closed, bolted, barred. "It was far out." A building condemned. "Nobody will ever be that close again."

Bush-hippies were the ones who headed for the hills after the sixties, dropping further out of society, looking to live independent of the world. They pretended it was perpetually 1969, the revolution was still coming, peace, love, and dope would carry them to the higher ground like Kesey's bus. Time was marked by the price of an ounce of homegrown. They didn't check publication dates when they picked up their copies of *The Nation*, *The Guardian*, and *The Socialist Review* from their P.O. boxes, and failed to notice any subtleties as they digested the leftist propaganda whole, substituting old bogeys for new ones. At political rallies the cameras zoomed in on them to discredit the event; dirty clothes, distrusting eyes, dusty FBI files. Same old freaks. Remember what happened last time? The confusion? Civil rights? Vietnam? "One, two, three, four, what are we fighting for?"

Naive, Sarah concluded. But they had been there when the heavy shit went down. Maybe that was too much for them. Too much for anyone. It was up to their security-starved children now, Republican-voting Democrats, video-game-gazing, second-generation dysfunctional, temp-employed whiners from an age without identity. At least the bush-hippies were on the right side. Sarah was certain her contemporaries would be responsible for the disappearance of any rain forest, ozone layer, Communist Party, or poetry that might have existed into the twenty-first century. With bush-hippies, you just had to look past their pretensions and realize they were as self-indulgent as anyone, good instincts but overly nostalgic and severely dependent on drugs. Compared to her set, bush-hippies would be saints if they wiped their asses once in a while.

"Arrrrgh!"

A Future Primitive jarred Sarah from her generalizations, leaving her lumped in the last category: associative-hippie. It didn't matter who she was, what she thought, how she dressed, how much she hated the people that populated her daily life, she was a hippie by association. Mom was a hippie, Mom's boyfriend was a hippie, she lived on a commune. Hippie, hippie, hippie. She couldn't escape the scent of patchouli oil. Sure she had done her share of drugs, protests, Carlos Castaneda, astrological charts, and Ouija boards, but even if it was true, and Sarah felt falling into this fourth category left it open for interpretation, she hated to be reminded of her surroundings, to hear that stigma attached to her name. Sarah McKay, hippie. Not even.

"You better ease up with that shit," Sarah said, recognizing the snarling Jeremy Roth, a child psychologist who worked the local institutions prescribing Ritalin and Thorazine to children five times more subdued than himself. "I'm in no mood to fuck around. Tell me where my Mom went, and I'll let you get back to that voodoo that you do so well."

The Future Primitives, like everybody at the Waterfall, took it for granted that Sarah was in no mood to fuck around. It was a given. Even when she was in the mood to fuck around, Sarah took that seriously too, surrounding herself with friends and letting her hair down like torrents of cartoon rain. If someone suggested she needed to take a chill pill, she shot back, they didn't know what she needed. If they had a problem with her, tough shit. There was the door, don't bump your ass on the way out. So when the Future Primitives continued growling, Sarah knew she was in for confrontation.

"Unghhh!"

"Oh yeah?" Sarah responded, wishing she had brought her marlin bat. "Tell me where my mother went or I'm getting my camera and taking some pictures. We'll see how proud you are of your privates when they're front-page news."

The threat had leverage. The editor of the local newspaper was an ex-marine turned radical who told Sarah if she wanted to contribute a column and photograph about the commune, he would publish them. Knowing he once fabricated an interview with a Congressman and punched out the county's superintendent, Sarah was certain that the editor would print whatever she sent him, the more controversial the better. But her allegiance to the commune ran deeper than she let on, not to these fawning creeps, but to some of the bush-hippies. Definitely to Mom. Anything she wrote for the paper would not reflect kindly on Mom. But it was a good threat. She knew the Future Primitives only did their thing at the Waterfall because when their dope money ran low they had to venture into the county to support their lifestyle. There were standards to everybody's depravity. The Future Primitives weren't so out to lunch that they didn't understand that employers rarely hired sexually deviant, nonverbal dirtbags. They were susceptible to bad press. Pictures wouldn't affect Saffron's part-time position in the holistic health department at the Co-op in Ukiah, but Jeremy Roth had a Ph.D. from Princeton and was no doubt thinking about tenure, somewhere, someday, after his sex drive and field research slowed down.

"I'm going to count to three, mostly because I can," Sarah told them. "If I don't get an answer, I'll see your picture front page."

Mancub leered at Sarah and crawled to the couch where he humped the crease between the cushions. Sarah made a mental note never to look there again for loose change. Saffron fondled her breasts and did her best Clint Eastwood. Jeremy watched nervously. Sarah started counting.

"One . . ."

Mancub bared his teeth, wolfing a succession of barks. Saffron pinched her nipples, eyes never leaving Sarah's to further her excitement. Jeremy appeared uncertain, caught between getting his rocks off and a hard place.

"Two . . ."

Saffron reached for Mancub's hairy butt which she squeezed as they both found a rhythm, yawping and grinding. Jeremy waded in to their midst, but lent no limb or appendage. Sarah felt sick.

"Three!" she said, spinning on her heel to search for her camera.

"Wah ugh all," Jeremy grunted.

Saffron stopped stroking Mancub and gave Jeremy the sneer of a woman cheated out of her orgasm by a man who had given into his own. Mancub turned from his penetration of the pillows, lint clinging to his penis.

"What?" Sarah said, almost at the door. "Speak the language. I don't have a doctorate in primitive cultures."

"Wah ugh all," Jeremy repeated.

"Waterfall?" Sarah asked. "She went to the waterfall?"

"Ughh."

"What does ughh mean?" Sarah demanded.

"It means, yes, you little cunt," Jeremy said, his voice scratchy from lack of use. "It means someday I'll give you what you deserve and you better hope your diaphragm's in when I do."

"Really?" Sarah replied, used to this kind of vulgarity. "Didn't Hobbes say the great equalizer in the state of nature was that everyone had to sleep? Your cabin's by the water tank, isn't it? If you ever dream of touching me, Jeremy, you better wake up and pray you still have a penis. And if my Mom's not at the waterfall, pick up tomorrow's paper, I might misspell your names. Saffron, is that with one f or two?"

Sarah extended one, then both middle fingers. Saffron charged forward on her knees, baring her teeth. Jeremy grabbed her by the ankles, pulling her back. Mancub padded over and clamped his mouth tightly on the nape of her neck. Sarah was ready to kick Saffron square in the face.

"Let the freaker go," Sarah told them, but they didn't remove a finger. They were into the restraint. Sarah could see Jeremy's member was hard. Mancub pawed Saffron's breasts, turning her howling from aggressive to erotic. Saffron thrashed between them, but it was play-acting now. Sarah turned to go before she needed another lifetime of therapy, muttering, "Fucking experimental hippies."

The waterfall was a mile from the main house. A trail off the main road led to a path that curlicued to a ravine where water fell from a river into a pool sixty feet below, shattering into shards of sparkling light, shimmering rainbows, shadows of leaves tattooing your body. There was another pool at the bottom of the gorge, the water of the first pool filtering over the sides into the second, twenty feet lower, then flowing into a river that wound into the forest. Although there were two waterfalls and two water holes, the first was where residents hung out. It was a sanctuary, the inspiration for the commune, out of a storybook where nymphs bathed with fairies and unicorns. But of course Sarah could never be there alone, an assortment of hippies were omnipresent, messing with her boogie.

As a child, Sarah had prided herself on being able to walk from the main house to the waterfall at night without a flashlight. If she got lost, she pretended she was a wiccan and asked directions from animals and birds, the moon and stars. But she knew the way by heart, rocks and inclines, fallen branches and stumps. She was ready with word magic if evil spirits came to harm her. The hills were full of spirits, some bad. The worst wasn't a spirit at all, but Mom's ex, Marty the Poobah.

Sarah remembered a yellow crescent above the trees, fixed firmly with indifference as she ran, branches lashing at her arms. She turned to see a strawberry jam smile smeared across the Poobah's face, a bleeding animal in his hands. The juices of lust. She was a rabbit bounding in a predictable pattern, through the underbrush, over boulders and low limbs. His naked body flashed white whenever she snuck a peek to gauge the distance between them. She would die if he caught her, possessed her insides. "E pluribus unum," she shrieked, but the spell had no effect. He was on her tail.

Sarah had always been lucky enough to get away. Others at the Waterfall were less fortunate, girls and boys. As they aged, Sarah saw them develop violent and promiscuous dispositions. They became withdrawn, fascinated with fire, crying in their sleep and drawing pictures of monsters, sucking their thumbs and refusing to eat.

"All the men are after you," Mom had said, after Sarah blew the whistle on the Poobah for chasing her. "Do you know how hard that is for me? You're young and beautiful. I can't compete with that."

"Mom, he tried to kill me," Sarah told her.

"Hon, there's a difference between sex and death," Mom said. "You're gonna have to learn that."

For months, Sarah wouldn't let herself be alone. She became inseparable from Lisa, stopped going to the waterfall, bought a deadbolt for her door, and quit relying on Mom for protection. She turned to her friends, music, books, painting, the marlin bat, spirits. On her own, she learned the difference between sex and death, making love and rape. It wasn't clear to her whether or not Mom ever did.

Sarah heard splashing as she neared the clearing where the steepest part of the climb remained. Descending, she spotted someone swimming in the icy water and her mother lying out on a towel in her black Dior one-piece, looking like she was poolside at the Betty Ford Clinic. Today there wasn't much sun, even less heat. But since the glut of skin cancer reports and the depletion of the ozone, residents of the commune had started wearing swimsuits, large hats, and sunblock. Some swam naked, but covered up after they got out of the water. Even the Future Primitives and hard-core nudists kept to the shade.

"Aren't you cold?" Sarah asked, sliding down the last incline, almost losing her Walkman in the process, putting it back into her jacket pocket as she regained her balance.

"If Kate Hepburn can do it every day, so can I," Mom said, setting aside her paperback and lighting a Gauloise.

"What's his excuse?" Sarah gestured to the boy she identified as one of the Poobah's illegitimate children, Raven Newchild, who was climbing the face of the gorge and diving off its side with workmanlike repetition.

"Crank or X," Mom answered, taking a pull of the cigarette. "He was tripping when I got here. Drugs affect children differently."

Really? Sarah thought. No shit.

"What are you reading?" Sarah asked instead, deciding there was no need to start harshing right away.

"Something Aslan's into called Cyberpunk," Mom said. "It's sort of Raymond Chandler meets William S. Burroughs. Bleak landscape, lots of computer talk, virtual reality. Sort of literary acid house."

What a contradiction, Sarah thought, "literary" and "acid house." Sometimes people smoked pot and recited bad poetry, but not like they dropped acid and watched *Fantasia* or took Ecstasy and listened to shitty music. She had never seen someone embrace an altered state and reach for Tolstoy.

"Shouldn't you master one reality before you move on to another one?" Sarah asked.

"Cute, hon," Mom said. "You know negativity makes you tense. Look how clouded your crown chakra is. And your posture. You're so tight."

"I know, I'm slouching toward abrogation, the great black void," Sarah said. "Only happy thoughts and a good chiropractor can save me."

Sarah spied a newt in one of the tiny pools of water in the rock. She caught it by its slippery orange tail. As a girl, she used to hunt them for hours. It wriggled between her fingers, tail whipping. She stroked its back and belly, experiencing the tactile pleasure of its slimy skin before returning it to its home.

"Why don't you go for a dip and clear your channels?" Mom asked.

"Because it's freezing," Sarah answered, her hand cold from

catching the newt, wondering why Mom wasn't shivering.

"Temperature is a state of mind," Mom said. "The water is cleansing, not cold."

If Sarah didn't change the subject, she would have to listen to how Mom had walked on coals and made love on a frozen pond, the personal experiences she always cited in arguments about mind over matter.

"Where's the Poobah?" Sarah said, watching Raven plunge into the water hole, bobbing to the surface with frenzied eyes.

"I don't know," Mom said. "I think he's tending his hamsters."

The Poobah had been trying his hand at genetic engineering in a shack where he also cooked synthetic drugs. He was attempting to create a breed of designer rodents that could be put into the anal passage to heighten sexual pleasure during intercourse. The Poobah wanted to cash in while gerbil jamming was hot. He was toying with bone structure, crossbreeding hamster cells with armadillos and porcupines, trying to create rodents he could package as "ribbed" and "studded."

"He's so sick," Sarah said.

"He's a visionary," Mom said, flicking an ash. "You just don't like him."

"I try to stay away from people making a buck by helping nuts stuff small animals up their asses," Sarah said.

"You've never given him a chance, even when we were dating," Mom accused. "You've always been down on him."

"I've never been down on him, and he's never gone down on me," Sarah said. "With the exception of you, Mom, I try to avoid psychos."

"That's a mean thing to say," Mom told her.

Sarah stared toward the waterfall, distracted by Raven Newchild's bare body falling into an explosion of water.

Yeah, Sarah thought, it was a mean thing to say, but Mom had said worse to her even more impassively. And Sarah was serious, she had written off her father, divorced her husband, kept mostly to herself on the commune, and her friend Lisa, who received most of the attention she was willing to invest in another human being, was relatively normal.

"Whatever," Sarah said, unsure of what she really wanted to say now that she was here. "I heard the music, so I came out looking for you."

"You didn't have to do that," Mom told her. "You made a choice."

"I know, Mom," Sarah said. It was impossible for her to be anything around Mom but fourteen years old again. "Here I am. Rock me like a hurricane."

"I wanted to talk to you at the main house but some Primitives were there," Mom said. "They weren't grooving on the music."

"Nobody grooves on that music," Sarah informed her. "You're the only one."

"It didn't seem that way in the sixties and seventies," Mom said. "It's better than that heroin music you listen to. At least there's some life in Janis."

"Not any more," Sarah said.

"Very funny," Mom said, without laughing. "I suppose now I'm going to have to listen to you tell me the reason you identify with heroin music is because I fucked up your childhood. Everything comes down to me being a bad mother, right? I'm sorry for the millionth time. Can we get beyond that? I do have my own set of problems."

Mom had a way of turning conversations, heading off any conflicting viewpoints before they were presented, admitting guilt to everything and nothing at the same time, trivializing what Sarah felt by simplifying her thoughts into extremes, then discarding them because they were overstated. There was no discussion with Mom, just her voice skipping over yours to topics she wanted to lecture on.

"Why can't you let me feel something without acting like it isn't valid?" Sarah asked. "I came here because I wanted to see what was wrong. And to tell you to quit playing that music. It doesn't remind me of happy times."

"Lookit," Mom said, "If you're going to be venting, I'm not into it. I'm having a tough time myself. If you want to be there for me, fine. If not, fine too."

"What about being there for me?" Sarah wanted to know. "How about not playing music you know freaks me out? Not laying all your shit on me?"

"I've been there for you," Mom stated.

Sarah was interested to see how she would get out of this one.

"I offered to pay for therapy," Mom said.

Exactly, Sarah thought. Hit and run.

"It's not my job to be your mother anymore," Mom tried to rebound. "You're an adult, not an infant."

"Which one are you?" Sarah inquired.

"Here we go again," Mom said, stubbing out her cigarette and placing it on her paperback.

"That's right, here we go again. And don't give me any of your origami apologies," Sarah told her. "Sometimes I wonder if we're speaking the same language."

"I don't think we are, hon, you're just yelling," Mom said. "You can't see my point of context. I got you out of that middle-class bullshit, away from the mainstream where you could be what you wanted, independently as a woman."

"That's what you wanted, not me," Sarah reminded her. "I was a girl. I wanted Popsicles and dolls. Independence was low priority."

"You think you would have been happier with your father in Tahoe?" Mom asked. "Wearing a Catholic school uniform all your life, him trying to screw your friends."

"Dad wasn't like that," Sarah said.

"Your father wasn't around long enough for you to know what he was like," Mom informed her. "It's fine to fantasize about what a great guy he was, how everything would have been peach fuzz if you had lived with him, but he didn't take responsibility. I did. I said I was sorry I wasn't in the PTA, baking cookies and tying your hair into pigtails, but that shit was killing me. I didn't want it killing you before you even got started."

Sarah remembered Mom at her school's open houses back in San Francisco, the nuns making her nervous. After an hour, she would disappear with one of the cute fathers. Sarah, brimming with energy from cupcakes and fruit punch, would notice Mom missing from the proceedings. One of her classmates would eventually report someone was smoking in the bathroom. Mom would return, blouse askew. She had gone to Catholic schools herself.

"Maybe I exposed you to some things you shouldn't have seen, but at least you saw something," Mom said. "You didn't turn out so bad. I must have done something right."

It was an unfair argument. Sarah would have to confess to being a terrible person to win it. Mom was accountable for most everything that had happened in Sarah's life. Sarah hadn't gone looking for hippies and Future Primitives. It was irresponsible of Mom to subject her to that reality.

"I did the best I could, hon," Mom told her. "You didn't come with directions. Neither did the divorce. I was trying to have a life, something I never had before. I was improvising. I didn't have any goals of my own; I had your father and you, and when your father left, I only had you. What was I supposed to do? I moved on. I took you here, and now you can take yourself somewhere else if you don't like it. I don't hear you bitching about free room and board, a place to do your projects and grow your dope. You can't lay it all on me. The only person holding you back is yourself."

"That and twenty-six years of chaos," Sarah said.

"I can't turn back the clock, babe," Mom said. "And I wouldn't if I could. I don't know if I could do any better. You think you can, take your shot. But don't be surprised if you make mistakes too, staying in Mendocino, not finishing college, Daryl."

"I was nineteen, Mom," Sarah said, referring to her marriage with Daryl.

"I was nineteen when I married your father," Mom told her. "Twenty when I had you."

"Old habits die hard," Sarah admitted. "At least I didn't have any children."

"Cycles are made to be broken," Mom reported. "I don't regret having you, you shouldn't regret having me."

"That's easy for you to say," Sarah said. "I'm a nicer person."

"Says who?" Mom wanted to know. "Maybe if you spent more time with your spirituality, like you did as a child, you'd find the way within, the healer inside yourself. You say I don't help? I've got a great book for you to read."

"I don't need a book, Mom," Sarah said. "I've read that shit."

"It's not shit," Mom declared.

"It's self-help and it's an industry, every month a new angle, a sequel, nobody getting any better," Sarah said. "You've got a library, look at you. I spent my childhood in fear. What's the book going to say about that?"

"Get over it," Mom told her.

"Can I quote you?" Sarah asked, looking at her mother ill-advisedly remaining out here in the cold.

What did she expect? Mom wasn't going to change. What did she tell Squirrel Boy, you can't pick your relatives? That was for sure. There came a time when you had to cut your losses. Get over it.

"You're right," Sarah decided, turning away from her mother to struggle up the incline of the waterfall's gorge, Raven Newchild in her line of vision also climbing, then plummeting.

"Where are you going?" Mom asked, when Sarah was halfway gone.

"I don't know," Sarah said, not turning to face her. "Away."

8

John could tell this wasn't a good connection, even before Christina answered the telephone, "Michael?" There was static on the line preceding the first ring and he became aware of the space separating them, all the roads, pit stops, blown tires, traffic, wrong turns, mountains, malls, concrete, telephone poles. Forget the straight line, there were still over three thousand miles between them, fiber optics trying to make it seem like distance was an illusion, that someone's physical presence wasn't necessary as long as you could hear their voice in your ear. John leaned into the receiver, trying to force his way to Christina's lips. But telephone calls, at best, were sweet nothings whispered without the heated breath that made them worthwhile. He heard the weak signal, the ring, her voice, the almost imperceptible splash of a pebble dropped from the top of an abyss. He asked himself, "When did things go wrong?"

"Christina," he finally said. "Who's Michael?"

"John?" Christina said.

John considered hanging up, thinking maybe he shouldn't have paid to connect Grandma's telephone in the first place. He found little solace in experiencing the same sufferings that had plagued his fellow man for centuries: family, addiction, bad teeth. Hadn't getting beaten up solidified his union with humanity for the week? He didn't need to add heartbreak to the list, especially when hair loss was around the corner.

"Yes, this is John," he said. "The man you shared your bed with? Six feet, 170, brown hair, blue eyes? I think I left my toothbrush on your sink."

"John? Is that you?" Christina said.

"Yes," John repeated. "It is I, Ensign Gibson, I just threw your stinking palm tree overboard and what's this crud about no movie?"

"John? I can barely hear you," Christina said. "You're not making any sense. Where are you?"

"Where am I?" John said, feeling the pull of the current, sucking, sucking, out beyond the reef, floating, floating, soon to be lost at sea. "Where do you think I am? Joe's Stone Crabs? I'm in Boonville."

"I can't hear you," Christina told him. "I'm hanging up."

"You can't hear me?" John said. "Maybe you should tell Michael to take his tongue out of your ear."

Click.

"Fuck!" he screamed, hitting the receiver against its cradle, catching his finger. His knuckle cracked. He slammed the receiver down again, catching another finger. He held the scepter of communication away from his body until the pain subsided, feeling his insides being pulled taut. Someone had to let go.

"You can't be gone!" he yelled, nobody to hear his cry but Grandma's squirrels.

The receiver bleated in his hand like an electronic sheep: baa-ugh, baa-ugh, baa-ugh. He looked around the room, which suddenly seemed as foreign as a marketplace in Tangiers, dust playing in the window light, table and dresser elongated with trains of shadow, smell of bleached sheets and pickled citrus. The strength of Grandma's presence. Her space and his, colliding. His reality mixed with her dreams.

Get a grip, he demanded of himself, staring past the bedroom door into the living room where Grandma's metaphysics books were shelved alongside her volume of Emily Dickinson's poetry.

"Instability gives birth to art," Grandma had told him. "It isn't something to be afraid of, it's the human condition. It's something to embrace."

John agreed, chaos was order. Liquid order. To deny that was to go against the flow of life. You weren't supposed to ask for relief, you were supposed to want more, and more, and so much more that you could explode.

All my friends going to therapy and Al-Anon meetings, John thought, letting go, letting God. Seeking safety in the status quo, straightening up so they can find someone to screw missionary position every night, watch videos with on the couch, eat ice cream, plan vacations to Jamaica. Buy a cat and call it Mittens. They've all given up.

Heaven may be a place where nothing ever happens, just like the song said, but John saw a flicker reflected in the darkness of their pupils, one eye on the hunt, straitjacketed by fear, begging to bolt to the edge of themselves, to the euphoria of open air. It didn't ever go away, the continuous craving for one more drink, one more kick in the crotch. One more kiss. Everybody wanted to feel exalted and alive, but to pursue that instead of filling your life with excuses was an exercise in faith. It was dangerous to search for something you've never seen, having only caught glimpses of the Grail from films, paintings, French poetry. Baudelaire dreams and Marquis de Sade reality.

"You can't deny who you are, because eventually you will be revealed," Grandma had also told him. "You can only try to reroute your impulses and spend energy where it will pay off."

John understood it wasn't healthy to be compulsive, but what else did he know? Parents in separate bedrooms, never kissing except for an inch of air near the cheek on holidays—staying together for the good of the child—resigned to a sufferathon sponsored by the Catholic Church, a mutual agreement to wrap each other in barbed wire. Meanness, mistresses, curses, lies. A life they had chosen, other lives they had failed to choose. Where have you gone, Joe DiMaggio?

He couldn't help picturing Christina sitting in what used to be their home, waiting for a man named Michael to call. Was there a skip in her step when she went to meet him? If a street light was changing, did she dash through traffic to be with him that much sooner? Was she imagining him in different clothes, haircuts, underwear? Asking herself what it would be like to take him home to meet her parents? Was she thinking of his kisses now? Does he do it better than I can?

John remembered how in the beginning of their relationship they had poured out their love for each other like it was an exotic liqueur. But somewhere between ruffled sheets, their delicate touches became familiar, exquisiteness turned bland, intoxication became anxiety. They sobered, parched bodies thirsting for another sip. Anything wet. They looked at each other, not knowing whether their glasses were half-empty or half-full. It was this uncertainty that had separated them. They began confusing love with habit, a label for the irretrievable hours that had to be deemed special or else they were lost.

Baa-ugh, baa-ugh, baa-ugh.

John wanted to throw the telephone through the wall. To punch or kiss her. To see it hurl, line snapping from the outlet. Hssss. Wham! Don't cry, I love you. Right through the wall. Can you feel that? Splintered paneling, square thud. Temporarily out of service. "We're sorry, if you believe this recording to be in error, please check the number and try again." How could she not recognize my voice? She used to say that since I had been surrounded by retired Jews all my life, I had a distinct inflection, that I was the only raised-Catholic who could recite the Ten Commandments as questions. Now she can't identify it? Now she was expecting calls from someone named Michael?

John tried to imagine Michael's voice. It came across as the speech of a soap opera star, one of those schmoozers named after a disciple of Christ and a northwestern state, Luke Montana, all store-bought biceps and haircut, "I know it's a small ranch and a small mansion, but Miss Christina, we could be happy, especially if Blackie comes out of that coma and the child's really mine."

Child, sex, somebody else touching Christina. John's head was spinning. He's stealing kisses meant for me. Gasps and swallows. His hands are where mine should be, running fingers through the silkiness of her hair. Tickling the wetness between her legs.

He dialed Christina's number again, trying to convince himself that Michael was nobody, someone from the office, a friend calling for computer advice. He wasn't hearing any sound from the receiver, no dial tone or recording or anything. He jiggled the cord at the connection where the receiver met the phone. He heard the hollow rush of wind, saw telephone lines swaying somewhere in Nebraska, a loose end down in a cornfield. He envisioned himself, alone and bitter in a hotel room with the bathroom down the hall, heating coffee and tomato soup on a hot plate, reading Bukowski and smoking Camel straights. He might even start whittling squirrels from driftwood.

"What am I going to do?" he asked the cabin, hearing no sound in the receiver.

He hated technology, paying fees to depend on something

that was a mystery. What did he know about telecommunications? You dial a number, you get a voice. Was he supposed to grab a screwdriver and shuttle himself into space to work on the satellite or whatever it was they had cluttered the skies with in the name of convenience? He had given them his trust.

"Work, phone, work!" he screamed, fiddling with the connection, removing the plastic clip from the side of the telephone and reinserting it.

Dial tone. He held the receiver away from his ear to see if the noise wasn't coming from somewhere else, the refrigerator or a faulty electrical outlet. But it was the go ahead from AT&T to transmit his disembodied soul. He pressed the numbers that used to mean home, sadly confident that after years of shooting the shit, heart-to-hearts, pillow talk, and orgasmic utterances, this would be the last time he would speak to Christina.

"Hello?"

"Hello."

"John?"

"Christina."

"Did you just call?"

"Yes, I called, and you answered the phone, 'Michael?'"

"I thought you were somebody else," Christina told him.

"I gathered that," John replied. "The question is, who did you think I was?"

"Nobody," Christina answered, then realizing he wasn't going to believe such a bald-faced lie, "He's the neighbor who moved in before you left."

John remembered him: barrel chest, Le Coq Sportif tennis shirt, Suntan U. Law School, internship at Merrill Lynch. Four-star consumer. He drove a Mustang and smiled at Christina when he washed it in front of their building. He suggested that they all be friends, invited them to play a round of "goff" at the Doral Country Club, boasting about his handicap, and adding that his grandfather had been an original charter member. John declined for both of them, explaining that his grandparents had been killed by putters.

"Not too far to go for a cup of sugar," he said, hurt by the mediocrity of his replacement and the thought that Christina might have started with Michael before he had bought his plane ticket.

"In case you didn't notice, you left!" Christina told him.

"Two days ago!" John matched her indignation. "Thanks for your period of grieving, but you should find some way to go on with your life. It isn't right holding this torch. I don't even have an IRA account."

"Two days is right," Christina retaliated. "You didn't even bother to call. How do I know what you're doing out there?"

"They didn't turn on my telephone until today," John said, Sarah entering his mind for the first time since he had been sober. "And I got sick."

"Too sick to find a pay phone?" Christina demanded. "They don't have pay phones in California, only ashrams?"

"I did call from a pay phone, but the line was busy," John said. "Then I got sick."

He didn't add that he had also been hung over, attacked, and Maced. Essentially he had told the truth, the chronology was just wrong.

"Anyway, what difference would it make?" he said. "You would have been talking to Good Neighbor Michael, discussing jurisprudence and tanning lotion. Tell me, when you graduate from law school at U.M., do they give you the police radio with your diploma or do you have to go buy it yourself?"

"If I want to see someone else," Christina said, "you can be certain I will. You left."

"You didn't follow," John said.

"I was supposed to follow?" Christina asked. "Is that your patriarchal take on things? I'm expected to waste away or follow my man because I don't have my own identity?"

"Did I say that?" John replied. "If anyone's called the shots in this relationship, it's been you. And if anyone's been in danger of losing their identity, it's me."

"When did you join this men's group, John?" Christina said. "Before you left? Or did they recruit you on the plane?"

"I wanted to leave Miami a long time ago," John said. "I followed you by staying right there. I didn't mind either, until I realized we were both unhappy and standing still. That's when I made this move, for both of us."

"If I've been so awful," Christina said, "then you should be happy with your decision. Bon voyage."

"I didn't leave," John insisted. "You didn't come!"

"You left!" Christina screamed. "You left! You left! You left!

I'm here in what used to be our apartment, surrounded by everything that used to be ours. Everybody keeps asking, 'What happened?' My parents, your parents, our friends, the fucking dry cleaner. I tell them John's an asshole, that's what happened!"

John rubbed the back of his neck. He had to admit that it must be awful to be in the apartment alone, looking at extra hangers in the closet, empty drawers in the dresser, doing the dishes without bumping elbows. No sounds coming from any room but the one you were in. As improbable as it may have seemed, it was probably easier to be out here where everything was unfamiliar.

John turned to the picture of Christina resting on the nightstand, glassless now after Blindman's visit. He recalled how they had met, second semester, sophomore year, English 250. Stumbling in late, the professor signed John's transfer, telling him, "Ask a student who arrived *on time* what you've missed." Filling a desk in the back row, John asked the girl to his left if he had missed anything worth writing down. It was Christina, before hardship or happiness, expectation or fulmination. Completely intact. Before the static electric longing that precedes a couple's first kiss. Her pink tongue had appeared from behind pearl-white teeth to tap seductively a single word, "Lo-lee-ta." That became their first private joke. Later, as they ate lunch in the cafeteria, John told her, "She was plain Chris in the morning, studious Christine in the afternoon, but in English 250 she became Chris-tee-na."

This wasn't the time to dredge up fond memories, John warned himself. Nostalgia can navigate the most jilted of hearts.

"I killed your fish," Christina said, breaking the silence. "Instead of giving them away, I flushed them down the toilet."

"Well," John said, searching for something to say he wouldn't regret, "I love and miss you too."

"Don't give me that shit," Christina said. "For the record, it was you who stood still, I was moving. I brought home a bigger check. I paid for the health club, the dining room set, birth control, anything we wanted that was nice. If I left things up to you, we would have spent every weekend at the beach."

"You're right," John admitted. "I would have given us both melanomas."

"Never serious when you should be," Christina said. "I hope you're happy with your decision."

"I hope you are too," John said, realizing they had come to a point beyond apology or reconciliation; even if she were to ask him back, or suggest that she move to Boonville, or if he requested permission to return, it wouldn't work.

"Christina?" he said. "Do you remember that night we went to Bean Bean's and left with a bottle of champagne? We walked on the beach, acting like I was on shore leave and going off to fight in the war. We pretended we might never see each other again. You filled my glass and then poured the rest of the bottle on yourself, saying, 'Drink up soldier.' We made love and you said, 'I hope I'm pregnant, because you're the only man I'd want to father my child.'"

"I remember," Christina answered, conceding nothing.

"For the first time in my life, I felt a part of me was squared away and I could begin fixing the rest." John told her. "I couldn't imagine a future without you."

John could hear Christina moving around the apartment, padding across the carpet and then the unmistakable sound of a refrigerator door opening, followed by the crack of a soda can. Diet Coke, no doubt. She would cut a wedge of lemon and pour it into a glass with no ice. He heard the slide of a drawer, then her fishing around the cupboard. She was walking again, settling back to wherever she had been sitting.

"Do you remember the next day?" John said.

"When you puked all over everything?" Christina asked. "I washed our comforter about a dozen times before I got out that smell."

"No, I meant the morning," John said, wondering how he had forgotten that part. "It was my first month at Leggiere and Philips, and I felt horrible. You said, 'Come back to bed.' You held the sheets open for me. I crawled back in, and you smiled the most satisfied smile I've ever seen."

"Then you threw up," Christina said.

"No," John said, upset she wouldn't lend herself to his sentimentality. "I threw up after I ate that shitty takeout from the Chinese place I hate but you always order from anyway, Rat Scabie Szechuan."

"Poo Ping," she corrected.

"Fuck it," John said.

"That's the Thai restaurant," Christina replied.

This was why it didn't work, John thought. We can't even

have a basic conversation without breaking into a hostile Abbott and Costello routine.

"What's your point?" Christina asked. "Or did you call to reminisce?"

"No point," John said. "For some reason, I wanted you to remember that for me. Regardless of what happens, wherever we go, I will be grateful for having been at peace with myself in your arms. But apparently we don't share the same memory. That's our problem though, isn't it? We don't exactly complement each other."

"I guess we don't," Christina agreed. "I'm just glad I didn't get pregnant, because if I did, I have the feeling I'd be taking care of a baby by myself right now. Someday, maybe I'll be able to forgive you for being an asshole, but if we had a child, I don't think I ever could have. At least you did something right."

John didn't know how to respond. He almost said, "Thank you."

"Take care of yourself, John," Christina said, abruptly, "I gotta go."

"All right," he replied, wondering where she had to go, suddenly aware that this was goodbye. "Take care of yourself too."

"I already am," Christina said.

"I love you," John said, but the connection had been terminated.

He sat on the edge of Grandma's bed, holding the receiver, running everything through his mind, the conversation, his old apartment, the cabin, champagne kisses, 60-40 memories, Christina, Good Neighbor Michael, bad Chinese food, Miami Beach, Boonville. The possibility of children. He searched the room expecting a response from somewhere between the planks or above the light fixtures. He put the receiver back in its cradle and reached for Christina's picture. He laid it face down on the nightstand in exchange for the telephone, which he rocked in his hand, feeling its weight and significance. Then he fired it across the room, scattering squirrels like bowling pins.

"Fuck you!" he yelled.

There was no answer except for the echo of the telephone's broken ringer, which John imagined emanating from his cabin, drifting down off the hill through the weeds, past the fence, sifting through tree branches, over graveled roads, vibrating by busted bottles, beer cans, torn truck tires, road kill, and into the town of

Boonville like rings of pond water set in motion by the stone of a mischievous child.

9

John was trying to write a letter to Christina, but the first line kept wanting to become a haiku:

> You'll probably end up
> being a lesbian,
> and I'll have another thing
> to figure out.

The wastepaper basket overflowed. He stared at the page, two-thirds blank, waiting for the rest of the words to come. Something had been left unsaid during their telephone conversation three hours ago, but it wouldn't reveal itself. He realized there was no product to sell, but he wondered when his marketing experience would pay off with a series of tight sentences. Chewing on his pen, he was gaining new respect for Margaret Washington.

A knock interrupted him, not a violent rapping, but a normal request to see if anyone was home. John decided it couldn't be anybody he had met recently, they would have just kicked in the door and started swinging. He abandoned the letter and looked for a weapon to be on the safe side, settling for a squirrel sculpture with a long tail that he could brandish as a club. Holding it behind his back, he approached the front door.

"Who is it?" he said.

"It's Sarah," the voice answered. "Is that you, John?"

"Maybe," he said, not wanting to fall for the old "bait and switch." It sounded like Sarah, but Daryl could be behind her holding a hatchet to her throat and when he opened the door, hack!, hack!, hack!, both of them would get it in the neck.

He grabbed another squirrel off the coffee table.

"Are you alone?" John said.

"What's the big deal?" Sarah asked. "Are you O.K.?"

Element of surprise, John told himself, flinging open the door and leaping into the threshold with a squirrel in each fist.

Sarah jumped back. John could tell she didn't know whether he was going to assault her or start juggling. She was by herself, a mud-streaked Toyota pickup parked in the driveway next to the Datsun. It had to be her vehicle, Daryl undoubtedly drove something American and with a gun rack. John lowered the squirrels.

"Sorry," he said. "I'm a little edgy."

"No shit," Sarah said, before noticing his swollen face, split lip, and the hypnotic swirl of purple beneath his eye.

John knew his bruises were at a point where they appeared worse than they felt, although it was debatable, and he could see that Sarah recognized the signature in his contusions, the handwriting of a closed fist that spelled DARYL.

"Jesus," Sarah gasped, "please tell me you fell in the bathtub."

"I thought news traveled fast in this town," John said.

"It does, but they're not exactly into current affairs where I live, or town gossip, or most types of communication for that matter," Sarah said, stepping forward and putting a hand to John's face. "God, I'm sorry. Does it hurt?"

"Only when I breathe," he said.

It wasn't the pain that bothered him now so much as the I-want-to-go-to-sleep-for-the-rest-of-my-life feeling that had accompanied him ever since the scuffle, intensifying with Blindman's visit, and nearing a state of narcosis after his goodbye to Christina. He had thought writing a letter would revive him, but that had backfired. So, seeing how there were no tall buildings to jump off, he was resigned to jeopardizing what little life-force he still possessed by conversing with Sarah. Since his coming to Boonville, death didn't scare him half as much as living a long life.

"Apparently your ex got the worst of it," John said, and told Sarah about the aid he had received from Pensive and her can of Mace, how Deputy Cal, Billy Chuck, and Hap had been no help at all. Then, as if talking in his sleep, he related his experience with

Blindman, the nightmares, and his phone call to Christina.

"It hasn't been a good week," he confessed, wondering what it was about Sarah that made him spill his guts.

In the sky behind her, John saw a large bird circling without flapping its wings, round and round, descending with certainty toward its prey. The wind pushed it off course for a moment, but it spiraled back, a holding pattern.

"Would you like to come in?" John said, realizing they were on the porch. "I could make some tea. You could fill me in on our night together. I blacked out. Maybe I did something worth getting my ass kicked?"

"You were a gentleman," Sarah replied, still examining his busted face as if she had hit him herself. "Tea would be nice."

Inside, John asked Sarah to make herself at home while he went into the kitchen to put a kettle on the range. He selected an herbal, non-caffeinated Zinger, thinking it might be what hippie girls drank when they weren't bottoming quarts of whiskey. In the cupboard he found some tea biscuits, a purchase made in the heat of his shopping excursion. Out of the corner of his eye, he watched Sarah take off her jacket, suppressing her amazement at all the squirrel sculptures. She adjusted the flue on the wood-burning stove to generate more heat, took notice of the busted telephone and the matching fracture in the wall, saw the kindling box full of more squirrels, read the first sentence of his letter, and sat down on the couch.

"Is it the fear of every man that their lover will leave them for another woman?" she called out to John.

"I don't know," John answered from the kitchen, pouring steaming water into two cups. "That was supposed to be a love letter."

"I think if I found out Daryl was gay, I'd be relieved," she said, examining one of the squirrels John had selected to defend himself, passing her fingers from teeth to tail, searching for meaning in its texture, feeling its heft, then lifting its end to determine the sex; smooth as a Ken doll, nutless. "He'd have an excuse for his anger, denying his sexuality, trying to be somebody he wasn't. As it stands, he's just an asshole."

John handed her a mug and put the plate of biscuits on the table in front of them, proud of his domesticity. He sat down beside her. Not too close. Sarah set the sculpture aside and blew on her tea, looking like the-girl-next-door, no makeup, hair tousled, wholesome as a borrowed cup of milk.

"You know, you look like one of them," she said, nodding toward Grandma's handiwork. "You shouldn't burn any, you might be incinerating your own spirit."

John was disturbed that Sarah could see his countenance in the carvings. He had tried to put the idea of intentional likeness out of his mind, but again was forced to wonder if he had been the source of Grandma's inspiration. Maybe that day on her lap had been indelibly etched in her memory too? His flight from her scent the final repudiation? But she must have known he had never deserted her in his heart.

"I'm not sure what Grandma had in mind," John said. "But it's unnerving to have so many of them looking at you with that expression."

"I'm sure that's what she thought," Sarah said, withdrawing her mouth from the lip of the mug. "I always thought it was weird that 'Chip 'n' Dale' out front faced the house and not the valley. Then I snuck up here once and stood in front of them for the full effect. It's as if the whole world is scorning you. I wonder why your grandma did that to herself?"

"You want milk or sugar for that?" John said, taking a drink of his tea, not wanting to talk about the squirrels or to be linked with Grandma's ostracism.

"No, I'm O.K.," Sarah answered. "I wish I had met your grandmother. I saw her in town, sometimes with Margaret Washington and Step, but I never talked to her."

"Step?" John asked.

"That's what they call Margaret Washington's boyfriend because he's always walking two steps behind her with his head down," Sarah said. "It might have to do with Stepin Fetchit, too, but her boyfriend's white. I don't know. Everybody has a nickname around here, Digger, Swoop, Squirrel Lady. The intimacy of a small town. I think I'm locally known as Megabitch."

She tried her tea again, letting that one sink in.

John remembered Christina saying that for men, women fell into three categories: bitch, virgin, or mother. For women, men also came in three flavors: assholes, guys you'd screw, and your boyfriend. "What about father?" he had asked. "Whether women want to admit it or not," Christina had replied, "Father fits into one of the first two categories." She never said what the categories were for women classifying women or men classifying men. But now John knew where Boonville had lumped Sarah.

"I always meant to talk to your grandmother," Sarah said. "I sometimes work with wood too. I'm applying for a grant to sculpt an exact replica of every citizen of Boonville and then stick them on crosses to line the downtown on both sides of 128."

"That's creepy," John said, biting a stale biscuit. "I'm not sure everyone would want to see themselves and their neighbors up on the cross."

"A lot of people didn't want to see Christ up there either," Sarah answered. "It's not the point of art to show people what they want to see. It's important to make them examine themselves and reflect what the artist sees. I'd like to do their pets too if I got enough money. I doubt I'll get anything with Bush in the White House. See how they treated Mapplethorpe?"

John wondered what Grandma and Sarah would have talked about if they had been given the chance. Art? Emily Dickinson? Divorce? The future of the Women's Movement? Her grandson in Miami who was just about Sarah's age?

Grandma had never met Christina, although they had spoken on the telephone.

"A woman has got to see something beyond her house, husband, and children," Grandma had told her more than once before Christina could hand over the receiver to John. "And a boutique's not good enough." Grandma would have liked Sarah though, might have even noticed her in the market or on the street, commenting to herself that there was still hope if that was the next generation.

"How many have you finished?" John inquired, trying to estimate the hours of work involved in such an undertaking, the fevered nights of sawing and sanding, shaving and chiseling, living with something trapped inside you until it finally manifested itself outside your mind: an entire town crucified. Nails pounded through their pets' paws too. Not only would Sarah's project offend the religious right, the animal activists would shit bricks. They'd flip for the honor of crucifying Sarah, not in effigy either.

"Just one, of myself," Sarah said. "Before I decided to go life-size, I made 715 three-foot crosses; then it occurred to me the project was about scale. I photographed those as a model to submit with my proposal, so it wasn't a total waste. But the funny thing is I don't live in Boonville. Technically, I'm a resident of Elk. But if I used Elk, I'd lose scope, metaphor, and audience. Everybody on 128 will be forced to look if I use Boonville. Tourists will think they're approaching Dracula's castle. And I'm sure there would be an excess of reds left in the tasting rooms, especially if I used the tentative title for the exhibit, 'The Blood of Christ in Wine Country.'"

"You should do it whether you get the funding or not," John told her.

"Yeah," Sarah agreed, her attention drifting to a corner of the cabin containing the picture of Grandma on the front steps of the Arizona homestead.

She sipped her tea and said nothing for a while, reached for a biscuit, and then thought better of it. Her enthusiasm had disappeared faster than fuel in a jet engine. She looked at John with the same sullen introspection he had seen at the Lodge when she had stalled in her speech on "sneaking away from the inevitable."

"Is there anything I can do?" John said, laying his teacup aside.

"No," she answered. "I just had another fight with my mom, that's all. I have to get out of here before I go totally berserk. I can do my projects somewhere else, L.A., New York, San Francisco, somewhere people can't enter my life unless I invite them."

Sarah's statement reminded John of his reasons for leaving Florida. But he had learned, the first person you meet at the airport is yourself and the first thing you do is claim your baggage. Nobody traveled light.

Sarah elaborated on her problems, filling in specifics for the generalizations she had alluded to at the Lodge. Real specifics: abuse, neglect, addiction. Who, what, where, when, how. Observations on her childhood, relationships, orgasms, periods, parents, constipation, the afterlife. John listened, thinking how true it was what people said about Californians sharing their private lives like other people discussed the weather. When Sarah got going, it was difficult to do anything but say "Uh-huh." She locked in on you with her eyes, then fired her ballistic confessional, only pausing to rhetorically ask "You know?" or "Ever feel that way?"

John learned they had a lot in common. Not the specifics, apart from not having siblings, but a compatibility of chaos in their lives because they had both been raised in the "Me Decade," which had been followed by the "Me Again Decade." During those twenty years nobody had wanted to do much parenting. The television transformed itself from entertainment to baby-sitter and educational tool, fostering an inability to express even the simplest idea without referring to a sitcom or ad campaign. Then there was the day-in day-out dilemma of "paper or plastic?" Do I weaken the world through destruction or debris? No plans to create a third option. Landfill. Despair. Tucked into bed with the feeling that everything had been done before, better. The inescapable attitude that it was coming to an end anyway. Searching for love in an age of nuclear proliferation.

"The thing for me was a day up in Oregon," Sarah confessed. "It's not as if my mom didn't come back, she couldn't have been gone any longer than five minutes before she turned around in the car and came back. But she did leave me."

Sarah told John that when she was thirteen, she and her mother had headed to Eugene, Oregon, for a job interview. Her mother had recently split with her boyfriend who had been taking daily doses of LSD for the past year, and she was thinking of shucking the commune for a career in civil engineering. Mom had a degree, and oddly enough, an interest in traffic flow theory. A meeting had been scheduled on the basis of her resume. Sarah had been delighted at the prospect of leaving the Waterfall.

"Everything was fine until we left the motel," Sarah explained. "We turned onto a street that had three names. We couldn't figure it out, every time we crossed this certain intersection, the road had another name. If we followed it for awhile, it changed names again. But I noticed there wasn't a break in the address numbers, they kept increasing, so I told Mom to drive further and see if the office wasn't where the address would be if the street had one name."

Sarah said her mother would follow her advice for a few blocks, then turn around before the numbers were large enough to be in the area of the office. Mom started screaming, "I'm late! Where the fuck is 2036 State Street?" Sarah could only reassert they shouldn't worry about the name of the street but follow the numbers. Swerving through traffic, her mother asked Sarah one more time, "Where the fuck is it?" When Sarah repeated that she didn't know, her mother wheeled the car to the curb, reached across Sarah's lap, and unhitched her door. "Get the fuck out!" she demanded. "You're no help at all!" Sarah protested as her mother kicked her out of the vehicle with her feet, yelling, "Get out! Get out! Get out!"

"And there I was on the sidewalk, watching my mom pull away," Sarah recalled. "I didn't think she was ever coming back. I had thirty bucks in my pocket because I carried my life savings with me whenever we took a trip, and I went into a store and bought a sandwich, a carton of milk, and a map, and asked the cashier for directions to the Greyhound station. For the first time in my life everything seemed clear, I was going to buy a ticket to Tahoe and live with my father. I was free."

John could tell Sarah remembered what kind of sandwich she had ordered, whether she had taken a left or right after leaving the market, and what time the bus had been scheduled for departure. She was there again on the streets of Eugene, formulating a conclusion about the universe: what she could depend on, what she couldn't. Her mother had dropped the pretense of taking care of her. Sarah could move forward now without constraints. A street with three names wasn't that complicated.

"I smelled the Ghia before it screeched to a halt in front of me," Sarah said. "She honked the horn and I didn't move. The passenger door flew open. I would have never come back, I swear to God, not in a million years. I heard her say, 'Hurry up, get in.'"

John had run away from home when he was fourteen, after being grounded for a C on his report card, even though he had received A's in the rest of his classes. His father told him he had to come straight home after school until the next semester, no extracurricular activities or hanging out like a punk. If he didn't like it, he could leave. John did leave, and a squad car picked him up six hours later, depositing him on the front steps of his house. His mother cried. The neighbors peeked through their windows. His father grabbed him by the scruff of the neck, promising the officers he would take care of things. It was the first time John had felt he could escape the pull of his procreators. But the parental magnet had clicked on and he slid back, helpless as a bobby pin.

"It feels like my mom's pushing me out of the car again," Sarah said. "This time I want to hit the ground running."

That had been John's mistake. He had walked to a friend's

house, misjudging the field of influence. John was proud that this time he had put enough distance between himself and home base. But he remembered another saying, "If you get far enough away, you'll be on your way back home."

"What's your plan?" he asked, feeling he was about to be involved in something he could never have conceived of a week ago.

"I started fasting," Sarah said. "I haven't been feeling right lately. I know I'm full of toxins, so I'll go a week or so without food and do a few café bootés."

"Café booté?" John asked.

"Coffee enemas," she clarified. "You never heard of a crappuchino? The caffeine stimulates peristalsis of the intestine, flushing you out. The only problem is if someone asks you how you take your coffee, you have to say, 'Black, and up my ass.'"

John didn't know if she was kidding; the last bit may have been the only part intended to be funny. Medical trends were reverting to primitive states, acupuncture, herbs, homeopathics. Everybody had a remedy for lower back pain and the common cold. Some of it made sense, in theory, but it sounded as if sick people had an overactive sense of adventure.

"What are you going to do after you cleanse?" he said, the thought of pushing Folgers up the down poop-chute giving him a new slant on the coffee jitters.

"I need money," Sarah said. "I can't leave here if I don't have cash."

John changed his position on the couch. He didn't have much money. He was in marketing. Sarah couldn't possibly believe he had excess funds to lend a woman he had met in a bar because she had divulged some secrets and had a violent ex-husband. He needed his nest egg for future hospital bills. Grandma's inheritance wouldn't last long. He was worried about his own finances. But he wanted to help out. If Sarah needed it, he would see what he could do.

"If I asked you something and you said 'No,' would you promise to forget about it and not tell anyone?" Sarah asked.

"Sure," John answered, thinking, how much do you need and who would I tell?

"Would you help me harvest my crop?" Sarah said. "I wouldn't ask, but you seem like a nice guy and I've got to get it out of the ground. I'm not supposed to have it."

"Nobody is," John responded, somewhat shocked. "It's illegal."

"Yeah, but I'm really not supposed to have it," Sarah explained. "We got rules where I live on private patches, even though everybody's got one. The weather's been weird too, and people are getting CAMPed. I need the cash."

John put down his cup and reached for a biscuit. He didn't know a thing about marijuana and now he had been propositioned twice to get involved in the industry. Maybe he was being set up? Blindman or somebody needed a fall guy and had selected him. Maybe a sheriff's election was nearing and the incumbent wanted to boost support by busting an outsider. Or was he being paranoid? It was grass, not crack. Boonville, not Miami. What was the danger in helping a friend pull a few weeds?

"You're not a Republican, are you?" Sarah inquired.

"No," John replied, uncertain if his liberalism was being goaded to the point where he would have to respond with action. Man or mouse? Mule or elephant? Did he believe in personal freedom, the Constitution, the Bill of Rights? Who was the government to tell adults they couldn't smoke marijuana when alcoholism was rampant, when they did nothing to stop the influx of cocaine, when the tobacco trade was legal and killed tens of thousands every year? When little Johnny can't read?

"Look, if you help me out, I'll give you two hundred bucks," Sarah said. "That's not bad for a night's work. And I'll check into something that might mean big money for you. Something you ought to know about anyway."

"What would that be?" John said.

"Don't worry," Sarah told him. "I feel bad about the way Daryl treated you, so I'll look into it anyway. But I have to know, John, can you help me? Otherwise, I have to find somebody else."

John looked at one of the squirrels on the coffee table. He was getting used to their scowls. Sarah's blue eyes were another matter. Half the town had probably fallen in love with them. Even amidst the rubble of his relationship with Christina, he could feel himself giving something to Sarah based on faith and the distant promise of a kiss. He knew it was irrational, a reaction to being alone for the first time in his adult life, but it was happening, however untimely and inappropriate it seemed. Maybe if he ran around the block and jerked off a couple of times, it would go away.

"Do I have to fast?" he asked. "Hunger isn't a prerequisite for a life in crime, is it?"

"No," Sarah said. "In fact, I'll buy you dinner."

"That's all right, I've got a few things to do," John said, thinking, like run around the block and jerk off a couple times, and I don't want to push the envelope by showing up in town with you just yet. "When do we have to do it?"

"Tonight," Sarah said, excited with conspiracy. "I'll bring everything we need, just wear black. I'll pick you up at midnight, like grave diggers."

Tonight didn't give John much of a chance to think about consequences. How many plants were they talking about? What were the personal consumption laws in California? What was the sentencing for possession of marijuana with the intent to simply help out a friend? How good was his lawyer?

"Who's grave are we digging?" John said to himself, but Sarah heard him.

"My mother's daughter's," Sarah replied, putting her cup on the table and gathering her jacket. "Are you sure you want to do this? I wouldn't blame you if you backed out."

Of course you would, John thought, everybody else did. He had been backing out of things for so long, he had finally cornered himself into a place where no more backward steps were possible. He had to take the consequences of his actions, however impulsive and idiotic. Maybe he would have better luck writing prison fiction than haikus.

"I better get things ready," Sarah said. "I don't know why, but I knew I could count on you."

John walked her to the door, standing on the porch as she got into her truck. The bird that had been circling had repositioned itself closer to the cabin, joined by a couple of cohorts who seemed to think it was a good day for something below them to die. The squirrels in the driveway looked as if they smelled the carcass. Sarah waved goodbye. John realized he had forgotten to ask her what they had done after he had blacked out during his first night in town. Apparently reading his mind, Sarah applied the brakes and stuck her head out the window.

"Sorry about your car," she yelled. "It won't happen again."

There was something about Sarah's earnestness that elicited hope. John believed she wasn't talking about the car, but telling him their future wasn't going to be nearly as destructive. The squirrels disagreed. The birds continued to circle.

Of course it won't happen again, John thought. How could it?

IO

It was time to run. John grabbed his jogging shoes, threw on a pair of sweatpants, a Speed Racer T-shirt, his University of Miami baseball cap, and began to hum the opening bars to the Beatles' "Revolution." He had a plan, and if it held firm, he would be back in the cabin in forty minutes with the codeine and alcohol purged from his system, leaving him plenty of time to take a sulfur shower, make dinner, eat, masturbate, and prepare himself to harvest Sarah's dope.

Laced up and stretching against one of the squirrels in his front yard, John realized what a contradiction the lyrics to "Revolution" were in comparison to the music. What seemed to be a call to arms had the underlying message that everything was going to be all right. He remembered what Hunter S. Thompson wrote in regard to another of Lennon's political odes: "When punks like that try to be serious, they just get in the way."

John hit the driveway repeating the refrain anyway, understanding that most things in life didn't hold up under analysis, functioning strictly on an emotional level. He had always been vulnerable to pop music's seductive hooks. Once Neil Diamond's "Forever in Blue Jeans" had lodged in his head for a week like elevator music caught between floors. At least "Revolution" had a good beat and a cathartic scream, he could go the length of a jog with that tune, but Neil Diamond was torture, one song segueing into a medley, "Sweet Caroline," "Song Sung Blue," "Coming to America." All songs he knew word for word, but couldn't specifically ever remember having heard.

John's favorite workout music was Phil Spector girl group stuff, Ronettes, Crystals, Marvelettes; "Da Do Run Run," "Be My

Baby." The rhythm punctuated his breathing, kept him pounding the pavement. Sometimes he would make up his own Motown doo wap ditty. "Well, she walked up to me and she asked me if I wanted to dance . . ." Gasp, gasp. ". . . Something, something, something else that rhymes with dance . . ." Wheeze, wheeze. ". . . When we danced she held me tight . . ." Pant, pant. ". . . All the stars were shining bright . . ." Puff, puff, okie-blow, cough, snort, hack. ". . . And then she kissed me."

But it was "Revolution" as he hit Manchester Road, centering each step heel-to-toe so he wouldn't twist an ankle running down the incline. Getting back up the hill was going to be a bitch. But he had resigned himself to health, at least for the next half hour. If Sarah could go a week without food, he could jog four miles. He steadied his pace. Surrounded by foliage, he could almost see the greenery giving off oxygen in return for his sickly breath. A gang of deer, one with antlers, bounded from the shoulder of the road into the trees. John quickened his stride, unsure if they attacked. A flock of wild turkeys gobbled at him from a turn near a culvert. A chill shuddered through him as he stepped past a dead raccoon. This wasn't the track at University of Miami where you could run round and round, only worrying about the number of women who lapped you. This was nature's obstacle course, shoddily paved.

The unfamiliar terrain gave him a shot of adrenaline. He passed more obliterated animals; frogs, birds, lizards. Squirrels. Flattened and overcooked, sun-dried guts spilled out their sides. A flash in the weeds caught his eye, one of the Datsun's headlights was resting alongside a piece of the front end. Neither appeared to be in good enough shape to warrant further investigation, the headlight broken, metal framing crumpled. John wasn't mechanically inclined anyway. Christina had been in charge of the tool box. John could barely pump gas, and that had come after years of practice. Besides, a blue-bellied lizard had claimed the salvage. They might bite. He jogged on, passing more crushed critters. Despite the lizard's victory, nature was losing about 30-1.

When John came out of the last curve, the slope of the hill leveled and he could see the high school in the distance. The sun had finished its daily arc. He was covered in sweat. He would chug back when he reached the intersection of 128. He wondered if he would make it without stopping. John was accustomed to finishing what he started, bad meals, boring novels, stabs at fitness. Not finishing something felt worse than never having broken ground. It wasn't that difficult to take one more bite, turn another page, take another step. Closure. Replay the song in his head one more time: You say you want a revolution?

John spied a pickup turning off 128, coming toward him in the opposite lane. For all the animal carcasses, this was the first vehicle he had seen. It passed, blowing debris into his face. Forty yards beyond him, the driver hit the brakes and the truck spun out of control, fishtailing, smashing into a fence separating a field of horses from the road. It skidded into the pasture, trailing a path of churned-up dirt. Ponies bucked and bolted. John wiped grit from his eyes. He couldn't see who was inside the vehicle. The truck's motor fired up again and it peeled out back toward the road, bouncing over the crumpled fence and up the slope, onto the asphalt and into John's lane. John started to jog again. Gears shifted. The driver leaned on the horn. John began to run, really run. The truck gained ground fast. John couldn't bring himself to stop or face the headlights. He smelled gas. Somebody whooped a cattle call. Just when he thought he was going to take a tour of the tail pipe, the truck zipped past with a squeal of brakes and slid into a half-donut in front of him. John tried to stop, but inertia vaulted him onto the hood, rolling him to the windshield.

With his face pressed to tempered glass, John saw two men smiling as if they were at a drive-in, watching a movie in which cars routinely spun out of control with the hero on the hood.

"That's the biggest bug I ever seen!" the driver said.

Kurts.

John forgot which one was which, but remembered Billy Chuck had told him it didn't matter, they were all called Kurts, whether one or the whole family was standing in front of you, every half-brother and kissing cousin. These were John's drinking buddies, two of the surviving triplet brothers Wayne, Dwayne, and Blaine. Billy Chuck had also told John that one of the triplets had died in a logging accident while setting chokers. The triplets had made a pact to drink a case of Coors in hell together and the surviving Kurtses were looking forward to the reunion the way most people anticipated their twenty-first birthday. Heaven was for pussies. Hell was an amusement park full of everything they enjoyed, family, friends, loose women, consistent work. Place like that, what did it matter if the beer was warm?

"When you're done with the windshield," Wayne, Dwayne, or Blaine said, "You wanna check the oil?"

The wipers flipped on and cleaning fluid streamed into John's face. He climbed off the truck unable to identify new bruises from old ones. A career as a stuntman had to be considered. His wrist was jammed, but he shook it to life as he retrieved his hat. It was a relief Kurts and not Daryl had been behind the wheel, otherwise the truck would have hit him, not the other way around.

"Squirrel Boy, we need one at Cal's Palace," Kurts said. "You play softball as good as you do speed bump?"

"I haven't played in a while," John said, disoriented by the overload of adrenaline, but not enough to think any interaction with the Kurtses wouldn't be dangerous.

"Get in," said the Kurts in the passenger seat.

"I don't have a glove or cleats," John protested. "And I have things to do."

"I bet it would be tough to do them," the driving Kurts observed, "if you were run over."

John saw that he was directly in front of the truck. Open space surrounded him. Even if he hopped a couple of fences, he wouldn't be safe. The truck engine revved, helping him make his decision. Passenger-seat Kurts stepped out of the cab to let John in, claiming he rode shotgun, not bitch. On the bench seat, John noticed the driver was wearing a baseball uniform. Not exactly a uniform, because it didn't match the other Kurts's outfit, but baseball gear: pants, stirrups, cleats, a cap with the brim shaved to a nub that read "Mustache rides 5¢." The other Kurts wore pin-striped pants, no stirrups, metal cleats, and a hat advertising Loomix. They both wore green T-shirts with the words "Spotted Owl Eaters" across the chest.

"Shouldn't you fix that fence before we go?" John asked.

"Why?" driving Kurts answered, gunning the pickup. "It ain't mine."

John was thrown back against the seat. Shotgun Kurts twisted the knob of the radio, and both brothers joined in a song about guitars, Cadillacs, and hillbilly music. They took the intersection of 128, ignoring the stop sign and swerving into a dirt path near a chain-link fence, cutting onto the highway in front of a sports car. Kurts leaned into John with more pressure than the g-forces made necessary, squishing him into the other Kurts, who squished back.

They slowed to a crawl. Kurts flipped off the sports car behind them and waved to the girls outside the drive-in. They drove the rest of the strip at erratic speeds, honking to familiar faces, raising fists to enemies, slapping the sides of the vehicle to the music, until they turned into a stadium parking lot with a grandstand that had a painting of an apple riding a bucking horse and the words "Mendocino County Apple Fair." Driving beyond the grandstand, they came to a Little League field with floodlights and a sign that read "Cal's Palace," in the same lettering that usually warned, "Beware of Dog!"

This must be the place, John told himself. Boonville's cultural center.

Kurts tossed John a glove that hung off his hand like a jai alai cesta. The fingers were a foot long with Day-Glo green splashed on their tips and a palm the size of a salad bowl. There was writing embossed on the interior to explain the construction, and an explanation seemed necessary: "double-lock webbing," "grab-tite pocket," "snap action." The only thing it lacked was rack and pinion steering. Wearing it, John felt like a third-rate superhero who had a weak gimmick instead of an actual power.

Faces in the stands turned as the three men approached the field; most of the faces belonged to overweight women consuming snacks, gossiping, and trying to gain the attention of the men strutting on the miniature diamond. Periodically, they nursed babies and wiped the snot-clogged noses of children. They didn't seem interested in John or his prosthetic.

"Ain't gonna be no forfeit!" someone shouted.

"The Squirrel Boy ain't on your roster!" a player from the other team objected.

"The hell he ain't," Kurts said. "We recruited him."

John followed the Kurtses to a dugout with a partially caved-in roof. The players sat spitting sunflower seeds and gobs of tobacco juice, drinking beer, and using the collapsed end to store equipment. There was a hole in the far wall where men leered at the women in the bleachers. The first teammate to greet John was Hap, wearing a St. Louis Cardinals hat and what might have been Dizzy Dean's glove, a museum piece that gave balance to John's futuristic fly-catcher.

"Glad to have you aboard, Squirrel Boy," Hap said. "Didn't know you pleeble."

"I didn't either," John said, figuring Hap meant "play ball."

Hap introduced him to the rest of the Spotted Owl Eaters. Each player wore a different outfit depending on their enthusiasm for the game: batting gloves, sliding pants, half-shirts, tube-socks, jeans. The other side had matching uniforms and enough men to fill two teams. John's squad looked ready to drink beer and watch them go at it. In fact, the manager, Big Jack, after telling John he would be playing right field and batting ninth, pointed to a cooler at the end of the bench, saying, "There's the beer." Game plan revealed. When they took the field, most of the Spotted Owl Eaters had a cold one by their side, which they pulled from between pitches.

"Hey batter, batter, swig, batter," John heard their second baseman chatter.

Hap explained they were playing "moon-ball," so named because each pitch had to reach the height of six feet, not to exceed twelve, and then land on home plate, or the rug stretching a foot behind it, to be called a strike. Flat pitches were balls. Fouls were strikes. Ten players per team, but you could play with nine, which was what the Spotted Owl Eaters were doing. An umpire stood behind the catcher to keep score, deciding balls, strikes, and close plays at the bases. There were seven innings, but if either team got ahead by ten runs after five innings, it was declared the winner.

It seemed to John more of a social event than a sport. Then he got a better look at his opponents: Cal, Billy Chuck, and Daryl were pointing fingers at him with a group that had to be the local all-stars, men who had been high-school heroes, played college ball, maybe a cup of coffee in the minors. After attending an athletic factory like University of Miami, John could tell real jocks from weekend warriors, and the athletes on the cusp who had the talent but would never refine it. That's who they were playing today, the boys who might have been. In contrast, John was suiting up for the alkies who couldn't have cared less.

John spit in his glove, pounded it twice, and braced himself for another beating. It was a good day for two.

The first batter, smelling weakness, lashed a line drive to right. John charged it but the ball didn't bounce as high as he had expected and sailed beneath his glove, impossible as that seemed, caroming off his shin and rolling to the fence. He tracked it down with a limp, firing it back to the infield. Without any warm-ups and not having thrown a ball of any kind in a while, he put too much oomph into it and not enough accuracy. The ball flew over the cut-off man's head, past Hap who was backing up the play, and into the opposing team's bat-rack. Stand-up triple. E-9.

"Hell of an arm, Squirrel Boy!" Hap yelled, repositioning himself on the pitcher's mound. "But if you can't aim, don't aim at all!"

The next batter drilled a seed off Kurts' chest at third, which he gathered, looked the runner back to third base, and threw the batter out at first. Kurts was the perfect third baseman, cheating down the line, daring grown men with aluminum bats to hit the ball through him at a distance of less than sixty feet. There would be seam marks embedded into Kurts's skin by the end of the inning. John was glad he was far away in right field.

The other Kurts in left, but probably equally capable of playing third, caught the next out, a lazy fly that carried to the warning track. The runner at third scored after tagging up. The clean-up man made his way to the plate. The only lefty so far in the line-up, and the only one to land that left to John's chin.

"Move back!" the center fielder warned.

Seeing the swollen nose of his teammate in center, John recognized him as the man Daryl had punched in the parking lot of the Lodge before getting to him. He had every right to respect Daryl's power. He knew how hard he hit too.

Daryl swaggered into the batter's box. The women in the crowd cheered as he called for time out, holding up his hand while he made himself comfortable, wiggling his ass, tapping the plate with his bat. The Kurtses chanted, "DAR-ryl, DAR-ryl" in high-pitched voices. Nobody else joined in. Most were taking the opportunity to finish off this inning's beer.

Daryl finally coiled into his batting stance. Hap's first offering tumbled in a spinless drift. As soon as it was struck, John knew it was gone. A child was released from the stands to hunt it down. The ball landed in the weeds fifty feet beyond the right field fence. Hap's head drooped while Daryl circled the bases, meeting his teammates at home plate. John walked to the fence to help the gofer find the ball, not wanting to watch the celebration.

"I think it's more to your right," John said, trying to steer the boy to the spot.

The boy ignored John's directions, stamping into a thicket of foxtail and vanishing from sight. When he reappeared, he held the oversized pearl, barely able to grip it in one hand. The boy used both hands to heave the ball back over the fence. Confused by the kid's throwing style, John got a bad jump and the ball hit the ground after grazing his outstretched glove.

"Mister," the boy called out, "you suck!"

John did his best Ted Williams, extending his middle finger.

"Same to you," the boy said, replicating the gesture. "But more of it!"

John retrieved the ball, noticing there were black pellets stuck to it. He wondered if it had landed in something in the weeds. Then he saw the outfield grass was covered with the same orblets. Removing one from the ball, he squished it between his thumb and index finger and brought it to his nose.

"Any day now, Squirrel Boy!" Big Jack called, from first base. "You can play with the sheep shit later!"

The infield tittered as John tried to flick the turd away, the clump clinging to his fingers. He couldn't wipe it off in the grass either because that would only compound the problem. Not knowing what else to do, John rubbed clean on the ball. He tossed it to the second baseman who whipped it to Hap who threw another knuckler. This one dipped fiercely. The batter grounded out to short.

"Shit beats spit every time," Hap told John, back on the bench. "Ask Gaylord Perry. The great ones never went to their caps, they go to their grundies."

Hap also explained that sheep were the groundskeepers, mowing and fertilizing the field for free, and in the off-season making a hell of a stew. John apologized for his miscue in the field. Big Jack, who was braving the substandard section of the dugout for a trip to the cooler, told him the run would have scored anyway. A beer landed in John's lap. The sound of cans opening filled the cave, rounding off the competitive edge.

"It ain't whether you win or lose," Big Jack informed him, peering out not at the playing field but at the women in the stands. "It's who you fuck after the game."

"Lord have mercy on that woman's ass," Bo, the second baseman, said, grimacing as he stood next to Big Jack, taking in the same view.

"I'd fuck her sober," Big Jack confided.

"Out of what?" the second baseman said. "You'd need a bakery truck to haul those buns."

"Speaking of which, Squirrel Boy," someone called from down the bench, not loud enough for the other team to hear. "You get any from Sarah?"

Everyone, including the on-deck batter, waited for John's answer. But John didn't kiss and tell. He also knew whatever he said would get back to Daryl.

"We're just friends," John said, but might as well have told them he screwed Sarah twelve ways 'til midnight.

"I'd be her friend, too," the center fielder said, amid his teammates' snickering. "I'd be her butt buddy."

"I thought you was Bobby Dee's butt buddy, Hank," said Bo.

"Fuck you, Bo," Hank replied.

"You making offers or insults?" Bo asked. "Seems these days you want to be everyone's butt buddy."

"At least I stick it somewhere," Hank said. "You ain't had pussy since pussy had you."

The bench encouraged their insults, asking, "You gonna let him get away with that?" or "Did you hear what he said?" Meanwhile, the game proceeded; someone hit a single, someone flied out to left. The slow approach of ball to batsman inspired little attention. The jousting on the bench was more entertaining and good-natured, until the topic of mothers was introduced.

John understood by Hank's jokes that Bo's mother, Night Train Elaine, was a drunk who dated men for the price of a bottle. She also had the misfortune of accidentally shifting gears in a truck while engaging in oral sex in the parking lot of Cal's Palace. She and her partner had been too loaded to realize the truck's motor was running, too into the moment to notice the truck was moving, and then amazed to find themselves climaxing in the visitor's dugout. The incident had occurred between games so nobody had been hurt, but that was why the roof of the dugout was caved in. Hank retold the story, making puns out of "stick-shift," "softballs," and "double headers."

"Let's get off mamas, because I've been on yours all night," Hank finished. "I had a cold and I guess she smelled the Ny-Quil."

Bo took a swing at the center fielder. John slid down the bench, certain Bo was going to rebreak Hank's nose. But Big Jack was between them before the punch could land. Big Jack was about six-four, two-forty, with a burly chest and biceps that rippled from his jersey. In another era, he would have worked for the circus bending bars of steel. In this age, he was probably a local legend performing feats of strength like kicking two morons' asses without putting down his can of beer.

"Both you tinsel dicks shut up," Big Jack said, holding the two men at bay by expanding his chest. "I can't concentrate with all this yappin'. You're on deck, Bo. Grab a stick before I do."

"When you least expect it, expect it!" Bo warned Hank, before leaving the dugout to take his licks.

Big Jack returned to his concentrating, staring intently at the crotch of a woman in the stands whose dress had climbed up past her thighs. He sipped his beer, squinting at the hint of pink beneath the tunnel of fabric. But Hank wouldn't let the argument rest. He made a show of not being afraid of Bo, declaring loudly that he would fight anybody, anytime, anywhere, and his history proved it.

"Sit down, Suzy," Big Jack said. "Before I make you prove it for the last time."

Hank mumbled something about being a team player. He took a seat next to John as one of the Kurtses, returned to the dugout after sliding hard to break up a double play and taking a chunk out of his leg. Blood seeped through his pin-stripes. Not wanting to drink, John handed Kurts his beer, reminding himself that he had business to take care of later. Kurts splashed some on his leg and sat down to enjoy the rest.

"What'd I miss?" Kurts asked. "Sounded like Hank was gonna get his ass kicked."

Big Jack walked in front of them, choosing a bat by proximity, swinging it with one hand while he finished his can of suds with the other. John noticed a ring of stitches around Big Jack's thumb, the skin above the scar a shade paler than the flesh below it. Big Jack swatted his empty into the screen, dousing the bench with a spray of foam.

"Hey!" Hank whined, cringing from the beer.

"It's embarrassing," Big Jack said. "You look like Murdered Row."

John self-consciously raised a hand to his eye, Hank to his nose, while Kurts continued poking at his festering leg. Hank pretended as if he didn't hear Big Jack's slight. Kurts looked up from his wound when he realized he had been included in the indignity.

"You look like a two-hundred-pound bag of shit," Kurts called after Big Jack.

Big Jack turned to see who had insulted him.

"Don't worry," Kurts added. "We won't tell Tammy Lee you was lookin' up her pussy."

Big Jack flushed, continuing toward the plate without comment, not checking to see if Tammy Lee had fixed her dress.

It reminded John of why he didn't play sports anymore, he'd had enough of dugouts and locker rooms, the nonstop flow of sexist and racist talk. "The hours involved in athletics are the same ones that obliterate common sense," Grandma had told him. "There is no such thing as a thinking man's game." She was right, athletes were better off obedient, answering to the memory of repetition: ten thousand ground balls to the left, ten thousand ground balls to the right. Batting practice, base running, shagging flies. What's the meaning of life? Reaching your physical peak before the age of thirty, and then being disposed of. No wonder sports heroes were drug addicts and wife beaters.

John had bowed out of sports in high school after his best friend, who was black, was repeatedly called "nigger" by his own teammates. Not to his face, but when he was out on the field. "That nigger sure can play! Look at that nigger go!" John complained and was told by his coach he was disrupting team morale. His father felt the same way, not approving of John's choice of pals, making it clear he would face the music alone if he created any problems by "popping off." John wanted to make a stand, but his friend told him not to worry, it was part of the game. If that was true, the green fields and thrill of victory weren't enough. John didn't want to play.

"You ruined it for everybody, Kurts!" Hank moaned. "Don't you know some girls sit like this." He held out two fingers like a pair of closed legs. "And some girls sit like this," he crossed his fingers. "But girls who sit like this," he spread them. "Get this," he extended his middle finger. "Like that." He snapped.

Kurts stared at Hank. The inning was over; Big Jack had lined out and the Spotted Owl Eaters were gathering their gloves and heading for the field. But as long as Kurts kept his eye on Hank, the center fielder wasn't going to move. Instead, Hank bent over to retie his cleats. Hank was one of the players who took pride in his apparel. His uniform and cleats were spotless, until Bo kicked dirt on them in passing. But Hank did nothing in response, not wanting to give anybody a reason to start a pecking party.

"Who asked you to play on this team, anyway?" Kurts finally asked.

Hank didn't answer.

"If you don't get a hit today," Kurts told him, rising from the bench. "I'm kicking your ass. And taking your cleats."

Kurts followed the rest of the team to the field. John took his place in right, feeling the gaze of his own fans; Billy Chuck was watching him from the on-deck circle, Cal was talking to Daryl and a couple others who nodded when Daryl pointed in John's direction. John felt like a spy with a blown cover. Although Hap, the Kurtses, and Sarah seemed to accept him, he was a stranger in a strange land. And he had seen how they dealt with one of their own; Hank would be beaten and left cleatless in the streets of Boonville by the end of the game. Maybe John should take a hint and hightail it over the fence, back to Miami. But it occurred to him that he had already defected. These were his countrymen.

"I was on this team before Kurts," Hank complained from center field. "He touches my cleats and I'm pressing charges."

Night began to spread. The lights shined brighter on the men playing a boy's game on a boy's field. Crickets chirped. Insects shrieked at a frequency above the hum of the lights, only audible if you could separate the two sounds. The smell of burning wood drifted on cold air. The women in the stands made trips to their cars, returning with jackets for their children, thermoses of steaming liquid, flasks to be passed beneath their afghans and blankets. They watched, they waited, they endured.

John wanted the game to be over so he could blockade himself in his cabin and wait for Sarah. The thought of her blue eyes and manic enthusiasm excited him. He didn't know what the women in the bleachers had to look forward to, doing dishes, clipping coupons, being mounted? Tuna Helper? It seemed to John if they weathered the softball game, they shouldn't have to see their husbands for another week.

A foul ball curved down the right field line and out of play, bouncing off a parked car. The gofer was on it in a flash, climbing underneath a truck to recover it.

"Catch this one, Dorkface!" the gofer yelled, throwing the ball to John. It dribbled to a stop in front of him, not possessing as much spunk as the kid.

John lobbed it back to Big Jack. But before returning to his position, he noticed the boy's shirt, a pullover with the number 82 emblazoned in red. John didn't know whether the number corresponded to a player on a professional team or the year it had been purchased.

"Don't look down," John told the boy. "If you can tell me the number on your shirt, I'll give you twenty bucks."

The child realized the offer was serious and that twenty dollars meant a lot of Jolly Ranchers. He bit his lower lip, rolled his eyes downward trying to sneak a peak at the numeral that could put him in Candyland. All but defeated, he gave it his best shot.

"Four!" he answered.

"Sorry," John said, making the sound of a buzzer. "Thanks for playing."

The child checked his chest to see if John hadn't been lying. Finding the eight and two, he pulled a face, feeling John had somehow changed the number, gypping him out of a mouthful of cavities. His mother called his name from the stands. The boy stood trying to comprehend the turn of events before leaving, the moral finally dawning on him.

"I can change my shirt," he said, before dashing off for maternal protection. "But you'll always suck!"

The insult echoed in John's ears as he repositioned himself. He remembered how his father used to attend his Pony League games, sitting in the bleachers with a bottle of schnapps. John used to pitch and his father had a string of insults waiting for him after every toss, "That fast ball couldn't puff a lip at ten paces! You couldn't throw a strike with the Teamsters behind you!" The premise was John would become a pressure player. The outcome was his father was banned from the stadium. He argued with the cop who escorted him off the grounds, "Don't tell me how to raise my kid! I don't come to your house and tell you to quit fondling your daughter!"

Another reason John stopped playing sports, the fans. He

couldn't think of anything more pathetic than a grown man sitting in the stands with some undereducated twenty-eight-year-old's name sewn onto his back. When the time came, he would play pickle and pepper with his own kids, but he would make sure they knew the difference between the big picture and Little League, the division between church and sport, stressing an identity that extended beyond a team's insignia. Something only Grandma had encouraged him to explore.

Three up, three down.

John found himself holding a Bombat, and waiting his turn to swing it. Hap told him this was the last game of the season. The winner decided the league champion. They weren't in the running, in third place behind their opponents Stafford Logging and The Boys of Summer, a group of teenage upstarts who the Mexican team called "Menudo Atletico." The Spotted Owl Eaters were going to finish ahead of the Mexican team Los Diablos, and the hippie team, The Dharma Bleacher Bums, who were led by a six-foot-ten first baseman who played in a tie-dyed sarong. It was a point of honor not to lose to the hippies. Consequently, they were winless. But The Spotted Owl Eaters could play spoilers by winning this game against Stafford Logging, because a loss by Stafford Logging would drop them into second place. So, Hap was talking strategy.

"If I get on," Hap told John, "I'd appreciate you not hittin' more than a single. These days, I run bases like I juggle women, one at a time."

John replied he would probably hit into a double play. Hap said, whatever he did, not to do that. At his age, sliding was a last resort.

"Of course, if push comes to shove," Hap said. "It's spikes high."

John watched him head for the plate, the only wooden bat in the team's arsenal resting on his shoulder. He could barely read the autograph etched into the lumber, faded from countless collisions with a cushioned piece of cork: Joe Medwick.

"You got a final on this one?" said a large man with a friendly face, through the fence protecting the spectators from the playing field. He had a full beard and wore a tweed coat, wire-rimmed glasses, suspenders, and a gray fedora. In his hands he held a notebook and pen, poised for scribbling.

"We're still playing," John informed him.

"You want to make one up?" the man asked. "Nobody gives a shit anyway. The only people who care are playing the game."

John didn't want to predict the outcome. "That's why you play them," he said. The man smiled. John could tell he had played his fair share. The man had the look of an athlete who had hung up his jock decades ago to pursue a career.

"They play them," he told John, "because if they didn't, they would have to confront the fact that their communities have been destroyed, plundered by corporate giants who have stripped them of their jobs, natural resources, personal freedom, and left them behind with inadequate health care, faulty public schools, and a chain of fast food restaurants, all while they were out chasing a ball and giving each other high-fives. They play them because they're too dumb to realize the result is always the same."

"Are you blaming the decline of Western civilization on the national pastime?" John asked.

"That's right," the man said. "Apathy."

Hap took a pitch inside. The ball rolled away from the catcher and behind the umpire, who seemed oblivious to its location. The catcher walked around the umpire to retrieve it, instead of the umpire moving out of the way. John noticed the umpire's mask was strapped on over the bald head of a man wearing all white, and that he was calling pitches by leaning an ear toward home plate.

"The umpire's blind," John said, identifying Blindman.

"What else is new?" the man asked. "You're the Squirrel Lady's grandson, right? How would you like to write an article for our local paper on an outsider's perspective of the Anderson Valley?"

"I'm not an outsider, I live here," John said, but how could he live somewhere they let a blind guy umpire softball? Even if he was calling a good game. "I don't think my perspective would win me any friends."

"A newspaper has no friends," the man stated. "How about covering a missing persons? Reports say you were the last one to see a certain Tony Balostrasi, a native of San Francisco who told his roommate he wanted to taste the food at the Boonville Hotel, missed work and his mother's birthday party, and hasn't been heard from in a week."

"I don't know him," John said, not wanting to concern himself with the whereabouts of Balostrasi who was probably off selling his stolen dope. He would turn up to treat his roommate to an expensive dinner and his mother would get a VCR and an apology for missing her celebration. But then John remembered Balostrasi's gun. He remembered he was supposed to help harvest Sarah's marijuana.

"You're up," the man said. "If you change your mind, we might be able to pay you something in the low two figures."

"I'll think about it," John said. "Right now, I've got to take one for the team."

"I understand," the man replied. "The toy department of life."

John entered the batter's box. Aside from his domestic problems, there were two outs and somebody was on second. Daryl stared in at him from short, Billy Chuck in center. Cal delivered the pitch from the mound. His teammates were cheering. The ball came in unbelievably high, at a slant above his shoulders, and landed six inches behind the plate. Blindman called it strike one.

"Next time you'll say hello," he snipped, from behind his mask.

"I thought that was you, Blindman," John said. "How are your sinuses?"

The next pitch hit the dirt a foot to the right of the rug. Blindman called it strike two. The Spotted Owl Eaters objected from the dugout, realizing the fix was on. John told himself to swing at the next offering, regardless of its location.

"This is a hitter's league, Squirrel Boy, you can't beg your way onto the base path," Blindman informed him. "Ask your Itie friend from San Francisco, he had the right idea. My offer still stands if you want to do business."

John didn't have time to reply, another pitch was approaching and he started his swing, weight shifting, hips flying open. Way out in front. He drilled it foul down the third base line. Strike three. End of inning.

"Good contact," Hap said, tossing John his glove so he wouldn't have to go back to the bench. "Blindman needs to have his ears checked, those first two were balls."

As the innings progressed, John felt more at ease in the field, but increasingly nervous about his postgame plans. Something told him the newspaperman was trying to link him to Balostrasi's crimes. What crimes? he didn't know. But if something illegal had happened on the night of his arrival, a blackout wasn't much of an alibi. Especially if you were caught later engaging in similar activities. "Ask your Itie friend?" Why were people so quick to connect him with Balostrasi? Because they had exchanged a few words and were from out of town? Ask him what? Call it paranoia, but John had the feeling he should back out of Sarah's scheme. Maybe call a lawyer.

In spite of his fearfulness, the game began to take on a pleasant rhythm. He had always enjoyed playing at night, cheating the darkness of its rightful domain. He made a couple of plays from right, cutting down a runner trying to stretch a single, making a diving catch of a Daryl line drive. He could see Daryl's displeasure, adding the snag to a scoreboard in his head, the only place John might be considered to have a lead. John also gained some respect at the plate, driving a double to left-center and a single up the middle, both on first pitches. He wasn't going to give Blindman a chance to squeeze him or renew the conversation about contraband.

By the seventh inning, the Spotted Owl Eaters had the lead, 6-5. The first two of their batters had failed to get aboard, each trying to tie the game with a swing of the bat and falling twenty feet short. The opposing bench turned their caps inside out, trying to seduce a rally. Billy Chuck wore his with the bill extended upright like a dorsal fin in the "rally shark" position. Daryl crouched confidently in the batter's box. An old desire crept into John's heart: Win. But a bad-hop ground ball found its way through the infield. The next batter hit a double, advancing Daryl to third. Cal drew a walk to load the bases. John could feel the game slipping away as Billy Chuck stepped to the plate.

John began to worry, not so much about the game, but about what he would do after it was over: avoid Blindman and Daryl, that was for certain. His plan had fallen apart. It was getting late and Sarah would be coming over whether he was going to help her harvest or not. He hadn't decided, trying to recall his first night in town so he could confidently deny allegations of being Balostrasi's accomplice, thereby deflecting suspicion of conspiring with Sarah. But the things he couldn't remember kept hiding behind the things he couldn't forget.

Billy Chuck watched Hap's first offering hit the heart of the plate for a strike. The base runners retreated to their bases, readying themselves to sprint with the release of the next pitch. John focused on Billy Chuck's face, trying intently to remember his first night in Boonville. What had happened before he awoke on grandma's porch? Half-images of heaving came to mind, Sarah's monologue, shots of tequila, shouting out eternal alliances. Hap hurled one inside. John recalled a mob, country music, hands guiding his to a steering wheel. Billy Chuck lifted a shallow pop-fly to left, both Kurtses converging at full speed. The night had been cold. Runners raced around the bases, the Kurtses charging the ball. He had cursed Grandma, saw her ghost in his empty glass, crashed her car into signposts while singing songs of liberation. "I got it! I got it!" He had tried to throw himself into an abyss, only to have his fall cushioned by people who had jumped in ahead of him. The Kurtses collided, arms and legs flailing in a confused tangle, the ball landing safely at the feet of their fallen bodies. John blinked at the familiarity. It was déjà vu all over again.

II

There was no time to masturbate. John had arrived home three hours later than he had expected, even taking into consideration that he'd been waylaid. After Billy Chuck's bleeder fell in for a hit, the Kurtses had been revived to face a two-run deficit and splitting headaches. The Spotted Owl Eaters squelched the rally and scored a run in their half of the seventh, but when Hank flied out with two outs and the bases loaded to become an "o-for" on the day, Stafford Logging preserved their victory and Kurtses left the dugout for a piece of Hank's ass and both of his cleats. Shortly following, Big Jack coldcocked Billy Chuck in the handshake line, believing he was gloating too much for a man who had won the game on a Texas Leaguer. John was congratulating Cal when he found himself being shoved toward the backstop, the deputy twisting John's right arm to his shoulder blades and forcing John to stand on his tiptoes.

"You don't want no part of this," Cal warned.

Hearing the brawl behind him, John felt it was the safest place he could be. He could see a mound of bodies covering home plate while those on the fringe slugged it out toe to toe, their fights consisting of one or two decisive punches. When the dust settled, Cal released him, making the transition from one of the boys to Johnny Law. In the bleachers, bouts were scored; Billy Chuck, K.O., Daryl had beaten Bo on points, Big Jack flattened a couple of other takers, Hank was barefoot and unconscious near the foul pole in right field, T.K.O. Overall, each team would feel they had won the fight. Bruises would mark individual losers. John could tell by the way the two teams eyed each other during the aftermath that there would be new scores to settle next season, and for the rest of their lives.

But with Hank's cleats slung over his shoulder, Kurts was ready to celebrate. However, his brother was on his knees in the batter's box searching for his lower lip. He had been at the bottom of a dog pile trying to open up a can of flaming whup-ass when somebody had chomped onto the brim of his mouth. John saw blood dribbling from Blindman's chin as a Mexican woman led him from the field by the elbow. John didn't say anything. Kurts sifted dirt, one hand pressed to his mouth. Blood lay bulbous around him like breaded chitlins. Kurts dusted off a clump.

"Don't worry, it won't look bad from my house," his brother consoled. "I got Krazy Glue in the truck. We'll patch you up, good as new."

The players began to leave the field peacefully after Cal told them he was "on duty." Women gathered their men. John could tell they would be in the stands next week, hoping for more of the same, excited by any beating they didn't have to take part in. Meanwhile, the gofer wrestled an equipment bag into the rear of a truck while his mother called for a Stafford Logging player to hurry. A derelict speared aluminum cans out of the trash using a stick with a nail hammered to one end. Hap led a flock of sheep onto the diamond for maintenance. Stafford Logging was organizing a convoy to Ukiah to celebrate their title-tying conquest. John followed the Kurtses to the parking lot after Big Jack made him promise to suit up for his team in two weeks for the play-offs.

"We need your bat," Big Jack said. "We'll move you to center if Hank don't get his cleats back."

Inside their truck, the Kurtses refused to drive John home until he had a heave-ho with them at the Lodge. Maybe two. By the time John realized the Kurtses' intentions, there was nobody left to ask for another ride or any way out of the truck. He had a hard time swallowing his beer with Kurts sitting across from him, scraped knuckles and Krazy Glue'd lip. John suggested he get stitches. Kurts said it didn't hurt. That's not the point, John replied, what about infection? Kurts ordered a shot of whiskey. Melonie poured a double. Kurts let it trickle over his lip, slopping some onto the bar. John realized some people were immune to pain, the paralyzed, the dead, the insane. Kurts clamped a hand to John's shoulder for his concern, forming a crooked smile, and recommended they get a burger at the drive-in. John grimaced for both of them.

But now he was home, shaved, showered, and shitting, regretting having ordered his chili cheeseburger and not buying any roto-reading while shopping at the market. In Miami, Christina had kept a copy of *Elle* or *Cosmopolitan* in the bathroom. John was fond of leafing through *Bartlett's Familiar Quotations* while he did his duty, but Christina didn't want to encourage him sitting on the throne that long. The bathroom was part of her domain. John was in charge of the drawer in the kitchen that held the potato peeler. Whenever he left *Bartlett's* in the lavatory, Christina reshelved it and he was forced to read about "What Women Really Want from Their Mates," or "Ten Tips to Avoid Splitting Up." None of which mentioned having to surrender the bathroom.

John found himself scanning the directions on a box of Q-Tips, wondering, who needed instructions to wipe wax out of their ears? Then he studied the list of ingredients in his hair gel, searching for the longest word. Winner: 26 letters. Several times he tried to pronounce the word, but couldn't make it more than three-quarters of the way through. He would have been happy with a *Watchtower*. He sat. The bathroom was filled with the steam of his shower and the scent of hard water. Eau de toilet. It condensed on the ceiling in mold-spawning droplets. The only thing worse than taking a dump in shower residue was taking a shower after somebody had punished the bowl. When Christina was mad at him, she would shit while he showered. Typical passive-aggressive. She also used a ton of toilet paper when she wiped, so it took two or three flushes to whirl the waste away. She would wait by the bowl for it to refill, jiggle the handle, and then reflush until every last speck was gone. Wee-wee or poo-poo, nobody ever saw an ounce of her excrement or the rain forest she felled in the name of sanitation.

John finished. Washing his hands, he heard the knock on the front door.

Sarah was dressed in hiking boots, black jeans, black T-shirt, a camouflage backpack, and a hunting knife hanging from her side in a leather sheath. Her hair was tucked under a red baseball hat with the words "McKay Construction" stitched across the front.

"You ready, Dieter?" Sarah said, noticing John was also wearing black, but cultivating a different look, one more appropriate for going clubbing in Prague.

"Is anybody ever ready for anything they do?" John said, realizing there was no reason for him to be doing this. Friendship, rebellion, and money weren't substantial enough answers. Identity crisis, maybe. Death wish, closer.

He recalled the first time he had ever smoked dope, pre-Christina, at a fraternity party. He had been in a mind-expanding mood and followed the sound of Grateful Dead music wheezing from a back room to a group of stoners passing around a ceramic bong with the word "love" etched into it. John told himself, "If anybody gets naked, I'm leaving." He sucked from the hookah. Couples made out. Uncontrollable giggling. "It's all part of an energy thing," a guy explained to him, as psychedelic wall hangings blended indistinguishably into the paisley bedspread. "You, me, the grass, Terence McKenna, everything. We're all just energy looking for love." The next day, John awoke with one arm wrapped around a woman he had never seen before, the other clutching an empty bag of Funyons.

"No," Sarah said, recognizing her words. "They never seem to be."

"Well, then," John replied, "let's make it happen."

At Sarah's request, they loaded the pile of road signs into her truck to give to a bush-hippie on her commune who was doing a series of sculptures, shaping road signs into giant penises; "Men At Work," "Falling Rocks," "Xing," "Yield Ahead." John was happy to oblige. The Kurtses had told him he should disappear them before Cal found out; the deputy was looking to make an example of someone to halt the recent rash of thefts. Hopefully, Cal wouldn't be on patrol when they passed through town. As Sarah steered them down Manchester Road, Cal seemed to be the farthest thing from her mind.

John was getting used to riding in trucks. He had never noticed how nice it was to ride up high, the perspective and feeling of power caused by the extra height. Sarah told him there was a primal joy to riding in the back too, claiming it was the closest thing to being a German shepherd. One of her favorite memories was of crossing the Golden Gate Bridge in the bed of her mother's boyfriend's half-ton Chevy. The smell of the Bay, drift of fog, spitting over the tailgate, wind whipping your hair, red cable and impossibly high towers. Flashing the peace sign to passing cars.

John said his parents made him wear a safety belt and wouldn't let him put a hand outside the window of a moving vehicle.

"Of course they did," Sarah said, mistaking his parents for concerned adults instead of control freaks. "Now they have laws against even dogs riding in the back of trucks. Not that my mom would have cared."

"When did your parents get divorced?" John asked, figuring it was a common enough question, especially in California.

"Four wives ago for my father," she said. "I don't know when it was official. I was about eleven. They separated before that. It brought up some interesting questions. For example, what do you call an ex-stepmother? The last one made it easier when she checked into the Betty Ford Clinic and became my 'twelve-step' mother, but the others are harder to label. Bitch 1 and Bitch 2?"

"Your father married four times?" John said.

"He's on five now," Sarah told him. "The exes are waiting for him to divorce this one so they can put together a basketball team. Right now, they just compare alimony settlements and play bridge."

Again, John didn't know if she was kidding. Did women still play bridge?

When John was young, he had wished his parents would get divorced. No such luck. Most of his friends' parents were divorced, but John's refused to get with the program. "Nobody hurts me like your father," his mother would cry. John became convinced it was the reason she never left. Symbiosis. Both of them were bottom feeders.

"My mom never remarried, but she goes through boyfriends faster than Stephen King writes novels," Sarah said. "After every breakup, Mom goes to Ukiah to buy the latest and sometimes there isn't a current title. When that happens, she brings back a self-help manual or new boyfriend. They propose in a month. I swear, her ring finger is raw from indecision. But Mom loves herself too much to think about anybody else longer than the time it takes them to make her come."

They had passed by town without running into Cal. There weren't many cars on the highway at this hour, the occasional tourist in mid-journey to somewhere else. Sarah slowed down and veered onto a gravel road.

"Anyway, marriage for women is the equivalent of a man

joining the marines," Sarah theorized. "Essentially, you're saying you don't want control of your own life."

John had never thought about joining the marines, but some of his friends had after binges and breakups. Three square meals a day, they said. Get in shape, learn to kill. Something that might come in handy should they get back with their girlfriends. One went through with it. The others finished college, developed habits, abused credit cards, went bulk-food shopping, found even worse matches for themselves, and got married.

"What's the female equivalent of a man getting married?" John asked.

"Getting a pet," Sarah answered. "Maybe Jenny Craig."

John could see her in the light reflecting off the hood as they sped along the back road, shifting gears as she accelerated around potholes. She beeped at animals as they bolted through the headlights. The road narrowed. The grade grew steep. The shoulder fell off into what seemed to be oblivion. John's ears needed to pop from the change in altitude. He stressed his jaw on its hinge, expecting to hear the tiny air-releasing report.

"That's why I got married," Sarah confessed, sneaking a peek at John trying to control his bodily functions. "I wanted someone to make my decisions for me. And nothing was more rebellious to Mom than marrying a redneck. Major two-for-one. Daryl was different then too. Actually he was the same, but nineteen. He had an excuse."

John wanted to confess something, too, but didn't know what. It was difficult to think with the truck bouncing him around. He searched for the safety belt. Sarah had strapped herself in earlier and seemed unaffected by the ride. He wondered what would happen if a vehicle came in the opposite direction; there was hardly enough room on the road for one car and with so many blind curves, they wouldn't see another driver until impact. John found the safety belt. Sarah told him not to worry, she knew the road better than her menstrual cycle.

"Let's hope you're regular," John said.

She seemed to give that some thought, then began to hum the theme to "The Brady Bunch." It reminded John of Christina's friends who were always discussing old television shows. Somebody would say, "Remember 'Bridget Loves Bernie'?" knowing nobody could forget something that pathetic, especially when they had asked the same question to the same group of people two weeks earlier at another party. "What about 'Holmes and Yo-Yo' or 'Chico and the Man'?" John was guilty himself, his dialogue smacked with sit-com analogies, and he could tell by the way the Bradys' station wagon entered the driveway if it was the episode Cindy got the sniffes or cousin Oliver was visiting and Bobby was going to take Mr. Howell in pool for a wad of bubble gum. 534 packs? The difference was, John was ashamed.

"Sorry," Sarah said, stopping her humming. "Sometimes I do that."

"It's all right," John answered. "Sometimes we all do."

They came to a fork in the road and John spied a huge glass barrel with material draped on its inside like a shower curtain. If somebody parted the curtain, you would get the false sense of having x-ray vision. Even the doors were made of glass. To the left of the peculiar building was an immense sphere of rusted iron, over thirty feet in diameter, and perched on top was a sculpture of a man in the Atlas pose, back bent, legs flexed, arms stretched behind him, but with no world on his shoulders.

"The Earth carries the weight of man," Sarah explained. "Not the other way around."

"What about the house?" John asked.

"Fully solar-powered," Sarah answered. "Hot in the summer."

They unloaded the signs near a refuse heap that included hundreds of Sarah's crosses. Sarah said whenever anybody on the commune came across found-art or "ready-mades," this was the drop site. You could take what you wanted and leave behind material for others to transform. The bush-hippie they had brought the signs for lived in the Pyrex palace and was an old-time socialist. He was the one who had taught Sarah how to weld. As a young man, he had helped to build the Golden Gate Bridge. That was part of the reason Sarah's trip over the span in the back of the truck had been so terrific—she remembered his tales of the Mohawks working unafraid of the dizzying heights and the men who had fallen to their deaths. Sarah said she enjoyed holding a blowtorch but was searching for softer lines now. John confessed his artistic inclinations had faltered after he broke the vertical knob on his Etch A Sketch.

He asked Sarah about the McKay Construction hat. She said it was her father's company, consisting of her father and three pothead flunkies. Her father hadn't helped her learn to weld or do any carpentry. She hadn't learned anything from him except how to write a postcard. But she loved him and wore her lucky red hat when she worked on projects, or needed extra strength, or motivation, or some mojo to get through the day. She was convinced she was at her best when she wore it. She adjusted it on her head, making sure the good luck was flowing.

Returning to the truck, they drove on until the road ended. They would have to walk from here. Even with his eyes adjusting to the night and the glow of the moon, John could see about two feet in front of him. Sarah told him to take off his jacket, once they got moving he would be too hot. Her other advice was to stand still if they saw a bear and make himself look big if they ran into a mountain lion. Before John could mouth the words "bear" or "mountain lion," Sarah stepped toward the trees, saying, "Stay close."

John stumbled forward in a controlled fall, skiing without the snow. Slipping, tripping, crashing, cursing, smashing face first into branches, bushes, saplings, anything that got in his way as he rolled down the mountain blindfolded by the night. He would never have made it as a guerrilla. Aside from not being fleet of foot, he was afraid of the dark. Real dark. Not turn-off-the-lights-in-your-bedroom dark or the-bulb-burned-out-in-the-basement dark, but snakes-could-be-slithering-near-me-and-I-wouldn't-know-it dark. The kind of black that reduces you to your basic survival instincts, which in John's case had been dulled over the years by supermarkets, cable television, and alarm systems. In contrast, Sarah maintained her balance at all times, picking out the path of least resistance. Sandinista first-round draft-pick. She could have played for Fidel.

John continued his nose dive, thorns biting into his legs. He tumbled until the pull of gravity released him. Sarah stopped every so often to help him to his feet and request that he not fall so much. Head in a sticker bush, supporting himself on a root that felt as strong as teak wood, John suggested they use the flashlight he'd seen poking out of her backpack, so they could see where the hell they were going.

"The hills have eyes," Sarah said. "No light until we get there."

"How far until we're there?" John asked, playing the role of a child on a road trip.

"Soon," Sarah replied.

John didn't tell her he had to pee.

They were on their hands and knees, crawling through the thickest brush. The soil seemed to be swallowing him, a mulch of mushrooms, decaying debris, rotting logs. A forgotten autumn. John's fingers probed for handholds, coming up with palms full of bugs and mites. It was the perfect place to ditch a body. It would decompose before the FBI could say "serial killer." He remembered reading about a psychopath in California called "The Trailside Murderer," but for once John wasn't worried, there was no trail around here. They crept along like lost alligators for another fifty yards, finally arriving at a clearing where they could stand. Sarah reached into her bag for the flashlight. She fixed a beam on an area of stomped chicken wire, slashed garden hose, churned-over ground, and irrigation tubing cut into lengths of less than a foot. No plants.

"I've been CAMPed!" she screamed. "Bush and his bullshit war on drugs. How many marijuana-related deaths are there every year? How many from alcohol? That hypocrite supports dictators responsible for importing tons of drugs into this country, but for some reason, he makes it a point to get my plants. If my other patch is gone, I'll get that bastard."

John didn't know what Sarah was talking about. He was too busy having a *Homo erectus* moment, holding his hands above his head and stretching. But if using a flashlight was dangerous, it seemed to him, screaming at the top of your lungs about killing the president would also be a no-no.

After her tirade, Sarah scanned the area with her flashlight. John thought it was unlikely that someone would be out here, whether they were paid by the government or not. He was amazed that anybody other than Sarah could find this place. Given a map, compass, broad daylight, and a bag of popcorn, John couldn't locate this spot again to save his life. But he also could never remember where he parked his car when he went to the mall.

"We haven't done anything yet, have we?" he asked.

"They've got infrared video cameras," Sarah answered. "Last month they busted a school-board member watering his plants in the nude."

"That sounds like an entirely different kind of crime."

"At least one of those pricks hurt himself," Sarah said,

illuminating a piece of bloodstained fabric and a section of ground saturated with a coagulum of red.

John noticed something else caught in the chicken wire. He asked Sarah to redirect the light. Hanging from one of the wire octagons was a hoop earring imprinted with skulls. Still clipped to its clasp, a piece of an ear.

"Let's get out of here," John said.

"I have to check my other patch," Sarah told him.

"And I have to keep breathing," John said. "I don't like this."

"Don't worry," Sarah said, but John had no choice but to worry, it was genetic.

Sarah kept the flashlight on as they foraged through the brush to her second secret garden. John wondered if he should tell her about his encounter with Balostrasi. He couldn't help feeling his next step would have him tripping over the dope-poacher's dead body. There had been a lot of blood back there. It hadn't all come from one severed ear. John wondered if CAMP's standard procedure was "shoot to kill." It seemed excessive. Newsworthy. But he hadn't read a newspaper in a week. His television was in the closet. Wouldn't the boys at Cal's Palace have mentioned it? Surely the newspaperman would have said something if someone had been recently murdered in the area. It must be a case of vigilante vs. vigilante. But who would be out here crossing Balostrasi's path?

"Whose property are we on?" John inquired.

"It's part of the commune, sort of," Sarah said. "The government can take away your real estate if you're caught growing on your own land, so smaller plots are under our own names while the bulk of 'the outback' is under the name of a cofounder who doesn't grow. He takes a cut from the harvest. Technically it belongs to him, but just on paper."

"What's his name?" John asked, unsure if he would get an answer, not because he would use the information nefariously, but maybe there were other reasons he shouldn't know. Sacred commune vows of silence. Rituals. Sarah could be sparing him the burden of a certain kind of knowledge. Or maybe there were even limits to her honesty.

Sarah turned and lit John's face with the flashlight, looking for signs of recognition as she spoke the name, "Whitward," then stepped through the low-hanging branches to another clearing and plot of budding photosynthesis. Twenty plants, eight to fifteen feet tall. Money growing on trees.

"As in Daryl Whitward?" John said, stunned simultaneously by the name Sarah had spoken and the stalks of marijuana.

"As in Wesley Whitward, his father," Sarah clarified, unsheathing her knife. "But I don't want to talk about it right now."

Seeing the blade, John didn't argue. This wasn't the time or place to insult someone's taste in men. He held open garbage bags while Sarah stuffed them full, hacking away with her knife like she had spent a lifetime in the cane fields of South Florida. John had never seen this type of plant before, a bumper crop from the pages of *High Times*. After tying off the fifth bag, he wondered about the street value. They were dealing with a lot of dime bags here. Not that he was any judge. His only attempt to purchase marijuana had scored him three joints of oregano.

Sarah explained that she had a buyer in San Francisco that bought her product in one lump. She was no dealer selling stems and shake. The commune had their connections, she had her own. Even with her other patch CAMPed, she would make forty grand. If they could get it back up the hill.

Sarah looked over the grounds for fallen buds. John pushed the final plant into plastic, his hands covered with a sticky resin. He was officially a bagman. If the cops came, the excuse of a "nature walk" wouldn't be accepted, not at two a.m. on the side of Mt. Everest with enough product to tour with the Steve Miller Band. With his luck there would be cameras capturing their every move. Suspect number one, female, Caucasian. And suspect number two, blundering onto the screen. "That's him, your honor, the last one to see my Balostrasi alive!"

John wanted to run, but there wasn't anywhere for him to even crawl. Without Sarah, he would be lost anyway. She wasn't going to leave without her crop. Nine bags full. So they started on their journey up the mountain, sacks slung over their shoulders like twin Santas delivering presents to the Furry Freak Brothers. After a few punishing feet, John was ready to cut the contraband loose. He was struggling to follow Sarah's lead, the payload snagging and threatening to tear every third step. He had to create his own path by creating openings in the brush with a well-placed knee, dragging the bundles through the woods after him as he sliced his way through the forest using his shoulder as a dull blade. The only thing keeping him on course was the sound of Sarah humming the theme to "The Brady Bunch." He stopped for a breather, wiping sweat from his brow, trying to get a better grip on the bags.

The woods went silent. Not the kind of silence oceans afforded with their eternal crashing, numbing smaller sounds with the roar and anticipated repetition, nor was it the white noise of traffic or an electric fan. This was a complete absence of sound. The Earth almost ceased to be spinning. John was afraid to move, figuring every animal, redneck, and FBI agent within fifty miles would be able to track him. Inanimate objects seemed to suck a collective breath in an effort to bust him. He curled into a fetal position, remembering a theory that humans started to sleep because it was the simplest way to keep quiet during the night when they were most vulnerable.

He noticed a twig sticking in his arm and pulled it from his skin. It was too dark to see if he was bleeding. He hadn't been speared too deep. John tossed the stick aside to the sound of buckshot on a drum set.

"They're shooting at us!" John yelled.

He began to burrow, hands hurling themselves at the dirt. Sarah shouted something about staying calm, but John was clawing his way beneath the topsoil, half-burying himself in front of the bags of dope. When silence reclaimed the forest, he raised his head. That's when he saw the eyes, two bloodshot orbs as large as owls, glistening wet, with a row of Cheshire teeth beneath them. He tried to form a shape around the eyes, but they disappeared. He stared harder but they were gone. Or watching from another vantage.

"What the fuck?" Sarah screamed. "Are you having some kind of flashback?"

"I heard something," John said.

"You heard a twig snap!" Sarah said, her voice amplifying and warbling in John's ears, then softening and solidifying into a normal tone.

"It sounded bigger," John offered, his own voice playing the same trick, realizing he was under the influence of something. "I panicked."

"No shit," Sarah said, approaching him cautiously, taking his hands in hers.

Marijuana resin clung thick to John's palms, along with a generous sampling of the forest floor. She studied a couple of cuts slashed across his lifeline.

"This stuff's getting into your bloodstream," she said. "Maybe through your pores, maybe through these cuts. You didn't swallow any, did you?"

"No," John said.

"Take deep breaths," Sarah said, setting loose his hands and trudging back to her bags. "Nut up, Squirrel Boy."

John concentrated on his breathing, telling himself there was nothing in the forest except nature; no government agents, no armed criminals, no malicious eyes. Apparently, paranoia didn't impress the chicks, especially when it was linked with hallucinations. He lumbered after Sarah.

When they reached Sarah's truck, John wanted to plant a flag. The hike up had taken longer than the trip down. He hadn't fallen as much, but the strain of holding the bags had sapped him worse than the toppling. Soreness seemed to be the special of the day in Boonville, every day. Tonight's menu also offered assorted greens and a dirt glacé. He swung the sacks into the back of the pickup. Feeling light-headed, he almost collapsed. Stars were fading in a sky that had turned three shades brighter in the last half-hour. John pressed his head to the dew-covered truck. They hadn't encountered any wild animals or narco squads, and despite losing one patch, uncovering a possible homicide, and learning that Sarah still had ties to her ex-husband, the mission was a success. It would just take a few months to remove the dirt from beneath his fingernails.

"One last stop and we're done." Sarah said, tossing her bags alongside John's.

"What?" John said, his body beginning to stiffen. "A little reggae, some rolling papers, we've got ourselves a party."

"I've got to dry, separate, and clean this shit before anybody takes toke one," Sarah told him. "Maybe in two weeks, but I don't torch the profit. And you're cut off."

"That's fine," John said, rubbing his hand across his face but hardly feeling it. "I feel weird."

"Don't worry," Sarah said, seating herself in the truck. "It's a short ride and a potentially big profit. You'll thank me later."

"Can I curse you now?" John asked.

He climbed into the cab, tempted to let his head fall onto her shoulder. But the road was too rocky for a snooze and he became transfixed by the squid mating in the headlights, eight legs times two, tentacled and intertwined with a slick of ink floating between them, drifting into shapes of hearts and diamonds. For a minute, he thought he was having an out-of-body experience, then realized he was staring into the side-view mirror.

Sarah was telling him about a science fiction story she was writing about an alien zoo where humans were kept in a cage that resembled a 7-Eleven. At feeding time, microwavable burritos were dropped into the cage with hot dogs and nacho fixings. The humans lined up and paid for things without knowing why; one guy played cashier, an old woman was a compulsive shelver. But the aliens had gotten things wrong, there were refrigerators full of books, crates of soccer balls, religious artifacts stacked next to cereal boxes and jars of peanut butter. It was similar to apes given a tire to play with instead of indigenous vines. The humans began to understand that they were trapped somewhere other than Earth. The first line was, "The Slurpee machine had been broken for as long as anyone could remember."

It freaked John out. The whole thing. It had to mean something, that the eyes he had seen existed. Sarah was trying to tell him Boonville was an alien zoo. It would explain the inbreeding. But what about half-shirts and Juice Newton? What could explain them? Viruses? Mind control? Was he thinking these thoughts or just thinking he was thinking them? What about the expression "second nature." What was "First nature," or "third nature?" How many natures were there? And why was everything being numbered, "the fourth estate," "fifth column," "seventh heaven?"

John noticed they were outside, walking through another forest, not as dense this time. When did they get out of the car? Dawn was breaking. He could see in front of him, but he had no idea where he was. It was a pattern for him in Boonville, disorientation like a morning cup of coffee. He followed Sarah out of habit. She had her pack and knife and continued to move forward with a purpose. It was enough to warrant John's submission. He smelled something familiar, diluted by the open air. Someone's perfume. Something crunched beneath his foot. He looked down to see he had stepped on a Christmas tree ornament. Why would a tree be decorated in the woods? Especially this time of year? Then he noticed he was standing in another marijuana patch, but in this one the plants were drooping with red bulbs to resemble wild tomatoes. It seemed someone had staked, fertilized, watered, decorated, and then left the weeds to their own demise. The stalks had been hindered by other foliage, but there were still an abundance of buds.

"Whose garden is this?" John asked, disregarding the broken ornament.

John saw something else in the dirt, a mud-caked bottle. He kicked it with his foot. There were several in a row, quart-sized, made of sturdy frosted glass, all covered with dirt. He assumed they had been used for watering purposes.

"Yours," Sarah told him.

"What do you mean?" he asked.

But before Sarah could respond, light caught a label, and John identified the bottle, Gilbey's. Then the fragrance, gin. And finally the gardener, Grandma.

12

"Hold on! Hold on!"

Sarah couldn't help hearing Janis as she urinated on her fingers during her third attempt to fill the metrically-marked plastic beaker that came with the home pregnancy test. She wiped her hands on a washcloth and transferred her pee into one of the test tubes set on the toilet tank in the fold-out cardboard stand. The color was definitely pink. Not a hazy reddish-brown or indeterminate Rothko blotch like the first two. This was irrefutable Science, independent from emotions, unerotic and cold as bathroom tile.

"Hold on! Hold on!"

Sarah remembered how Daryl twisted in ecstasy or whatever it was that filled his body when he came, malice, longing, temporal adequacy, last month when she saw him on the sly for only the third time this year. Not bad for her. They had fucked in his pathetic double-wide trailer—the Double-Dumb, she called it—parked behind the airport. The night had been unbearably lonely before and after they had done the deed, everything pointing her to his trailer, the bourbon she had been drinking, the music on the radio, the wide spaces between the stars. It was inescapable, the destiny of a small town.

Sarah had needed someone to say the words that night, even if they didn't know what they meant or how to express them in a way that she or any other woman in the Western Hemisphere could understand. "I'm gonna cum a huge load for you." What kind of dead-fuck language was that? She wished Daryl could just follow the bouncing ball, kiss her with the kind of passion he had when they were newlyweds. At least he knew half how to touch her, that was better than some anonymous body on top of you, needing to turn off the lights and take one last swig from the bottle before they kicked off their boots. Or didn't. But they had been condomlessly careless, and now Sarah stood in her bathroom like she had been shot and had forgotten to fall down.

Pink.

She slapped the test tubes off the toilet tank and they broke with a tinkle. Urine splashed the shower curtain. The wet facts dripped. An alternate universe unembraced. Nobody whispered sweet nothings into the ear of Science, Sarah was sure of it, amidst her make-shift laboratory of failed results. Daryl would want her to have it too. Just like the last time. There wasn't a chance in hell she was going to tell him, she decided right then and there. This one would have to be taken care of solo.

A hard-to-breathe feeling entered her throat, the first sign of a panic attack. She had been fighting them off for the last few months, nearly fainting when she stepped from a hot bath or stood up too fast. She even borrowed one of Mom's books on the subject and knew to run through the H.A.L.T. list: hungry, angry, lonely, tired? Of course, she answered each question yes. Does it ever stop? She tried to take deep breaths and think about some better place, Hawaii, the Kona Coast, an uncrowded beach at sunrise. A room with a ceiling fan, a well-made bed, and clean sheets. One in a major hotel, not a hospital.

"Hold on," she told herself, reaching for a towel. "Hold on."

She began cleaning up her mess. The test tubes had broken into large enough pieces she could handle with a swath of toilet paper. She crumpled the rack constructed from the box of the pregnancy test and threw it in the wastepaper basket. Her hands were shaking. She wondered why they never showed this on the package. How come they always depicted an antiseptic couple who looked as though they had never had sex, smiling like they had won a new car? Just once she wanted to see a woman in the advertisement, upset and alone. A 16-year-old girl in a high school bathroom, crying. That was the way it had been for her the first time.

With a shudder, she cut her finger and flashed onto an intuitive moment: It would have been a girl. Sarah was struck motionless. She knew this as well as she had ever known anything: a little girl. With Daryl's stupid mouth and her blue eyes.

Sarah collapsed, hyperventilating in a heap of helpless tears. This was three. Too many futures to be stillborn. Sarah remembered the last time she had gotten pregnant, four years ago, and how Daryl had wanted to use that as an excuse to get back together, as if having a child would somehow solve their problems. She was so lost then, she had said she would think about it if he went with her to Planned Parenthood in Ukiah.

"It ain't football, there ain't no strategy," had been his sensitive, rural response. "You have babies and raise 'em. Nobody plans it."

"They do when they're not ready," Sarah had replied.

He said he was ready, and what their relationship needed was a "rally point."

"I'm not ready," Sarah had told him. "Not now. Not with you."

That's when Daryl smacked her. And Sarah forgot he had ever made her happy, that he possessed a good side, and that this violence was nothing other than learned behavior. His father wasn't a redneck, somewhat outdoorsy, but he came from Palo Alto with a degree from Stanford in ecology. He was a gentle man. Daryl was a first-generation redneck, self-taught. He had learned it from Boonville, by choice.

"Tell me when you get your abortion," Daryl had said, as Sarah held her jaw. "I'll go to the Lodge and pass out cigars that say, 'It's dead.'"

She didn't talk to Daryl for a year, except to curse in his general direction. Then the work of Susan B. Anthony, Virginia Woolf, and Mom's whole generation of women's libbers went out the window. Crime of crimes, Sarah kissed the man who had struck her. Even Lisa had a hard time swallowing that one. But nobody knew about their trysts these days. Lisa wouldn't believe her predicament, especially since she had escorted Sarah to the clinic that day of the slap four years ago. Although Sarah had returned the favor previously, when Lisa's boyfriend from Calistoga refused to take her to the hospital for her abortion.

"Ninety-nine percent effective when used correctly," Lisa had lamented the entire trip to Ukiah, leaning against Sarah's truck door, hoping it would accidentally open. "I don't think we even fucked a hundred times."

"It almost makes you rethink abstinence," Sarah replied,

patting Lisa's knee. "Don't worry, you're making the right decision."

To get to the clinic, they had to walk through the Burger Churchers and what seemed to be the entire religious right waving signs and blocking the sidewalk, screaming murderer, baby killer, slut, promising eternal damnation for them both. Sarah didn't know which denomination the Burger Churchers belonged to, but their church was behind the Burger King just off the highway—The Church of Jesus Christ Crucified with a Side Order of Fries. One held a Ziploc baggie of blood and threatened to sully their path, thinking better of it when Sarah closed her fist. There were no volunteer escorts. Sarah had decided long ago "Ukiah" was the Pomo word for "wasteland." Another Burger Churcher with a brood of mayonnaise-faced children, future panty sniffers and dentists, held posters of a mangled fetus with a caption that read, "Why are you killing me?"

The Romans had the right idea, Sarah thought, feed these assholes to the lions.

"Let's talk," a protester offered, holding out his hands to show there was nothing up his sleeve but the Scriptures. "If you don't love your baby, we will."

"How do you know I'm not just getting a checkup?" Sarah asked.

The protester looked from the two women to the rectangle building that seemed to be designed by an architect weaned on Legos, pondering what care the staff inside might be administering, tending to the ailments of the working class, gonorrhea, herpes, a yeast infection that untreated would lead to sterility. He only knew Sarah and Lisa were seeking medical attention probably for something caused by sex, and by the looks of them, out of wedlock!

"You're going to burn," the protester said, matter of factly.

Joyless pains-in-the-ass, Sarah thought. Instead of doing something productive, helping out underprivileged children or checking into the Kama Sutra for themselves, these fanatics were self-prophesying a hell on earth.

"Concubine!" one howled.

"Keep your cross out of my uterus," Sarah responded. "Why don't you go home and make Jell-O."

"Harlot! Whore! Sinner!"

"Ohhh, talk dirty to me some more," Sarah goaded.

"If God made you in His image," Lisa jeered, as a parting shot, "then He must be one ugly son of a bitch!"

They ducked toward the clinic. But the door, painted a daunting shade of orange like it was the threshold of something scientifically unnatural, was locked. There was a note printed on computer paper directing them to an intercom that appeared to have been broken and fixed. Sarah pressed the buzzer.

"Who is it?" a disembodied voice asked.

"Sarah McKay," she answered.

"How can I help you?" the voice said.

"We would like to see a doctor," Sarah said, spotting a surveillance camera's blinking red light.

"And what would this be regarding?" the voice asked.

"This would be regarding health and medicine," Sarah said, not wanting to have this conversation within earshot of the protesters. "This is a clinic, isn't it?"

"Do you have an appointment?" the voice said.

"Yes," Sarah said, beginning to wonder about the volatility of the crowd, feeling their unspoken support for someone going too far, the rhythm of heartbeats inaudibly chanting for a single purpose. More importantly, she was worried about Lisa. This process was uncomfortable enough without reactionary mob hysterics or getting the fifth degree from a Radio Shack speaker. Sarah could tell Lisa was resolved in her decision, although her body seemed to be cringing, eyes filled with hangover sadness. She was no doubt wishing this experience would be over. But Sarah knew it would always be there, bringing weight to her future choices. Good decisions resonate throughout your life as pervasively as bad ones, and with just as much regret.

"Check under the name Lisa Johnson," Sarah told the voice.

"Who are you?" the voice asked.

"I'm a friend," Sarah said, reaching out to put an arm around Lisa's shoulder.

Sarah was ready to leave, pay the extra money, and call a private practice, but the buzzer sounded and she pushed open the door, hearing the hermetic suck of a broken vacuum seal. They walked through a windowless hall to another formidable door where they again had to wait to be buzzed in, this time without further inquisition. The place was one gun turret shy of a fortress.

When they finally entered the waiting area, Sarah was surprised the gauntlet hadn't led them to a police station questioning room: one chair, a bright light, and a pack of cigs. On the contrary, the waiting room was cheery with plants and comfortable furniture. Along the far wall was a coffee table offering a selection of magazines including what had to be the only copy of *The New Yorker* in Ukiah, and ironically, *Woman's Day*.

Sarah was about to give the receptionist a raft of shit for the way they had been treated outside, but saw her workstation was enclosed in bulletproof glass. Cut into the glass was a double-sealed slot for returning the forms clipped onto the clipboards stacked on the counter.

"Sorry about this," the receptionist said. "We've had bomb threats."

"That's all right," Sarah said, certain the secretary must endure harassment on a daily basis. Religious whackos were nothing if not organized, with plenty of gilt crucifixes and bake sales to prove it. They probably had a file on this woman full of information most people wouldn't find the least bit significant or incriminating, lists of movies she had attended, photos of men who had spent the night at her house, suspect toiletries. For sure, the progressive forces out front knew her address, what make of car she drove, and the license plate number. That would be enough to scare Sarah. People who believed in Sodom and Gomorrah, Adam and Eve, and Jonah being swallowed by a whale were capable of anything. Except logical thought.

"Thanks for being here," Sarah said, by way of her own apology.

Forms.

Still sprawled on the bathroom floor, Sarah remembered the paperwork patients had to complete on each visit to the clinic, requiring you to recall every sexual encounter and to linger on all the bad ones, if not actually call the formally consenting partner with the not-so-great news that you had a painful rash or cluster of warts. It was no *Cosmo* quiz. When it had been her turn to fill out the questionnaire, Sarah checked off the methods of birth control she had used; sponge, foam, diaphragm, everything from condoms to "pull and pray." Each scratch of ink recalled memories of awkward moments and broken promises. Sarah realized it was difficult, if not impossible, to kiss someone with your eyes and heart wide open.

One question read, "Has someone ever touched you in a way that hurt, frightened, or made you feel uncomfortable?"

Sarah wanted to know, "Are they asking me if I've ever been in love?"

She wondered if having someone turn out the lights when you wanted them on counted. What about probing fingers? Stalkers? Lying about your name after a one-night stand? Receiving the wrong number on a cocktail napkin? Saying "I love you" and getting a grunt in return? Faking orgasms? The occasional grab-on-the-ass, copped feel, insults from construction workers. The Poobah would definitely qualify as a "yes." So would the Future Primitives, most of Mom's boyfriends, as well as a number of the Waterfall's rituals: drug fests, harvest parties, summer swims. But what about when the moon shone behind the Golden Gate Bridge in the early a.m. radio hours of the Marin Headlands after she had danced with the vaqueros and transvestites at Caesar's Latin Palace in the Mission and some beautiful boy who had never called her again mouthed the lyrics to Bobby Vinton's "Blue Velvet" between bites on her neck and single malt–scented kisses that stung like paper cuts? All she thought was, "Please don't put your disease inside me. Don't love anyone but me."

Sarah wiped her nose on her shirtsleeve and picked herself up off the floor. She decided if she was strong enough to have survived her past, she would make it through this calamity too. Endure, that's what she did best. She would sell her dope, find an apartment in the Bay Area, check out Cal Arts, fill out the grant applications, and follow through. Finish something. She had a hollow feeling in her head and a heightened sense of her surroundings. She splashed water on her face and looked into the mirror to see Mom and Dad staring back, their overlapping image creating a new wrinkle.

Bummer days, Sarah thought, exasperated, reminding herself of Dad during a coke jag, Mom after a run with the reefer and Chablis; "Down on Me Days." There was no need to intentionally repeat this unhappiness. She wanted to find Daryl right away, give him a final fuck-off while she still had the conviction. He'd say something stupid, and it would be easier to leave. She could pack and have her dope ready to go by morning, forgo Ukiah, and set up an appointment on Haight Street where they didn't treat you like a criminal. A reservation at the St. Francis sounded nice for a couple of nights, hot baths and room service. Before departing, she would swing up Manchester Road to see Squirrel Boy and say goodbye, make sure he was in better spirits, not having paranoid visions. What a lightweight. But she should talk, she used to see things in the woods too, sober. Maybe she would invite Squirrel Boy to visit her in San Francisco and have a drink at Tosca. She could use someone to talk to, someone who at least pretended to listen. Sarah wondered what kind of father Squirrel Boy would be. Would it be different if she were carrying his child? She felt guilty for thinking about Squirrel Boy, thinking about anything other than the operation in her immediate future.

Sarah dried her face with the last of the clean towels, then spied the dipstick from the pregnancy test poking from the debris in the wastepaper basket. There was an unborn child curled inside her. She was too old for excuses. The doctor had told her that because of the scar tissue a third abortion would be dangerous if she wanted to have children in the future. She gathered the trash to take out to the garbage. Her decision had been made. Nothing in Sarah's world had ever been pink.

"It's the color of weakness and submission," she said, defending herself from invisible forces. "There's nothing feminine about it."

She drove to the Double-Dumb and found Daryl in his carport underneath his car, a '78 Camaro painted primer gray and held together by Bondo. If Daryl was home, he was either asleep, watching TV, or working on the Camaro. Same as it ever was. The car was more than a hobby, it was a way of life. Every year he bragged about entering it into the open-class race at the county fair, but when the entry date came the car was either up on blocks or out of commission from some "deer swerve," an expression that meant he had an accident while driving drunk, but had been sober enough in the morning to file an insurance claim. The Camaro wasn't a racing car to Sarah, despite the black stripe running the length of its dented body. She used to tell Daryl that instead of an oil company he should find a Scotch tape factory to sponsor him. Once they had made out in the front seat, but she couldn't remember going for a drive. On the occasion when Daryl did get it running, he'd take his dumb-fuck friends to Ukiah with a cooler of beer. He would have another "deer swerve" on the ride back, which would mean six more months of carport. He used to say, "The difference between a Jehovah's Witness and a foreign car is that you can shut the door on a Jehovah," but it was his Japanese truck that got him around, the Camaro remaining as reliable and American as Daryl.

Speak of the devil, Sarah saw his head pop up from beneath the muscle car. After she had got the restraining order, Daryl bought the Double-Dumb, and, in an attempt at home improvement, dug a hole in the driveway in front of it so he could stand while he worked on his car instead of having to lie on his back. But it was just a hole. He hadn't laid cement or put in a set of steps or beams to secure the sides or any amenities other than some planks stolen from a lumber site to stand on. And a shovel to bail sludge. There was no runoff and the hole was deep enough to create a pool of freestanding water in its bottom from rain and seepage. Frogs made comfortable homes. Daryl peed with them. The walls sporadically caved in and Sarah used to worry he would be buried alive. Sometimes she feared he would fill in the hole with her at the bottom of it, the next local to hit national headlines. Each month the hole grew bigger, inching closer to the front steps of the Double-Dumb. Sarah had never spent the night in the trailer even if they had sex until the rooster crowed. The Double-Dumb was not a place she wanted to wake up.

Daryl looked excited, the way he did when he thought he might get some. The grin on his face was wide enough to carve into three pumpkins, the same cross between silly and spooky. He wore a work shirt and held a screwdriver in one of his greasy hands, a beer in the other. There was a rash beneath his eyes, reminding Sarah that he had mixed it up outside the hotel with Squirrel Boy and Pensive Prairie Sunset. Sarah would have enjoyed watching him get stomped by Pensive. There was something untamed in that smile of his, a certain amount of pleasure to be exacted from someone else's suffering that Sarah had always wanted to see knocked off his face. It was his half-smile that she had fallen in love with, the less assured boyish smirk.

Daryl finished his beer, tossing the empty to the back of the hole, pushing up his "T for Texas" baseball cap with the screwdriver, letting his head tilt to the left as if that side of his brain had gotten an idea and the weight of it had thrown off his equilibrium.

Go with your strengths, Sarah thought, even if they're also your weaknesses.

She couldn't help finding him sexy, his strong hands and transparent intentions. She hated to admit it, but men in holes trying to fix things turned her on. Not to mention Daryl's sturdy arms and husky back, his pliability, their heated past, the way he wanted to protect her, his willingness to kill one or both of them in the name of love, and how easy it was to flood his senses by just showing up. She knew most of her affection for Daryl was based upon his need for her. Instead of working on herself, she could focus on maintaining him, her own shortcomings never coming into question. There was always something wrong with Daryl to tinker with, pound out, and polish. He was Sarah's Camaro.

"They always come back," Daryl said, as a greeting.

Sarah knew it, he'd open his mouth and the first thing he said would piss her off. Which *they* was he referring to? The long line of girlfriends that didn't exist? And "always come back"? It was humiliating to think he had taken her visits as personal conquests.

Looking at him, Sarah realized how nice it was going to be to leave Boonville and not have an emotional investment in an ex-husband. The lyrics from an old country song came into mind and she dedicated them to the memory of Daryl, "I've been a long time leaving, but I'll be a long time gone."

"You want to crawl out of your hole?" Sarah asked, standing in the driveway, close to the front end of the Camaro. "So we can talk."

"It ain't a hole, Sarah," Daryl corrected her. "It's a work pit."

The wind blew across the open field of the airport where planes seldom took off or landed. The windsock pointed directly at the Double-Dumb. Only affluent tourists and wine-industry heavies used the strip, with the exception of a couple of old-timers who flew in WWII and Dwight Duchamp who dive-bombed the high school, usually around graduation time, to protest his denial of a diploma from that esteemed institution forty years prior, once dipping too close and taking out the metal shop. Like most events in the valley, it was called an accident, even after Dwight walked away from his flaming craft without apology, saying, "That's my present to the class of '48!"

Daryl's Double-Dumb had been tied down on a cheap plot behind a grove of pine trees planted to shelter a community of suburban-type homes from this very current and the bleak view of the airport. But his trailer was parked too far beyond the hopeful enclave and the prevailing westerlies hit it straight on, causing the screws of the Double-Dumb to rattle like a frightened man's teeth, as if Dwight Duchamp might be flying in on this vindictive draft to claim his diploma.

"You want to go inside?" Daryl asked. "You look nervous."

Sarah hadn't realized that since standing there she had been scraping her upper lip with her bottom teeth, causing a tag of dead skin to curl free. Her lips had already been chapped from drying her dope in the heat of the wood-burning stove, not to mention the countless trips to and from the main house. She licked them with the tip of her tongue. They dried instantly. Wetting them only made it worse, but she couldn't restrain herself. It made her long for the fog of San Francisco, the city's consistent, reasonable weather. She would be there soon if she continued to make smart choices.

"No, I don't want to go inside," Sarah said.

The Double-Dumb's interior was more depressing than the exterior, with its logger motif, dishes in the sink, reeking chew-spit containers, crumbs and hair balls accumulating beneath garage sale furniture. Empty bottles: beer, bourbon, tequila. It was like living in an alcoholic's pancreas. Television droning sports or pornography from the satellite dish, Daryl's primary source of information. Then there was his armoire of firearms.

"I'd rather have twelve men judge me," Daryl used to quote Evel Knievel, who also had a penchant for Colt pistols, "than six of them carryin' me to my grave."

Sarah could handle guns, but it made her nervous when other people did. And no different than any other redneck, Daryl was armed to the teeth. Open boxes of bullets, shotgun shells, and casings were scattered throughout the trailer. The Double-Dumb was the only place where Sarah felt claustrophobic.

"You want to climb down into the work pit?" Daryl asked, Sarah sympathizing with those women who married men on Death Row. "Wouldn't be the first time."

It would be her last though, she thought, the equivalent of hurling herself into her own grave, the Camaro for a headstone, the rattle of a busted timing chain for a eulogy. What did I ever find attractive about this man? But she remembered their walks in high school, beyond the special ed domes; Daryl quiet at her side, not asking any questions, holding her hand in a way that made her feel safe. He would listen to her for hours, going on about Mom and Dad, the Waterfall, how someday she wanted to be the next Gertrude Stein. When she showed him her poems and sketches, he would look from her to them and back again, saying in a gentle voice, "You're good, Sarah." That was the sum total of his criticism. Sarah believed him, catching him looking at her with proud wonder.

Having relocated to the Waterfall from Palo Alto at thirteen, Daryl knew the players in Sarah's life intimately. His father was a business hippie, a sub-sect of the experimental hippies, but Daryl managed to escape the hippie influence by aligning himself with the locals and staying away from the main house. Few linked him to the Waterfall, except fiscally. They knew his father, Wesley, owned the outback, on paper, and everyone on the commune, including Daryl, grew pot. But at sixteen he moved into town, renting a house with Billy Chuck's older brother Buck. After marrying Sarah, he came back to the commune. Following the divorce, he returned to town.

Because of Daryl's intimacies with the Waterfall, Sarah hadn't felt as embarrassed about her upbringing as she did with other men. Daryl protected her from the freaks, including the Poobah, who he once smacked in the head with a post-hole digger. At night in bed, when he was asleep with his body cradling hers, nothing felt more secure. But the division between them became greater, the art vs. ESPN split, and he more than anyone began using the Waterfall against her.

"You and your hippie mother!" he'd say, a whole subtext of uncomfortable knowledge carried with it. Daryl had seen Mom naked, watched her have sex with a number of different men on a number of different occasions. Mom had tried to seduce him. He knew all the drugs Mom had done. How horribly the Poobah treated her. How insane everything was in Sarah's life. The more Daryl condemned Mom and the Waterfall, the harder it became for Sarah to separate herself from them. And through his attacks, Daryl managed to sequester himself from the other residents and actions of the Waterfall, elevating his status to mainstream American.

"I'm moving," Sarah told him.

"You want to park your car out back?" Daryl asked, still hoping for a tumble, acting as if he didn't hear her, or worse, didn't believe what she was saying.

"I'm leaving for San Francisco tomorrow, and I'm not coming back," Sarah said, firmly. "Except maybe for holidays."

Why was she hedging? What holidays? They didn't celebrate Thanksgiving or Christmas on the commune. There were a couple of Hanukkah holdouts, lighting menorahs on the sly, but the only holiday the Waterfall observed was May Day, and that was a drug-filled orgy with everyone dancing naked around the May pole, gobbling laced baked goods. Except for the May pole, no different from any other day. And not exactly why you come home for the holidays.

"What's in San Francisco?" Daryl asked.

Sarah surveyed the flat behind the airport, the Double-Dumb, the satellite dish, the Camaro up on blocks. Daryl in his hole. Describing what was in San Francisco was having to redefine everything, not simply a semantics argument between a hole in the ground and a work pit.

"I'll be in San Francisco," Sarah said, and it seemed the clearest explanation.

"This ain't because of that yuppie, is it?" Daryl asked. "I'd be willin' to apologize for kickin' his ass, unless you're fuckin' him."

"This has nothing to do with him," Sarah said, knowing that wasn't entirely true, but Daryl wouldn't understand if she admitted that John was even one-one-thousandth of the reason for leaving or inserted that he was cute and she could date whoever she wanted. This wasn't about John, it was about her future as the unnamed presence grew inside her and expanded out in front.

"I didn't want you to hear it from someone else," Sarah said.

"You got a phone number or address?" Daryl inquired, but he was really asking if this were more of her unthought-out bullshit.

They would be fucking again in two months, Sarah saw him thinking. Three tops.

"I'll be where I'm at," Sarah replied, but she had let a beat pass.

"San Francisco, huh?" Daryl said, and flashed that smile again. "You know the difference between a guy from San Francisco and a faggot?"

He usually attempted to clean up his act around her. If he wanted to get laid, Sarah demanded he be on good behavior. There were rungs of a ladder to be climbed carefully, flattery, drinks, reminiscence. He was daring her to leave.

"No," Sarah said. "I'm sure you don't either."

"A faggot puts on a condom before fuckin' his pets," Daryl said.

"Am I supposed to laugh?" Sarah asked.

"I don't know," Daryl said. "You don't take me serious, maybe you think I'm funny."

He disappeared for a second, returning with another beer, which he opened by placing the cap's edge on a flat part of the Camaro's engine and slapping it with his fist. He sucked greedily at the foam. Sarah was thirsty. She waited for him to offer her a sip. Daryl took another long drink.

"You look like you're puttin' on weight," he said, and the insult passed because its tone held a casual observation. Sarah had put on weight, something Daryl used to pester her about. He preferred her with "some cushion for the pushin'" as he put it, and no doubt remembered her bulimia, the big meals and short trips to the bathroom. Diet pills, anemia, cottage cheese. Binaca spray for dessert. Back then he wanted her to be healthy and had helped her feel attractive enough to stop vomiting. Now he just wanted her.

"You retainin' water or Twinkies?" he said.

"I'm trying to retain a friendship," Sarah said. "But you're being a prick."

Daryl let his gaze wander to a place on the Camaro's engine. Without setting down his beer, he reached over and attended to it. Substituting a wrench for a screwdriver, he pried at the chassis, leaning into it with his whole body, but making no discernible progress.

Force things until they break, Sarah thought. That's how Daryl tried to fix everything.

"Whatever," she said, knowing that "whatever" was California passive-aggressive for "fuck you."

Maybe in the back of her mind she had hoped Daryl would say the right thing instead of everything wrong. But now she felt sad, bloated, and nauseated, the same way she felt in her bulimia days after eating her favorite meal of meat loaf, mashed potatoes, and a chocolate milkshake. Comfort food that never brought her any. Her eyes welled with tears, body mutinous. She felt like barfing on Daryl, right there in his fucking hole.

"You want to be my friend?" Daryl asked, looking up from

under the Camaro. "Because I'm a good conversationalist? Because we read the same books and like the same movies? Bed buddies is more like it. And look where that leads."

He knew.

"You married me for better or worse, until death do us part," Daryl said, recapping what Sarah believed to be the worst verbal contract of her life. "How many deaths you willin' to rack up?"

Daryl was telling her that this was her decision. If she was willing to scale down her expectations of life, they could work things out. Or maybe that wasn't the point. Maybe they were meant to suffer.

Sarah could see him thinking she would be back after it was over. He could work on his Camaro and drink his beer. They always come back. She had, too. Sarah was as predictable as he was, her pattern just slightly more elliptical. She couldn't blame him for being upset either, having been excluded from the decision when he was willing to father the child. Or do his version anyway, teach it football and how to spit. But Sarah knew she would be the one changing diapers and worrying for the next twenty years, waking up at age fifty wondering who she was and who she could have been. Daryl didn't care, as long as there was beer in the fridge and the Camaro in the driveway.

Sarah had thought about adoption, but she wouldn't be able to give up a baby after carrying it inside her for nine months and then experiencing the pain and elation of pushing eight pounds of life from her own flesh. She didn't want to think about it, or the possibility of never taking part in something that made her fundamentally human, that admitted her into the secret society of her gender. She saw how other women without children were looked upon, sad and incomplete, despite any accolades they achieved. But she had already been a parent, raising herself, and knew she didn't have a taste for it or want her identity, her life's work, to be that of "mother." It was fine for other women, but not her. She wasn't going to have children. She wasn't sure this world deserved more babies, and unlike most women, had no great urge to procreate except around her period, and then she did what she was supposed to do, cry and bleed.

The screen door on the Double-Dumb rattled. Sarah's lips burned. There would be no good-bye kiss. She had no intention of crawling into Daryl's hole. He wasn't going to climb out. There were no halfway points in these matters.

Sarah headed for her truck.

"You'll be back," Daryl said, and threw his beer bottle to the back of the hole.

And there was a moment when Sarah couldn't imagine a life beyond Boonville, the Waterfall, growing dope, good ideas and poor follow-through, drinking with Lisa, Mom blaring the feminist hits, the Poobah and Future Primitives, grapes and rolling hills, rednecks and migrant workers, rendezvous at the Double-Dumb. Feeling trapped. Her life had been full of these paralytic instances, an ammo clip of misfired momentum, shooting out in rapid succession a series of blanks that kept her pinned in no man's land.

"They always come back," Daryl said.

"Fat fucking chance," thought Sarah.

13

Waiting. Between the slamming of a car door and the next visceral response to the Earth's indecipherable spinning was a lot of waiting. John had called Blindman and set up a meeting for him to purchase Grandma's gin-scented homegrown, but recalling their prior conversation about the importance of time and how the over-the-counter drug addict was clockless, internally and externally, it came as no surprise that he was late.

In Miami, John's marketing colleague Bean Bean used to say "What could be better?" whenever he was left in the lurch. Most of Bean Bean's waking hours seemed to be filled with what John called DMV moments, stuck in traffic, lines at the bank, getting stood up by dates. But Bean Bean claimed the best experiences in life came unexpectedly at baseball games between innings or riding the bus watching the humanity parade pass by.

"How long can you come?" Bean Bean was fond of asking anyone unfortunate enough to be cornered by him, everyone finding him as dull as the tedium he reveled in, the lectures he gave near the water cooler on peasant uprisings in Spain from 1647 to 1683 or something equally without context or applicability: rainfall in the Eastern Bloc, the muffler size of foreign cars during the sixties, Brazilian tax law. "You better enjoy the foreplay, eh muchacho."

"You have to believe the small truths over the big lies," was the way John's grandma had put it, adding, "Only boring people get bored. Life may be tedious, but not if you brought a book."

Taking Grandma's advice, John flipped through her Emily Dickinson, and read "There's a certain Slant of light." That was the reason people hated waiting, the somber time it allowed for reflection. It wasn't just the lack of substance surrounding an incident, but the insufficiency of the event itself. The event of their lives. John realized that most people enjoyed being preoccupied, doing the mental equivalent of folding laundry, stuffing hours full of neat piles. The doubtful and difficult kept at a distance. Idle hands may be the tools of the devil, but John was convinced an intentionally idle mind was the work of a higher force for evil, mediocrity.

Grandma claimed everyone had an invisible lightbulb above their heads waiting to shine when they got an idea, just like in the cartoons. For most people, it never turned on. Some flicked the switch after losing a loved one or having a near-death experience, others discovered themselves in unbearable straits, and, tired of themselves and their situation, they groped in the dark for the switch, trying to engage. Then there were those that always had the tungsten burning, churning amperage into light and purpose, constant as Venus in a summer night's sky. Often you could see infants crying from the brightness in their eyes, predestined to do great things, already wanting to know reasons. Their problem would be storing the stimulus, finding outlets, and the magician's maxim, which John thought Blindman would agree with, if he ever arrived, "The more you see, the less you know."

John himself was often overwhelmed by flashes of light that froze him against walls of information like an atomic shadow. The worst for him was "the third day sober." After his binge and hallucinatory experience on the side of Greenwood Ridge, he had again experienced the phenomenon that occurred when his mind was done occupying itself with survival, leaving him with a calm that carried with it the sorrow of every Sunday evening that ever pointed toward the confusion and emptiness of another Monday morning, and the time in between, when the rent was coming due, and unmade phone calls piled up, letters were left unwritten, sentiments unspoken, conversations that only occurred in his head, and somebody else had moved away across town or into another way of life, or marriage, or divorce, or a dead-end job, or financial duress, or addiction. The third day sober was a summary of those things, namable and unnamable, that had caused him to pee the bed and suck his thumb as a child, create imaginary friends, and talk to himself. The desire not to get up in the morning, to fake sickness. It was a dark spot in the back of his brain that floated forward across his mental health. The sum total of himself that didn't add up.

In a way, the third day sober was like experiencing Grandma's squirrels; individually they were negligible, their stern disgust dismissible as a minority opinion, but as an army they were crippling. Why else would someone carve so much scorn into so many pieces of wood unless they too were paralyzed by the tremendous amount of evidence flooding in, fingering them as guilty of some unidentifiable crime, the continual chant of insufficiency that becomes the song you can't get out of your head? You begin to believe in it, rely on it, hum it while you work. Your mantra of inadequacy.

Each squirrel also seemed to be a science experiment for Grandma, a frequency exercise in which she charted the same answer of quantum guilt. The only way to cope with the eternal accusations was to make peace with the known facts. And on the third day sober you had to do something constructive: jog, write, clean the toilet. Make a beginning. Otherwise, you would be back counting the days all over again. Maybe for that reason, every third day sober Grandma had created the habit of whittling a squirrel. But looking at the plague of wooden vermin, the psychosis etched into their expressions, John doubted Grandma had ever lined up that many sober days.

John checked the closet where he had stored the bags of Grandma's dope, stems and branches poking holes in the green plastic. According to Sarah, everyone in the valley grew dope. It was as common in Mendocino County as planting grapes. No big deal. Maybe not for her, John agreed, but it was a leap for him. And you couldn't deny the presence of a criminal element in this particular growth industry, guys like Balostrasi lurking about, whether you thought hemp should be legalized or not. He didn't know why he was obsessing about Balostrasi. He guessed it was because the only people who didn't worry about breaking the law were criminals.

At first, John didn't want the twenty plants in Grandma's patch. But then Sarah had told him it was worth thirty grand. She would confirm the quality with a telephone call to Blindman. On that basis, they had set a price. Of course, with Blindman, it was sight unseen. Blindman would get his wifeback to do the tiresome work of drying and sorting while she was making his No-Contact.

Maybe lace a few joints for himself in the process. John couldn't imagine anybody wanting a more enhanced high from the marijuana. When he had returned home from the harvest, he had spent the remainder of the night contemplating his cleaning products, stacking his Wisk bottle on his box of Tide, and then his dishwashing soap on top of that, along with a teepee of green and yellow scrub pads, and a bar of Irish Spring soap. He rearranged the cleaning agents until secret messages began to appear. Then he scrubbed the grout in his bathtub, fighting an overwhelming desire to hear the Allman Brothers. The next morning, he thought about dumping the stash or giving it back to Sarah, but finally he drove to the hotel and asked Hap for Blindman's real name, Jerry Parish, which John thought was surprisingly normal. He called Information for the number, and kept a bud for a day when he was bored and the cabin was dirty.

At the hotel, after he had requested Blindman's name, Hap had noticed his red hands. He kidded John about the intensity of Braille lessons. John slurped his cappuccino and asked if Hap had seen Sarah. But he could tell Hap was connecting the dots, putting together the parallelogram; Blindman, Squirrel Lady, Sarah, Squirrel Boy. Someone was selling dope. And John was making it clear someone was sampling the product in too-large quantities.

"Nope, I ain't seen her," Hap had told him. "But Billy Chuck said she was out at Whitward's when he went to borrow one of them blooper videos."

"Blooper videos?" John had said.

"Blunders and foul-ups," Hap had explained. "There's one goin' around of celebrity porn bloopers; Chuck Berry peeing on a girl, Elvis with six cheerleaders and a monkey. That butt-ugly kid with the red hair used to be on a show about a family. Somebody filmed him with a transsexual."

John didn't know what Hap was talking about. What butt ugly redhead on a show about a family? Throw a cop into the mix with a buxom blonde, and that described half of prime-time television.

John was more concerned about Sarah's connection to her ex-husband. Why were the divorced couple talking? Did it have to do with Daryl's father and the Waterfall's "outback"? What was a redneck doing growing dope on a commune? John had been so disoriented during the harvest, he wasn't sure if Grandma's crop had also been on Waterfall land. Maybe there was a hippie crime syndicate and he would have to pay tribute? Maybe Sarah was working her deals through Daryl? Or maybe she was just working things out? She seemed adamant about her contempt for her ex-husband, but John knew enough about women to know he didn't know enough about women.

"The wife likes the ones where weddin' cakes slide off tables and cats fall into toilets," Hap had continued. "Some folks got other tastes."

"Do you know what Sarah was doing there?" John had queried, trying to skip over the video conversation.

"Same old same old," Hap had replied. "Daryl was fussin' with his Camaro, tryin' to get it ready for fair. They were arguin' and Sarah stormed off. Billy Chuck said Daryl looked too pissed to ask to borrow a video, so he came here and I lent him one from my Chuck Norris collection."

John had tried to put the information into working order. He wished Sarah had a telephone so he could call her. It was a long drive to the Waterfall to discover she wasn't home. He didn't know where she lived up there either. Not to mention, he might not be welcome. He had opened his mouth too much already: Daryl was due to pay him a visit. He'd postpone contact with Sarah until after he finalized the deal with Blindman.

"What you want with her?" Hap had asked. "Don't say business or pleasure, Squirrel Boy. No man could be that dumb."

John thought about the mistakes he could have avoided by taking other people's advice and what he had learned doing things the hard way. The strangest aspect was not having Christina's vote cast into the mix anymore, leveling optimism or solidifying his confidence, supplying an excuse and place to point his finger if things went wrong. Her answer to any impasse was to scream insults and withhold sex. His father, on the other hand, also part of John's morality meter, made his decisions based on what he thought Ronald Reagan would do in a similar situation, being a fan of both his films and anti-Communist work. Before John left Miami, his father had taken to describing his choices as "executive decisions," as if Reagan's two terms in office had somehow further validated his judgment. John's mother blustered at the fringe of the decision-making process like a poorly funded lobbyist. Both would be horrified to learn John was involved in a dope deal. His father would shake his head in embarrassment and disgust on the confirmation that Grandma had grown marijuana. The Gipper would not have approved.

"I want to talk to her about something," John had said, as a woman with nothing in her glass but orange juice pulp beckoned Hap for more bubbly.

Hap moved to refill her glass. The hostess stepped into the bar and called for a table of five. Although John had been drinking coffee, everyone else in the bar was getting sloshed on red wine and mimosas. It was eleven-thirty. Light flooded through the front windows of the hotel, a beautiful day. John didn't want to think about these tourists on the winding roads of highway 128, swerving in pursuit of the perfect pinot.

"That's what the rapist told the deaf girl," Hap had replied, catching John off guard. "Don't start dealin' that shit, Squirrel Boy. Or start smokin' it either. They call it dope for a reason. No shame in being a traditionalist, stay with the bottle. Your Grandma didn't leave you her place for you to become a pothead, otherwise she would have left rolling papers instead of them squirrels."

"I don't smoke marijuana," John had said, unoffended by Hap's paternal tone.

"I don't care if you're shovin' it up your ass in the shape of the First lady," Hap had informed him. "I've lived here long enough to see the signs and know the long-term effects. They ain't what you'd expect."

Hap had told John that aside from losing your volition, the worst side effect of smoking dope was that it turned you into a neat freak; the image of a messy room belonged to teenagers, it didn't apply to adults. He knew people who couldn't roll a joint without vacuuming first. They all owned white carpeting too. Marijuana made you paranoid, he had confirmed, but mostly of spills. You became anal retentive and interested in a supreme order, except the supreme order didn't extend much beyond your sock drawer.

"Makes your feet smell like moldy bread too," Hap had added. "Not a lot of people know that because serious pot smokers get a kitten to cover up the stench."

John had assured Hap he would never become a habitual pot smoker if for no other reason than he didn't want the responsibility of a pet.

"Never say never," Hap had said. "You fall in with the wrong folks, it don't matter if you're allergic to cats or Carlos Santana, things take care of themselves."

"It's a subculture I don't have much connection with," John had said, uncertain whether he was fooling himself or lying outright. There he was, jacked on caffeine while contemplating the stultifying effects of his third day sober, and in his next breath, asking for the name of a drug dealer. He had recently been stoned out of his gourd while taking part in two dope harvests in one night, falling for one of the gardeners and related to the other. And if Balostrasi didn't resurface, John was ominously the last person to see him alive. Or the second to last. So despite a gag reflex to the trimmings and trappings of the stereotypical pot smoker, some might consider John to have more than a minor connection with the subculture.

"Don't take up poker, Squirrel Boy," Hap had said, before assisting another customer. "You ain't got the face for it."

Later, as John rethought Hap's caution, he heard a car in his driveway, followed by footsteps on his porch. Blindman filled the doorway, holding his squirrel cane in one hand and a shopping bag in the other. In place of his white clothing, he wore a Hawaiian shirt with a yellow parrot on the right shoulder and a pair of blue-and-green-striped pants. He sported the same black sunglasses. It was a tourist's outfit, one looking for a gay bar in Tahiti.

"You ready to do business?" Blindman said, addressing the door frame two feet to John's left.

John looked past Blindman to the car in his driveway, a late model Chrysler with a figure slouched behind the wheel, a woman either fiddling with the radio or intentionally leaning out of his sightline. John thought it must be Blindman's wife.

"I was ready two hours ago," John replied, returning his attention to Blindman's outfit. "What were you doing? Looking for something special to wear?"

"Why do you say that?" Blindman asked, glancing over his shoulder in the general direction of his car. "I'm wearing white, ain't I?"

John saw the slouching woman shift in her seat. She looked at John and then the totem squirrels. She kissed something in her hand and begin to pray. Blindman's grip tightened on his cane. John could see the invisible world sending him signals, the Morse code inside sarcasm, the warning in a delayed response, the broken message of a stutter. Blindman was seething. He appeared ready to tap a course back to his car. The figure in the front seat reached over to the passenger side and locked the door.

"Of course you're wearing white," John said, and Blindman seemed to relax. "I've never seen you in anything else but an umpire's mask."

"Sorry about the other day," Blindman said. "Things haven't been the best on the home front. I'm getting ready for a run with some Robitussin. Either that or I'm calling Immigration and getting a new wife."

Again Blindman turned to where he thought his wife had parked, but was actually staring in the direction of the woods. John wondered if certain reflexes were instinctual and you performed them even if you didn't have the senses to back them up, like trying to scratch the itch of an amputated leg. There was a threat in Blindman's gesture, but what was he going to do? Pin the tail on the donkey?

"Come in, Blindman," John said, taking a step back into the cabin.

Blindman tapped past the threshold to the couch in the living room, knocking over several squirrel sculptures on his way. John shut the door. Blindman made himself comfortable while John reset the statues. John sat down in a chair opposite his guest.

"Squirrel Boy, I believe you have ten trash bags of Edna's product and it's as good as Sarah says it is, and in return, I have thirty grand," Blindman said, recapping the deal. "But if you're trying to pull a fast one, recording this conversation or trying to shortchange or blackmail me in any way, I'll have you killed faster than you can say, 'Who was that fat Spic with the knife?'"

John hadn't considered those options, except in regard to their being used against him. He wasn't going to say anything. He figured Blindman wouldn't either.

John's father wouldn't have approved of his son's trusting nature. "Never put all your cards on the table," he used to say. "Something is worth what you get for it." When John had refused to play their stock market game anymore, his father took him to work to get him interested in sales. For such an unscrupulous guy, his father's office sure was crappy. It was then that John realized there were other ways of knowing, the threadbare confidence in the cut of your suit, the frame surrounding your wife's photo, the cadence of your voice. His father oozed the fumes of failure.

"I'm presuming you'd rather not have me make a phone call to Miami," John said, hoping Blindman couldn't smell bluff. "Anything strange happens, it's your ass and the price of a plane ticket."

Dueling tough guys. But whereas Blindman might have some south-of-the-border connection to do his dirty work, John would have to do it himself or call Bean Bean and try to set up an opportunity for him to bore Blindman to death, arrange what seemed to be an innocent luncheon and then unleash him over dessert with a speech on farm reports during the Truman era or the history of slippers.

"I'd expect nothing less," Blindman said. "I'm easily found."

With that gentleman's agreement, Blindman owned a permanent part of John's guilty conscience.

Leafing through the seventh envelope, each containing fifty bills with the face of Andrew Jackson looking blankly to his left, John realized he had never had this much cash in his hand before. The previous high had been 6,200 dollars, which he had carried on his person for two hours after he and Christina had withdrawn the amount from their savings to buy a used car. He had taken the wad from the bank's envelope, doubled it over and secured it with a rubber band, and then slipped it into the pocket of his khakis to pretend it was walk-around money. He put a ten at the center and went to eat breakfast. He had a secret crush on a waitress, sexily full-figured and unflappable, who never gave John more than a refill on his coffee. For some reason he wanted to impress her. He knew she wouldn't be impressed by a large sum of money, but maybe by the mystery surrounding where it had come from, a layer of intrigue suggesting John was a complex character. It was a careless move, even at John's breakfast nook where the toughest customers ordered eggs Florentine. But he felt like Scarface flashing the roll, until the waitress casually said, "Buying a used car today?"

John was up to twenty thousand, stacking the envelopes on the coffee table, when he thought about where he was going to hide it. He couldn't put the money in the bank, the IRS would think it was unclaimed inheritance. Coffee cans in the backyard seemed too retro. There weren't that many inventive hiding places thieves didn't know about, under the bed, in the Bible, a shoebox. If you had any idea about the person you were robbing, you knew where the money had been hidden. There was an energy that drew you to that hollowed brick above the mantel. The same reason the most common combination for a briefcase lock was 666. The feng shui of secrets.

In college, John had friends that raided dorm rooms for pornography. Nine out of ten times they found it beneath the mattress. Then it was the embarrassing question of what that student had found arousing; *Playboy*, *Hustler*, *Juggs*. *National Geographic* photos of starving pygmies. The more off-beat it seemed, the more difficult it was to find; a tribute to the link between the sexual imagination and shame. In one room, they found a folder of historic pictures of Chairman Mao bathing in the Yangtze along with a specialty Asian men's magazine called *Yellow Inches*, a tube of Vaseline and a package of plastic forks carefully hidden in an empty typewriter case. Someone knew what he liked. It was either the design major or the foreign exchange student from Austria. John never went on the raids and didn't purchase pornography he felt he had to conceal. Daryl's sex blooper video was safe. John was strictly a *Sports Illustrated* swimsuit issue man, hidden in plain sight, just creased and kept around for an extra couple of months.

"It's all here," John said, finished with his counting. "Do you want to test the product?"

"No way of me telling until I get it separated and dried," Blindman said. "It's about trust, Squirrel Boy. Get me a drink. We'll close this thing."

"What would you like?" John asked, returning the envelopes to the shopping bag, still uncertain where he was going to hide the money, but the problem of having too much cash wasn't something to complain about.

"Edna had a bottle of Germain-Robin in the cabinet above the refrigerator," Blindman said. "We used to have a belt to finish our business. It was her favorite."

"What is it?" John asked, moving to the kitchen.

He didn't like Blindman knowing more about the contents of his cabin or Grandma than he did. He hoped the bottle wasn't there. Blindman would realize he couldn't lay claim to memory in John's home. He also hoped Germain-Robin wasn't gin because unless gin was ice cold with a Greek festival's worth of olives in its midst, he couldn't stand the taste. Or the smell.

"It's brandy from Ukiah," Blindman answered. "Supposed to be the best in the States. They serve it at the White House."

John found the bottle. Above the name Germain-Robin was printed the word, 'reserve.' He opened the cork and sniffed the caramel-colored liquid.

"I thought Grandma's favorite was gin," John said, now looking for glasses.

"That was every day," Blindman answered, as John set the bottle and glasses on the table. "This was special occasions."

John didn't want to hear any more about Blindman and Grandma's special occasions. He poured what remained of the brandy into the glasses and handed one to Blindman who stuck his nose into the drink, then began swirling the liquid.

"Needs to warm up," Blindman proclaimed. "You don't send your children off to school without putting clothes on them."

Blindman leaned back into the couch holding his glass like it was a tin cup full of pencils. John didn't know whether he should slug his back and tell Blindman to do the same or wait to savor his grandma's favorite drink. Maybe it would take the bad taste from his mouth knowing she preferred something with a little more complexity and style than bargain gin.

"You going to do any gardening next year?" Blindman asked. "Read a couple issues of *Sunset* magazine and the *Anarchist's Cookbook*, and you could set up a fine future for yourself."

"I'm not planning on it," John said, whose plan was not to plan anything for a while. "This was a one-time deal."

"If you develop a taste for the easy green," Blindman said, "you'll develop a green thumb."

"I don't mind working," John answered, and it was a good thing because he was no trust-fund baby. Forty grand of inheritance, twenty plants and a thousand squirrel sculptures was hardly a legacy to insure a secure future. But planting and tending a crop of marijuana seemed like more work, not to mention stress, than it was worth. He'd rather punch a clock.

"Think of it as a civil rights issue," Blindman suggested. "Performing a community service in the face of tyranny."

John tried to rationalize growing dope in this light but it wasn't the same as running a clean needles program, supplying AIDS testing in poor neighborhoods, or donating time at the YMCA. None of which he had ever done, but was more inclined to participate in than farming cannabis for justice. He felt the freedom to cultivate marijuana was the sort of single issue that had already garnered too much focus, draining energy from pressing issues and larger problems. What was the end result anyway, smoking a joint? It was like worrying about suicide being outlawed, people were going to take the leap if they wanted to. There was no need spending your life building tall platforms for them to jump off.

"Not my battle," John stated. "I'll sign a petition but I'm no permanent supplier."

"What am I supposed to do?" Blindman pleaded. "Edna's gone, CAMP's killed my other perennials, and your pal Sarah's leaving town. If you can't count on hippies for grass anymore, who can you trust? I'll be back making opium from Cost Plus poppies."

"Sarah's leaving town?" John said, skipping over the question of opium production. "Where's she going? When? How do you know?"

"Who woke you up?" Blindman said.

John had questions for Sarah, not to mention an extracurricular interest, despite the warnings and understanding that he needed time to reconcile his relationship with Christina, half the length of the relationship according to what he had gleaned from her woman's magazines. Three and a half years of soul searching. Christina was already rebounding with Good Neighbor Michael. Why shouldn't he start the healing process?

"How do you know Sarah's leaving?" John repeated, thinking he was going to be left having to get a shrink and keep a dream journal.

"Word is she's pregnant and moving to San Francisco," Blindman explained. "I heard she ain't having the bambino. Cutting two cords with one snip."

The report didn't seem right, even if it was a shock to John's infatuation. How many people had distorted the story before it had reached Blindman's ears? Leaving? Sarah had said she wanted to go, but that was quick. Maybe it had something to do with her talk with Daryl? Why hadn't Hap told him? Was this the evening edition of the news? But if it was true, no wonder Daryl was jealous. John had to admit, he didn't know Sarah very well. But pregnant? She certainly wasn't showing.

"Everybody should grow up once in a lifetime, Squirrel Boy," Blindman said.

"Who's the father?" John asked, and noticed he had knocked back his drink without tasting or toasting anything. Germain-Robin my ass, he thought, moving his tongue to search for remnants of Grandma's favorite flavor, a fading burn of the alembic brandy in his throat tasting like another shot of something. John thought better than to refill his glass; no use creating the need to start counting days sober. The bottle was empty anyway.

"I'm assuming it's Daryl," Blindman said. "Maybe somebody got her up at the Waterfall? I'm certain there's more than one trying. It ain't yours, is it, Squirrel Boy? You better looking than folks say, a lover not a fighter?"

"It's not mine," John said.

"Cheers then," Blindman said, raising his glass to John's empty one. "Otherwise you'd be blowing that money I gave you on child support."

John waited for Blindman to finish his drink. He decided he would make a trip to the Waterfall after his guest left. He knew it was none of his business, but John believed that he and Sarah had a real connection, something beyond the present circumstances. But if Sarah was carrying Daryl's child, paying her a visit wouldn't be a move in the direction of self-preservation. He'd have to be careful. Like Hap had told him, "Leek bee'n."

"It's a wrap," Blindman said, drink finished. "You mind helping me load the bags into the car?"

"They won't all fit into the trunk," John told him. "You want to make two trips?"

"Just stuff the rest into the back seat," Blindman answered. "Folks will think I'm making a dump run."

John did as he was told, having his own bad decisions to worry about.

On Blindman's command, his wife popped the trunk and helped John heft the bags from the cabin into the vehicle. John said, "Hello," but she ignored him like she had been ordered not to speak. Or maybe she was scared that John possessed the supernatural power of the squirrels. On their first trip to the cabin, John heard her mumble "Dios mio!" upon seeing the hundreds of carvings. After looking sideways at John, she took a rosary from her pocket and kissed it.

Blindman waited in the passenger seat looking as absurd as the parrot on his shirt. With the dope packed into the backseat, there was no view through the rear windshield. Blindman's wife didn't seem to care, stealing another nervous glance at Blindman. For a second, John thought she was going to crack a smile at her brightly dressed husband, but she started the car and made a three-point turn. Before leaving, she looked at John and made the sign of the cross.

"Think about next year," Blindman called from the car. "Keep the tradition alive."

"No way," John said, flanked by the gigantic squirrels. "See you later."

"Not if I see you first," Blindman yelled.

John heard him laugh. The unlikely couple drove away in a cloud of dust.

14

John made his way up Greenridge Road toward the Waterfall commune with a couple of wrong turns and only a few parts shaking loose from the Datsun, nothing so important that he felt the need to stop: a hub cap, a windshield wiper, a chunk of the rear end. He thought he had fixed his headlights but when he flipped on the hi-beams, the left one pointed into the trees, spotlighting squirrels. Driving slowly, he avoided the deer and rabbits that ran onto the road from the forest. He located the glass yurt near the inverted Atlas sculpture and parked next to the found-art heap, which the Datsun blended into seamlessly. John saw a trail not wide enough for a vehicle, leading to a building lit in the distance. He hiked toward the light.

The first person he encountered on the deck of the main house was a naked woman with wild blonde hair and pendulous breasts, crawling on her hands and knees. Trying to act cavalier, John asked her if she had lost a contact lens. The woman glowered at him. She had definitely lost something. Not only was it odd to be naked on all fours, outside, at night, but it was far too cold for that sort of behavior. John could see his own breath and steam misting near the woman's orifices.

His first question having been ignored, he politely inquired the way to Sarah's cabin. The woman barked twice and began to pee, in no particular direction. John watched urine dribble down the side of her leg, reminded of his first sight of a woman's pudenda; he was nine years old at Billy Fulbright's house. He went to use the bathroom in Billy's parents' bedroom and found Mr. and Mrs. Fulbright locked in a love embrace. John didn't quite know what the physical in-out in-out meant. It was still humping to him, and nobody used the word "hump" once they knew its definition. Mr. Fulbright was behind Mrs. Fulbright, graciously saving John the sight of his penis, both of them panting with the expression of stumbled race horses. Mrs. Fulbright stood, and there it was, coming down the home stretch, a length out in front; Mrs. Fulbright's sunshine. She shrieked. It would be years later until John saw another woman's connie in the flesh and never would it seem so vague and forbidden. But more troubling was how he incorporated Mrs. Fulbright's scream into his idea of sex; it turned into an anxiety of being caught. John was certain someone other than he and his partner were coming. The first play of foreplay was to lock all doors. He wouldn't do it with anyone else nearby or if bedroom walls seemed thin. But the final effect was whenever someone mentioned sex, he still thought of Billy Fulbright's parents. Now this naked hippie woman on her knees was also going to be lodged in his memory like an insoluble dream.

"Can I help you?" a deep voice queried.

"Yes," John replied, before seeing it was the giant who called himself Aslan that he had seen acting strange at the Boontberry Health Food Store. He was barefoot, wearing the same sarong, and his eyes were as glazed as two donuts. In his hands, he held what appeared to be a bushel of rabid weasels, clawing and squirming.

"I'm sorry, I found her like that," John said, referring to the naked girl, deciding the best approach to the giant would be to apologize for his presence, immediately, and as often as possible.

"She's beautiful," Aslan said. "Don't you want to take hold of her and push yourself inside? Feel her buck and squeal? Doesn't she sing to something animal in you, an ancient calling?"

John didn't answer. He was thinking about how he had made a series of bad decisions that had culminated in this final mistake of driving to the Waterfall commune.

"You can't reason away instinct," Aslan told him. "We are the dominant sex, designed to spread our seed."

"I'm looking for Sarah McKay," John said, and even the naked girl looked nervous in the presence of the giant. "But I can go."

"There is something special about a female on the verge of becoming a woman," Aslan continued, and John saw the giant was bleeding at the wrists from weasel bites and weasel scratches. "It takes a man who has tasted the cycle at every spoke to understand her natural self. We are men and the Earth holds our destiny if we listen to its rhythms: fire, water, air. Women are trained to hear those rhythms and follow those messages with their bodies. Men turn deaf ears to their natural calling. We should feel no guilt for what we do to the flesh. It is just a boundary for our conscience alone. And our conscience is not our soul."

John was beginning to pray for some David to appear with a slingshot when a naked man crawled from the main house. He made his way slowly across the deck to the naked woman and sniffed at her brown eye. Then he barked. To John's dismay not very fiercely, and not at the giant. Sensing something amiss, the naked man looked up to see Aslan. A weasel thrashed loose from his hand and scurried into the woods. The naked man started to back away. The woman followed suit, leaving John flexing the muscles of his bladder alone on the deck with the giant.

"If you kill a man," Aslan said, taking a mammoth step toward John, "all that is required is to return his body to the Earth."

The giant's face twitched. He shrugged his shoulders and blinked. John was reminded of his father's Parkinson's. Something in the giant had also gone haywire, but John guessed it was pharmaceutical, not biological.

"I've put travelers into the ground without ceremony," Aslan said, speaking faster and past John, not just above his head because he was taller, but addressing his words to the mountaintop. "I am not the son of God. I will not forgive those who trespass against me. I have boundaries that won't be crossed. If you steal from me, I will take from you what is most precious and return you a poor man to the dirt."

John thought about the recently disappeared Balostrasi. It wouldn't have surprised John to notice his earring hanging from Aslan's lobe or to see that the Italian's blood had been splattered across his sarong. It also wouldn't have shocked him if the giant used his skull for a porridge bowl and started shouting, "Fe fi fo fum!"

"A thief steals nothing of value," Aslan said, words seeming to rise up from Middle Earth as he took another step toward John. "To feel a person inside is what they desire, but they reach for objects instead of flesh. They touch the conscience, not the soul, and die without knowing either."

"Dad," someone called from the main house, halting Aslan's progress. "Can you help me with my math homework?"

A boy appeared in the main house doorway wearing a hooded sweatshirt and unlaced basketball shoes. He had a large forehead and not enough hair. His hands were the paws of a puppy who would someday grow into a big dog. They held an opened textbook. He seemed unafraid, although leery of his father.

"What did I tell you about interrupting, Raven," Aslan scolded. "Can't you see I'm in the middle of something?"

The middle of what? John wanted to know.

"You said you'd help me with my homework," the boy whined, picking at a patch of acne beneath his ear.

"I'm working, Raven," his father countered, thrusting his hands forward as proof.

Which, for John, still didn't explain the weasels.

"Do you have any idea how many children I have?" Aslan said. "I can't play favorites."

"What about Basil and Radicchio?" Raven asked, as if he had decided to order a salad.

"Those two are at a special age," Aslan answered. "Remember the bedtime stories I used to tell you?"

Raven looked ashamed, cowering into himself with the humble body language of a boy half his size. It was then that John identified the most disturbing aspect of Aslan; he was "the man at the end of the block." The dark presence in the shingled house his mother had told him to beware of as a child. No rides, no candy, no games of "I'll show you mine, if you show me yours." Certainly, no bedtime stories. Physically they were different; "the man at the end of the block" was hardly a giant except in the minds of the children on John's street. He had been a pale specimen who defied the Florida sun by wearing dark suits and never sweating. He sat in his weed-ridden front lawn reading books wrapped in covers he fashioned from brown paper bags. His house was the first to be egged on Halloween. One day he moved. A fat woman with cats took his place. The end of the block was no longer off limits.

"What would you learn if I did your homework for you?" Aslan asked. "You have to become your own man."

John's initial reaction was to ask if he could help Raven with his studies, but he didn't want to overstep any more boundaries or deal with any more naked hippies doing whatever it was that naked hippies did in the privacy of their homes. He could hear Janis

Joplin music coming from inside the building. He couldn't resist looking through the door that Raven had propped open with his foot. He saw a leather couch and a mural painted on the wall that seemed to commemorate the building of the structure, complete with a figure twice as large as the rest of the barnraisers. In the center of the room was a tree the building had been constructed around, only the trunk visible, the top disappearing through the roof. There was a crafts fair of mobiles, weavings, pottery, and mosaics. Paintings filled the wall adjacent to the mural. A couple of hippies sat reading magazines, *The New York Review of Books*, and a foreign *Vogue*, in armchairs built from telephone books and clear packing tape, one drinking a Diet Coke, the other smoking a joint. The naked woman John had met earlier was splayed on the floor with the naked man in a Greco-Roman wrestling pin. Another woman, clothed and standing, spritzed houseplants with an atomizer. Everyone was engrossed in their own activity, oblivious to the others.

"Are you the Squirrel Boy?" Raven asked.

For the first time, John felt like he might come out of this alive. Aslan was still standing too close for comfort, but the giant had become preoccupied with the crease in his arm near his elbow, staring deeply into the fold.

"Yes, I am," John answered, nobody else seizing on this opportunity for further introductions. "I'm looking for Sarah McKay?"

"She's leaving," Raven said, looking at his father. "I think she went to Mendocino with Lisa to say goodbye to somebody."

If she were pregnant, John wondered if Sarah might not be seeing the father of her child, discussing plans, maybe even marriage. Eloping would be more her style. John could imagine Sarah having a quickie ceremony in Seattle or Buenos Aires or wherever people on the West Coast did that sort of thing. Las Vegas? Some blackjack, a wedding band, and then doubling down.

But he remembered Blindman saying Sarah was leaving town to have an abortion. John understood not being ready to have a baby, especially if Daryl was the father. But with a child, there was hope. With death, there was only death. An abortion may offer the chance for others to live fuller lives, but at the core of the decision was the loss of a life.

He recalled his own close call on the baby front with

Christina and how different things would have been if they had had a child. It had made him realize that they were playing for keeps every time they made love. Luckily, it had been two missed periods due to stress and diet pills. But if she had been pregnant, John wouldn't be in Boonville. He would be back in Miami appeasing Christina's desire for them to "get somewhere," arguing over whether their child should attend public or private schools, and if it should be named Holden or Christopher, Helena or Caitlin, shamelessly jockeying for its affection.

John also remembered how Grandma would well up with tears when she heard a woman had "withstood" an abortion. That was her terminology, "withstood." She was fervently pro-choice, saying, "A woman's body is not a man's decision," but she had lost two sons in Korea and a daughter in a car accident, and was left with only John's father. No grandchildren other than John. "There is no worse suffering than for a mother to bury her child," Grandma had claimed. "And to be the cause of that death, today or twenty years from now, there will be regret and a certain amount of self-hatred. It doesn't matter whether you have the operation in a hospital or in an alley with a coat hanger, the gravity of your actions will resonate within you. It is a viable option, but never a gratifying one."

John understood there were decisions that altered the course of your life, whether you made them cautiously or not. But he also knew sometimes things just happened.

"Her mother's inside," Raven said, interrupting John's thoughts. "She might know when Sarah's coming back."

John now wondered what comfort or assistance he could possibly offer Sarah. Reports suggested that she had made up her mind about the next phase of her life. Looking at Aslan and Raven, the inside of the main house and her comrades, and knowing more about Boonville, John could see how Sarah could come to the conclusion that having a baby and sticking around the Waterfall weren't progressive decisions for a headstrong woman with artistic intentions. But he decided he would leave a note with his address and telephone number. For polar opposites, he felt they had too much in common to lose contact.

"Greta's inside?" Aslan asked, looking up from his elbow.

"Don't you hear the music?" Raven said.

Janis Joplin was singing "Get It While You Can." Aslan

seemed to understand this was part of Greta's personal soundtrack, if not her theme song.

"Tell her I'm at the lab," Aslan said. "I'm working on samples that glow in the dark."

"Tell her yourself," Raven said, trying to punish his father for not helping him with his homework, the same way, John thought, the young giant would later experiment with drugs and wear goofy clothing, dye his hair purple and not write home except to ask for money. Aslan looked ready to pound Raven into mincemeat for his insubordination, but was hesitant to approach the doorway to the main house. Obviously, the big man wanted to avoid Sarah's mother at all costs.

"That's why people have children," Aslan explained, tightening his grip on the weasels whose mouths popped open, tongues hanging agog. "So they have someone to do things for them. Now do as you're told."

Raven looked at his shoes.

Aslan's remark reminded John of his own father once calling him "a sorry excuse for a milk bill." He would have done anything to hurt him in that moment, but he too could think of nothing else but to remain defiantly silent.

"Do it on the paper!" a woman screamed from inside the main house. "You primitive motherfucker! Not my prayer rug! Not my yoga mat!"

John was having trouble believing this had begun as a neighborly visit.

"Would you mind getting Sarah's mother for me?" he asked Raven, thinking it was a way out for all of them. "I could relay your father's message for you."

Raven thought it over. Aslan was walking in place as if to dramatize the fact that time was wasting, then he started shaking his hips and flailing his weaseled hands above his head, moving to the beat of his own drum. He was unable to respond paternally to his son. In this way, John could tell, Raven knew his father would always be consistent; he could be counted on not to be counted on. With the proper perspective, it was a foundation to build on. John's parents were also consistent in their behavior. If they hurt your feelings accidentally, they went back and did it again on purpose.

"Is that all right with you?" John asked Aslan.

"I'm having problems with the flavored ones," the giant answered, straightening his sarong the way a businessman fixes his tie. "The French Tickler's fine, a hint of truffle and champagne, but the rest taste like chicken."

John didn't know what Aslan was talking about. He caught Raven's attention, signaling him to retrieve Sarah's mother and anyone else inside who might be wearing white and carrying a butterfly net.

"Bring me a glass of water too," Aslan told his son. "The rainwater from the purifier, not that slimy Evian. I'll help you with your math if you help me clean cages."

"Clean your own shit," Raven said, before slipping inside.

Shockingly, the giant didn't become violent. Instead, he bent over and scattered the rest of the rodents who loped away like fat kids in a game of hide and seek, resigned to poor concealment. They didn't look like weasels to John now, too small and furless, tailless and short-limbed. Not that he had seen a weasel before, but these were something else. He knew it the same way he would know a hyena was not a Saint Bernard even if a sign at the zoo claimed it to be true. Each of these animals was unique in their body and markings. They weren't lemurs or chipmunks. Marmots, voles, mongoose? John noticed what he had mistaken for the animals' hair were quills. Dwarf porcupine?

Fox food now, John thought, certain none of them would survive a night in the forest. One was already dead.

"It isn't easy playing God," Aslan said, his zoological explanation.

John looked at the giant. It all seemed like science fiction, their names, the main house, the space mammals. But while Aslan stood before him, a futuristic Hun ready to ransack the planet, all John could think of was how people tended to vote for the tallest candidate in a presidential election.

"Marty," the woman's voice called from the main house, and Aslan bolted into the woods, "don't leave that fucking dead hamster on the deck, they're attracting skunks!"

The woman walked onto the deck wearing a pair of jeans and a blue cableknit sweater. Her eyes were somewhere between the two hues and locked on John with the same intensity that he had felt from her daughter. Her hair was held in a bun at the top of her head by a pair of chop sticks, a few loose wisps. Experience had drawn lines to accentuate a portrait aimed at flattery. There was something in her body language, straight back and high chin, that John recognized in Sarah. Greta was also the first hippie John had met to wear a bra.

"Men always want someone to clean up their messes," Greta said, telling John in advance she wouldn't be granting him any favors. "I hope Marty didn't scare you. It's close to harvest and we tend to get provincial if not downright paranoid around here. We've had our share of problems. I'm sure Sarah told you."

"Not exactly," John said.

"Well, she has a penchant for exaggeration," Greta said. "You know, water signs."

The Janis Joplin music inside the main house stopped. Greta turned to stare back through the open door. She told someone to be careful with her vinyl. John saw she was holding a glass of wine and a cigarette that wasn't hand-rolled.

"So, what brings you to this neck of the woods?" she said, pulling on the cigarette and taking a swig of wine.

"I'm looking for your daughter," John said.

"She's leaving tomorrow," Greta said, and there was something in her statement that seemed to be offering herself as a substitute.

"That's what I heard," John said.

"If you so much as think something in this town, everybody knows it by lunch," Greta told him, taking another drag of her cigarette, flicking an ash toward the dead animal that Aslan had left behind. "It isn't yours, is it?"

John could tell that Greta was the kind of mother friends probably admired for her no-shit attitude, not to mention her looks, which couldn't have escaped Sarah's suitors. But if you were her offspring, it would drive you insane. The tonal quality alone. Constantly trying to rattle your confidence with false concern. For all Greta knew, John could have come to the Waterfall to borrow a book or to see Sarah's art work. But she had chosen to believe the worst-case scenario and deal with it flippantly. He heard everything Sarah's mother had to offer in the question, "It isn't yours, is it?"

"I don't know what you mean," John said, wanting to put the conversation into a less casual arena. Everyone in California might be comfortable with airing their dirty laundry, but he wasn't there yet. It would take him longer than two weeks to ascend to local custom. He believed there were topics you didn't discuss with someone's parents the first time you met them. John thought it was inconsiderate and rude of Greta to bring up the delicate subject of Sarah's pregnancy, let alone pry into his involvement.

"I'm just trying to find your daughter," John insisted.

"Really?" Greta said. "I think she's trying to find herself too. Good thing she's formed a search party."

"She wasn't expecting me," John said.

"I have a feeling you weren't expecting her either, the messenger always appears before the message," Greta said. "If Sarah took the time to center herself, she'd be easy to uncover. I keep telling her, 'You become what you most resist.'"

John knew another old adage, "If you want to know who you're marrying, meet her mother, and add the father's worst trait." Greta was a flashing warning sign.

"You look like you're searching the more conservative routes," Greta said, giving John a once-over as if she were considering buying him a new aura. "I don't think you'll find her there. Ask yourself where your grandmother would hide."

"If she's not around," John said, "Could you point me to her cabin, so I could leave a note?"

"You sure you wouldn't rather come inside?" Greta asked, gesturing with her wine to the main house.

"Yes, thank you," John declined. "I'm sort of on a mission."

"A man on a mission," Greta repeated. "What in the course of history has caused more harm?"

How about a woman without direction? John almost answered. How about jealousy, spite, and fear?

Her suggestion about Grandma irked him. It was a dangerous question, one John continued to pursue despite the upsetting answers he received. But he didn't want to get into it with Sarah's mother. He felt lucky to survive the giant and wasn't up for picking a fight. It wouldn't serve him to be branded a sexist either, not with Sarah, Pensive Prairie Sunset, or Grandma's ghost. The only place it would help was at the Lodge where they would buy him a beer if he could relay his story in the form of a lesbian joke.

"We're all on a mission," Greta said, taking her last drag of her cigarette and letting the butt drop from her fingers, squishing it with her foot, then picking it up. "Then we come to Boonville. That does us all in."

From what John had seen of Boonville, there was nothing

inherently evil in the hills, woods, or vineyards, except maybe the residents. If these people had become sick, it was in spite of their surroundings.

"You should be happy your daughter's leaving, then," John replied.

Greta fixed him with her blue eyes.

How long had the women in Sarah's family been using the suicide calm of their eyes so effectively? John wanted to know. The Gibson females had no such trick, no way of rendering men docile with the mere omission of a blink.

"It's not such a bad thing having a child, you know?" Greta said, still holding her crushed butt. "You get to relearn everything, tying your shoes, learning how to walk, the pleasure of ice cream."

Greta patted herself down in a search for more cigarettes, coming up empty.

John wished he had one to offer her for a distraction. They would both feel better.

"People are less judgmental if you don't have children," Greta said. "You can go on forever as an eccentric if you do it by yourself. Once you make a bond with someone or have a child, that's when you're subject to society's scrutiny."

John felt Greta's eyes again. She wanted him to agree with her. He realized that despite her apparent confidence, she was the kind of woman who didn't believe in her existence unless a man was nodding at her.

"Nobody judges you on what you were like before you gave birth," Greta said. "Sarah doesn't care who I was as a young woman. What color my demons came in."

John looked from Greta to the dead animal. He doubted if the little beast knew whether to shit or go hibernate when it was alive. He wanted to miraculously jostle it back to life. Sprinkle holy water. John the Baptist, patron saint of genetic mutation.

"Even if I had been a bad person, everything would have been forgiven if I was a 'good mother,'" Greta said, slashing physical quotation marks in the air with her fingers. "Who knows what that means?"

John didn't want to hear any more of this woman's State of the Union address on parenthood. He wanted to know where her daughter had gone, physically, not spiritually. Did every request for information in California have to become a share session? He was one step away from singing "The Bear Went over the Mountain," which was what he did as a child when his parents fought.

"Nobody has the answer until it's too late," Greta stated. "After they've had children and have been allowed to be children."

She checked her pockets again for cigarettes out of habit or extreme need. John didn't know how long it would take for a full-on nic fit to take hold of her. Some people needed constant self-medication.

"That's the thing about having a baby and watching them grow up, they surprise you." Greta continued, hands still searching for a cigarette. "And you can't do a thing about it, except try to accept their choices and forgive your own."

In his head, John heard himself singing, "The bear went over the mountain, the bear went over the mountain, to see what he could see, to see what he could see, and he saw the other side of the mountain . . ."

"Being a grandmother is your second chance," she added. "I hope Sarah lets me have it."

John tried to brush that statement aside, but couldn't help wondering if Grandma had regarded him as a second chance. Was he supposed to redeem three dead children and his father? Grandma obviously hadn't felt good about herself, her marriage, child-rearing, facing the squirrels, discovering a kind of life she didn't have the tools to fully create. Would it have been worth it for her if John came out the other end? Was it enough that he had come this far?

"I hope she does, too," John said, and Greta smiled with wine-stained lips the way some girls do when you tell them they look pretty.

"I have to find a cigarette," she said. "Are you sure you don't want to come inside for a drink or something?"

"I just want to leave a note for Sarah," John answered.

He almost told Greta she should be looking for someone ten years her senior, not twenty years younger. John could picture her on a sailboat in the Keys with an older man, retired and searching for answers himself. He'd have an interest in untying knots and he'd view her idiosyncrasies as kinked rope, excited by her energy, responding to her Earth Mother monologues with amusement and a spin that expressed that he took her seriously, happy to end each evening in bed with an attractive, complicated woman. John thought Greta needed to leave the commune more than her daughter.

"I don't know if I'll see her before she clears out," Greta said. "Sarah's having exponential mother issues. I'm low on her list of confidantes."

"Where's her cabin?" John asked.

"Did you see the glass house down in the flat?" Greta said.

"That's where I parked," John told her.

Greta said there was a path on the left-hand side of the glass house that headed down the mountain; a quarter-mile down was Sarah's cabin. He couldn't miss it. And, if Sarah was home, she asked John to tell her that her mother would appreciate it if she dropped by to say goodbye. Not just because of the electricity bill. She had something for her.

John said he would and thanked her for the directions.

"All you can do is all you can do," Greta said, walking back inside the main house but checking over her shoulder to see if John was watching her, testing her powers.

John was watching, trying to figure out what promise could have lured a woman like Greta up to a place like this. He almost wished he was an old burn-out able to follow her inside to dissolve into something larger than himself. Janis Joplin music filled the air again. John doubted love had ever been free, even in the sixties. It certainly had become costly in the seventies and eighties, especially when it splintered into divorce. There was always a price. Sometimes you just paid in installments.

Layaway, John thought, amused by his pun, turning away from Sarah's mother and the main house, saying goodbye to the prickly lump of flesh left lying in the dust.

Returning to his car, he wondered if he should report the giant to Cal as a suspect in Balostrasi's disappearance. He seemed a prime candidate and had practically confessed to a killing: "I've put travelers' bodies into the ground without ceremony." What more did you need to warrant an investigation? If not Balostrasi, somebody else was taking a dirt nap in these hills, tucked in by the giant's hand. But maybe nobody cared. More than likely, Cal knew more about the case than John. The newspaperman at the softball game also seemed to be tracking it. Hap, Blindman, Sarah, all probably had information they hadn't disclosed. Everybody seemed to know more about everything than John. He just wanted to synthesize the conflicting stories into something tangible to avoid further trouble. But he realized that in order to do so, he'd have to adopt Boonville's two unofficial mottoes: us vs. them, and, live and let die.

John found his way back to his car. His sense of direction was improving. Light was emanating from the transparent house, despite the drawn shades. As he approached the Datsun, the front door of the house opened and an old man appeared with a pair of goggles pushed back on top of his thinning head of hair. He wore work gloves and a mechanic's jumpsuit. His face was slug-lipped and sweaty as he stood with large forearms and a chin that sprouted from his barrel chest. He couldn't have been four inches taller than five feet. If Aslan was the first giant John had met, this gentleman was the first troll.

"You lost?" the troll said, and John saw a crowbar in his hand.

"Not anymore," John answered, cautiously. "I got directions at the main house."

"That doesn't mean you have any more idea of where you're going than before," the troll said, leaning the bar of steel against the door frame and taking off his gloves. "They're not the best at giving directions. Where you trying to go, young man?"

"I'm a friend of Sarah's," John said. "I'm trying to find her cabin to leave a note."

The troll tilted his head, indicating he had a neck tucked somewhere behind his stalactite chin. Then he recited the same directions as Sarah's mother had given, adding that there was a reflector on a broken bit of fence on the opposite side of the road from the turn for Sarah's place. It was the only way John would spot the break in the trees, otherwise he'd drive too far or turn at the next left, which would lead him to the Teepees, which were worth avoiding at all cost, giving a bad name to hippies, naturalists, and Native Americans alike.

"Only dumb white people would live in a teepee when they didn't have to," the troll said, patting the sweat on his head with his gloves. "These days even Indians think of a group of teepees as a Native American trailer park, without the kitsch."

The troll told John if he ventured into the Teepees, he'd have to powwow with someone he called Chief One Man Slum, the leader of a sect of Indians from Newark, New Jersey, and the self-proclaimed last member of "the lost tribe." The troll believed "lost" described Chief One Man Slum and his minions to a T. He was certain The Chief was lying about his heritage and "the lost tribe" was a group of Puerto Ricans. In the troll's opinion, The Chief was another fat slob with a Joisey accent and an East Coaster's enthusiasm for Devil Dogs. Every six months the Waterfall had to pay a cleanup crew to scour their compound so garbage and disease didn't overflow into the rest of the commune.

Having met enough legends in the forest for one day, John said he would keep an eye open for the reflector.

But the troll continued talking, telling John his name was Francis and he was eighty-two, a welder and a sculptor. When he was young he'd worked on the Golden Gate Bridge and punched out Orson Welles in a bar fight in Sausalito during the filming of *The Lady from Shanghai* because Rita Hayworth had given him the eye. He'd drunk all the Beats under the table in North Beach during his day, which wasn't a boast because although they were lushes and Benzedrine addicts, none of them could hold their liquor. He had drunk his fill now and didn't drink anything anymore except a glass of red wine with dinner, along with eating half a raw onion.

"Bernini was my god," Francis said, because John didn't know how to excuse himself and the troll had a quality that made you want to listen, something more than his age or plainspokenness. John felt that something important might be discovered that would otherwise remain hidden if he didn't pay attention, that certain information had an expiration date that was coming due. He had felt the same way listening to an interview of Henry Miller that had been aired on the day of his death, the last words of a dying era that pertained more to you than the one you were living in. He had sat in his driveway until the radio show had finished—Miller teaching him a thing or two about art and Paris and being alive—well aware that Christina was upstairs in the apartment burning dinner.

All the answers to life could be found in Rodin's hands, Francis told John, who wished he had a tape recorder. Christo was a chump who relied on cleverness, and clever didn't have any place in art that was going to last. But nothing lasted, so maybe Christo was onto something. But he was no technician, and an artist had to know his craft. There was nothing better than melding two objects together and having their sum total equal something greater than their separate parts. He said his friends called him Franny, and they all said he worked and talked too much, but he was a Greek and healthy as an ox and had lived through two world wars and a depression and had never married, though he'd had plenty of opportunities, and it was tough bananas if people didn't like it. He identified the Datsun as having once belonged to the Squirrel Lady, and he pegged John as the Squirrel Boy. He said he admired the old broad's work. She was tough and a survivor and any grandson of hers could call him Franny.

"Your grandma helped inspire the project I'm working on now," Franny said, with a broadfaced grin, happy to have an audience. "We were both interested in quantity and repetition and taking everyday objects and transforming them into something startling with the subtext of a preexisting language that shapes an object as masculine or feminine. Releasing what is already trapped inside. Road signs are masculine. I'm turning them into giant penises because subconsciously they are orders to obey male power."

Franny said Edna had believed that there was a force behind large quantities and repetition that made people uncomfortable because of their direct link to time and its fleeting nature. She called it the nostalgia pool and thought it could be filled with the liquid of positive or negative experience, triggering emotions of loss or hope.

"Never underestimate your own ability to repeat yourself," John's grandma had advised Franny. "Or your inability to see the variation within that repetition."

As an exercise to demonstrate an aspect of that point, Franny had welded a dozen baby carriages from abandoned refrigerators, one for each month of the year, filling them with the smashed remains of his wine bottles and Edna's gin bottles that they had emptied during each month of that year. The same kind of bottles held different experiences within the same action of containing spirits and being used to imbibe from, he explained, and they fragmented into different-sized pieces and patterns when they were broken in the carriages. And the carriages, which were the same vehicle of the same size and design, also carried dissimilarities because of the materials they had been forged from and the variables of being produced by human hands. Just like memories.

John was trying to visualize the project and follow Franny's explanation, also thinking about the wheelbarrow of broken glass back at the cabin and what that could possibly mean.

"It's also eerie to see something other than a baby inside a pram," Franny said. "There is a sense of violation if the object you replace it with isn't its equal or in some way at least equally cute, a stuffed bear or doll. Overall, the installation emanated a sense of futility and vulnerability. It was purchased by a winery in the Valley and transported to an estate in Kyoto, Japan. The Japanese understand tragedy better than Americans. They know it's not supposed to teach us how to create a perfect world, but how to live in an imperfect one. Maybe the bomb did teach them something, the second one anyway. The deliberate consideration behind repetition."

Franny divulged other projects he had undertaken that involved filling various transparent containers or cages he welded into different shapes, a giant hole, a cow, a lung, with used toilet paper rolls, milk cartons, and empty cigarette packages. One project included constructing a see-through dumpster loaded with the debris he had found on a hundred-foot strip of highway over the period of a year. Each day at five o'clock he would collect the "tourist flowers" in bags. If what he discovered was too cumbersome, an engine block, a mattress, a 1932 National cash register, he piled it into his car after enlisting a passing motorist's support. On completion, he rolled the dumpster to the strip he had patrolled, erecting a sign that read, "You dropped something!"

Franny thanked John for contributing road signs to his latest effort. John saw the sheets of metal stacked near the pile of Sarah's discarded crosses, which were next to Franny's glass yurt and the metal Atlas standing on top of the world, keeping watch, holding his imaginary burden. He also spied the wooden replica of Sarah discarded in the found-art heap. John realized it was one thing to have inspiration, another to complete your undertakings.

"The process is more important than the result," Franny said, as if reading John's mind. "We often make art to purge ourselves. It's not the end product that relieves us but the work. Picasso once said, 'When I'm painting, I'm God, and when I'm not painting, I'm not.' It becomes an easy choice. The problem is that sometimes, as much as we want our art to be personal, it becomes co-opted, a collaborative effort, even if it's just someone stretching your canvas, developing your film, etc. It's impossible for an artist to organically create all the tools and means for his medium. Not to mention the lack of control over the audience or its ability to interpret meaning, an object's spatial context and the question of why it exists in a certain place and time."

John looked at the found-art pile and thought if you could transport it to a museum, it could be an art piece in itself.

"It's a conversation spanning man's existence," Franny said, and he could have been describing the heap of discarded material before them. "Starting and stopping, backtracking at junctures and occasionally synthesizing wholly in a painting, sculpture, or single sentence. That's if we're lucky. Nothing stripped to its core meaning hasn't been done before. All we're doing is trying to make it new. That's what Ezra Pound said."

John noticed something crawling in the pile of crosses. It was one of Aslan's hybrid weasels, dragging its hind legs, pulling itself up and across each piece of wood, blood trailing from its head and feet, climbing until it reached the cross at the top of the heap. It stopped where the two pieces of wood intersected. In the light from Franny's house, John could see its thorny body expanding and contracting with each breath. After a pause, it stretched its front legs forward to climb higher, only succeeding in clawing one last inch. Then it died, front limbs collapsing at its sides.

"Ultimately, you have to chose life, which is the work, pursuit, and creation, instead of death, which is inactivity, stagnation, and decay," Franny said, unaware of the weasel's plight. "Better to be a ghost proper, than a shadow of a man."

John stared at the dead weasel spread out on the cross.

And it hit him, not like a bolt from the blue, but like something that had lumbered out of the forest to show itself in daylight. He knew what he had to do. He wasn't sure what it meant, but he knew all the elements involved, the pieces that had been left behind for him to put together. The first steps of his own life.

"Franny, would you help me with an art project I inherited from my grandma?" John asked. "It might be illegal. Unfortunately, I need to finish it tonight. But I think it's right up your alley."

The old Greek smiled, obviously amused by the Squirrel Lady's straight-looking grandson suggesting that a stranger in his eighty-third year on the planet help him with an illegal art project, when minutes earlier, he was getting into his car to deliver a message to the hippie girl, Sarah McKay.

But Franny seemed to feel the force and sincerity of John's urgency, and maybe felt partially responsible for that enthusiasm after his speech. He had said he respected John's grandmother as an artist and understood how artists work, striking while the iron was hot. It didn't matter how crazy the idea, ultimately it was action that mattered.

"Sure, I'll help," Franny said. "What do you need me to do?"

15

"I'll give you something to scowl about," John said, driving the first nail through a squirrel's forehead and pinning it firmly to one of Sarah's three-foot crosses.

He set the crucifix upright and pounded it into the ground so it stood by itself. The dirt was hard and didn't give way easily. He brought the sledge down again, the base of the cross wedging another half-inch into the earth. They would have to make stands for the crosses in the section of Highway 128 where there was a sidewalk, in front of the Lodge, drive-in, AV Market, and fairgrounds. But it was cathartic to see even one of Grandma's squirrels up there on the cross, cooling his heels, looking alive and pissed off. The icon of a new faith. Now the expression carved into its face seemed to stem from the nail cleaved through its forehead.

John paced off twenty steps and banged another crucifix into position. Franny was making another trip in his truck to the Waterfall for more crosses. Pensive had been telephoned and was on her way with a "lifetime supply" of nails. So it was just him, the squirrels, and an empty stretch of asphalt leading two ways into the darkness. He didn't care if the crosses were equidistant, it wasn't an exhibit that hinged on accuracy. As long as there were 715 of Grandma's squirrels, crucified and lining the main strip of Boonville from the turnoff for Manchester Road to the dented population sign on the south side of town, with half the crosses on one side of the highway and half on the other with the life-sized replica of Sarah at the end, everything would be fine. That is, if they managed to complete the project before Sarah left and Cal didn't bust them for creating a public nuisance.

John regretted that Grandma wasn't alive to offer input on the overall schematic. It was why he had called Pensive. Aside from wanting protection from Daryl, if he should happen out for a drive, John felt one of Grandma's friends should be involved for the sake of her spirit and the benefit of a woman's touch. Rightfully, Grandma should have been the one to crucify the myriad of her critics. But it wasn't her battle anymore. She had done her part, leaving behind the weapons to fight the war, even if there was no plan of attack or well-defined enemy. After death, John decided, and this included Christ too, you weren't responsible for anything done on your behalf. Wills were written before people died, in their daily movements and influence. What Grandma had bequeathed John was an instinct for the grand gesture and a longing to see it manifested. The pioneer spirit. "Come west, young man!" All formal instructions were open for interpretation. What the dead left behind was what you chose to acknowledge; objects and money were token symbols of a legacy. The final wealth was dispersed in memory.

If she were alive, Grandma might not have sanctioned this project, taking offense at John converting her whittlings. Nobody had been struck by her ability to collaborate. In her mind, the squirrels were probably autotelic, each a study in the discrepancy within mass repetition. A testament to her inability to belong. Perhaps the missing link between mother and child. But John didn't care anymore; that was Grandma's cross to burn. He hammered another squirrel to a cross and into place along the roadside. He was deep into his own creative process.

He looked at the squirrels stacked next to the Datsun. It was nearing midnight, light spilling from street lamps and the insomniac signs burning in shop windows. The handful of homes on the downtown strip were quiet, a television glowing in a second-story window. Sleepy time in sleepy town. The Buckhorn was closed, as was the drive-in. John saw the Lodge around the bend in the road, trucks parked out front waiting for their owners to stagger out and fumble with keys, in defiance of the rest of the valley. Lonely time in lonely town. By last call, none of them would notice or care what John was doing with his squirrels and crosses. No designated drivers in that group, or art critics. Nobody would cry sacrilege tonight.

John decided the best approach to the job would be to create an assembly line and work crews, one to do the crucifying, the next to lay the crosses in place, the last to erect them in the hallowed ground. They would need all the materials and artisans present to run the drill efficiently. He would be the foreman, although he wasn't sure he had the skill set for the position. Organization and authority outside the office were not his strong suits. There were already problems. He didn't know if he had brought enough squirrels. He had started counting at the cabin, but decided to pack the Datsun full, accuracy giving way to speed. Grandma's supply was inexhaustible, so he didn't have to worry about running out, but they would have to build more crosses if Waterfall residents had taken any from the found-art pile for personal projects. Sarah said there were 715, but who knew how many remained? They were as suitable for kindling as the squirrels.

What else had he overlooked? Franny would no doubt be better suited for the supervising role, although he was an invaluable line-worker, the Golden Gate Bridge a strong bullet on his résumé. But where were the Mohawks when you needed them? Maybe Franny could send a smoke signal to his old Native American welding cronies? Otherwise, John figured they had seven hours before morning traffic or someone called Cal, if everyone was willing to work through the night.

The one thing they had going for them was that Sarah didn't strike John as an early riser. She wouldn't be leaving town at the crack of dawn. So the trick was going to be maintaining the exhibit after it was finished, keeping locals and tourists from running the crosses over with their cars or tearing them down with their bare hands. Art involving the cross tended to cause a stir. Christians always welcomed something to crusade against. He wasn't sure about the Moonies and Krishnas, none of the squirrels were bald or passing out flowers. Still, they would have to stand guard; Franny with his crowbar, Pensive with her Mace, John with his ability to take a punch. They were going to need lots of coffee, and maybe the Kurtses.

John saw headlights. Whenever a set approached, he thought it was Cal's cruiser and his body stiffened. Given the opportunity, he felt he might be able to convince Cal that there wasn't anything wrong with the project, maybe even enlist his support. This was anarchy, right up Cal's alley. And the deputy had a sense of humor, John was sure of it, but more often than not the joke was going to be on you.

The car reduced its speed, steering to the side of the road and parking in front of John, who squinted as he stood in the overlapping center of the headlights, holding an armful of crosses. There was no siren or flashing lights. The headlights cut and John couldn't see anything until his eyes adjusted, forming objects around the smears of color burned into his view. Then he saw Pensive unstick herself from the front seat of her Pacer.

"I am an instrument in the shape of a woman trying to translate pulsations into images for the relief of the body and the reconstruction of the mind," she said, getting out of the car. "We recite that at the beginning of every meeting at the Radical Petunia. Edna loved it. She said for artistic women, it should replace the 'Our Father.'"

Pensive was wearing another culturally unspecific outfit, a purple caftan large enough to double as a banquet tablecloth. In her arms she juggled a cardboard box, an extension cord, and a nail gun. She set down the box. Catching John off-guard, she gave him a hug. He tried to shake loose, but Pensive's body had swallowed him alive. When she finally spit him out, John was convinced he had experienced what they called in California "rebirthing."

"I'm so glad you telephoned," she said. "I tried to enlist Margaret Washington but she said the project left her open to bad publicity. She has to go on NPR in a week to promote her new book, *The Altar of What I Know*, but she wanted you to know Edna would have been proud. Although she didn't want to be quoted."

Pensive scrutinized the squirrels that John had finished the way a victim identifies a perpetrator in a police lineup. She nodded. Justice was being served. She set down the nail gun to lift open the hood of the Pacer, propping it wide with a metal rod.

"I rallied a group from the Albion Nation," she told John, connecting the extension cord of the nail gun to the car battery with a makeshift adapter. She seemed pleased with the hookup and returned to the driver's seat. There was a burst of sparks. She waddled out of the car holding a pair of protective goggles and made her way to the cardboard box that she had placed next to the squirrel pile. The box was full of nails.

"I had to tell them the squirrels were all male," she said, slipping on the goggles and loading the nail gun, test-firing a shot through the crotch of a squirrel with a resounding pop.

John winced.

"They're sticklers for those kind of details," Pensive said.

John wasn't going to argue. Hippies, dropouts, inbreds, lesbians, everybody was invited. No undertaking had ever turned out the way he had planned by the means that he had planned them. As the gamblers used to say at the track in Hialeah whenever a long shot came in, "That's why they run the race." Pensive's contribution of a nail gun was already a fast start out of the gate. It would subtract hours and blisters from the first leg of the project, as long as she didn't point the thing at him.

Pensive began nailing squirrels to crosses, making a stack out of the completed crosses. Some of the wood had rotted from exposure to the elements outside of Franny's yurt, splintering as the nails bit hard against the grain. John didn't know what kind of wood it was, having never set foot in a lumberyard. He knew palm trees, walnut and oak when he saw it in furniture. Formica. But once a tree had lost its leaves and been processed into lumber, it was anybody's guess. Pensive doctored the damaged crosses as best she could with an extra nail or piece of wood, then moved on to the next. She had a flair for carpentry that must have come from years of living in the country, doing-it-herself. John had wanted to create a series of How-To-Fix-It books for guys like him; the first volume would be entitled, "*Jostling, Jiggling and Jerry-rigging*," the next, "*Coat Hangers and Spit*."

He loaded Pensive's finished product into the Datsun and drove down the road, setting each crucifix in its appointed spot. He tried to keep a count so he would know when to switch sides and decided not to erect any more until he had laid them all out, not wanting to give passing motorists any reason to notice the spectacle until it was done. With the crosses lying flat, drivers would breeze by the way they normally traveled through Boonville, holding their breath and counting to ten.

In no time, John had placed close to three hundred crosses along the strip. Franny arrived with another shipment of crosses. He inspected their progress. Pensive had created two stacks of squirrels near her Pacer, those she had nailed to crosses and another pile waiting to be sacrificed. She got another box of nails from her car. John wondered what she was doing with so many nails, but was afraid to ask. Meanwhile, he had made it three-quarters of the way to the fairgrounds without incident. Another trip in the Datsun, a recount, a slight realignment, and he would start on the other side. To his surprise, after a rocky start, he had estimated the spacing fairly accurately. But they were going to need more squirrels.

"Looks like the Judgment Day is approaching," Franny said, clapping John on the back. "Come hell or high water."

They took a break. John bought coffee at the Pic 'N Pay, making no conversation with the cashier, who was cleaning a rifle and hardly looked up from the firearm, which was laid out in pieces near the register on a towel. He was oiling parts when John entered the store and wiping the stock clean with a chamois rag when John left, only pausing from his work to ring John up and point with the disassembled barrel to the sugar and creamer on the condiment stand. John grabbed a fistful of pink and blue packets, never looking back. He doubted the Pic 'N Pay lost much profit to shoplifters.

Outside he stopped himself from peeking into the Lodge, hearing the jukebox and patrons whooping at whatever was passing for excitement inside, missed pool shots, bad jokes, Melonie bringing the next round. He noticed the Kurts' truck in the lot and had the feeling that his drinking buddies would find him before the night was through. The project was becoming a Tower of Babel. He had forgotten how that undertaking had ended, except in rubble. God or the Assyrians or somebody had gotten pissed. Bad architecture? Attacking Mongols? Maybe he should have tried to enlist the cashier from the Pic 'N Pay; they could use a sentinel.

Sitting on the tailgate of Franny's truck, the three laymen caught their breath and sipped coffee. There were few stars in the sky, but the trio looked toward the heavens as if they were scheduled to light up like the ceiling of a planetarium, perhaps looking for a sign, or something that could be interpreted as a sign.

Franny said that working at night gave him the feeling of getting away with something, a predatory energy. Pensive confessed that she had gotten hooked on reading with a flashlight and a Judy Blume novel for just that reason. She felt she was having a naughty conversation. That, and as a child nobody would play with her. She blew into her Styrofoam cup.

Franny said he had had no use for school after the eighth grade himself. He had jumped a northbound train one night in

1919, back when the stars really knew how to shine and the horizon was full of promise instead of fluorocarbons and a man with a strong back wasn't afraid to work an honest day for an honest dollar and he could always find that kind of work and get an education on the railroads and in the timber camps of Oregon and Washington making fortunes for other men who sent Pinkertons to do their dirty work, busting heads and unions, while he spent his sweat and script on women and bathtub gin. Another night, when he'd had enough of the rain and trout fishing and train whistles and the felling of trees, again under the cover of darkness, he left to come home to his parents' coldwater flat in the Mission District of San Francisco, which wasn't all Mexicans then, and watched his parents die of consumption while he learned to weld from the auto-body mechanic who ran a garage down on the corner of 19th and Folsom.

John didn't know how to follow that story; coming to Boonville was the most adventurous thing he had done and it had been on a three o'clock flight. Broad daylight. He had a couple heave-hos and watched a movie, ate beef bourguignon. As for school, he was a deviant but within the pack, and mostly in his head. He had friends, none he kept in touch with after his school days, but he always had a group to sit with during lunch and at assemblies.

Franny and Pensive drank their coffee, waiting for his offering. John agreed night lent itself to the feeling of mischief with the exception of sex, which seemed to him more risqué during daylight hours. His cohorts giggled, remembering impproprietous moments in the sun. If you didn't have a good story yourself, John decided, sometimes it was enough to spark them in your audience.

They switched subjects and began discussing the inherent power of the image of the cross and its value as something more than a religious symbol, making the aesthetic decision that the imperfect crosses would add to the exhibit, giving it an immediate sense of age. After watching Franny use three creamers and all the packets of sweetener in his coffee, John wondered if his aesthetic could be trusted. Not that the coffee was good, even though Pensive and he roughed it black, but he had noticed over the years that the people whose opinions he trusted preferred the same things as himself. Not just in one area either, food extended to books, which extended to politics, etc. He found it was unlikely someone who thought highly of Ronald Reagan, James Michener, and succotash, would think well of Bernie Sanders, Carl Hiaasen, and oysters. There was no empirical right or wrong when it came to aesthetics, just people with bad taste.

Franny advised them that if they wanted to sell art, they should use aged materials whenever possible, frames, newspapers, anything thirty years older than the present day option. Buyers lapped it up. New meant untested and undefined. Too much thinking. People wanted to be walked through art, hands held the whole way.

"In this country consumers long for older objects because they haven't created a tangible history or link to the past themselves," Franny said. "Everything is disposable these days."

John looked at the Greek's stubby legs hanging over the tailgate. His feet didn't reach the ground, even with the help of the truck's full load and Pensive's full figure.

"Especially people," he added.

Pensive shifted her weight and the truck wobbled on its shocks. She took a sip of coffee. The grimmest of smiles bent her lips. John was surprised that she had remained quiet, not thinking she was the type who could just listen. But she was very respectful to Franny, letting the old troll ramble.

"Nobody listens, nobody remembers." The caffeine was speeding up Franny's already charged speech. "Nothing seems as full as the past because there are so many versions. It can be overwhelming. The present has only your own observations to contend with. But people don't want to know history, they want to fabricate a new one that jibes with their idea of a noble lineage. To hear it told, nothing in this world has ever been anybody's fault. We're all just going to hell in a handbasket."

Franny removed a pouch of tobacco from his pocket and began rolling a cigarette. Pensive looked at the makings. John thought she was going to ask him for one, but instead she inched away from Franny. The truck shook as she moved, spilling coffee down John's front. Fortunately, it was no longer hot and only dampened his shirt. He dabbed at the fabric with a napkin, spreading the wet spot and widening the stain until it was hard to believe so much liquid had come from one splash.

"Nothing makes me more upset than when Americans talk about how old everything is in Europe compared to here," Franny said, the rear of the truck tilted to a forty-five degree angle with

John leaning into him. "Let me tell you something, this planet's the same age the world over. You don't like arrowheads and pictograms, Chinooks and Aztecs, tar pits and toxic waste dumps, that's as much a part of who you are as England and Germany, London Bridge or Auschwitz, or even Greece is to me. There is one history of propagation and genocide, heroism and tyranny, and it belongs to all of us on these seven continents. Don't be fooled by a few quaint churches."

Pensive tried to ignore Franny's cigarette but the wind was blowing the smoke in her face. She coughed dramatically. Franny didn't notice, finishing his universalist diatribe against the Eurocentric world. Maybe he thought her objection was to his argument. Franny began waving his arms to emphasize points, increasing the amount of smoke drifting in her direction. Pensive coughed again, this time in earnest.

John didn't mind the smell of smoke. He thought hand-rolled cigarettes weren't nearly as bad as the store-bought kind. He remembered when Christina had a run with Virginia Slims, finding something she identified with in the packaging: "You've come a long way, baby." North Florida condo pool culture. John didn't begin to understand it. He hated the way she had smelled during that period, the dead cigs clinging to her hair, her clothes, her body. She stopped when crows' feet appeared near the corners of her eyes. Vanity, not death, always her great motivater.

John thought smoking cigarettes only made sense in the wee hours of the night when there wasn't any handier way of killing yourself than to wait for cancer to come calling. When he drank, the two seemed to go hand in hand. But when he drank, a plastic factory could be on fire and he would inhale deeply. He had never bought a pack of cigarettes. He'd give his money to Blindman for heroin before he pussyfooted around with death and supported R.J. Reynolds.

Watching Pensive squirm in Franny's dragon's breath, John decided people were defined more by what they didn't tolerate than by what they did. "No bare feet, back talk, leftovers, liberals, or loud music," that was his father in a nutshell. It was difficult to say what the man supported, except Reagan, which meant in a roundabout way the seven deadly sins. Maybe in his own manner, patricide. John had developed a lengthy list of annoyances himself, starting with people who picked their noses while they drove and running to inedible garnishes. He would never make it as a Buddhist, unless there was a less publicized branch who were uptight.

He found it odd Pensive didn't move out of range of the smoke. Instead she began eating something she had brought with her, a hockey puck made of weeds. She said she had baked it using sunlight and all-natural ingredients, taking five days to cook it in a special oven built from mud and a flat rock she had fished out of the river. The last batch had been stolen by raccoons, which to John was hardly a four-star culinary endorsement. Didn't they eat grubs too? Maybe raccoons in this area were to muffins what pigs were to truffles in France? Since John hadn't done the research, he politely declined Pensive's offer of a taste. She tried enticing Franny by revealing there was also gingko root among the ingredients.

"And walnuts," she said, the final hook.

Walnuts, John thought, wondering why people tried to improve every recipe by adding nuts. He hated their texture in cooked food, even kung pao chicken. Christina had a recipe for pork chops breaded in crushed macadamias that she prepared for dinner parties, knowing John hated them and looked finicky scraping the crust away with his knife. Considering the price, John thought, macadamia nuts were the biggest con job since saffron. What was the big deal? Was saffron 20 times a better spice than cumin or paprika? John would take old-fashioned salt and pepper and the money he saved passing on the saffron to buy a bag of pretzels. Nobody, not even a hippie, would throw pretzels into a main entree.

Franny passed on his chance at the ginkgo puck. He told Pensive that coffee and cigarettes had brought him safe thus far, and like grace, they would bring him home. He started rolling another butt. With no other bribe or recourse at her disposal, Pensive asked if Franny wouldn't mind not smoking near her. Holding his lighter behind the cup of his hand, Franny had caught her double negative and said no he wouldn't not mind. Pensive clarified her request, adding statistics about secondhand smoke. Franny said he would refrain from lighting up if she could name an artist worth their weight in finger paint that hadn't smoked. Pensive suggested Margaret Washington. Franny flicked his Bic, taking a pull from the rollie and exhaling two puffs through his nose that floated toward Pensive. She made a sour face, her ginkgo puck backing up on her. Franny didn't say another word. Break was over.

John and Franny unloaded the crosses from the troll's truck, then Franny left for the Waterfall for another haul. Pensive continued to churn out crosses in her smokeless work environment, humming "If I Had a Hammer," keeping rhythm with the pneumatic blast of the nail gun. Folds of arm fat shook with each shot. Rosie the Riveter had nothing on her. She could get a job at any shipyard in America. The only thing missing were the anchor tattoos on her biceps.

John resumed dropping off the crosses. As he drove, he noticed a rise in the road as it left town. It would add to the cumulative effect for the southbound traffic, the same as the entering and exiting of the Vietnam Memorial in Washington, D.C., a sense of descent, immersion, and then release. Who knows what it would feel like going the other way, a flip-book of a crippled cartoon character? Cheating death? Although the project was becoming something more than he had expected, with greater meaning and combined purpose, Sarah was still the target audience. Her review was the one that counted. She would be heading south.

Finishing the fairground side of the street, John felt strange about leaving crosses in front of a church with a high steeple that was tucked just off the highway near a row of trees. There was a picnic area in the churchyard and an unlit neon sign that spelled "Good News." John could picture teenage newlyweds racing from its boxy congregation hall in a rain of rice. He thought it must be Lutheran or Baptist, not knowing the difference, guessing that one ate barbecue and the other didn't. He had seen a bumper sticker once that said Southern Baptists believe in a second coming. But that implied a different kind of conviction. John killed the working headlight of the Datsun, which was shining on the house of God. He didn't want to wake anybody up, least of all a Supreme Being. The project wasn't ready for Divine Criticism.

He began working his way back the Lodge side of town, the spacing coming more naturally since completing the first side. He had developed a system of tossing crosses out the open passenger door without having to stop, traveling slow enough so there was minimal damage, a few scraped faces and scratched tails. Nothing that didn't add flavor. He would straighten them when they were all in the street, not repeating the process every hundred yards as he had done in the beginning. Time was of the essence. They had to make stands so the squirrels could be erected on the concrete areas, and the rest still had to be put into place. John didn't know where they were going to get the wood to make the stands or what the best design would be. Franny's engineering expertise would be called upon. Maybe Pensive would have an answer. He could also ask the Kurtses if they had any logging secrets, since they had just flipped a U-turn in their truck near Pensive's workstation and were coming his way, horn honking, music blasting, bottles flying, accelerating with reckless abandon.

So much for a covert operation, John thought.

As they approached, John could hear the Kurtses screaming in strange unison, one voice climbing higher than the other, warbling loudly, then dropping low as a background for the other to solo, neither voice faltering entirely, but growing together like two farmers calling for a lost pig. A bottle exploded off what was left of the Datsun's front end. John didn't know if it was a warning shot or a greeting. He also didn't know when the Kurtses were going to start applying their brakes. Maybe they planned to swerve past to give him a scare. But they were headed dead-center, homing in at ramming speed. John braced for impact as the Kurtses truck swung in a skid toward him, turning in a quarter-arc, rubber smearing asphalt as the high-pitched squeal of the tires sang out at an octave above their own trilling voices. John's cry joined theirs in a chorus of holy terror. He felt his body jerk, slamming into the car door with his shoulder as the truck's rear caught the back of the Datsun, both cars coming to an immediate stop, facing in the same direction.

"You know them pine cones you put glue on and sprinkle with glitter around Christmas time?" Kurts asked, leaning out the window. "I practically invented them."

Given the speed the Kurtses had been traveling, John was shocked that he hadn't been laid out on the concrete with the steering wheel embedded in his chest. The impact from their truck had been minimal. The Datsun's open passenger door had whipped shut, snapping a cross in half, but other than that, what was one more dent? No insurance papers would exchange hands.

"I ain't never made no art," the other Kurts admitted.

Under other circumstances, John would have asked for more experience and checked references on the glue-glitter-pine-cone precedent—next Kurts would be taking credit for the milk-carton rocket ship or Popsicle-stick puppet man—but he needed all the help he could get.

"But I'm bhell wimth a bchainsawm," he added, making m and b sounds where none should have been enunciated.

John could see his lip hadn't healed properly since the brawl at Cal's Palace. No surprise there, given the medical attention they had applied, Krazy Glue and bourbon. John didn't want a closer look. He'd be able to tell the two apart from now on, regardless if they answered to one name.

"We need to make stands for these crosses," John explained. "Do either of you know how or where we can find the materials?"

"I got some ideas on the subject," Kurts said. "But I hear you got some lickin' daggers comin' from Albion."

John hadn't heard that expression before and pictured a gang of leather-clad lesbians carrying knives and ice cream cones, castrating everything in their path.

"Better put on yer nard-guard," Kurts said. "Them dykes know more than their way around a three-pronged outlet."

"Prarieb Mamab moo," the other Kurts stammered.

It took a second for John to understand what he had said.

"What'd Franny say 'bout them stands?" the first Kurts asked.

"He's getting more crosses from the Waterfall commune," John said, realizing again, everybody knew everybody in this town and in their own way had a relationship, even if it was an understanding to leave each other alone. Franny had probably worked with Kurts' great-grandfather, just as Billy Chuck's and Lisa's grandfathers had spent time together logging. John wondered when Franny had moved to the valley. How long did it take to become established as a local, truly accepted, not just acknowledged to fill out a softball team or a drunken pause down at the Lodge? Was Grandma's name coming up for membership before she died? Did that give him a leg up? Or one foot in the grave?

"Tell 'em we'll take care of the stands," Kurts said. "By my account, Hank still owes us for losin' to Stafford Loggin'."

John noticed the pair of cleats hanging from Kurts' rearview mirror. He told himself that Hank probably had a woodpile and the Kurtses would liberate a few sticks. It was a good cause and they were on the same softball team. What more explanation did anyone need?

"You got the crossbow in case he wakes up?" Kurts asked his brother.

"Yeb."

"Be back in an hour, Squirrel Boy," Kurts said. "You can count on us."

They burned rubber down the road, launching one last bottle at the Datsun, hitting it where the grille would have been if it hadn't already fallen off. John got out of the car to retrieve the crucifix that had been cut in half during the Kurtses' stunt. Pensive would have to stitch it together with her nail gun. He put another crucifix in its place and continued his work, telling himself there was nothing to worry about, everything was falling into place. This was the way things got done in Boonville.

Setting the last of the load's crosses in place, John could see the Albion Nation had arrived, dressed in overalls and hiking boots. Pensive was explaining the project to them. The women seemed to be coupled off, half of the group wearing baseball caps pulled down low. It didn't take a genius to understand John didn't fit the description Pensive had offered to garner their support. Who knows what she had said? "The sex change is coming soon"? He could see them thinking that this breeder couldn't be the reason that they had taken to the streets. He was the evil rapist Margaret Washington had cautioned them about. Not that they were what John had expected; no leather, knives, or ice cream cones. There was a standstill of misconception.

If they hated men so much, John wanted to know, why did they dress like them? They shouldn't be allowed to wear jockey shorts, sweat socks, or rodeo belt buckles. No Bruce Springsteen bandannas or crew cuts either. No hating your cake and eating it too. If he were a lesbian, he would accentuate his feminine curves with dresses and skirts. Which was probably the kind of thinking that made homosexual women want to ban straight men from discussions. But being ignorant didn't make him homophobic. He was a big Jodie Foster fan, Marlene Dietrich too. Instead of marking him as the enemy, they should try to educate him. Not that any of them appeared to be the official spokesperson for lesbians, but they did call themselves a nation. There must be a manifesto lying around somewhere. There seemed to be a dress code.

John would have liked to ask what they thought about his theory that aside from people born gay, women were more likely to turn to homosexuality than men, becoming gay after bad experiences with the opposite sex, failed marriages, physical abuse, rape. Something a man would rarely do, partially because of the larger taboo of homosexuality among men, but mostly because men, along with most women, didn't view other men as sympathetic. You never heard a man say, "I feel I can be vulnerable around you, Bob, in a way I can't around Mary. Let's fuck." Also the overwhelming media opinion was that women were beautiful. You couldn't blame them for wanting to sleep together. Men were portrayed as clunky and dumb. How could you screw someone you couldn't trust to order a pizza?

Maybe men were missing an opportunity, not branching out within their gender. It would be a battle won for population control. Fewer arguments on Super Bowl Sunday. Not that men and women were that different, although sometimes they seemed to be. Maybe they just wanted different things out of sex and relationships. John wouldn't be the first to propose such a notion. What those things were, he didn't have a clue. But there seemed to be a liberating power these days for a woman not to need a man, some of it economic, some of it spiritual. For whatever reasons, biological, social, or both, John was attracted to women and what they could or couldn't offer him. He almost wished he was gay, to widen his options. As he introduced himself to the Albion Nation, sensing their misplaced anger, he also realized that if he ever did become gay, he would never hate women entirely.

"John," Pensive said, helping him speed up the process, "This is Chris, Steph, Pat, Reggie, Sue, and Mike."

Mike was the only one who smiled. It was clear God had played a trick with her body and she had received more than her fair share of testosterone. She reminded John of a boy who hadn't gone through puberty; clear complexion, youthful face, soft demeanor. But Mike also had an understated strength. Unlike the others, she seemed comfortable to be out at night in Boonville.

Reggie averted her eyes when John said hello. She was the youngest, the rest of the group was somewhere in their thirties or earlier forties. Reggie couldn't have been much past drinking age. She stood, slouching. Uninvited fingers seemed to be jabbing at her sides with pins and needles. She was a voodoo doll of herself.

But aside from her bad posture, she was pretty, with wet brown eyes and a sensual but down-turned mouth that appeared to be in a permanent pout.

"We don't allow the male species on the grounds of Albion Nation," Sue said, trying to blame John's presence for Reggie's discomfort. "That goes for everything; humans, birds, animals. No penises on the premises."

John knew Reggie had bigger problems than proximity with males. She wasn't allergic. Someone had hurt her in a way she couldn't forget and she was going through life waiting for the next bruise.

"Well, I appreciate you all coming here tonight," John said, trying to focus on Reggie to show he meant no harm by being male. "We really needed the manpower."

Oh shit, John thought, realizing his slip, trying to recover with platitudes and by praising Pensive's contribution. It wasn't that careless a thing to say. What was the substitute word, "personpower?" He would have felt like an asshole using that term. And if he had said womanpower, he would never have forgiven himself.

"My grandmother would have been grateful, too," he said, trying to end his blundering. "She believed art was a binding force, one that reaches across race, religion, and gender, bridging prejudices to our commonality. An organic language. In the end, I think this project will reflect all of us."

Unfortunately, there was no keynote speaker or podium to step away from. John stood among the lesbians, holding his broken squirrel cross. There was a hard silence, followed by a scary moment when he realized that all of the Albion Nation had brought hammers. He could feel everyone trying to figure out the next move. Then Pensive stepped forward and took the pieces of wood from John's hands, firing nails through them at an angle that reconstructed the cross and its martyr. Without this gesture, John was certain the Albion Nation would have climbed into their van and driven away. They had their own order and didn't need it upset by some oppressive hetero who chose his words ineptly. But they seemed to accept this ritual as part of John's apology. He didn't know where he had conjured the art jargon or cleverness to attribute their sentiments to Grandma. California must be rubbing off on him.

Before the Albion Nation dispersed to erect squirrels, Franny returned with the final load of crosses, greeting them with a hardy "Evening ladies."

Back to square one, John told himself. So much for an organic language.

Franny didn't seem to have any intention of demeaning the women with the word "ladies," but he was demanding that they use his reference point instead of theirs for any interpretation of the salutation. They seemed to take it in stride. Old age inspired respect if not tolerance in most people. Apparently, they also knew Franny. Mike appeared to be genuinely flattered by his greeting, a cordiality rarely offered in her direction.

"Aren't you dead yet?" Mike said, jokingly.

"You know statistics show women outlive men," Franny answered, with a wink. "I just haven't found the right one to bury me."

John could see Mike was enjoying the novelty of talking with a man, any man, especially a flirting octogenarian. Franny was past posing any kind of threat to her sexuality or politics. It was like someone saying you looked good when you were in a hospital bed. You didn't call them a liar, you just waited for the doctor.

"I'll bury you," Sue said, clearly the hard-liner of the Nation, the only one who hadn't extended Franny her regards.

She was half Franny's age, with the body of a gymnast, limber and powerful, ready to spring into a series of somersaults and flips if the need arose. The features of her face also leaped at you, angular jaw and full lips, dark eyes and thick brow. There was something about her that spoke of cobblestones, black market vegetables, and cast-iron pots. Winters spent in the pelts of dead animals.

Rather than spin a cartwheel, Sue took off her baseball cap and ran her fingers through her stubbled hair. Her muscles flexed. John wondered if she and Mike were a couple, or had been, even though they were both wearing baseball caps. Did butch date butch? He hoped not. Mike seemed nice. Sue was a ballbuster.

"I'll dance on your grave when all of your archaic sexism is dead," Sue said, staking territory nobody had laid any claim to.

Franny looked up from his truck, where he had walked to start unloading crosses. In another time, John could tell, he would have taken a swing at anyone who addressed him with such animosity, male or female. He didn't now, not because he was too old for fisticuffs or was afraid of losing a fight to a fitter member of the opposite sex, but because there was no winning.

"I survived two world wars, young woman," he said, lifting down the tailgate. "I lived through the Great Depression, when I saw people stronger than yourself lining up for stale bread. I've seen things, the depravity of the human condition, that I hope you can't imagine. But never in my eighty-two years did I ever look someone in the eyes and wish them dead."

"Times have changed," Sue said, trying to goad Franny into a cruder reply. "You haven't had to live your life as a woman, then or now, bombarded by repressive language in a male-dominated society."

"However hurtful you may think words are, they aren't bombs," Franny told her, the tailgate locked into place. "Slander isn't hunger. Name calling isn't the end of a rope. They can lead to those things, but there's a difference between the two. I've been called names during my lifetime, believe me. Words nobody uses anymore, Wobbly, Red, slacker, bum. They once kept me from work and incited me more than once to strike my fellow man. And I'm not the tallest fellow in town. Nor am I the lightest of skin. Swarthy. Another word not often used kindly. Not too many people know a Greek when they see one. I've been called most everything, Hebe, Wop, Spic, Kurd. But I allow my actions to describe me, not other people's words."

"You don't know what it's like to be a homosexual in this country," Sue said.

"It's always difficult to be yourself," Franny answered. "When I saw Emma Goldman arrested in Portland for passing out pamphlets, and then again after a lecture in a workers' hall in Walla Walla, talking sense about one big union, only to be deported from this country, I protested her deportation and was clubbed by policemen and thrown in jail. I did it not because I believed in what she was saying a hundred percent, Russia didn't turn out so well, Stalin was no panacea, but because she had a right to say what she thought. She lived under the conditions you described. In my book, no woman more thoughtful or principled, humanitarian or forward thinking, has walked this earth. *She* was a lady."

The Albion Nation was stunned that someone in their midst had seen Emma Goldman lecture in person, and had been arrested on her behalf; it made campaigning for Geraldine Ferraro seem lame. Even Sue was speechless. What could you say to out-feminist that unless you had gone down on Virginia Woolf?

"I'm sorry if I offended you with my wording," Franny said, with diplomatic bite. "It was my mistake. It's clear you are no lady."

John could tell the Albion Nation would no longer object to being called a lady by Franny. From his lips, they would consider it both a polite term for an adult member of the feminine sex and a compliment, the way he had intended. But John wasn't sure, if she were alive today, Ms. Goldman wouldn't have objected. Grandma hadn't liked the word either, but was tolerant of "civil lumpings" as she referred to them. Her official line was: "There are larger battles to fight than semantics."

Sue had a point, there was a psychological load behind the word "lady." It had become a cheesy term implying manners and compliance. John didn't know a better alternative; dame or broad didn't seem any more liberating. Womyn, as he had once heard suggested, was ridiculous. Given a vagina, he thought he would rather be a broad. It sounded stronger and put you in company with the femmes fatales of the forties; Barbara Stanwyck, Rita Hayworth, Lauren Bacall. Seduce and destroy. Heels and a gun holster. John was certain that someday women would reclaim all those words as a part of their history and a source of pride, eventually every group did, among themselves anyway: nigger, fag, redneck. Any unacceptable term could become safe, just as any acceptable label could turn offensive if it were continually used in a derisive manner. It was more tone, intent, and circumstance that mattered. Money and a good army.

Enough of linguistics, John thought; he had already learned that much from trying to talk to Christina when she was in a bad mood. Given the problems implicit in language and people's inability to listen or empathize, it amazed him that anything got accomplished or that two people could cohabit without ripping each other's heads off. But this was no time for a rhetoric debate. Night was turning to day and they were a far cry from finishing the project. Despite the coffee, John was tired. He didn't check his watch. Knowing how late it was would only make it worse.

"Enough small talk," Sue said, appearing to come to the same conclusion. "I came here to do a job, not to be insulted. If you have to address me, my name is Sue."

John was tempted to sing out, "How do you do?" in the voice of Johnny Cash, but restrained himself.

Without another word, Sue headed toward the first cementless area of crosses with her hammer, the rest of the Albion Nation following. Pensive took up her position at the nail gun, shrugging off Franny and Sue's exchange as if the conclusion was as good as could be expected given the fact that lions were lying down with lambs. Mike squeezed Pensive's arm before joining the pack, seeming to say, "You know how Sue gets."

"If she does dance on my grave," Franny told John, one man to another, as they wrestled crosses from the back of his truck. "I hope it's a striptease. Maybe she could raise two things from the dead."

Franny had brought the carving of Sarah in this haul. They lifted it from among the other crosses. Weather had marred one side of the statue with water blotches and there was a long blemish of dirt where it had been resting against the ground. Mites had wormed away a section near her leg. There were patches of fungus on the lower half. John could see it hadn't been a flattering self-portrait to begin with. Sarah's arms were folded across her chest in a guarded manner. She had cut her features accurately, but in doing so they had become distorted; the softness of her skin and grace were lost in the rigidity of the wood, along with the ease of her stance and vitality of her eyes. She would have been better off cheating, distorting her attributes to reach a closer approximation. Sarah was a beautiful woman. The statue was haggard. It was odd that she would choose to chisel herself this way. At least she hadn't whittled her face onto the body of a squirrel.

They slung the statue with a caber toss motion back into the truck after emptying out the rest of the crosses. It belonged at the other end of town in front of the population sign, the last thing Sarah would see as she was leaving. They should have tilted it in the truck bed to get at the crosses underneath instead of pulling it all the way out. Being tired was making them work harder. John didn't know how Franny had managed to load it into his truck at the Waterfall. Someone must have helped, maybe the giant in training, Raven. Either way, Franny was agile, which John attributed to his being so short, keeping a low center of gravity all these years. But if John got to be Franny's age, forget about lifting heavy objects or mixing it up with lesbians, if he was still blowing his own nose he would consider it an accomplishment.

John saw another set of headlights coming from Manchester Road, pausing at the stop sign. He thought it was Cal deciding on a plan of action. The vehicle rolled into the middle of the highway, through the intersection of lanes and across the street, where it parked with its engine running on the skirt of the road, facing them. It was some kind of seventies muscle car.

"Which way are you going to run?" Franny asked him.

John had started to fill the Datsun with crosses to spot the unfinished area so the Albion Nation could do their work. He didn't want to break stride. The phantom driver was going to have to do more than lurk in order to scare him.

"Ignore him," Pensive advised, testing the limits of her extension cord. "He just wants a reaction."

"A man that crazy is liable to get one," Franny said.

"Not the one he wants," Pensive said, firing a couple of nails into the air, which landed in the street with dull thunks.

John couldn't make out Daryl's face at this distance, but he knew it was him. The car idled, missing on one of its pistons. John wondered if Daryl was trying to figure out the meaning of the exhibit or if he had come looking for him.

"Pensive, you want to call Sue and the ladies over," Franny asked.

"He's perpetuating his own negativity," Pensive said. "He wants us to meet him with resistance because it's the only thing that feeds him. He doesn't have the positive energy to join us. He can only destroy us if we let him grow on our anger."

"Or if he has a gun," Franny said, a scenario not in line with ancient myth or the universe's perpetual battle of good versus evil, but one Pensive must have realized was a possibility, because she reloaded her nail gun.

John wasn't worried. If Daryl had planned on taking him out, he wouldn't be fooling around with stalker tactics. He wasn't wily enough to engage in psychological warfare or in control of his emotions to the point where he wouldn't just drive up and start shooting. He must have understood that John and Sarah weren't an item, although the project in some way included her, seeing that her crosses were laid out in the street. What John hoped to achieve with them, Daryl couldn't have known. John wasn't fully aware himself. He only knew he was seducing a side of Sarah that Daryl didn't understand.

"It seems there's always a threat of violence in this town," John said, looking at Daryl and his car. "I'm learning to live with it."

He retreated to the work, believing that doing anything else would give Daryl reason to assume his guilt or cowardice and to attack. Franny and Pensive stood watch for a minute to make sure Daryl wasn't setting up a rifle. Apparently, Daryl had a reputation as a gun nut always up for target practice. A truck neared and John turned at the sound in time to see Daryl drinking from a bottle in the wash of light. Whatever he was consuming wouldn't add to the levity of his mood.

Having committed to ignoring him, John switched his attention to the arrival of a truck whose headlights had left Daryl looming in the dark. By the loud music and skidding brakes, John knew the Kurtses had returned. In the cab, wedged between them, he saw Billy Chuck. In the rear of the truck was an overflowing stack of wooden slats all about the same size, two inches wide and five feet long. They were painted white, peeling in some spots and flecked in others, with a tangle of wire linking them together. John guessed this mound of wood had been Hank's fence.

"Ask and you shall receive," Kurts said, stepping from the truck, waving to Daryl's car across the highway.

The three men looked like a quarter of the Dirty Dozen come straight from the front, tired expressions of recent combat on their faces, pockets of sweat beneath their armpits, fresh mud on their boots. Billy Chuck was wearing the only clothes that John had ever seen him in, causing him to wonder if he had any others. By the way they tugged on their belts, adjusting and wriggling inside their jeans, John suspected they were freewheeling too. Underwear for them was probably considered a middle-class affectation.

"You got two choices for them crucifix stands," Billy Chuck said, spitting dramatically, playing the munitions expert called in for the bombing of a single bridge. "Like for Christmas trees or like for picture stands."

John thought if they could erect the crosses perpendicularly with the picture-stand design, he would prefer that approach to keep the braces out of view. They tested one on a squirrel and it toppled sideways with the slightest touch. It wouldn't be able to sustain the winds. John thought the Christmas-stand model would have to be employed. They did another experiment and found that wouldn't work without shims beneath the top slat on both sides. Too much work, not enough time. Finally, they nailed a slat to the bottom of a cross as if the squirrel were a diver at the end of a platform, then another using the picture frame model, forming a stiff triangle. Perfect. Braces out of view, squirrels stable.

Billy Chuck and the Kurtses emptied their truck, dislodging the wire from the wood. Pensive began attaching stands, Franny driving her Pacer as she went along to keep the nail gun juiced. John was ready to lay out the last of the crosses using the Datsun, but the final ones had to be set near Daryl's car, which got him thinking he should switch roles with someone else. He saw Reggie and Sue returning from their group to check on the next phase of the project. As they approached, John heard Sue tell Reggie that everything was going to be O.K.: "He won't try anything."

John thought the remark was more overreaction to his penis, uncertain what it was they expected him to try? But then he understood they were talking about Kurts, who had dropped what he was doing on his brother's foot.

"Regina?" Kurts said.

Reggie curled into Sue who draped an arm across her back, pulling Reggie close. Kurts' brother shouted something unintelligible from behind his torn lip from either the pain of a crucifix being dropped on his foot or the surprise of discovering Regina was a member of the Albion Nation. Either way, his brother told him to "Shut the fuck up!" Pensive stopped her nailing to listen in, along with Franny. Billy Chuck laughed, understanding what was taking place before John could piece it together.

"What happened to your hair?" Kurts demanded.

"It's Reggie now, dumbshit," Sue told him. "She doesn't want to have anything to do with you."

Reggie peeped at Kurts from beneath Sue's arm.

"I thought you were staying at your folks in Fort Bragg," Kurts said.

"Fort Drag, maybe," Billy Chuck threw in, for the sake of nobody.

"You don't own her," Sue said. "She can do whatever she wants. She doesn't have to answer to you."

"What do you have to do with this?" Kurts asked.

"Everything," Sue clarified, tempting fate. "I'm a woman. I'm her neighbor. I'm her lover."

Kurts clearly believed one of Sue's answers didn't belong with the others.

John thought if Kurts had been the one to hurt Reggie, she had every right to leave him for the next ride out of town, regardless of who was driving. And if Reggie really was a lesbian, she had no business with him in the first place. John was getting into the spirit of small-town meddling. But Reggie had also acted out one of John's fears, the topic of his haiku, being displaced for a member of the opposite sex. How could you argue with that? Reggie couldn't have been asking for much upstairs, given Kurts' conversation and Sue's trite polemics, but downstairs his plumbing was all wrong, a faucet where she wanted a drain. Or something like that. She wanted what Kurts couldn't physically offer. John's heart went out to him, although he thought Kurts would make any woman curious about her own sex.

Watching the couple, John understood why Christina had been so upset; rejecting was the easier end of rejection. It might not be fun pointing someone to the door, but it was better than having it closed in your face. The other part of rejection that cut deep was when your partner found someone else, especially if they did it before you did. That's why John had been so distraught by the news of Good Neighbor Michael. He noticed that happy couples didn't care how other people lived; they were too busy being happy. Rejected single people had time on their hands, hours of it earmarked for resentment and advising others how to conduct their business. They kept photographs and trinkets, recalled memories in diaries, wrote bad poetry, left nasty messages on answering machines, wasted their time praying in vain for their partner to resume a failed relationship. People's problems were the same all across America, only the dialects changed. Sometimes genitalia.

It could have been a physical thing with Christina, too. She wasn't a lesbian, but she hadn't been hardwired to understand John's dreams and fears. You couldn't learn that sort of compassion or line of reasoning. It was everything that lived and breathed in a ghost world that surrounded your senses, sending you messages from everywhere and nowhere at once. You were born into your phobias and unobtainable purpose. Christina hadn't been enough for him, just like Kurts could never satisfy Reggie. But that was the cruelest thing you could say about someone, that they weren't enough.

The current tragedy between Kurts and Reggie played out as theater of the absurd—squirrels filling the stage instead of chairs. Kurts was too dumbfounded to become violent, even with Sue egging him on, calling him names and belittling the power of his appendage. John could tell that Kurts had invested emotion into this woman being ushered inside the Albion Nation van. He stood with his hands hanging uselessly at his sides, mouth open. Sue told him not to follow, threatening personal retribution backed by the Albion Nation; they were armed and trained to defend themselves against male intrusion.

"Wag your weenie within a hundred yards of Albion," Sue warned, "and we'll shoot it off."

Kurts couldn't have heard anything, concentrating as he was on Reggie, who waved apologetically from the front seat of the van. Kurts waved back.

John had seen enough of these scenes to know it would be followed by another. Whether they knew it or not, there was more dialogue to come. They would be incapable of dropping the curtain with so much drama left to play out. They had nothing else going on in their lives. Even rednecks longed for resolution and a better ending than dyke gets girl.

"If Regina's a lesbian, what does that make me?" Kurts wanted to know, watching the van drive away.

"Shit out of butt sticks," Billy Chuck told him, punching his shoulder.

"Hell, I'd give anything to have my heart broken again," Franny said. "You get to be my age, you wonder if the damn thing still works. The last time I fell in love, Truman was in office and she left me for a sonofabitch whose job was to uncover Communists and who probably started his investigation with me. She moved to San Diego and had a whole brood of snitches. She's probably dead now. Since then it's been the heat of a blowtorch for me. That's a long time not to feel your heart beat."

Kurts looked to his brother, who was readjusting his lip with a finger. Pensive drifted back to her workstation. Billy Chuck started breaking slats of fencing with the heel of his boot to make stands for the crosses.

"I should have known somethin' was fishy when she shaved

her pooter," Kurts said, starting in with a hammer. "Those k.d. lang cassettes were a hint too."

John wanted to know if the rest of the Albion Nation was going to continue to help. They weren't going home in their van unless Sue came back for them. It was a long way to Albion on foot. Someone would give them a ride after they finished with the exhibit. If they didn't have something against men driving. Until then they could lend a hand or start walking.

Behind their truck, John saw Billy Chuck share a consolatory line of white powder with Kurts, who rubbed at his nose and gums after jerking his head away from a piece of mirror with a rolled up bill in his hand. His eyes watered. Billy Chuck lifted the mirror toward John. He declined, climbing into the Datsun to do a cross count. He drove by the Albion Nation working vigilantly under Mike's direction. They must have been curious where their other members had gone, but maybe they thought they were running an errand or making out. John didn't say a word. He calculated they were eight crosses short, not including the special cross they would have to construct for Sarah's statue. Twenty-nine more squirrels were also going to be needed. He didn't want to retrieve them alone because Daryl would surely follow him, insisting on a showdown.

John turned to look for Daryl's idling car, thinking he had heard the noise of the engine coming from somewhere else. It was gone. He listened, trying to discover its new location, but the revving seemed to come from everywhere at once in the echo of the valley. It could have been another car. Maybe Daryl went home. Psychopaths had to sleep too, John thought, although probably not as much as normal people. As a precautionary measure, he sent Pensive to his cabin for the last squirrels, relieving her of the nail gun.

In an hour, he was standing in the middle of Highway 128 in the predawn light, near the spot where he had blacked out. The exhibit was coming together, gathering force with each erection. Looking down the road toward the south end of town, he was flanked by two growing rows of crucifixes. Everyone was making stands now and the hammering was as loud as a stampede. In another hour they would be done. Tonight he wouldn't need a bed with Christina in it, he would just need a bed.

He saw another car turn from Manchester Road. It was

moving slowly, taking in the squirrels as it cruised the strip, waiting a good hundred crosses before switching on its flashing lights.

Cal didn't bother to get out of the car. John saw he was still in his pajamas, his gun holster looped around blue flannel marked with little gold badges.

"Your friend Daryl says you're keepin' him awake," Cal said, not angry so much as perturbed. "You want to explain to me what the fuck you're doing?"

John squatted next to the cruiser so he was eye level with Cal. The morning air was cold and full of potential. He looked at his hands. They were blistered and cut from hammering and handling the wooden squirrels and slats of fencing. Then he turned his head to see Franny putting up another crucifix, not bothering to stop even with the police car present. The others continued as well, the town more than the exhibit looking like it had been built overnight.

"I wish I could," John said, and knew he was speaking for all of them, even the residents of Boonville who hadn't helped in the project other than to be counted in their own way, up on the cross in effigy or in their homes for real, but would wake up to confront the spectacle of 715 squirrels nailed to crosses lining their small town, and be forced to make some kind of connection. "I think it has something to do with Christ."

16

"The road don't even end in Katmandu," Sarah reminded herself, walking the path to the main house, ready to say goodbye to Mom, the Waterfall, and Janis Joplin, all with one tearless farewell, hating that Janis's bit of lame improv had been imbedded in her brain and recalled like a line from Keats. Like it actually meant something. It was a stupid thing to say, even during a live performance when you're reaching for something extra, high on dope and Jack Daniel's, in front of an audience full of hippies and bikers, all potted and plowed themselves, even considering the gobbledygook political mysticism of the times when Katmandu must have meant something to a bunch of freaks in training. Nepal, wow! Sitars, wow! They've got good hash and the Dalai Lama, right? Janis was a dead drunken dipshit. She almost had an excuse. But it was an unforgivable thing to quote to your daughter whenever you conveniently failed her as a mother.

"I know you're upset, but I can't drop what I'm doing every time you need me," Mom would say for any number of reasons, forgetting to pick Sarah up at school, leaving her with perverts in potential rape situations, and Sarah could feel it coming, whether it made sense or not, more of a crutch in Mom's speech than words of wisdom. "You know, hon, the road don't even end in Katmandu."

Sarah would rather listen to the whole Bob Seeger song "Katmandu," than hear Mom or Janis say that one line ever again. Bob Seeger was another dipshit. Dad listened to him. At least Dad had the good sense not to go around quoting him, telling Sarah when something went wrong, "You know, hon, it's funny how the night moves."

Sarah paused, trying to steady herself by putting a hand to a tree and bending at the waist. Her body felt hot and swollen, insides pressing to get out. Having Janis stuck in your head was enough to make anyone physically ill, but she knew this was a different kind of nausea. Shutting her eyes, she cursed Daryl and felt her stomach muscles tighten. She inhaled deeply, but the air had gone sour. "Shit," she said, and her dinner from last night at Cafe Beaujolais came up almost as it had been served; salad, mushroom soup, grilled rabbit with new potatoes and baby carrots, and an acidic local Cabernet that no longer complemented the meal.

Wiping her mouth with her shirt sleeve, Sarah couldn't wait to have the rest of it out of her body too. Before Lisa had shown up at the restaurant last night in Mendocino, she had to fight back tears. The sound of the ocean crashing in on itself, couples from the B & B's coming in for romantic dinners, holding hands in candlelight, walking the beach looking for shells. She wanted to scream at them, "There are no shells on this beach, just broken bits in the sand!" She had to go to the bathroom to compose herself. A waitress was washing her hands. Sarah didn't know how, but every woman on the planet could tell when you were pregnant. They saw it in the pallor of your skin. Prenatal curves. Men didn't have a clue, they were beasts. They couldn't even tell when a child was their own. Women were mammals, they knew, sensing when one of their own was manufacturing milk and if that female didn't want to be gestating. They knew by the way you skulked past, not looking into their faces when you should have been happy to greet the world.

"I'm sorry," the waitress said.

She wasn't talking about using the last of the paper towels either, although she acted like that's what she meant after she saw Sarah recoil and hustle toward the lone bathroom stall, which was occupied. Sarah rattled the door, freaking out the patron on the other side who yelled, "I'm hurrying! I'm hurrying!"

"I'll be all right," Sarah reassured the waitress.

"I hope so," she said. "I'll be out here if you need anything."

Sarah didn't want her sympathy; that wasn't solidarity. Fuck sisterhood and fuck motherhood, you couldn't rely on anyone but yourself. She was making the right decision. Her body was just switching on its defense mechanism of hormones and guilt, trying to have its voice heard. It would be quieted soon. And if the waitress understood, she would wipe that stupid merciful look off her face and get back to her tables. Someone must need their overpriced sprigs of salad identified.

When the waitress left, Sarah realized that she had to get out of the bathroom without the woman in the stall seeing her, otherwise she wouldn't be able to sit through the meal knowing that the woman was somewhere in the restaurant watching her. Lisa would sense something was wrong. And Sarah didn't plan on telling Lisa she was pregnant. They had pledged they wouldn't go through this shit again, even if they had to raise a baby together. But Sarah didn't want Lisa raising her child. It wasn't a houseplant. Lisa was great, Sarah loved her dearly, but it was still Lisa, not a real father. They weren't a lesbian couple who wanted to live an alternative lifestyle. They were friends who had told necessary lies in order to distance themselves from what had happened, trying to convince themselves it wouldn't happen again and that they could take care of it together if it did. But here she was. The toilet flushed.

Sarah splashed some water onto her face and hurried from the restroom. She grabbed a napkin from the busing station and dried herself, then threw it into a bus tray. If Lisa asked any questions she would blame her mood on her period and the stress of moving, the redness of her eyes on allergies. She would call her in a couple weeks when it was over. They'd go shopping with harvest money and get sloppy on sidecars and eat foie gras, forget about the whole thing.

"You want me to come down with you?" was the first question Lisa asked.

She would have just offered to help move if she didn't know, Sarah thought. "Coming down" implied emotional support. For what, unloading boxes? Sarah didn't need help dumping Daryl. Leaving Mom at age twenty-six? Ordering rabbit probably put a weird vibe into the air, telling Lisa this wasn't the only dead bunny Sarah was responsible for lately. Why did she think Lisa would be less perceptive than other women? She was her best friend. Sarah could say, "Remember that guy at that place that time?" And Lisa could fill in the blanks. They were linked at the subconscious.

"Is something wrong?" was Lisa's second attempt to elicit a confession.

"No," Sarah said.

The lie sat there between them, untouched, like an hors d'oeuvre neither wanted to taste but both knew had taken a long time to prepare. Lisa loved her too much to call coup. It wasn't in the nature of their relationship. Lisa worshipped her, had followed her through years of trouble and bad fashion, would rob a liquor store in white pumps after Labor Day if Sarah gave the order. Since Sarah's first day at the junior high, she was the older sister left in charge. But it wasn't supposed to be acknowledged. With this lie, Sarah had told Lisa that despite all they'd been through there were things she didn't trust her with. Didn't trust anyone with.

From now on, Sarah told herself, looking at her closest friend, who seemed a million miles away, no man is going to enter me without protection. But that's what she had said last time. Then came the heat of the moment, her defenses falling away as easily as her panties, believing she could create something miraculous from her fumbling limbs. It was becoming more difficult each day to maintain faith in the future. Sex was easy, the next day was hard.

Sarah spilled her wine. The waitress from the bathroom arrived to clean the mess though it wasn't her table. Sarah didn't apologize for the overturned glass, but tried to keep her eyes from the waitress. She took an inventory of the diners as a diversion, coast hipsters and tourists, dressed in a way that suggested that they spent their paychecks on patio furniture instead of clothes. Nothing revealed in their faces, the comfort of wine and anticipation of the meal. Nobody in the restaurant had noticed the spill except one woman who must have been in the bathroom stall Sarah had rattled. She was whispering to her husband, who nodded in a consoling manner, reaching across the table to pat her hand. The waitress didn't bring a fresh tablecloth, but replaced their napkins and Sarah's wine. Sarah wanted to leave. She felt like a fish in an aquarium, the one everyone suspects of eating the other fish.

To get back on track, she and Lisa talked about old times. Some things never changed, regardless of how hard you tried. You only had the available materials to build from. Sarah ate her dinner and thought about the blood spots she sometimes found on the embryos of eggs, because her rabbit tasted a lot like chicken.

On the trail to the main house the air still seemed rancid. Sarah took a deep breath and on the strength of it straightened herself. Harvest was over. She was reaping what she had sown, eighty grand and a belly full of Daryl's love child. At the close of the sixties it wouldn't have been so bad a proposition, but it was twenty years later and she had seen where that same deal had landed Mom. She was climbing to that very place.

She had been going to cut out without saying goodbye to Mom, but the Squirrel Boy had left her a note in the form of a poem, too good for him to have written, but appropriately confusing: "Safe upon the solid rock the ugly houses stand: Come and see my shining palace built upon the sand!" Whatever, Squirrel Boy, she had thought, what did you do, fix your lopsided porch? But then he had added, "Your mother hopes to see you before you leave. She has a present for you." It was enough of a guilt trip to work. For Mom, not the Squirrel Boy. It was going to take more than a couple, copied verses of poetry for a man to get on her good side right now. Squirrel Boy was sweet, but in his own way as clueless as anyone else around Boonville. Sarah had packed her truck and was ready to vamanos, roll with the momentum that told her to run and don't look back. After her dinner with Lisa, she didn't want to face anyone. She had decided to skip Squirrel Boy and forgo the farewells to everyone but Mom. She would write. Or she wouldn't. The whole town must know the dirt and that she was leaving by now anyway, for whatever that was worth, about a pound of catshit in her book. They could read about her someday in *Art Digest*, the ones who could read. The rest could look at the pictures.

She had told Lisa that she could stay in her cabin rent-free until she decided what she wanted to do with it. Sarah would rather not grow dope next season, though it was hard to pass on the easy money since the irrigation system was already in place and that was the difficult part of growing, aside from worrying. She would rather sell her portion of the commune, but who knew how much she could get for it? Without a good lawyer, nothing. When push came to shove, hippies were litigious; all those arrests in the sixties had gotten them used to going to court. And Communists knew the value of everything, never relinquishing any capital without bloodshed: "What's yours is ours" was their underlying sentiment. A historical fact. The contracts were in Wesley's and the Poobah's names too, and they would try to screw her worse than Daryl. A clean break sounded better. They could fuck themselves, which she knew they did anyway, in twos, threes, and clusters. It would be a cold day in hell before she had another conversation with any Whitward or any Waterfall resident.

She tugged at her lucky red hat. She didn't like to wear it unless she was doing something artistic, or harvesting, not wanting the magic to run out by using it in an unwarranted context. Lucky red hats didn't grow on trees. And there was probably a specific kind of hat for leaving town or talking to your mother, most likely a helmet, but she needed something extra to get her on the road. Sometimes the definition of creation was to keep something alive. Her survival would be an achievement in itself. Dad would understand. If he knew anything, it was the art of making an exit.

When Sarah reached the main house, after stopping twice more to heave on the way, she found Jeremy Roth lying on the deck looking like he would lick his balls if he could. She heaved again. Jeremy seemed amused. Sarah knew Mom was inside because when she had checked her cabin she found an empty video-store bag, the first sign of a Jill Clayburgh festival. Or something equally foreign. The main house had the VCR. So she had no questions for the Princeton Primitive who probably had one of his own questions answered when she puked. He was laughing at her as she climbed the steps. Sarah thought it was a breach of his grunting oath. Not wanting him to stray too far from his natural self, she kicked him as hard as she could.

"Hasta los huevos, butthole," she said, putting all of her weight behind her foot.

Jeremy didn't retaliate. None of the other Primitives were around and they didn't get tough without the pack. She had only managed to kick him in the leg too, missing his vitals when he moved at the last second to cover himself. It probably hurt though, and there would be a bruise. He deserved worse. For years she couldn't bring friends over to her house because of these assholes; either she was too ashamed of the freak show or her friends' parents wouldn't let them come. Rednecks may be stupid, but they had sense enough when it came to hippies. Lisa had been the first, only because her mom was dead and her dad was a drunk. It was a month before she came back, asking if the nude giant was going to be there before she accepted an invitation to dinner. There was a certain lure and fascination with human oddities, as long as you didn't have to live with them. But from the first day, Sarah would have paid her quarter not to look.

She paused before going into the main house because it seemed Jeremy was ready to break his Primitive vow and speak, maybe even stand and attack. Sarah picked up a rusty antique iron lying on the deck seemingly for the purpose of smashing across this pervert's skull, or maybe it was a door stop. Take your pick. Jeremy thought better of it and limped to a corner of the deck. He didn't want a piece of her. Not the piece he was going to get anyway.

"What are you going to do with that?" Mom asked, when Sarah walked inside carrying the iron.

"I haven't decided yet," Sarah answered, seeing they were the only two in the main house. "Where is everybody?"

"I think they went to the waterfall," Mom said. "Marty and Raven were watching the movie but they got bored."

Sarah saw the video boxes on the coffee table next to a bowl of popcorn, a bag of carob-covered raisins, and a half-smoked doob. Mom had rented *The Rose*, *Looking for Mr. Goodbar*, and *The Turning Point*. She held a wine glass in her lap, hunkering down for a triple feature of depression. On the screen, Diane Keaton was also having a drink. Sarah identified the movie as *Looking for Mr. Goodbar*, far from a feel-good crowd-pleaser. Nobody but Mom had any desire to revisit these films. Watching the credits was enough to bum you out.

"I think you took me to see this in Ukiah when I was twelve," Sarah said, putting down the iron.

"It's a classic," Mom said. "They don't make films like this anymore."

Thank God, Sarah thought. Maybe we are evolving as a species.

But she had the feeling that if she came back in twenty years, Mom would be doing the same thing, getting high, drinking wine, taking inventory of her anger, acting out her own version of *An Unmarried Woman*. Mom hardly went out to the movies anymore and rarely art films because she didn't get down to San Francisco except to shop for clothes. Museums and galleries had been crossed off her list. She had the money to travel, but outside of flying to Bali in the winter, where she sat on the beach and read whatever paperback the Poobah recommended, she didn't go anywhere. To Mendocino for dinner, that was it. Boonville, to the hotel. Ukiah, for self-help books. No bars, no men. She used to make the scene, cavort and carouse. Sarah didn't know if Mom saw her friends outside of their healing circles anymore. This wasn't menopause, this was a conscious decision to stop.

Mom turned from the television, glancing at Sarah's lucky red hat, then at her stomach. If she didn't believe the rumors before, Sarah thought, they had been confirmed now. She could tell Mom wasn't taking it lightly. Her distress was coming from somewhere other than their last conversation at the waterfall or Sarah wearing the lucky red hat, which Mom hated because it had Dad's name on the front and Sarah relied on it as a source of Higher Self, calling on some aspect of her father that Mom couldn't tap into and failed to inspire in Sarah. It couldn't be the coming abortion; Mom was pro-choice. She had made the same decision herself, before and after Sarah had been born. And she couldn't have known about Sarah's appointment at the clinic, not even intuitively. Nobody's radar was that good. Sarah concluded that Mom's problem was that she couldn't stand the thought of anything else having Dad's name on it. If Sarah were to have a baby without a father, it would bear the last name McKay. Another scotch-guzzling potato eater. Charming and unreliable. But there was no way she was going to raise a child in this X-rated carnival atmosphere. No absent fathers. No pot-smoking, alcoholic, hippie, agoraphobe grandmas influencing her children.

"I guess you heard I'm moving to San Francisco in about ten minutes," Sarah said. "Squirrel Boy said you had something for me."

"You know, hon, I don't know when we stopped being friends," Mom said, reaching for the remote and pausing the movie.

Sarah didn't know when they ever had been friends. And was the point of having children to be their friends? Find someone else to tell your troubles to and borrow money from.

"I miss you," Mom continued, Diane Keaton frozen behind her. "I used to think it was you and me against the world. I look at you now, and I see myself at your age. I don't know where all the time went."

Sarah didn't care where all the time went so much as where all the time was going, the next few minutes in particular. Up the hill, down the hill. Listening to Mom lament. Same old shit. She was ready to establish her own clock and punch in overtime without Mom.

"It doesn't seem fair. I'm not that old," Mom said. "My life can't be coming to a close. I'm not through with it yet."

You're not even 50, Sarah wanted to point out, but instead crossed her arms, trying to guess what Mom had swallowed recently other than a carob-covered raisin. She could hear the fear of a drug crash in her speech, the paranoid arc of too much speed coupled with the fatigue of being awake too long. But her voice wasn't racing, her pupils weren't dilated. It definitely wasn't dope or wine, unless one or the other had been laced. Mom was riding something unknown to Sarah, something from the medicine chest cut with the stimulus of isolation, old videos, and her daughter's imminent departure.

"I wish we could talk," Mom said, and the heaviocity in her voice was gone, stripped to a tone Sarah remembered hearing as a girl in San Francisco when they ate peanut butter and jelly on crackers in the park and Mom pushed her on the merry-go-round, reciting her own made-up song that delighted them both no end, "Here we go round on the merry-go-round." One line repeated until their sides split.

"I don't know what happened," Mom confessed.

Sarah looked at her, trying to find that woman in the park somewhere inside this middle-aged hippie lying on a $5,000 couch in a self-made funk of booze and bad vibes. Nothing was sadder than a dropout who had sold out and then been passed by.

"Here we go round on the merry-go-round," Sarah said to herself.

But maybe Mom had swallowed a truth serum and was speaking from some distant place in her heart that was dormant but not yet dead, smothered by smoke and denial, choking on the remnants of pills and regret, but still fighting for a kind of release and sobriety. The Poobah could have mixed a batch of sodium pentothal in his lab for kicks. Sarah knew residents of the Waterfall, Mom included, would take anything if they thought it would alter their state of consciousness.

"I really wish we could talk," Mom repeated.

Sarah's head seemed to be coming apart at her temples. She didn't want to have this conversation. She thought this might be her nineteenth nervous breakdown. Hers, not Mom's. Mom was well into the hundreds, severe depressions not included. Sarah could feel her body revolting against her mind. Mom knew how to manipulate her worse than a snake charmer working a cobra. Soon she would be dropping words like "home" and "family" and Sarah would become defenseless, seven years old again. The strain of standing in the same room with Mom was becoming too much. Sarah thought she might hurl, but didn't know what she had left inside of her to come up. She knew anger was the way out. Focus on everything that had been fucked up. No forgiveness. But she wanted to believe Mom so badly, wanted to play the traditional roles of mother and daughter for even an hour to see how it felt, that whenever Mom threw down bread crumbs, Sarah followed the trail not knowing which one of them was more lost.

"I wish we could talk, too, Mom," Sarah replied, wanting to know if having one parent who cared about you was asking too much. "But I'm on my way out of here."

"Wait, I do have something for you," Mom said, reaching for a small box on the coffee table. "A going-away present, I guess."

It was a ring box with the name of a jeweler stamped on the felt exterior, gray with silver trim. Sarah had never seen it before and she had gone through all of Mom's drawers at one time or another, including her metal strongbox in the back of her closet. The ring box reeked of yellowed letters and birth certificates. Sarah wondered if it had been purchased at a pawn shop or if the box held something other than its original contents. Neither of them wore jewelry, except for earrings and the occasional necklace. They were that rare breed of hippie that didn't go in for beads and bracelets. Too gauche for Mom's taste, who even in her hard-core days snuck peaks at *Mademoiselle* down at the market. The only ring Sarah had worn was her wedding band, which she still wore, but on her friendship finger. Mom's fingers were bare as the day they headed north, when she had made a pit stop at China Beach—the same spot where Dad had proposed to her with the Golden Gate Bridge behind him—and Mom tossed her wedding ring into the waves, claiming she was as likely to find that ring again as she was another husband.

But when the box was in Sarah's hand, she knew what it held. It was the same feeling in a cemetery that draws you to a family grave. There was a heat emanating from the box like she was holding one of the biscuits Mom used to make before cooking became identified as part of the conspiracy against women. "Careful, don't burn yourself," Mom would caution and Sarah would take a big bite anyway, the taste of milk and butter filling her mouth. Dad chirping, "That's my girl." But maybe that never happened. Maybe there never were drop biscuits and happy family dinners. Maybe she invented them to have something to long for, telling herself another convenient lie for survival. Sarah was more afraid now to open the box than she ever was to burn her mouth on one of those biscuits. She swore to God, Mom used to bake.

"You might not believe this," Mom said, waiting for Sarah to accept her present, "but having you was the best thing I ever did."

Sarah snapped open the jeweler's box and stared at Mom's wedding ring. Of course Mom didn't throw it away, she wasn't nearly the revolutionary she wanted to be. How could she toss ten years of her life into the ocean and pretend they didn't happen? There wasn't enough water to cover it up.

"It's hard to peak when you're twenty," Mom told her. "Knowing you'll never create something as beautiful ever again."

Sarah was going to start crying, and not stop.

"I was happy once, you know," Mom said, and Sarah knew she hadn't invented anything, there were simply different versions of the same facts. "As delusional and short-lived as that happiness may have been, there were days in my early twenties when I didn't have to think, I just was. That's what happiness is, not having to think. Doing everything right on instinct. But when the time came for your father to be the bullfighter and for me to feel like a princess, it didn't happen."

Goddamn, Sarah hated goodbyes.

"Take it," Mom said. "It's yours."

Sarah's first instincts were to shut the box and return the gift. But she knew there was more to it than that. She decided whatever bad luck followed the wedding ring was a spell cast upon the world and it could be broken by the promise of the hope and strength of the original giving. She slipped it on, remembering how she had cried the day she and Mom left for the Waterfall, knowing it was truly over between Mom and Dad, and the day she herself walked down the aisle and how Mom's tears mussed her mascara. The ring fit snugly on her friendship finger, up against Daryl's offering. A true marriage.

Mom put down her wine and stood. Sarah was unable to remember the last time they had hugged. There was a distinct smell to Mom's flesh that Sarah recognized as being not unlike her own, masked slightly by stale dope smoke and the leather couch. It was important to Sarah not to cry and to be the one to release her hold first. Mom clung to her after she had stopped squeezing. Sarah focused on a spot beyond the walls of the main house where she would soon be living the rest of her life.

"I love you, hon," Mom said.

"I love you too, Mom," Sarah said, breaking from her grip, "but I've got to go."

Before she knew it she was inside her truck, driving the winding road she had traveled a zillion times away from the Waterfall. Go, go, go, she told herself, the sun powering the heat of an Indian summer that couldn't quite get rolling, one of those days twenty degrees cooler than you thought it was when you looked out the window. It would become hot soon after this cold front left, but until then leaves were beginning to turn and it was the start of another fall. Sarah's favorite season. She opened the window to feel the air against her face, temporarily relieving her nausea, and pushed her Cowboy Junkies tape into the cassette player. It was always fall in San Francisco, cool and a bit damp. "Put on a sweater if you're cold," Mom used to say, but Sarah didn't want to remember any of that now.

Don't look back, she reminded herself.

But she should have been looking forward with more care. As Sarah approached Boonville, near the Anderson Valley Way turnoff, she didn't see the lamb that had wandered into the highway and she hit it squarely in an explosion of mutton and wool before it could bleat a defense. The wheel jerked in her hand. She applied the brakes with a rush of adrenaline. She could feel the animal's life force rushing through her. She turned off the music. When she backed up to the lamb, she saw it was dead. There was nothing she could do. It wasn't her fault. Dumb fucking animal. It should have stayed in its pen. She was too rattled to get out of the truck for a closer inspection or to assess the dent that would be imprinted in her bumper. She'd wait until she had to stop for gas in Santa Rosa or made it to the St. Francis before she checked the damage. She couldn't look the sheep in the eyes. The sight of blood would make her puke. It was a bad omen.

I'll stop in town and tell Hap or someone at the hotel, she thought; the lamb probably belonged to Hank. He should check his fence before the whole flock got out, stupid goddamn redneck.

If the leader had got loose, the rest would follow. Sarah wasn't certain she would stop. She wanted to put distance between herself and Boonville, not go back on any of her decisions. But when she reached the turnoff for Manchester Road, there was a traffic jam and a mass of sheep milling within the sporadic movement of cars.

It was a sign.

She knew it was a sign even before she saw the first squirrel nailed to one of her crosses. And then the next one. And the next. And the next. And realized there was a row of them on each side of the street as far as she could see. People were inspecting them, causing more of a delay. Hank had his big rig and was trying to round up his livestock, causing more congestion. Sarah spotted Billy Chuck and Kurts laughing at him from the back of their truck. Cal's cruiser was parked nearby and he was explaining things like there was an answer other than the end was near and the Messiah was walking amongst them. Sarah could see a group of angry motorists calling for the messenger's head, giving Cal an earful. Franny was standing next to him with Pensive Prairie Sunset and Ms. Manly Mike of the Albion Nation, smiling at the commotion. Sarah was certain that Franny was somehow involved with this, but the others, although capable of deviant behavior, who knew why they'd become a part of this spectacle? Franny waved at Sarah but she didn't acknowledge him, more determined than ever to find her way through this maze.

It was like the project she had planned, "The Blood of Christ in Wine Country," except the Squirrel Lady's squirrels had replaced the wooden sculptures of the town's population. They scowled at her as she passed. This was what Squirrel Boy must have meant by his note, "Come and see my shining palace built upon the sand." He knew it wouldn't last. As soon as the locals counted the number of squirrels and made the connection, they wouldn't stand for the effigies of themselves to remain. Frightened by their reflection, they would destroy that part of themselves they couldn't heal.

As Sarah drove past the hotel, she could see Hap with a microphone stuck in his face. There were two network news vans and a small crowd in the parking lot, rubberneckers bringing traffic to a halt. Sarah could hear Hap harping Boontling above the noise of the sheep. She never paid much attention to the local tongue spoken by a few of the old-timers. She could only pick out the general meaning of some of the words. Hap would be tonight's local-color sound bite.

"Bahl or nonch," he said, "You got a classic johnem of a crayzeek cock-darley and a lizzied appoled ready to pike. Turn this cow-skullsey Boont into a skype region, a kingster of squeekyteeks. Any oshtook ridgy could see that. But I ain't one to harp lews 'n larmers."

Sarah felt her pulse in her ears. She tried to remain steady in the driver's seat, not looking toward the cameras. Her life was nobody else's business. Gawkers. They had the same problems as her, whether they knew it or not. Minus the sheep. An image of the animal she had left in the highway resurfaced as she watched its family filling the streets to stop its killer from leaving the scene of the crime. The squirrels resembled a jury of her peers ready to bring in a guilty verdict. She knew Boonville was the jail, but who would dare preside as judge? There was no God. Her early days at Catholic school were enough to teach her that.

Her heart was pumping fifty miles an hour faster than her truck was moving, her mind running at a pace close behind. Hungry, angry, lonely, tired, she ran through the H.A.L.T. list again, reminding herself to breathe. Too much was happening. She knew she was partially responsible for the chaos, but she wanted off this fucking merry-go-round.

"It's aliens tryin' to communicate like them patterns in the wheat fields in Iowa," she heard Skeeter telling someone outside the market. "A sure case of first contact."

The traffic lessened as she neared the edge of town, but it was more than simple road rage she felt building as she approached the city limits. Something was about to burst. Something the St. Francis, an abortion, wedding rings, or leaving Boonville could not repair. Not all the king's horses or all the king's men. Not any man, woman, or child. Nothing could put her back together again.

Sarah checked her rearview mirror and saw Boonville in an upheaval, sheep and locals, tourists and cars roaming the highway, hemmed in by the two rows of crucified squirrels as if their expression of shame and disgust would forever contain them. She thought she saw Daryl's Camaro in the middle of the turmoil but turned her eyes away, having seen enough. But there before her, at the end of the row of squirrels, in front of the town's population sign, looming above the hood of her truck, was the carving of a woman affixed to a cross with a nail pounded through her head and stomach. She steered to the side of the road, parking in front of the crucifix, and studied the image of herself that she had created.

Sarah began to cry.

17

John was dreaming when he heard the knock on his door. In the dream, he was a teacher correcting tests for an English class at Anderson Valley High School and the students were getting perfect scores by answering all the true-false questions true. At first he thought they were cheating or it was his mistake for having designed a test with only true answers. But when he graded the essay question, "How can art affect our daily lives?" he discovered their responses were unique and insightful, although written in a language he didn't recognize as English but was able to understand anyway, a slangy dialect of American full of odd nouns. He looked up from one of the exams to praise a student, but found himself looking out on a classroom of squirrels, all with a red apple in front of them, missing a bite.

John decided to answer the door, thinking it would be Blindman or Cal or one of his cohorts come to tell him that the crucifix project had been dismantled and a mob was forming to string him up. "Dancing at the end of a rope without music," he told himself, forgetting where he had heard that expression. He walked from his bedroom, tucking his shirt into his pants, having slept in his clothes again. He wondered if there was special attire for a hanging, aside from the rope necktie the guest of honor was required to wear. He didn't want to be underdressed.

"Hello," Sarah said.

The sun was bright behind her. John could hardly see. By the glare, he figured it was late afternoon.

"Nice work down in town," she said. "What better way to spend your Sunday than to see yourself crucified? You really know how to get a girl's attention."

John raised a hand to shade his eyes. He saw Sarah's eyes were red and her nose needed wiping. She was trembling and looked like she had climbed out of an over-chlorinated swimming pool, except she wasn't wet.

"I borrowed your crosses," John said.

"I saw that," Sarah answered. "You hammered a few nails through my sculpture too. It was quite a statement. Tell me, what did I ever do to you, Squirrel Boy?"

John felt the stare of the two squirrels towering behind her. He had grown tired of their criticism and sledged two smaller squirrels into their sides when he had returned home this morning, trying to use the smaller squirrels as handles to rotate the big ones to point away from the cabin. But they were too heavy to move by himself. He almost threw out his back trying. They remained frozen in their position and dissatisfaction.

"I meant it as a compliment," he said, noticing Sarah's face now looked as much like one of the frowning squirrels as his own.

"Next time send flowers," Sarah suggested. "I like tuberose."

John could tell she wasn't exactly angry, more disturbed by the experience of the crucifixes. He couldn't have expected any less of a reaction, but there had come a point in the project when he was no longer in control, working on instinct, uncovering a piece of himself that had been hidden. It was strange, but when he was finishing the exhibition, he didn't care or think about any specific individual. There seemed to be a greater force guiding him. It surpassed his needs or Sarah's, a common agony and indefatigable hope that was bigger than Boonville. That became his motivation.

"It was your idea," John said, getting his bearings.

He wasn't trying to deflect blame. The truth was that without Sarah he never would have conceived of the project. He tried to explain to her the events leading up to the first nail, starting with his visit to the Waterfall and meeting her mother and the giant and the troll, then rambled into stories about his family, Grandma, and Christina. He mentioned the others' involvement, Pensive, the Albion Nation, Billy Chuck, the Kurtses, and how they had put their own marks on the crosses. He tried to lay bare his intentions, but it still wasn't clear to him why he had done what he had done or its full significance. The meaning would vary depending on the understanding and compassion each viewer brought to the work. For him, like Franny had suggested, it meant release. He had pieced together order, a reflection of himself that felt truthful, linking him to a specific time, place, and community.

"I hope you're not mad at me," John said. "I heard you were leaving and it was all I could think of to do."

"I'm not mad at you," she said, shaking her head, turning to face the valley, then setting her eyes directly back to his. "In fact, you might be the only person in the world I'm not mad at right now."

"Maybe this isn't the time to tell you," John said. "I made a deal with Cal to keep the crosses up so you could see them."

"What kind of deal?" she said, eyebrows lifting.

John told her about Balostrasi and the earring and what the giant at the commune had said about "burying strangers." Sarah asked how that affected her. John said that, without naming names or telling him what he was doing on the side of the mountain that night, he told Cal the approximate location of the ear they had uncovered. In return, Cal guaranteed to guard the project until she saw it, providing it was no later than tonight. John figured with the dope harvested and Sarah out of town, they were off the hook if Cal found the stomped site or the other patch, which would be a miracle because his directions were vague to say the least.

Sarah shook her head, asking John if he knew how long it took to set up an irrigation system, to find natural springs and water sources, to lug hoses and dig trenches. How expensive it was to start from scratch? How hard it was to scout locations? The risk involved? How everyone in the valley knew who was growing on that ridge, so the Waterfall was in deep shit if there was an investigation. And with her gone, everyone at the commune would think she ratted them out. Unless the Feds found her first.

"Cal doesn't care if you're growing dope," John said. "Especially if it's gone. That's not his job."

"That's what you think," Sarah said.

"I couldn't have it on my conscience," John said. "If Aslan killed Balostrasi he should be put away."

"Poachers disappear in these hills every year," Sarah said. "They know what they're getting into. Not that that makes it O.K., but I didn't set up the dynamic. I wouldn't kill someone trying to boost my crop, but I wouldn't steal someone's hard work either. If he's guilty, I hope they lock the Poobah up and throw away the key. But let me tell you, if he did do it, it's the least of his crimes."

"What could be worse than murder?" John said.

"I'll let you answer that yourself," Sarah said. "I don't want to think about it."

"I'm sorry if I got you in any trouble," John said.

"Don't worry, the Feds coming after me is a long shot," Sarah said, cutting short the lecture. "The Poobah's been surfing a wave of bad karma for years. It's about time it closed out on him."

Enough said, John thought, ready to leave the subject alone. He knew a lawyer who could get him out of whatever he had stumbled into so far, as long as he didn't fall any further. Bean Bean's cousin routinely cleared citizens in Miami unlucky enough to be in the proximity of large quantities of cocaine at the wrong time, usually a straw's length away in a Porsche parked in a staked-out parking lot of a convenience store. They walked with probation, donating their vehicles to the judge's favorite charity. That sort of help was a telephone call and a nonrefundable cash retainer of five thousand dollars away. But he was worried about Sarah. Although she seemed to be taking everything in stride, it could be more out of habit than choice.

"The golden goose always dies," she said. "I'll be all right, nothing's in my name up there. I needed to make a clean break anyway."

John could see that despite the problematic nature of the information he had disclosed, it had come as a relief for Sarah. Decisions had been made. It was out of her hands now. She seemed grateful for the intervention, regardless of the outcome. She could take care of more pressing issues.

"I'm pregnant," she said.

"I know," John answered.

He wondered who the father was but knew it was Daryl. Sarah confirmed this with a silence. The ass-kickings made sense now. Sarah's early harvest and flight. The crime was always simpler than its confusing evidence.

"What are you going to do?" John asked.

"I thought I knew," she said. "But what was right for me before, isn't now. And I started seeing signs everywhere. I'm not religious, but I feel like someone is trying to tell me something."

"I think we create our own signs, to tell ourselves which way to go," John told her. "I think we always know what's right inside, but sometimes we need to manifest physical proof."

"Well, I slaughtered a lamb on my way over here," she said, with a nervous laugh. "Hit it with my truck. Dead as fucking dead."

She choked off a snuffling, her chest beginning to heave with hiccups of grief.

"Tell me that's not a fucking sign," she said, looking up at him.

John stepped forward through the doorway, enclosing her in his arms. She accepted his hug, her lucky red hat falling from her head as she leaned into his chest. John felt the heat of her body and strength of her arms as she returned his embrace. He rested his chin on the top of her head and patted her back. He could feel her tears wetting the front of his shirt. A breeze blew across the porch, but he felt warm. Sarah's hair was soft against his cheek and he felt he could fall asleep right here, standing up. They swayed together on the deck, not quite a two-step.

"Thank you," she said, letting go. "I needed that."

John reached down for her hat. Sarah wiped her nose. John wished he lived in an age when men still carried handkerchiefs. But he knew Sarah didn't need anyone to blow her nose. He wasn't the man for that job anyway. He just wanted to do the right thing once in a while. He held Sarah's hat out for her.

"You keep it," she said, the blue of her eyes radiant beneath the remnants of her tears. "You're going to need it more than I am."

"Are you sure?" John said.

"No," she said, finding a lighter tone in her voice. "Just wear it when you visit me in San Francisco. And don't flinch when I ask you to run out for ice cream and pickles."

"You're certain?" John asked, unsnapping the plastic strap on the back of the cap and adjusting it so it would fit his head.

"Of what?" Sarah asked.

John remembered Sarah asking him on his first night in Boonville, "Is anybody ever really ready for anything they do?" Sometimes until the event takes place, you don't know. You can only hope you've prepared yourself, because ready or not, the episodes of your life unfold without much rehearsal. He felt he had a different answer for her question now.

"Thank you," he said, pulling the cap on over his tousled hair.

"It looks good," she said, coming forward and kissing him lightly on the lips.

It could have been a hippie girl thing, but there seemed to

be more than friendship in the kiss. John was determined not to read too much into it, although Sarah smiled with Mae West sassiness as if to say, "Think whatever you want, big boy." John knew they would meet again under better circumstances. He would need a break from the loneliness of Grandma's cabin. A night in San Francisco might be the ticket; dinner, candlelight, conversation. Strolling along together in the fog. He'd gladly try to satisfy Sarah's cravings.

Sarah told him to check at the Boonville Hotel in a week or two and she would leave her new address or a telephone number with Hap. She needed to be alone for a while, set up a home and a studio, create a stable environment for the change coming in her life. She wasn't going to fuck this up. John said he knew she wouldn't and he looked forward to seeing her again when they both felt better.

"Before you go, would you help me with something," John asked, adding, "It's not even illegal."

"If it doesn't take too long," she said. "I really have to go."

"It will only take a minute," John said.

He led Sarah off the porch to the giant squirrels. As the two stood at the base of the sculptures, John thought the squirrels seemed like overly protective mothers guarding their young. John grabbed onto one of the makeshift handles and told Sarah to do the same. They leaned their weight into the large piece of wood. John thought the squirrel handles might snap, but the totem began to turn, damp soil churning from beneath as bugs and spiders scurried from their hiding place. The outer rim of a dark circle appeared in the ground, the base of the sculpture moving a few inches to the left. They paused, counted to three. Using all their strength, they turned the squirrel so it faced the valley.

"One more to go," John said, moving to the other squirrel.

Before taking hold of the handle, he looked up at the giant carvings facing in opposite directions. They seemed confused, a weather vane pointing both north and south.

"I don't know how your grandmother carved something so huge," Sarah said. "She must have had help, at least putting them in place."

"I don't know, either," John replied, willing to let that remain the eighth wonder of Boonville. "I guess Gibsons think big."

They took their grips on the second squirrel. This totem

moved easier than the first, joining its partner in the new view. Seeing both squirrels pointing in the right direction, John felt a surge of relief. Sarah seemed to feel the shift too, acknowledging they had accomplished something by giving John the thumb's-up signal.

It may not have been what Grandma intended, John thought, but it's what he could live with.

He wriggled one of the squirrel handles from the side of the second sculpture. It's face was mashed from being wedged into the larger piece of wood, but it still held John's features enough to be recognizable. He tossed it to Sarah.

"Here's a souvenir," he said. "Don't bother making a cross."

"I won't," Sarah said, walking to her truck and propping the squirrel on the dashboard.

John remained standing in front of the cabin wearing her lucky red hat, flanked by the two giant sculptures. Sarah closed her door and started the truck, leaning her head out the window and looking back before she drove away, her blue eyes appearing as if they had never seen a tear.

"Take care, Squirrel Boy," she called out. "You're a local now."

John watched the truck pull out of his driveway, heading for the winding road that led to the floor of the Anderson Valley and then into, and out of, the town of Boonville. He turned to go back inside, but stopped on the steps of his cabin to take another look at the view and the backs of Grandma's squirrels, reflecting briefly on the last two weeks and the changes they had brought into his life, understanding he lived here now, this was his home, and thinking to himself, "Yee-haw."